PENGUIN BOOKS

Monty Jay is a dark romance author with titles published in multiple countries. Their books are for hopeless romantics with wicked hearts looking for their next morally grey hero. They call the Appalachian Mountains home, along with their two furry friends, Poe and Maeve. When they aren't writing you can find them reading anything by Stephen King, in a tattoo chair or binging a new true crime documentary.

Also by Monty Jay

*The Truths We Burn*

*The Blood We Crave: Part One*

*The Blood We Crave: Part Two*

*The Oath We Give*

# THE LIES WE STEAL

The Hollow Boys Book One

MONTY JAY

PENGUIN BOOKS

PENGUIN BOOKS

UK | USA | Canada | Ireland | Australia
India | New Zealand | South Africa

Penguin Books is part of the Penguin Random House group of companies whose addresses can be found at global.penguinrandomhouse.com

Penguin Random House UK,
One Embassy Gardens, 8 Viaduct Gardens, London SW11 7BW

penguin.co.uk

First published 2026
001

Copyright © Monty Jay, 2026

The moral right of the author has been asserted

Penguin Random House values and supports copyright. Copyright fuels creativity, encourages diverse voices, promotes freedom of expression and supports a vibrant culture. Thank you for purchasing an authorised edition of this book and for respecting intellectual property laws by not reproducing, scanning or distributing any part of it by any means without permission. You are supporting authors and enabling Penguin Random House to continue to publish books for everyone. No part of this book may be used or reproduced in any manner for the purpose of training artificial intelligence technologies or systems. In accordance with Article 4(3) of the DSM Directive 2019/790, Penguin Random House expressly reserves this work from the text and data mining exception.

Cover Art by Opulent Designs

Set in 10.86/14pt Fanwood
Typeset by Six Red Marbles UK, Thetford, Norfolk

Printed and bound in Great Britain by Clays Ltd, Elcograf S.p.A.

The authorised representative in the EEA is Penguin Random House Ireland, Morrison Chambers, 32 Nassau Street, Dublin D02 YH68

A CIP catalogue record for this book is available from the British Library

ISBN: 978–1–911–74687–4

Penguin Random House is committed to a sustainable future for our business, our readers and our planet. This book is made from Forest Stewardship Council® certified paper.

To the ones who love the darkness and all that lurks there.
And to Stephen King: because of you, I am.

# TRIGGER WARNING!

*This is a* ***dark romance****. It deals with sensitive subject matter. That includes, but is not limited to, graphic sexual scenes, graphic violence, serial murder, sexual assault, human trafficking, mentions of suicide and suicidal ideations, kidnapping, and torture. If you find any of these triggering, or those similar, please do not continue.*

# PLAYLIST

Beyond the Pines – Thrice
Baby – Bishop Briggs
37 Stitches – Drowning Pool
Chalk Outline – Three Days Grace
It Was a Sin – The Revivalists
Control – Halsey
In Chains – Shaman's Harvest
Into the Fire – Asking Alexandria
Happy Song – Bring Me The Horizon
Skeleton Key – Love Inks
Help – Papa Roach
The Devil – BANKS
Killer – Valerie Broussard
Black Honey – Thrice

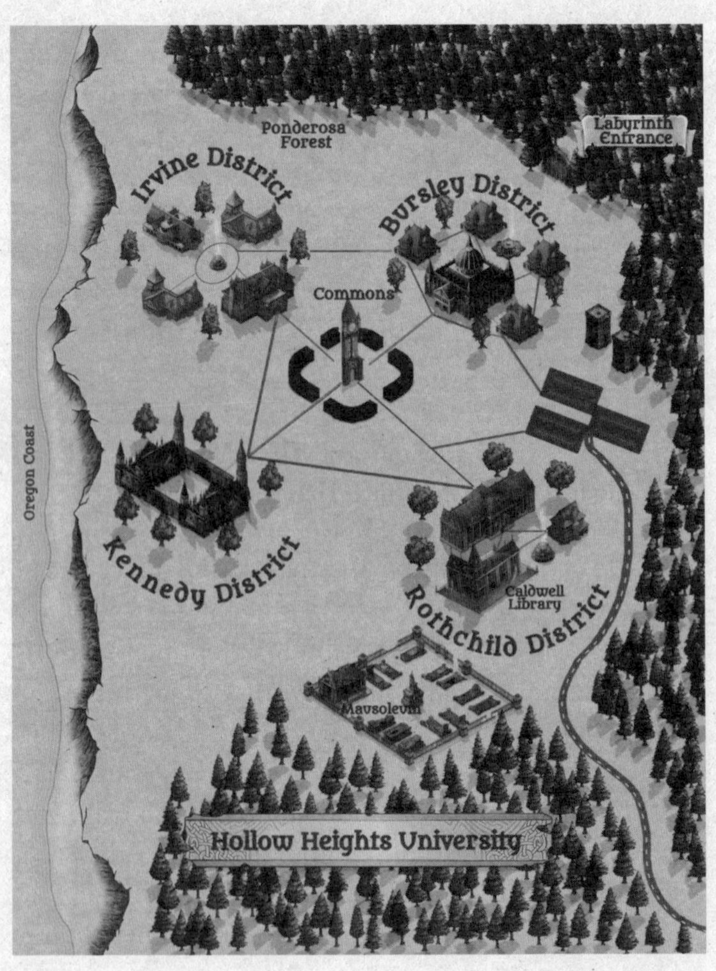
Ponderosa Forest
Labyrinth Entrance
Irvine District
Bursley District
Commons
Oregon Coast
Kennedy District
Rothchild District
Caldwell Library
Mausoleum
Hollow Heights University

# CHAPTER ONE

## When Darkness Calls You Home

### Alistair

I always knew I was born with a ravenous appetite for violence.

Destined to be the black sheep of my family.

They should learn to warn others about the children who are left to cultivate with the absence of light. When you take away their luster, the darkness doesn't just become a part of them, they become the darkness.

Power rippled through my arm as I felt this kid's nose shatter. My knuckles dug into the flesh of his face, chasing the only thing that could sustain my hunger.

Pain.

The tall, lanky moron who'd thought it would be a good idea to challenge me fell hard to the ground with a thud.

In official mixed martial arts, you're supposed to stop when your opponent falls that hard.

Fortunately for me, this is The Graveyard. The abandoned racetrack on the outskirts of town, where kids gather from surrounding areas in search of trouble. Illegal street racing, fights, drugs, and half-naked girls. It's the Garden of Eden for rich kids. The grass in the middle of the cracked asphalt circle was where the fights took place, all while engines roared and echoed, seeing whose daddy-bought machine would pass the finish line first.

The Graveyard is the place you come to get buried. Especially if you're up against me.

I charge forward, mounting him while pressing my knee so far into his gut I could feel his organs shift below me. My agile fists heaving punch after punch to his already inflamed face. My breaths rush out methodically, each point of contact I let out another breath. There are hands grabbing at my shoulders, clawing at me to stop.

I don't care, it only makes my knee press harder. My fists bludgeon him mercilessly.

Why should I let up because he was stupid enough to step into this ring with me?

Seems like a personal problem.

My heart is thrashing inside my chest, the energy coursing through my veins like drums in my ears. It blends with the screams of the people around us, the revved engines, and the smell of oil.

Fuck, what I wouldn't give to feel like this every second of the day.

I deliver a right hook, watching as my ring imprints my initials onto the tender skin of his cheek, splitting it right open above the letters A.C.

A gush of searing blood from his face splatters across my chest. A ferocious roar rips through me, the crimson liquid acting as gasoline to the flames inside my body. It wasn't the blood I wanted, though. I wanted his agony. I wanted to see him hurt. I wanted to know that he'd need to be carried to his car tonight, driven home, and he'd probably crawl to his fucking bed. Where he'd stay for the next week because the bruises I imparted were too much to handle.

It made chills speed down my spine.

That's my not-so-secret secret.

I'm always, *always* angry.

"Jesus fucking Christ, Caldwell, let him up! That's enough, man!" The voice rings between my ears, but I throw one last punch before shrugging the eager hands off my skin.

The circle of people around us chants for the brutality that has just taken place. The inability to turn away from tragedy or disaster. All of them are the same as me on the inside, addicted to the cruelty. They're just too afraid to admit it.

I hate cowards. And every goddamn person in this fucking town is one.

Monsters behind masks terrified that their neighbors will see the skeletons they keep shoving into their closets. What they don't know is you can't keep anything a secret in Ponderosa Springs. Not for long.

I know that better than anyone.

Shades of red flash behind my eyes as I stand up, hot spit coming from my mouth and landing right next to his groaning body. He's lucky he's able to make noises, even more fortunate he isn't dead.

Besides the blood on my chest, there isn't a mark on my skin. Which almost makes me angrier. Nothing challenges me anymore. I clench my jaw as I turn around, the mass of people parting like the Red Sea, leaving me an open pathway to exit.

"Money for the bets." One of the older guys running this chaotic shit presses crumpled-up bills into my chest. I look down at it, then back at him.

"Keep it." I grunt.

I don't need or want that money. He could do fuck all with

it, I didn't fight for cash. I fought because if I didn't, I'd kill someone.

I quickly scoop up my leather jacket, shrugging it easily over my shoulders. My T-shirt was somewhere in the muddy grass and I don't feel the need to search for it.

My breathing begins to regulate as I make my way to my car. Even if the fight was bland, releasing even just a little of my fury would mean I could sleep tonight. With everything going on, sleep was not something I could afford to lose.

Music poured from my speakers as soon as I turned the key over. The sound heavy and exhilarating. My left-hand grips the wheel tightly, I can faintly see the white beneath my blood-soaked knuckles. They throb so hard that it almost feels good.

I quickly throw it into gear, ready to make the drive to my parents' home. Twenty-eight thousand square feet, nine main bedrooms, ten spares, seven bathrooms, twenty-six acres, and there still isn't enough space between myself and my family. My grip tightens. I was supposed to be on a flight to the East Coast next month, putting an entire country between them and me.

Instead, I'm trapped here for another year at least, chasing a ghost.

Making a hard right, I turn into our driveway. One that's covered by towering trees, the paved road stopped momentarily by the large steel gate blocking the entrance. I click the button on my remote to automatically open them, pulling past them and into my family's estate.

Driving around the tacky marble fountain in front, I slide into my parking spot easily. None of the usual cars are here, meaning no one's home. It wouldn't matter anyway; even when they are here, I'm invisible to them.

I always have been.

Lightning cracks across the sky behind the house, lighting

up the fog for a split second before thunder rattles the ground beneath my feet as I walk towards the door. The keypad glows under my touch as I enter my passcode and step inside.

When my parents and brother are here, this house is shining with light. Its glow can be seen through the trees on the road. Extravagant parties celebrating a clipped toenail, family dinners that I'm never invited to. But when they are gone, it's just me and the dark.

My boots echo off the floor, step by step until I'm in the kitchen turning the faucet on. I run my swollen hands beneath the lukewarm water. The blood begins to flow down the drain, some of it anyway. There is some stuck between my fingers, already dried.

There shouldn't be noise inside the house. It should be how it always is when I'm here.

Dead silence.

Except it isn't. My ears twitch, picking up on the familiar click, followed by a whoosh at the lighting of the flint.

"Trying to scare me?" I say out loud, drying my hands slowly before I turn around.

I peer into the dark of the parlor room, Rook's face illuminated by the single flame of his Zippo as he flips it across his knuckles and through his fingers. I spot the single diamond strike match resting in his mouth, the scarlet tip peeping out of the side.

He's leaning back in the leather beveled chair, arms resting on the sides as he stares at me through the dark.

"If I was, you wouldn't have heard me," he retorts.

I navigate myself into the chair across from him. Pulling the lamp string, illuminating the room in an amber glow. Just as I sink into the stale material, resting my arms on my knees, I hear footsteps approach behind me. I don't bother looking over my shoulder.

"Thatch." I greet, as I see his shadow walk past me, taking the seat to our left.

At six-four, Thatcher is the tallest one of the group. Not like he needs his size to scare anyone.

He slings one leg over the other, his ankle resting on his knee, "Get your rocks off battering some poor kid's head in, Ali?"

I grind my teeth, the pompous asshole knew I hated being called that. Known that as long as we've been friends, but it wouldn't be him if he wasn't trying to get underneath *someone's* skin.

You see, Thatcher's veins were constantly pumping with ice water and mine were always boiling.

"You really wanna talk about what gets people off, Thatcher?" I raise one eyebrow at him, taking in his Armani suit. I'd learned to stop questioning his extravagant wardrobe a long time ago.

"I wouldn't want to give you nightmares." He smirks, and I can't help the matching one that appears on mine.

I'd be lying if I said I haven't wanted to rip each of their heads off at some point. We knew how to push each other's buttons. However, right now, I was reminded of how I'd kill anyone who'd try to do the same.

It's why I'm willing to stay in this godforsaken town—because one of our own had been scorned.

"Where is Silas?" I ask.

"Sleeping for the first time in . . . fuck . . . I don't even know," Rook answers.

"Don't be naive, Rook. Silas doesn't sleep anymore. When he does, he sees *her*. We all know that," Thatcher interjects, reminding us all why we are here in the first place.

The grandfather clock in the hallway chimes, signaling that midnight has reached us. The weight of his words filters into the room. The wrath I'd tried to release earlier started to creep back up. I could feel the flames licking my heels, the copper taste in my mouth.

"Speaking of her." Rook reaches forward, tossing a cream-colored folder onto the table in the middle of all of us. Perks of being the district attorney's son.

I lean forward, grabbing it, "You look inside yet?"

He shakes his head, "Wanted to wait until we were together." Raising up a bit, he reaches into his back pocket, grabbing the white pack of cigarettes. Pulling a single one out, he rakes a hand through his long brown hair.

"Mind?" he asks, referring to the smoke.

"Burn it down for all I care." I say honestly. Rook leans back in the chair, pulling the match from his mouth and lighting it with his fingers, a trick he'd taught himself when we were at summer camp. He lights the end of the cigarette, inhaling deeply, a cloud of smoke gathering around his face.

Since I was six years old, the only things I'd ever cared about were Rook, Thatcher, and Silas. We'd sworn to protect each other always, even if it meant wreaking havoc on others in the process. Nothing else mattered besides them, to any of us.

You never see one of us without the others; we are the kids that were never made to be good. We were always meant to be crooked and broken.

"We are all aware of what will happen when we start looking into this, correct?" Thatch asks, "There will be blood on all of our hands. Not just the little destruction we've done around town all our lives. We won't be burning down historic churches or playing wicked games. We will be killing someone."

We should flinch or cringe at the idea of taking someone's life. But we all knew what each other was capable of.

"It's their own fault. They should've known better than to hurt someone we care about."

I remember that night. I remember the smell of that house

we found her in. Like pig shit and vomit. A trap house where druggies hide out and shoot their liquid gold. I remember what her body look liked, bent and left hopelessly fragile on the filthy ground.

Like an angel who'd gotten lost and found herself in Hell. She didn't deserve to die there. And Silas didn't deserve to find her like that.

I could still hear his screams when I shut my eyes. Hours and hours of shouting. A wounded beast whose pain was growing into unfiltered rage. An emotion that coursed through all of us.

"We find out who did it. We end them. And he can move on. He'll be able to move forward."

"He won't move on." I shake my head, "Even if we find what we are looking for. You don't move on from something like this."

I open the folder, revealing the white pages stuck between. The patient's name in black, bold letters that make my jaw twitch. Rosemary Paige Donahue. My eyes scan through the report, all the questions asked. Was the patient's death expected? No. Was ACLS performed? Yes.

*By one of my best friends until we pulled him off her,* I think to myself.

Flipping to the next page I find the drawing of a body from the front and back, but instead of having circles around certain areas like I assumed it would, it was blank.

My eyebrows inch together as I read the coroner's findings.

*No visible signs of trauma or contusions.*

So, the scratch marks on her hands? The purple circles from the obvious bruising on her arms? I saw those. They were there.

*The most significant finding on the autopsy was the presence of methylenedioxymethamphetamine (MDMA) in the patient's system. After a thorough investigation, it is my conclusion that the amount ingested caused heatstroke in the patient. The core body temperature was raised leading to cardiac arrest which led to death. No foul play was detected.*

So, the dirt underneath her fingernails, like she'd been clawing at something? That was just a coincidence? The police didn't investigate further into the fact Rose had never touched drugs up to that point?

There were things that weren't adding up. That weren't sitting right with me.

"Here, genius, you read it. Tell me what you think." I toss the files at Thatcher, watching as he rests his hand on his chin while his eyes scan across the paper.

"No evidence of foul play? No documentation of the bruises or the marks on her skin?" he says out loud and I nod in silent agreement.

"We saw her body. I don't know about you two, but I've got twenty-twenty vision. Rose was not there of her own free will. She never even went to parties with us, made Si stay home with her all the time. Is Ponderosa Springs really trying to hide the murder of the mayor's daughter?" Rook comments, taking another puff of his cancer stick. One that I'm about to steal for myself.

Rose was not only Silas's girlfriend, she'd become . . . one of us. Slowly she'd weaseled her way into our group, making herself a friend. We wouldn't admit it out loud, but we all cared for her like a sister.

Her death was eating at all of us.

"Wouldn't be the worst scandal here."

"So, if a pathologist would lie about something like defense wounds and foul play, what else is he covering up? Better yet, *who* is he covering up for?" Thatcher asks.

"I think we should pay the good doctor a visit." I scan my

eyes across my two friends. Rook's mouth quirking up into a smile as he flips his Zippo across his fingers, snapping it shut.

"Don't have to tell me twice," he mutters.

Thatcher grins sharply, "As long as I get to cut first."

We made a deal.

A promise to one of our best friends, that we'd figure out who did this to his girl. Left her dead and dirty. All of us giving up our plans to leave this toxic place for an entire year, just to get the revenge he needed.

Not even God could save the people who got in the way of that.

# CHAPTER TWO
## Through The Fog

### Briar

*We are all thieves, Briar. I just got caught.*

That's what my father used to tell me every time he was whisked off in the back of a police car.

To an extent, he was right. We're all thieves.

We steal air from the atmosphere so that we can breathe. We steal happiness. We steal lighters. There is no such thing as, "Hey man, can I just borrow your lighter?"

If you believe they are going to give it back, well, you're just an idiot with one less lighter.

But most of us, all of us really, steal time.

We aren't owed any set number of minutes on this earth, yet we take it anyway. Every day you wake up, is another day yanked from the inside of the hourglass.

I was eleven by the time I learned how to pickpocket. Nearly a professional, I'd mastered the art of seven bells within six months and soon I'd become a criminal prodigy.

So, while my mother was flipping burgers, my father would set up mannequins all dressed in men's suits, strewn with pockets, and they would be rigged with seven strategically placed bells.

My goal was to pick the mannequin clean, without ringing a single bell.

I was his mini-me. His pride and joy. His little criminal.

I had dexterity, speed, and I was agile.

Pickpocketing, lock-picking, safecracking, all the things to make a perfect crook I'd excelled at by thirteen.

Other little girls learned ballet. I could break into a fire safe without breaking a sweat. I mean, hell, there wasn't a lot I couldn't do. Even when he'd first started guiding me, I knew it was wrong. Stealing was bad. Everyone knew that.

But those moments I spent with my dad? Those late nights perfected my technique and were the best time of my life. His profession kept the lights on, food on the table, it kept my family together.

Yeah, some families probably bonded over board games; mine bonded over larceny.

*"There is honor among thieves, Briar. Honor among us."*

I'd been used to him going in and out of jail, spending a few months here and there, but he always came back to me. He promised he'd always come back to us.

But one day he didn't.

My moral compass never did have true north. Maybe it was why I was always so curious about things I shouldn't be. I was aware that my behavior was not socially ethical, but I didn't regret anything I'd ever done. I did it for my mom. I was working with the skills I'd been given.

When life gives you lemons, steal a fucking juicer.

"Are you excited about this fresh start? It's a huge deal they accepted you, even with my recommendation. They tend to accept locals only." My uncle, Thomas, my mother's brother, speaks to me for the first time since the plane ride.

He's shy like that. My mom says it's because he was born crooked, all that knowledge and no social skills. I'd always liked him, though, since he gave great Christmas gifts. Instead of talking he was always paying attention to the little things.

"It sounds more like a cult than a school, T."

It probably was a cult. Actually, I know it's a freaking cult. It's the only university in the states with enough money and power to only accept people in the area, alumni students or children who come from extremely wealthy families.

Everyone with their head out from under a rock knew about Hollow Heights.

How does a thief with a record, split ends, and barely two dimes to rub together get accepted? That's a good damn question.

It had little to do with my 4.0 GPA, high test scores, and extensive athletic ability, and everything to do with the fact Thomas was the biology professor and had been for the past three years.

My uncle was somewhere in his late thirties, the younger of the two siblings. He and my mother had grown up poor all their life, just like me. Except when Thomas turned eighteen, he tucked tail and ran far away from his family. Came back years later with a snazzy degree, and a Rolex.

No, I didn't try to steal it.

"It's not nearly as pretentious as you are imagining. It's surprisingly down-to-earth," he says, with a smile.

I scoff, "The brochure included an entire segment on how a prince, an actual prince, graduated from there. It looks like every single ivy league school came together and had an orgy." I yawn a bit, "You're gonna look at me and tell me that place isn't filled to the brim with entitled rich kids with Amex cards?"

I cross my arms across my chest, staring at him with one eyebrow raised.

Don't get me wrong, I'm thankful to be attending. The education I'll receive from here will guarantee me a job after I graduate. I'm just not excited to be the "scholarship" kid. It's a lot like being the brown-paper-lunch-bag kid, or the one who picks their boogers and eats them.

It's not a good look.

"Don't be so judgmental. There might be quite a few people here who don't have a ton of money, Briar. This is going to be the greatest four years of your life, I promise." He reaches over, squeezing my hand reassuringly, and I wasn't aware how badly I'd actually needed that.

The longer we drove down this unending entranceway towards the imminent black gates, the worse my nerves got. While it was a dream to be accepted, this place looked a whole lot like a nightmare.

I stared out of my window at the baby rain drops that clung to the glass. I inspected the rows and rows of pine trees. At any moment it seemed they would reach forward and grab the car.

The sun used the wet clouds as a guard so that every single moment here felt gray. Devoid of all colors. Vacant of warmth.

It seemed, to me anyway, these kids were paying a shitload of money to live inside a Stephen King novel.

I cleared my throat, sitting up a little straighter, tugging my hoodie up on my head and placed my headphones in my ears trying to settle my stomach. The eerie silence that had settled around us was giving me serious haunted house vibes.

Even with the music playing, I could hear the gravel crunching beneath the tires as he continued to drive inside the campus. The first piece of the college you see, welcoming all new students and returning ones, was a large, weathered brick arch with a mocking metal plaque bolted to the front. The rust and ivy attempted to shield the written words on it, but it was no use.

*Hollow Heights University*
*Est. 1834*
*"We invited success."*

The plaque was engraved in bold letters, bearing its name to all who enter.

Where the leather-bound books whisper in dead languages and the empty marbled hallways creak with defiance.

Outside, the light never touches the ground, a constant blanket of fog dances through the towering pines.

The infamous university for wealthy boys and girls. One of the most secluded and elite colleges in history. It's rumored to have homed some of the wealthiest young minds in the country.

Hollow Heights insured parents would not be disappointed after their child completed the program here; they would return after graduation diplomatic and refined. Ready to take on any job thrown their way.

The college was situated on the coast of Oregon, three hundred acres and Victorian architecture that felt older than dirt. I'd toured it online, but the computer didn't do it justice.

The town it was built in was Ponderosa Springs, known for, you guessed it, the pine trees of the same name. I didn't know a lot of its history except that it was filled with wealthy families, you had to drive through it in order to reach the campus, and it was hard to ignore how rich it all looked.

Whether it was on purpose, or by accident, the architects of the school had made this place feel miles and miles from any real type of civilization. It was like its own world beyond the trees, built on somber wetland, and the seclusion made me queasy. Ya know, like after you eat gas station sushi.

"Your thing is freaking me out again with its beady red eyes," Thomas says as he pulls up to the drop-off spot for the dorms.

I peep down at the small animal in my hands, her pure white fur soft underneath my fingers and her little nose stuck up in the air smelling her surroundings.

"Her name is Ada and she is not a *thing*. She is an albino

dumbo rat. If you call her a thing again she's gonna bite you," I warn, even though both Ada and I know she wouldn't harm a fly.

When my dad let me pick out a pet when I was young, I chose a rat. Not because I was trying to be different or outside of the box, but because there was just something über-cool about rats. I'd had three, each of them living to their expected lifespan of two-ish years before they died. I waited a few months to mourn, cried every time, and then I started looking for a new companion.

Ada and I have been going strong for about a year now.

"Do you need help gathering your bags to your room? Or do you think you can manage?" he asks from the driver's seat.

I look out at the dorm, Irvine District, where all the lowerclassmen stayed. A circular water fountain rested in the center, a large saint doubling as a water spit. The cracked marble made me feel he'd crumble at any second.

Crows squawked from above, their black wings darting through the haze. My eyes tried to count the number of gargoyles that stood guard on the top of the pedestals and pilings.

I wave him off, "I can handle it. Thanks, though." I open the door, tucking Ada into my hoodie pocket, where she stays most of the time when she isn't in her cage.

I automatically wish I had thrown on a pair of jeans instead of these athletic shorts; I'm not used to the cold. Texas didn't have cold weather, or this much fog.

Walking to the trunk of the car, I lift it up, placing my book bag on my shoulders and grabbing my suitcase.

A cold gust of wind hits me, like something had run across my back. I turned my head slightly, gazing over at the buildings, expecting to see someone standing there staring in my direction, but I was only met with students shuffling across school grounds, lugging their suitcases inside. My brows furrow, I could've sworn I felt like someone was watching me.

"You alright?" Thomas asks beside me.

"Yeah," I shake my head, smiling, "I'm good."

"This is going to be really great for you. I just have this feeling." He rubs his hands together, "Here is your dorm key and lunch card. If you need anything you have my number, my apartment is in town, but it's a short drive so don't hesitate to ask." He wraps an arm around my shoulder, giving me the most awkward side hug in history.

"Thank you, Uncle T."

Affection wasn't something I was huge on to begin with. You can't be poor *and* soft.

I should've been nervous walking towards a school that makes Harvard look like a backwoods community college.

But I wasn't.

It wasn't in my nature to be nervous or scared. When you live the life I've lived. The one where you have to fight for your survival, the meals on your table, the roof above your head. You don't have time to be afraid of anything.

You do what needs to be done.

# CHAPTER THREE

## *Way Down We Go*

### *Alistair*

"Took you two long enough," I mumble pushing myself off my car with my boot, tossing my cigarette onto the ground, stomping out the dying ember.

"Thatcher had to press his suit." Silas shoves into Thatch's body with his shoulder, his body covered with an entirely black hoodie. The moonlight reflecting off his hardened face.

"Versace? To a crime scene? A bit pretentious, even for you." I eye his outfit, looking like he's attending some fucking political debate about global warming or health care.

"Good to see you don't hate mommy and daddy too much. Seems you at least learned your brands from them." His voice levels, "We know you oppose all things wealth, Alistair, but there is no need to be jealous of my incredible style." He straightens his collar.

I step closer to him in warning, but the sound of a high whining engine disrupts my temporary anger towards my best friend.

Rook's steely gray colored bike swerves into the morgue's parking lot. The revving of the bike ends suddenly as he turns the key. Pulling the matte black helmet off his head and shaking his hair like he's some kind of boy band member.

"Glad you could join us, Van Doren." I remark.

He walks towards the rest of us, keeping his riding gloves on, the only one of us with a smirk on his face. He raises his book bag up.

"Got everything. Extra, in case we decided on—"

"We are not blowing anything up today, Rook," Thatcher cuts him off, already knowing where his thoughts are headed. He holds his hands up in defense.

"Let's go find out what the good doctor knows." I turn on my heel, the gravel crunching beneath my boot as we walk towards the back door of the building. Rook had come by earlier, ran a little errand for his father at the D.A.'s office today.

Maybe Theo Van Doren thought Rook had turned a corner, wanting to help his old man out. It's a good thing Theo doesn't know his son, and that he was only playing nice so he could unlock this door so we would have an easy way inside.

My knuckles sting with anticipation as I pull the door open carefully. I hear Silas click the lock behind us, just so no one else follows behind. We fall in step as we make our way through the receptionist area, my heart thuds inside my chest. Metallic flavor spreading through my mouth as I clench my jaw.

What did it say about me and who I was that this situation had me exhilarated?

I can see the glow of lights, just before I press my hands into the double doors, opening them with a loud thud. The smell inside the medical examiner's office is horrid. It clings and permeates. A cold body with a sheet pulled up to its chest.

To the left, Doctor Howard Discil jumps at his desk, the chair squeaking underneath his weight. Quickly, he adjusts his glasses, trying to recover from us spooking him.

"Excuse me," he clears his throat, trying to sound a bit more stern, "but you boys can't be here right now." He readjusts in his seat, eyeing us each warily.

I look over at the boys, all of us making eye contact for a brief moment, as if this was someone's last chance to back out before we started really dirtying up our records. When no one says anything, I turn back to Howard.

"I don't remember us asking for your permission."

It's quick work after that. Silas and Rook retrieve the nylon rope from the bag, securing the doctor to his chair. He struggles, hopelessly, but still struggles. Wiggling in their grasp as they wrap the black rope around his body, binding him completely.

"What the hell do you think you're doing!" he yells, his face turning an ugly shade of red.

Rook presses his foot into the doctor's back, shoving the rolling chair to the middle of the room, staying behind the desk as he starts to open drawers and sift through papers.

I reach into my jacket pocket, pulling out a pair of golden brass knuckles. The metal is cold in my palm, the heat from my skin warming them up quickly. Stepping towards Howard, I slip my fingers through the loops, allowing the curved end to nestle into my palm, squeezing it tightly in my grasp.

"Rosemary Donahue," I say, still looking at the reflective metal on my hand, my initials etched into the tops of each knuckle. "You did her autopsy report, right?"

"That's privileged information. I can't just tell you something like that," he argues, struggling against his restraints.

The muscle in my jaw tics twice as I tilt my head to the left, cracking my neck.

My arm strikes forward, sudden and forceful. My hand is protected from the impact with the steel shielding it from the outside, but I can still feel the metal digging into his cheekbone.

A whoosh of air passes between us as his head snaps to the left at the impact. A groan of pain falling from his mouth, along with crimson liquid. It splatters onto the floor, onto his shirt. I probably knocked out a tooth.

The skin where I made contact is split, bleeding from the nasty cut already starting to swell, turning burnt red.

I place my hands on either side of his chair, bending down so my face is close to his, shaking my head and clicking my tongue.

"Wrong answer, Howard."

Something sharp like electricity fires through my body as his eyes glint with fear.

The adrenaline of knowing he's terrified for his life right now makes my toes curl inside of my boots. I could live off this. His fear. I could feed on it like a hungry fucking dog.

"I'm going to ask again," I say as I stand up to my full height. "Rosemary Donahue. Her autopsy."

"Yes! Yes! I did her autopsy! Why does it matter? It was just an overdose!" he yells frantically.

I nod, "Good, that's really good. Now, tell me, why'd you forget to mention the defensive wounds on her body?"

Shock registers on his face, like the dots of why we're here are finally connecting. He knows we know something. The question is, will he be stupid enough to lie to our faces?

With a short shake of his head, "There wasn't. It was just an overdose."

I was almost glad he lied again.

Another sharp, murderously hard punch lands in the same place on his face. This time, he really does spit out a tooth, maybe two. The weight of the brass knuckles makes my punches even worse.

This anger, the one I'm always so quick to release, has been there a while, escaping every time I open my eyes. I'm angry at store clerks and drivers. Everything and anything.

And every time I throw these punches, every single time I'm hurting someone else, it's them I'm picturing . . . the people who gave me my last name, and all the ones attached to it.

The ones who made me nothing but a spare.

I change my direction, digging a savage hit into his ribs, and I swore my ears could hear them cracking inside of his chest. Bone-crushing pain, that made me feel like I was on the best drug on the planet. Nothing could touch this euphoria.

"I was there, you fucking scum," I spit out the words. "I saw her body before the police arrived. Her nails bloody and filthy from clawing at something. Bruised like she'd been held down. Are you going to lie to me again? I promise, if you do, you'll regret it. Believe it or not, Howard, I'm going easy on you compared to what my friend will do."

"I'm not lying." His lungs wheeze for air. "I swear, all of my findings were in the report. That was all of it!" Blood drips from his mouth onto the stark white lab coat.

I wonder if when he pressed his slacks this morning he'd thought he'd be bleeding on them later.

If he wanted to be difficult, then we could do difficult.

"Don't say I never warned you."

I turn my back on him, pissed I couldn't get him to spill more information.

"He's all yours," I mutter.

Giving Thatcher the go-ahead to do whatever it was his twisted mind had come up with. I wasn't so cruel that I would let him go first. I at least tried to give the good doctor a chance.

The click of his Oxfords bounce off the wooden floor. The weight of his sinister intentions vibrates off the walls of this office. I lean my back on the wall, resting there as I watch Thatcher take part in one of his favorite pastimes.

Making people bleed.

He sheds his suit jacket, tossing it onto the desk, while he takes his time rolling his sleeves up to the elbows. All of this a part of the mental game he plays.

We were a good contrast, he and I. He was cold and calculated. I was instinctive and hot-blooded cruelty.

The perfect pair of sociopaths.

Howard violently shakes his head, "Why do you even care? Come on, boys, think about this. If someone found out you assaulted me your futures would be ruined!" He argues frantically, "She's just some rich girl. Just some dumb girl who overdosed, probably partied all the time. You know that type!"

The air runs cold, no sounds to be heard except for his labored breathing. From behind him, like silent water, Silas moves from the shadows. His black hood hiding his face as he grabs the back of Howard's hair, twisting it sharply in his grip.

With one fluid motion, he jerks his head back, the doctor groaning in protest,

"Her name was Rosemary. And she was not just a girl." His voice is coarse, not swift and sharp like Thatcher's, or sarcastic like Rook's. It's coarse, rough, battered and beaten. It's full of anguish and vengeance.

"She was mine. And now, you're going to see what happens when someone fucks with things that belong to me," he snarls in his ear.

Thatcher grabs the circular stool near the morgue table, sitting on top of it and rolling his way in front of the tied man. Similar to how a doctor would do when examining a patient. Silas backs up again, arms crossed, leaning into the wall, continuing to watch.

"You make a modest living don't you Dr. Discil? Sixty-grand a year? Presumably more here in Ponderosa Springs. That's a pleasant life for your two sons, isn't it? How old are they again? Five and ten?" he asks evenly, waiting politely for his reply.

While doing so, he lays out a black leather bag that's rolled up. With relaxed hands he undoes the buckles on the side, flipping them up, and slowly starts to unroll them onto the desk. The metal of the objects inside catches the moonlight, glimmering in the darkness like deadly stars.

"You twisted little shit . . ." Howard hisses, trying to jar himself out of the chair.

Thatcher's long, icy fingers run a path down his collection, back and forth, "I ask because your hands are vital to your work. I of all people know how important hands are to the art of dismemberment, so I correlate to you, Dr. Discil."

I grind my teeth, watching as the doctor eyes all of the sophisticated blades on his table. His Adam's apple bobbing.

"Still haven't learned to stop playing with your food before eating, have you, Thatch?" Rook says as he continues looking through the office.

Thatcher just grins, continuing his line of questions. Getting inside of his head is half the fun for him. He doesn't just like to make them bleed on the outside, he craves the fear on the inside.

"My father granted me this one," he says, picking up one of the knives. "You know my father, don't you?"

The question makes the doctor shake.

"Yeah, I presumed you did."

"You see, with this knife, I could use this tiny hook here and embed it into the flesh of your back before peeling your skin clean off. I've been in the market for a new pair of skin boots."

"I don't know anything! This is pointless!" Howard continues, his voice shaking at the thought of Thatch making him into a pair of shoes.

Done with the teasing, he grabs a thicker, long blade, feeling it in his hand for a moment before grabbing the doctor by the wrist to hold him steady. With precision and grace, Thatch slices straight through the first knuckle of the doctor's pinky finger. The piece of the appendage falling helplessly to the ground.

White bone is quickly covered with a fountain of blood, squirting from what is left of his small finger. An inhuman cry erupts from him as he looks down at his hand, horrified of the lengths we'd be willing to go to.

"You think what he did hurt? Several punches to the gut and a split lip? I will show you pain, Dr. Discil. Extreme pain." He seethes, "Until the last words you croak from your vile mouth are, 'Please, just kill me.' So, I suggest you answer our question before there isn't anything left for me to cut up." For a moment the facade of Ponderosa Springs's most wealthy, future politician cracks. The creature that lurks beneath coming out to play.

"I didn't, I just—" He stutters over his words, ready to crack. Except it's not fast enough for us.

The sound of someone chopping a carrot fills the room once again, another knuckle cut off, leaving just a sliver of finger left. Blood soaks the front of Thatch's white Versace button-down.

Another scream fills the room and I'm grateful we were able to get in here after-hours.

Howard is trying to catch his breath while Thatcher lines up again,

"Wait, wait, stop, please! I'll tell you! I'll tell you, just stop!"

Finally, the words we have been waiting to hear. I lean off the wall, walking towards them a bit.

"I don't know who it was. All I know is I received a letter when Rosemary's body got to my office, asking me to cover up any evidence of foul play on the body." He breathes, whining in pain between words,

"And this has to do with Rose, how?" Thatch applies pressure to his finger.

"Wait, wait, I'm getting there," he begs. "At first I was against it; I was going to put my findings in the report anyway b . . . but . . ."

"They do what everyone in Ponderosa Springs does. They

gave you money for silence," I finish. My blood pumping hot in my veins.

"Yes, and I needed the extra money! I couldn't pass it up. I'd checked my bank account and, sure enough, there was the money."

"And Rose? What was her cause of death?" Rook asks from behind the desk, his hands gripping the edge of it so tightly I thought the wood might splinter beneath his grip.

"She had an allergic reaction to something in the drug. It was injected into the side of her neck, I'd found an entry wound. But when I did my examination I noticed someone had shoved a few of the pills into her throat, trying to make it more believable she'd taken them herself, but they did it postmortem, so . . ."

"So, she couldn't swallow them." Thatch finishes for him.

He nods, "She died of anaphylactic shock! That's all I know, I swear to God!" he cries, the blood leaking from his hand pumping out to the beating of his heart.

There is a quick silence that passes between all of us. We'd expected maybe someone with money was covering up the fact they'd killed her in order to attack the mayor.

I guess we weren't the only monsters lurking around town.

Thatcher looks over at me and I nod, giving him the go-ahead. He starts to clean up his knives, wiping them on his slacks, placing them neatly in his case.

"The pills in her throat, where are they?" Silas asks from behind him.

"Bottom-left drawer. They are in a ziplock baggie. Please, please, just don't kill me!" he wails.

Rook retrieves the baggie, all of us walking towards one another, creating a small circle.

"They are marked, some kind of symbol on them. It's faded, though, I'd have to check it out." He squints, looking down at the bright pink pills, "I can call a few people, see who is selling Ecstasy with this tag on them."

Fucking drug dealers marking their shit.

"And following the drugs is going to do what for us?" Thatcher imposes.

"It's all we have right now. It's that or nothing," I point out. "Thatcher, finish up and let's get the fuck out of here."

Looking over at Silas I ask, "You good?"

He nods, shoving his hands into his hoodie pockets, "Fine."

Knowing that's all I'll get from him, I don't bother asking again. When he needs something, he'll let us know. Silas doesn't talk unless absolutely necessary.

"Wait, wait, what are you doing? I told you everything!" Howard screams as Thatcher stalks towards him.

He bends down, grabbing the back of his head with one hand while the other presses a blade into his throat, a small trickle of blood leaking from the pressure,

"If you say a word, I'll come back for the nub. Then I'm taking your treacherous tongue. Or maybe, I'll go after your kids. You think they'll like my knife collection?" There is a mumble of words from Howard, some form of a beg,

"You've been good at hiding things lately, make sure it stays that way Dr. Discil. Do. Not. Make. Me. Angry," he pushes. "Is that clear?"

Thatcher scoops his case up, grabbing the black suit jacket and folding it over his forearm, falling in step behind me as we make our way out of the office.

I could feel the weight on my shoulders as we walked towards our cars in the parking lot, a snake slithering down my spine, knowing that was the last person we'd leave alive in our journey to revenge.

Mercy is no more.

# CHAPTER FOUR
## *Welcome Home*

*Briar*

Black and gold, colors of extravagance, riches, and mystery are noticeable everywhere across the campus. They are the school's signature colors and could not be more fitting. I wander down the hallways of ornate decoration. Tall, arched kaleidoscopic windows that gave me vertigo with how the light dazzled through them. Everything around me felt . . . expensive.

I saw groups of girls huddled together as they walked past me arm in arm, giggling about something. Their heels clicked in sync, each with their hair braided neatly down their back. Lost in their own world. Ada squeaks in my pocket, nudging her head out, only to hide again when I duck to avoid a ball that was launched over my head, turning sharply to see a guy catch it with a lacrosse stick. He raises his arms in celebration, as his friends trample past me, knocking into my shoulder, chuckling and high-fiving each other.

Another girl was handing out fliers for a debate team, her pressed plaid skirt and sweater vest told me she probably wanted to do something important in life. I felt so outside of my element, like I was just a shadow in their lives.

I mean it wasn't their fault they were born into wealth and I wasn't.

This wave of understanding, of realization, hits me as I walk through these winding corridors, through the pointing arches and up a flight of embellished stairs. My earbuds snug inside my ears, vibrating with the force of the music I'm listening to.

No one here knows me.

Not a single soul knows who I am.

I made my way through classmates; I shifted and moved through the reuniting hugs from sophomores. Barely noticed, not because I was weird or being ignored, but because I was new.

I reached the room all the way at the end of the third floor. Tucked on the left, the gold numbers 127 on the front. My hand grabbed the doorknob right as someone tapped on my shoulder. I pluck my earbud from my left ear, music still blasting in my right.

"Yeah?" I ask, looking at the tall, pretty blonde with super white teeth. There is a soccer ball tucked underneath her arm, and she's popping her gum, over and over again.

"Lizzy Flannigan," she shoves her free hand out towards me.

I return it, "Briar, uh," I pause not knowing why we are introducing ourselves with last names, "Lowell."

Nerves bubble in my stomach. Fear of automatic rejection that usually comes attached to my last name.

"Hmmm, never heard of Lowell before. Anyway, it's Flannigan as in Flannigan Oil. Yeah, my dad owns it. Pretty cool. I just wanted to give you a little heads-up before you entered the bug palace." She nods her head towards my dorm, popping a bubble as she does.

A breath of relief passes through my lips because, like I said, they don't know me here.

"Bug palace?" I ask, deflecting the attention away from myself.

A place this nice has a bug problem? Maybe if they stopped paying so much for the mowers to make perfect checkered patterns in the lawns they could get an exterminator.

Budgeting goes a long way, ya know?

"Yeah. Sucks for you, but you're rooming with Lyra Abbott. Super weird goth chick with an obsession with nasty bugs. You're welcome to hang with us in the student lounge if you don't want to be in there. You might even be able to get a roommate swap." She rocks on her heels, back and forth.

I get this feeling Lizzy is being nice because she hasn't found a reason to be either, A. threatened by me, or, B. hasn't sniffed out my weakness.

I like to make my own assumptions about people and I'd like to do that about my own roommate.

"Thanks for the warning. I think I can handle it, though."

Texas has rattlesnakes, I think I can handle some bugs. I start to turn away from her when she speaks up again.

"Anyway," she sighs, "I'm supposed to hand these out to all the freshmen." She hands me a black flier. "It's a homecoming party. Jason Ellis is hosting it this year, which means his parents are out of town on business, so we have their entire estate to rave on."

I'd never been invited to a party before, let alone gone to one. I'm sure people in my high school had them, I just never went. This felt like a step in the right direction.

I wondered what parties here would be like. From what I'd heard, rich kids loved to get into things they shouldn't. Something about having everything they could ever want, but still needing more.

"Sounds cool. Thanks for the invite," I say coolly.

"Are you, like, a local? Or from one of those big monopoly families on the east coast? I've never seen you before." She tilts her head, eyeing me up and down. Taking me in.

Here it is, she's trying to figure out if I'm competition or just another weird chick she can gossip about to her friends.

"Um, no," I shake my head. "I'm from Texas."

"Ohhhh, southern money, huh? That's dope."

I open my mouth, wanting to correct her, I don't want to give her a false impression. I'm not ashamed of being poor. Fighting for what you have just shows strength. There's nothing I need to feel embarrassed about.

"Lizzy! Let's go!" someone hollers from down the hallway.

"That's my cue, I'll see you tomorrow night?" she offers.

"Ugh, sure thing, yeah, totally." I stutter over my response, smiling a little.

Finally opening the door to my dorm, all I want to do is drop down on the mothball-scented mattress and cover myself with the scratchy comforter I bought from Walmart.

"*Yeah, sure thing, totally* . . . What a fucking idiot." I mimic myself, wanting to smash my head into a wall for being so awkward.

Ada started moving around in my hoodie pocket, meaning she was ready to get settled into her new cage. Thomas had moved some of my stuff inside before I'd arrived, thinking it would make my transition a little easier.

Two matching twin beds on opposite sides of the dorm, a desk at the end for each of the students inside. I waltz to the desk, opening the medium-sized cage filled with ropes, toys, and bridges, letting Ada go inside so she can get used to her new surroundings.

I take my time looking at my roommate's decor. I am now aware of why they call it the bug palace. Her walls are full of glass boxes and posters of dead bugs. Mostly beetles and butterflies, but I'm pretty sure I spot a spider there somewhere.

I hear the toilet flush just as I turn, seeing the bathroom door open. Out walks my roommate, wearing bright yellow rain boots that are caked with soggy mud, drying her hands on a paper towel.

We don't speak for a second, she takes me in just like I am her. Her frizzy brown hair that's trying to hide underneath a black leather bucket hat, the pieces of her straight across bangs popping out a bit. I note the oval, amber ring on her pointer finger that looks like it has some type of bug trapped inside of it.

"It's dead," she says, catching me staring at it. She wiggles her finger before pointing at the ones on the wall, "All of them are dead. So, you don't have to worry about anything crawling around on you at night."

The way she says it makes me think she's had to say those words before and she's used to defending her hobby. She likes bugs and I steal things, who am I to judge?

"They don't bother me," I say, scanning the room, laughing a bit. "I mean the spiders are a little creepy, but it's kinda cool. I've never met anyone who's collected them before."

A little weight falls off her shoulders, a pretty smile breaking across her face as she reaches her recently cleaned hand towards me, "I'm Lyra. It's called entomology. The study of bugs, but I'm mostly a lepidopterist nowadays, just butterflies and moths, minus a few beetles."

Ah, just first names. What a good start.

"Briar. Kinda jealous I don't have a cool hobby. Is there a reason for it? Or have you always just liked bugs?" I return the handshake with a smile.

"I have a thing for dead stuff. It's a long story, so Briar Lowell, right? I heard you talking to Lizzy." She starts walking towards her side of the room as she keeps talking, "Princess of the oil industry. Four-year state soccer champion, graduated fourth in our class and she pushed her best friend in a pool at senior prom by accident, because she accidentally wore the same color as her." *Accident* and *accidentally* are spoken with finger quotations.

"So, she's the queen bee around these parts then?" I toss my stuff on the bed, sitting on the springy mattress. I was trying to not be judgmental, but Lizzy gave me the vibes of the kind of girl you were friends with only because you didn't want her as an enemy.

"That's the thing about Ponderosa Springs." She mirrors my movements on her own bed, kicking her boots off. "Other places have one Regina George. Here, there is never just one. Every piece of the hierarchy has their own mean girl, the jocks have Lizzy. Nerds have Emily Jackville, future aerospace engineer. Art nuts have Yasmine Poverly, daughter of not one but two art tycoons, and is said to have swirls like Picasso. Or whatever that means."

"This place is just every teenager's dream, huh?" I joke sarcastically.

She snorts, "Basically."

"So, how do you know all of this? Are you local?"

Twirling the ring on her finger and staring at the ceiling, she answers, "Yeah. Ponderosa Springs born and raised. I'm not from a crazy wealthy family, so for me that means I'm a ghost. I'm not really bullied but no one talks to me either. I don't benefit anyone, so I'm not included. I just kinda float around this place, watching everyone else." She turns her head to look at me, "Anything you need to know about this place and the people who live here, I probably already know about it."

I nod, "I know what that's like. Being invisible, it's easier that way when you know the alternative. Back home, I didn't have many friends either."

"Welcome to the loner society, Briar Lowell. I'm the president, but there is an opening for a VP."

I laugh, leaning up and sitting with my legs crossed. Loner

Society, party of two. I liked the sound of that. Having a friend, being a part of something. I bend down, grabbing the flier Lizzy had given me.

My fingers graze the thick paper, reading the words over and over again.

When I was in middle school, I got invited to a sleepover birthday party. Nothing big, just a few girls from my English class. I'd never been over to anyone's house before and I was stupid to get excited.

Long story short, my fun ended after mani-pedis when my dad got busted trying to rob a bank. It was all over town within a matter of seconds and I'd quickly gone from Briar, quiet girl in English, to Briar Lowell, trailer park trash whose daddy stole to get by.

I was told to leave the party that night.

And I never talked about it again.

But things are different here. No one recognizes my last name. No one knows who I am. I can be whoever I want. There is no limit. I no longer have to be a criminal prodigy with a stained reputation.

I no longer have to be the outsider. To conceal myself so I can steal things. Because here everything is already paid for. All because I was worried about the lights being shut off or not having food on the table.

I wanted a life, I didn't just have to survive.

One I could enjoy.

And I knew just how to start.

# CHAPTER FIVE
## Meet Your Devil

*Briar*

This idea made a lot more sense inside of my head than it did right now. It had seemed like a great plan all evening, getting ready, driving here, even the first twenty minutes seemed promising.

"I can't believe I let you drag me here," Lyra laughs, hiding her face behind her red solo cup that's still at the same amount from the time we arrived.

We were clustered in a corner outside people-watching.

In my head, when I got here I was going to be a social butterfly. Lyra and I would be chatting with girls about classes or boys we thought were cute. Maybe I'd even be talking to a guy who I might give my phone number to.

That was not the case, at all.

"Okay, so maybe—" I make an *oof* sound as someone slams into me drunkenly, muttering a sorry before continuing to walk past me, "Maybe this wasn't the best plan. In my defense, I didn't think the party would be like this!"

I looked out from where we stood on the back patio of Jason's house, watching all the drunken bodies filling the backyard and in-ground pool. It was a beautiful pool, one that made the swimmer in me envious. It was the only sport I was decent at and not even my high school had one this nice.

Well, minus the bodily fluids and trash at the moment. The DJ blared music from multiple speakers around the house, and, God, if you thought the backyard was packed. Bodies were filling every square inch of this mansion, pouring out of the living room, kitchen, and even upper bedrooms.

I watched through the haze of the fog machine and weed, at people grinding together to the thumping beat.

"I told you, the kids of Ponderosa Springs aren't normal. Everything they do, they have to do ten times harder than regular teenagers. It's the money. Gives them all this complex that they are untouchable," she yells over the music.

I'd practically dragged my new roommate to this place, spewing some bullshit about us trying to be something more than ghosts. This was our freshman year of college; the next four years were supposed to be the best of our lives.

I thought a party was the perfect way to kickstart that.

Obviously, I had the right intentions, the execution was just a tad off.

"I vote we leave and hit up Tilly's Diner for greasy burgers and fries, what do you think?" Lyra offers, seeing how uncomfortable we both are.

I take another look around, couples, throuples, and more with their tongues down each other's throats. Watching the sly transaction of pills in little plastic baggies. My lungs burned at the recycled air even though we were all outside, I wanted to be anywhere else but here right now.

"Hell yes—" I start, but my voice is drowned out by the chant of someone's name.

Lyra and I both shift our gazes to the roof where a guy stands on top of it, wearing only what God gave him and a lacrosse helmet.

"Dear gods . . ." Lyra mutters, shielding her eyes just as he screams something incoherently and propels himself off the roof and into the pool.

Those around us lose whatever sense they have left, screaming, laughing, completely immersed in the moment.

"If I never come to one of these again, it'll be too soon," I mutter and Lyra nods her head in agreement, tossing her drink over her shoulder.

"I have to go to the bathroom real quick, then we can leave."

"Do you want me to come with you? I don't know if I trust everyone here," she yells over the chaos.

"Yeah! That way we don't lose each other."

Together we make our way through the yard towards the back door, the heat inside the living room slaps me in the face, taking me aback a little. It's pitch black inside, the only light is the silver strobe bulbs that sporadically span across the room. It's a snug squeeze inside, people crammed impossibly close to each other.

How does anyone even enjoy this?

My sweaty hands clutch Lyra's as she navigates through the people as best she can. It feels like we are making headway through everyone until someone jostles into the middle of us.

My hand slips out of hers, my drink spilling down the front of my shirt, and to make matters worse, it's so dim I can barely see anyone's face.

"Lyra!" I shout over the derangement, squinting my eyes trying to catch a glimpse of her wavy brown hair and patterned shirt.

My breathing shortens, my mouth dries as I lick my lips to wet them a bit. Wishing I wasn't wearing my drink now because my throat feels like the Sahara. I try to remain calm, not wanting to freak out, and suddenly develop a fear of closed spaces.

My feet scuffing forward, my eyes spot the front door and I'm assuming that's where Lyra would go too if we lost each other. There's just a mountain of people I need to get through first.

The music changes, no longer an upbeat hip-hop song with a strange remix, instead it's a piercing screech of a guitar paired with frenetic drums. A sudden icy breeze races down my spine, unwanted chills sprinkling across my skin. My senses heighten. My skin tingling, breaths settling deeper in my stomach. My ears almost twitching at every tiny sound.

I know this sensation. I've been trained to notice it; even when other people don't recognize the subtle feeling of being followed, I do. You have to always trust your gut as a thief, knowing the right time to strike is just as important as the skill itself.

So, I think, actually I *know*, there is someone here watching me. I turn swiftly, checking my left and right, everyone is caught up in the elation this party has given them.

Someone blows a cloud of smoke in my face, making me cough, waving my hand to clear it out of my vision.

My body flinches back, my heart sinking to my feet, spooked from what I found. The strobe light catches the angles of his face in glitches. One second he's there, the next it's darkness.

He comes to me in sections, like a jigsaw puzzle.

His broad shoulders were sheltered by black leather, a white shirt plastered tightly across his chest, stretching against the rigid muscles that lay beneath. The perfect swimmer's body. Tall, wide, all tapered to a fitted waist. I find one of his hands suspended by his side as he props himself up against the wall, his boot keeping him there. Lengthy legs covered with dark-washed jeans, a standard for college guys, minus the wallet chain that hugs his pelvis and it makes my lungs throb with adrenaline.

There are at least twenty people from me to him, enclosing him on both sides, yet he sticks out. I'm unmoving, continuing to piece him together. My mouth starts to water, my hands sweating profusely, and there is a thumping inside my stomach.

Smoke from his cigarette creates a veil of mystery around his face, the strobe revealing him gradually. I catch the veins in his dominating hands, protruding, looming too-large fingers that are embellished with silver rings.

I shudder unconsciously, blotches of blood are clinging to his knuckles. He'd recently connected them to someone's face and I wasn't sure if it thrilled me or scared me. Was he someone who could put up a fight? Or someone violent by nature?

I was so curious. My nosey self wanted more. More than the pieces of him I could see. That was until I started putting together the edges of his face. The beat in my stomach dropping south, crawling between my legs.

I clinched my body together, biting harshly on my tongue.

The harsh scowl that adorns his otherwise angelic face sucks the breath out of me. How anyone so handsome could look this bitter was beyond me.

I'd always been good at math, angles, points, and numbers. Everything about him was flawlessly proportioned. Aligned, sharp, and intense.

Dark hair, the color of onyx. Dark eyes like strings of licorice, sugary enough to eat and tart enough to make you sick. It wasn't one of those instances where you thought someone was looking at you but really they were looking somewhere else.

His eyes left no question. He was staring at me.

But it was what I perceived the shade of his heart to be that scared me. Such a terrifying level of black varnished the organ inside of his chest that recycled blood over and over again. It made me wonder if I sliced him open would his blood even spill crimson?

The lowest part of my abdomen quivered from dread, from desire. There was a gravitational pull in his appearance, luring me in. But I could feel the sensations that rippled off him like a stone in a still pond. He was filled with ruckus, anarchy, he was violence personified and it struck a chord in me that hadn't been plucked in a long time.

Fear.

Hot-blooded fear that boiled in my throat, ate at my skin, and gave me the sudden need to run far, far away from him.

While my brain was moving on high alert, screaming to leave and hit the road, my body had an entirely different reaction. It was refusing to leave his gaze. The outside of me, frozen. But the inside buzzed. The feeling stuck between my legs intensified because there was something about trouble that I'd always loved.

When the strobe light went dim for a split second, then relit the room, he was no longer leaning on the wall. Now he was a few lengths closer to me.

One second he was there, the next he wasn't, only to reappear another inch closer to me.

He was an apex predator on the prowl for something to feast on. Something he could sink his teeth into and shred apart by the seams, stoking his need for the hunt and curing his hunger.

I wrap my hand around my wrist, digging my nails into the soft flesh of my arm. Forcing myself to stay put. I needed to see what would happen.

What he would do.

Another burst of light, and then, I could feel him in my space.

He was so very close to me. Sucking up all of my oxygen. Looking over my body. Just another step forward, just another inch, and I could touch him. Smell him. Feel his presence tenfold.

As if he could sense that knowledge, he poked his tongue

into his cheek, running it across his canine teeth and dropping his head, jaw tensed. His eyes beckoning me, giving me this urge to show him something . . . special.

He knew I was nervous. He was ready for me to turn and run for the hills. I think a piece of him wanted to chase me, wanted me to try and get away so the wolf in him could hunt me down.

Darkness encases me for another second, and I'm holding my breath, ready to face the consequences of my decision. To deal with whatever destruction he was ready to do to me, prepared to see his face light up with something like surprise that I stayed put.

For a millisecond, I could smell something spicy and warm. I could feel his proximity right on me, even hear his breath fan down on my face.

My eyes shut, floating in the seconds before he attacked.

"Briar!"

Lyra's voice pierces through the haze, my eyes snapping open, realizing the mystery man is gone, disappeared into the crowd with not so much as a word.

"Hey, do you know who—" I stop myself, knowing Lyra is full of knowledge about the people who live here, but how would I even explain him?

Tall? Hot? When he looks at you, you feel like he might eat you alive? She'd think I was crazy.

"Know who?" she yells, eyebrows coming together in concern.

I look around me once more, trying to catch even a glimpse of his leather jacket or silver rings.

Only to be disappointed.

"No one, it was nobody. Come on, let's get out of here."

## Alistair

"Well, did you get your fix, Alistair? I haven't known you to be the kind of guy who only watched. I kept waiting to see when you'd pounce. You let me down, pal. I was ready for a show."

I jog down the steps of the front entrance, lighting a cigarette as I do. The smoke burning my chest, setting fire to whatever good that's left in there.

"Not getting enough action, perfect one? Need to get off watching me now? All you had to do was ask, Thatch, and I'd let you."

His arm rests on the driver side window, staring up at me with a glare. Slowly he raises his middle finger, the ruby gem with his family signet reflecting in the night.

"Move over, sugar." I open the driver's door, with a sarcastic smile.

"This is my car!"

"And you drive it like you're an elderly man with cataracts. Now, move the fuck over."

He grinds his molars, lifting himself over the middle console and on to the passenger seat. Readjusting his three-piece suit. I hated this car. The Lamborghini Huracán was one of the best on the market, dipped in Thatcher's signature color. Dark red. But even I could respect that this car needed to be driven correctly and going ten over the speed limit wasn't it.

"Buckle up, honey. Wouldn't want you to hurt yourself."

I can feel his glare on the side of my head as I put it into drive, pressing aggressively onto the accelerator, the tires squealing loudly.

"You break it, you buy it," Thatcher says with snark as we

tear out of the driveway and towards the address Rook had sent us.

His right hand grips the side of the door. It's subtle, most wouldn't even notice his already pale hand turning another shade of white as he squeezes the handle.

Except I know this is the one thing Thatcher can't deal with, and that's not being in control.

"Oh yeah? With what money? You think I can fork out the two hundred grand for this?"

"Oh, don't be modest, Alistair. We all know you have more money than God. One of the perks of having your last name on everything in town."

My hands grip the steering wheel impossibly hard. The animal in my gut waking up, as it does any time my family's money is brought up. My family in general.

"Not my money. It's theirs."

He relaxes in his seat a beat, laying his head on the headrest with a sigh,

"Whatever you say, Ali. Whatever you say."

The drive goes by quickly; this car eats the pavement for breakfast. It's not long before I'm turning the car into the dirty driveway. A rickety old mailbox marking the house.

I see the fire before we even pull in front of the house, the orange glow between the trees crackling and building higher.

"I'm gonna fucking kill him," I groan, running a hand through my hair with agitation.

The car crawls to a stop when we are parked several feet away from the blazing trailer. I'm quick to hop out of the car, seeing Silas looming over a kneeling body, a wooden baseball bat in his grip.

"Where the fuck have you been?" Rook hisses, stalking up towards me, anger radiating off his body.

"Yeah, what took us so long to get here, Ali? You wouldn't have gotten distracted?" Thatcher asks, cunningly. He has a tendency to ask questions he already knows the answers to. Boosts his monstrous ego.

I push Rook's chest before he can get in my face, pointing my finger at him, "I told you to wait. I told you if worse came to worst you could light it up, but not before I even got here."

The anarchist in him refuses to back down, let alone admit what he did was reckless. I should've known better than to let him take the lead on this one. Rook is as unpredictable as the roaring flames behind us.

I got distracted. It's my fault I wasn't here earlier.

Distractions make you weak. Make you stupid. And I am none of those things.

I allowed myself to be both of those tonight.

I usually don't enjoy parties. I went tonight because we needed to watch Nate. Wait for him to leave. I typically only go when we have a plan to cause some type of chaos, scare people, fight someone, burn something down, ruin everyone's fun. Never going to *actually* party. However, this Hollow Heights Homecoming proved to be . . . interesting.

I should have been focused on the task at hand. There was a lot at stake right now, but instead I stopped to watch her.

The one who never looked away from my eyes, not even when my presence started to scare her. Her cherubic face glowed in the darkness, reflecting off the strobe lights. I couldn't see a lot of her, I wasn't sure if her hair was brown or if it was that dirty shade of blonde that I seemed to have a thing for.

I wasn't so sure it mattered.

There was something inside of her that was more interesting than her looks. The way she didn't run from me. She didn't allow her fear to overcome her. No, she was curious. She let her curiosity win, she wanted to see what I would do.

My cock twitched.

Wondering how far she would let me go before she cried mercy.

"You are not the goddamn boss of me, Caldwell. If I want to torch up this shithole because I think it's the best bet at protecting us, then that's what I'm going to fucking do."

"Careful, Rook," I warn him.

"Or what? You gonna hit me?" He raises an eyebrow, "Do it, I'm sure I can take it." He is baiting me. But this isn't sparring in my basement like normal, this is me letting out my anger and him needing pain. I'm about to rip his balls right off and put them on a shelf in my fucking bedroom.

"Ladies, we have more pressing matters at the moment. Put your dicks away, you're inadequate compared to me, let's focus on not dying or going to jail for the time being."

Thatcher slaps our shoulders, pushing between us and walking towards Silas. Knowing this is nothing to concern himself with because it's like brothers arguing over the last piece of pie.

"Did you at least cover your tracks?" I ask Rook as we follow Thatcher's moves.

He gives me a sideways look, "I'm not an amateur. Broken bulb in the oven, turned it to high, took ten minutes before it exploded. However, we have to make this quick, he's got a lab in the back bedroom, and I hear meth is highly flammable."

Goddammit.

"Batter up!" Thatcher howls like a wolf at the full moon.

Silas straightens up, like he's at bat for a World Series title. Rearing the wooden barrel back, he slugs it forward, swinging his hips and upper body with it. A thud followed by popping of what sounds like Rice Krispies electrifies the night.

Apparently, Silas had grown tired just watching all our fun.

A charge of excitement zipped through my blood, my dick

twitching again. Tonight had been full of things that got me going apparently.

"Who is he? And what do we know?"

"Nate Robbins, self-proclaimed Candy King. Sells everything from weed to heroin. Only person in town you can get Ecstasy from with a crown on it," Rook tells us, "Hasn't said anything about who he gets it from, though. It's just the normal responses, 'stop,' and, 'don't kill me.'"

I peer up to the trailer, the entire left side is encroached with orange fire, moving quickly towards the back. I wasn't interested in being burnt to a crisp tonight, so, we were going to need to wrap this up.

Thankfully for us, it was secluded. Placed in a plot of land that was surrounded by towering trees, miles away from anyone else. The perfect place to commit murder.

The wind howled, owls sang in the branches, and I could smell the rain on its way. There is always a scent that settles into the air when a thunderstorm is coming.

Nate could barely sit up on his knees. If Silas was smart, and I knew he was, he took his legs out first. Dirt covered his clothes, blood dripping from his face too quickly to be healthy.

I doubt he'd be able to walk out of this, if we let him live that long.

He bellows in sheer pain. I knew this one would be a little harder to crack than Doctor Howard. Nate was a criminal, he had more to lose if he told the truth.

"I'm not telling you assholes shit!" He spits saliva and blood onto the ground in front of him.

"How heroic," Thatcher grunts.

We didn't have time to pussyfoot around with this guy, not like with Howard. The clock was ticking and we needed answers.

I crack my neck, grabbing Nate by the back of his greasy hair. Silas had done a number on him, open wounds oozed blood and bruising had already started.

"Thatcher, give me your knife," I reach my free hand towards him, feeling the cool metal of the Swiss army placed into it.

I flick the blade open easily, hooking it underneath an already open wound, lifting the skin up, shredding ligaments and nerves. It's severely painful, something I wouldn't want to happen to myself.

"Son of a bitch!" he cries. I can feel his warm tears on the back of my hand as he withers in my hold. Every bone Silas struck is probably broken or shattered. They ached with all his movements.

I couldn't imagine what kind of pain he was in.

"I wouldn't lie again, Nate. Tell me about the Ecstasy."

"Goddammit! Fuck! HELP ME! SOMEONE HELP!" he wails into the night like a banshee.

Rolling my eyes, I fillet the skin back even more, pulling it up and pressing the tip of the blade into the tissue beneath. I feel the blade hit his cheekbone, so I begin to rub it back and forth.

"Scream like a fucking pussy all you want, Nate. No one can hear you out here. There is no one that is going to save you from this," I seethe.

"Fuck! Agh, fine!" he groans, then bawls like a little baby. I don't blame him, though. "I'll talk, please, I'll talk!"

I smack the opposite side of his face, "Smartest move you've ever made, Nate."

"I get my X from a teacher's assistant at Hollow Heights. Name's Chris. It's good product, only guy who makes it like that in the state. I just, I—" He stops.

"Uh-uh, keep going, Candy King," I add, wiggling the knife in front of his face.

"I just mark it with my symbol, okay?! Make people think I'm the one making the shit. I meet the guy in the parking lot of Tilly's on Saturdays, he drives a white Volvo. That's all I fucking know I swear."

"A teacher's assistant? You're fucking joking," Rook breathes.

I sling Nate's body down onto the ground, he hits it with a thud. The windows inside the house shatter, an audible explosion resonating from inside the walls. The fire hisses and crackles, warning us of its rage.

I throw my arm up to shield my face from the wave of heat. We need to leave. Now.

Leaving Nate there, unafraid of him talking or if he dies, either way he can't touch us. He's a drug dealer and we are four of the most important sons in this fucking shithole.

I jog to Thatcher's car, using the knife to quickly slash Nate's tires, making it that much harder for him to get help.

"Is everyone in this fucking town involved? Who's next, the fucking priests?" Rook mutters, slinging his bag over his back, helmet in his hand as he turns to face me.

I glance over at Silas who's staring at the flames that climb higher and higher every second. Lost in his head and I wonder if he's seeing something other than just flames. Wonder if the voices are there, or if he's imagining people dancing through the fire.

Wonder if he is seeing her.

Red flashes in my eyes, knowing I can do nothing but watch him in pain right now. I can't help him, not yet anyway. But I can slaughter the people involved in her death. I can't bring her back, but I can avenge her.

For Silas.

I return my eyes to Rook, "If they are—" an eruption shakes the ground, a gust of hot wind hitting all of us. Nate screams, the fire probably spreading to outside the house and creeping up on him.

"—Then we'll watch the whole town burn for that mistake. For Rose."

# CHAPTER SIX
## *The Hollow Boys*

### *Briar*

"So, come on, spill it. Tell me what I need to know about this place. Where to avoid, secret societies." I ask Lyra as we start picking at our lunch.

The weather was nice enough to eat outside, no sunshine of course, but there was no rain and I needed to give my allergies a rest from all the dust inside the building walls.

I stab a tomato with my fork, popping it into my mouth as Lyra starts tearing the pits out of her black cherries, the dark juices staining her fingers. Today had been a mandatory orientation for all students. Classes started tomorrow and I wasn't sure if I was excited or wanted to throw up on my Chucks.

Orientation was a snooze fest. Teacher after teacher, then the dean expressing his need for obedience and excellence. Teachers enforcing rules that had been here longer than most of us had been alive. I'd barely listened, I didn't plan on doing anything too scandalous that would even require me to know the details of their authority.

"What do you want to know?" she answers, tucking one of her chunky black Doc Martens beneath her.

"Everything, anything." I shrug, "Is Kennedy Hall really haunted?" I raise an eyebrow with a playful smirk.

Lyra laughs a little, "Who knows? Story says there was a girl who was sleeping with one of the English professors back when the school first opened. Apparently, he tried to end it and she was so broken-hearted that she jumped right off the edge of one of the colonnade's openings. They recovered her body at the bottom of the cliffside, stuck on one of the jagged rocks. Rumor says that if you walk Kennedy Hall past midnight, you can hear her screams as if she's falling."

The wind brushes my hair behind my shoulders, a thought brewing in my head. What is it about love that makes people want to die if they can't have it? I'd heard once it was a chemical in your brain and I was beginning to think I lacked the biology to feel that way.

"Crazy how people love that deeply, isn't it?" I say aloud.

Lyra bites into her pit-less cherry, chewing softly, "That's not love. It's obsession. Two very different things."

"Yeah? You don't think that's the same thing?"

"No," she shakes her head. "Love is real. A tangible thing you can run your fingers over, warm and safe. Obsession is living a fantasy in your head, over and over again. Obsession is living in a nightmare, but never wanting to wake up."

I squint my eyes, suppressing a smile. Her face is so serious, staring down at her cherry-soaked fingertips, like there is something staring back at her. I'm aware there are skeletons in my roommate's closet, everyone has them.

Something that makes them tick. A core secret that motivates their every move and when she's ready, she'll tell me. But a part of me thinks, this conversation is a clue to who Lyra Abbott really is.

"Whoa, that's deep," I mutter sarcastically.

She snaps back when she hears my voice, shoving my

shoulder playfully, "I'm serious. It's a thin line between the two, but there is a line nonetheless."

Cracking open my juice, I peer to my left at the sound of loud noises, seeing a small group of guys playing tag football in the middle of the commons. We'd picked one of the tables that was nestled beneath a tree, away from the busy areas, because as we realized the other night, socializing was something we were going to have to learn.

One of the players breaks through, the rest trying to tackle him while he crosses their agreed line for a touchdown. He raises his arms above his head in triumph, his dirty-blonde hair dusting the top of his forehead. The kind of boy built for attention.

His long-sleeve white shirt leaving little to the imagination, its see-through material allows a direct view of the deep-set torso muscles that contract as he laughs and cheers with his friends.

"Easton Sinclair," Lyra whispers. "Dean Sinclair's son. One of the most beloved sons in Ponderosa Springs. Athlete, student body president, volunteers at the local animal shelter. A perfect human if there ever was one."

I chew the inside of my cheek, having a problem not looking at him. You couldn't blame me, though; we didn't have guys like that back home. Ones that look like Abercrombie models.

Pretty sure that my staring is burning holes into the side of his head, he turns in my direction, eyebrows furrow on his handsome face as he searches for the eyes looking at him.

I quickly turn back to Lyra, face flaming a bright red.

"Yeah," Lyra giggles. "He tends to have that effect on girls. Let's see, who else . . . Oh! Scottie Campbell," she points to our right, "his parents own a bunch of steel mills, and he poured his entire tray of food on me the first day of fifth grade. Then he fell down an entire flight of steps at school the next day. I started believing in karma after that."

The guy is tall, lanky, and looks like the kind of guy who picks on other people until someone bigger comes around.

Not being able to help my curiosity, I turn my head back to Easton, just enough to catch a glimpse of a pretty brunette tossing her arms around his shoulders and placing a kiss on his lips.

"What about her?" I ask, slightly envious of the way her plaid skirt fits her shape. A pretty little cardigan dressing her shoulders and a headband holding back the flyaways. Poised, elegant and stunning.

All things I am not.

"Mary Turgid, parents are owners of chain stores. One of the most academically competitive people in our grade. Double major, with goals to be a defense attorney for one of the biggest law firms in America. Driven, pretty, and the master of killing people with kindness."

Yeah, definitely the opposite of me. They make a cute couple, though. The young John F. Kennedy and Jackie O.

I wonder what it's like to be that girl. Miss Americana, the one everyone loves, who thrives in the spotlight. I'd been here a week and I was already thinking about things I know I'll never be.

Even if Hollow Heights was foggy and a little mysterious, it had something Texas never did.

Hope for a better life.

A frigid gust of wind flips the pages of Lyra's book violently, howling between the trees, making them groan and sway. The once silent sky cracks with thunder. A warning for a storm brewing. There goes our lunch outside.

I start to pack up my things, not wanting to get caught in this downpour, when I hear Lyra inhale deeply, like someone had punched her straight in the gut.

"Why are they here?" she croaks out, her voice sorta trembling with fear. Pressing her book into her chest like it was going to protect her.

I look around quickly, noting the murmurs and whispers spreading out across the common. All of them either glancing or staring in the same direction. I can feel the mood shift in the air, like a dark force had just swept across everyone.

"Who? What is going on?" I furrow my eyebrows, looking towards the main hall, the door opening as a police officer walks out. Was there a drug bust already? Why is everyone so freaked out?

I'm answered by the doorway giving way to a tall body that made a small flash of something a lot like fear zip down my spine. The light of day illuminates the four men, one by one as they appear, hands cuffed behind their backs. They couldn't have been twenty feet away from me.

Even bound by metal bracelets, the hysteria erupting throughout the students around me told me the handcuffs did little to restrain the power they reverberated.

"The Hollow Boys."

It's spoken like a satanic cult's prayer. I half expect the ground to start shaking and hellfire to start raining down with the weight of her tone. It was obvious this wasn't the first time these guys had done something like this.

People were afraid of them for a reason.

It was hard to deny how attractive they were. Beautiful enough to pull you in, but the air that surrounded them made you want to take a step back. Multiple steps back.

They walked out, one after the other like demonic dominoes, falling in perfect alignment. Each of them so different, yet they looked like they meshed so well. Like knives and blood.

The sound of someone sucking their teeth vibrated through the area,

"Couldn't start the year without some type of chaos, isn't that right, boys?" he howls loudly.

The students physically shivered, the hair on the back of

my neck standing up straight, painfully aware of the uneasiness coursing through my body. I prided myself on being afraid of nothing, but there was something contagious about fear. Once it grabbed ahold of one person, it rubbed off on the ones around them.

The first one stood with his shoulders back, bearing a wolfish grin while a single match sat on his red lips, like a warning. Every time his mouth moved, he would roll it to the other side of his smirk.

"Is that a match?" I ask, ridiculously.

Lyra nods, "His name is Rook. Rook Van Doren. Son of the district attorney. He's the most . . . approachable of the four. You'd think his boy-next-door features would make him the sweet one. But the match is there for a reason." She mumbles like she's telling me a spooky story around a campfire.

"People joke that the match is there to light his short fuse. Last year, he burned down the town's oldest willow tree. No reason behind it. Just did it because he likes to watch things burn. Every fire, every arson crime, everyone knows it's him. But that's just what I've heard."

I wanted to roll my eyes. Tell her she was being dramatic, silly even. But I could feel how feral he was, it was in his eyes. The way they flared and crackled like a forest fire, just waiting to tear down anything in his way.

"A lovely welcome home, I believe." The person behind him says, his voice echoing like screams in an empty cave. It bounces off the inside of my chest and his ice blue eyes sting everyone in front of him, including me. They are the bluest eyes I've ever seen on a human. He's the tallest, and skinner than his counterparts, but by a long shot I think he might be the most intimidating.

Porcelain skin, paired flawlessly with his charcoal topcoat, an ironed black turtleneck, and plaid slacks, I was envious of how well he was dressed. Everything about him told me he cared about how people saw him. Making sure every cotton blond piece of hair was in place at all times.

"Thatcher Pierson. Death manifested into one perfectly-made human." Lyra breathes the same way she does when she's admiring one of her dead bugs. With excitement.

"Capable of choking you with his bare hands and not feeling anything in his cold, dark heart. He is incapable of feeling anything. Which is why it's believed the apple didn't fall far from the tree. His father was Ponderosa Springs's one and only serial killer."

"You're fucking joking. A serial killer?" I hiss. I thought my parents were fucked up. Psycho dad beats broke parents in fucking spades.

"Do you—" I can't believe I'm actually asking this, "Do you think he's like his father? Does he, ya know, kill people?" I whisper because I'll be damned if he hears me.

All she does is shrug, watching him walk every step of the way to the cop cars.

"I don't know and it's not a theory many have tested out. So, until then, no one will know." Still moving her eyes with him, even when I ask her about the others.

"Uh, Silas Hawthorne," she nods. "Heir to a technology empire. Diagnosed with schizophrenia when he was twelve. Of course, his parents tried to cover it up, but there is nothing that stays quiet in Ponderosa Springs. Not forever, anyway. He never used to talk much, but now, since Rosemary, he's practically a mute."

I fan my eyes across the golden-skinned one. An outside appearance designed for sunlight that carried eons of darkness on the inside. Pretty golden-brown colored eyes that were supposed to carry warmth, but I had a feeling they only harbored demons.

"Rosemary?" I question, feeling like I was being caught up on the local workings of a gang or some killer club.

She nods, shushing me, wanting me to keep my voice down, "Rosemary Donahue, mayor's daughter. I'm not sure what exactly happened, but everyone else says she overdosed. Silas was her boyfriend. They'd been together since I think middle school. He is the one who found her body. They all did."

It made sense. I could see the wrath that sat upon his shoulder. The reason darkness pooled off him in waves. The loss of someone he loved had turned him into something else entirely.

I had so many questions. So many feelings. There wasn't enough time to clear up my thoughts.

It was then that the clouds began to cry, heavy, wet tears that splashed on my thin, gray cloth jacket. It would be doused soon. The cheap material didn't hold out water well.

We needed to get inside before the rain came down full force, but I stayed sitting in my seat. Because the last member filtered down the cobblestone steps and I wasn't sure he needed an introduction.

I knew him.

I'd remember those eyes anywhere.

The other boys had been dressed sharply, designer clothes, wearing their wealth as a badge of pride. But he was sporting a worn-down leather jacket that molded to his powerful shoulders. A gray Henley underneath and simple jeans.

The same feeling I'd had the other night slithered up my legs; in the dark he was alluring, but in the light of day he looks so striking it takes the breath out of my lungs.

"That's Alistair Caldwell. They'd never say it out loud, but everyone knows he's the one calling the shots. His family owns half the town, one of his great-grandparents founded Ponderosa Springs. He fights at The Graveyard every weekend, and he's never lost. I doubt anyone has even laid a hand on him."

*Alistair.*

So that's the name of the mysterious guy I'd seen at the party.

My breath comes out in visible puffs, the chain on his waist, the rings on his fingers. It all worked so well to fit this image of an angry boy. An angry god. Not a single emotion registered on his face except rage.

I could feel it even from over here.

"The sons of the torturously wealthy. Ponderosa Springs's worst nightmare. They are the Black Death of this town. Not because they are popular, but because they have the power to scare people. Legends. Pretentious and they own every single bit of it. I just, I don't know why they are here," Lyra says, confused.

They were enjoying this. Each of them. Evoking terror and questions. The student body so concerned with what it was that required them all to be led out in handcuffs. They were loving the fear. Like hungry monsters and it was the perfect meal.

"They live here, why wouldn't they come to Hollow Heights?" I somehow find my voice enough to ask another question.

"They hate it here. All of them. They were supposed to leave after senior year. I thought . . . I don't know. They just aren't supposed to be here."

The wind nips at my exposed skin, sweat pools on my palms, and a shaky breath escapes me. The rain comes down harder, yet we sit there watching them get shoved into the back of the black SUVs.

The adrenaline I felt near him, Alistair, rivaled any crime I'd ever committed. My heart pummeled my chest cavity. As they were tucking his head inside, his dark eyes pierced mine all the way over here.

I knew he saw me. Just like he did at the party.

The corner of his lip twitched and I sucked in a breath.

Slowly, he winked before the door was completely closed and they headed to the police station.

That day there was a dark cloud following me, even after I'd shed my wet clothes and stood underneath the warm shower. I stood there, this feeling looming over me that Alistair wasn't done with me, yet.

# CHAPTER SEVEN
## *Shadow Children*

### *Alistair*

Over the course of my life, there were many things I'd never felt. Things I couldn't care less if I ever experienced now.

Trivial things like peace, comfort, love.

You see, a child needs those things to grow. It's vital to how they turn out. However, I had accepted a long time ago that what nurtured me wasn't something soft and sweet.

I wasn't raised with kindness or joy. From the moment I'd come into this world it was made very clear my role in my family.

Nothing but a spare. A backup.

Unless something happened to my older brother, I was nothing but a waste of perfectly good furniture space.

But there was one feeling I knew. Not because of my blood family. Not because my father taught it to me, or my mother showed me it as a young boy.

It was something I could feel in my bones and rushed through my veins. Something I'd learned from years of experience. It was one of the only things I felt sure about.

Loyalty.

Knowing that there was someone out there who had my

back just like I had theirs. Knowing if it came down to them or me, I'd throw myself under the bus every single time.

And that's how I knew this douche with a badge was full of shit.

"Give it up, Alistair. The other boys have already told us everything, pinning everything on you. You don't wanna go down for attempted murder and arson now would you, son?"

My upper lip twitches, I have to physically swallow the urge to stand up and smash his face into this metal table separating us. However, I don't move, keeping my cuffed hands in my lap.

I'm impressed with my own self-control.

"Yeah? Tell me, *Daddy*, what is it that I've done? You gonna tell me how I did it? Hmm?" I hum, unfazed by his games.

Aggravation eats at him. He's probably getting the same shit from Rook and Thatcher. Silas I doubt has even muttered a word since they lugged us down to the police station.

They would get nothing from us and soon they'd realize how pointless it was in the first place to even bring us in.

"I ain't your daddy, boy. If I was, you'd be headed to military school quicker than you could open your smart-ass mouth." His southern accent bothers me; it's obvious he'd moved here later in life because locals don't sound like back-woods hicks.

"And I'm not your son or your boy, you inbred hillbilly. And I'm not saying anything else, so you're wasting your time."

Nonchalantly, I throw my legs up onto the table, the mud on the bottom of my boots falling off onto the surface. Putting my hands behind my head and leaning back, shutting my eyes. I'd never been more unbothered.

We were not hungry dogs who were ready to tear each other to pieces the moment our loyalty was tested. For years we'd been covering for each other. We didn't even need to know the details of what one of us had done and yet we could have lied so flawlessly they would never be suspected.

Did they think we would snitch on each other because they put us in separate rooms? Turned down the thermostat? Kept us in handcuffs and left us in here for an hour before coming in? That they could scare us into turning on one another?

We were not fucking dogs.

We were wolves. Rabid, feral, and fiercely loyal to our pack and only our pack.

"You think this is a joke? These are serious charges; you are looking at years in prison. You think that tough guy act's gonna work in a state penitentiary?" He raises his voice, I hear his fist smash the table loudly, but I don't bother opening my eyes.

"If you had a shred of proof, I might, and I mean this, I might bat an eyelash. Until then I'm going to catch up on some sleep. You mind?" I crack one of my eyes open, nodding towards the light switch.

The screech of his chair vibrates the room, heavy footsteps approach me, I feel his fingers dig into the edges of my leather jacket, jerking me up closer to his face. I can smell his morning coffee and cheap aftershave.

"I'll nail you for this, you little prick. If it's the last thing I do, I'll throw your ass into prison myself," he hisses.

I grind my teeth, my eyes opening, and I'm positive there is nothing but pure evil behind them. The bubbling of red starts to filter across my irises, the room spinning in fast circles, the cop whose name I'm not even sure of starts becoming nothing but a black silhouette.

Something I need to obliterate. I can't stop the shaking in my hands, or the way my hands swing up, even bonded by cuffs, knocking into the underside of his arms. His hands fly off me.

"Lay hands on me again, and I'll stick my fist so far up your white-trash ass you'll lick my fucking knuckles."

I stand up, my height giving me maybe an inch on him. I

stare down at him, wondering if he'd have the same balls if I wasn't in cuffs and he didn't have a fucking gun. I doubt it.

"Yeah, big boy? Do it. Give me a reason to throw you into the pit." He smirks, all cocky like I won't smash his face in.

My restraint isn't something I'm known for and the only thing that saves me from watching him collect his jaw off the ground is the interrogation room door swinging open with a thud.

"Your knight in shining armor is here!" Rook sings as he waltzes into the room.

Officer Dickhead takes a step back from me, "You can't be in here, this is an ongoing interview."

"Well, see, the thing about that is," Rook starts but doesn't get to finish because I can hear his father in the hall behind him.

"Does anyone want to tell me why my son was arrested because of something a drug dealer said?" he booms, and I know the officer beside me is realizing that he has fucked up.

Rook's father, Theodore, was not an enemy people made lightly. His father was once a judge and Theodore was well on his way from Ponderosa Springs's district attorney to Your Honor in just a few years. And like his father before him, he'd slowly become his own son's worst nightmare. But letting him go to jail wasn't going to happen. That would taint his name too much.

I look at Rook, something like understanding on my face for what I know he'll have to deal with later tonight. If anyone deserved to leave this place, it was him. If anyone needed to get away from his toxic family, it was Rook.

He shakes his head, silently telling me to drop it.

I lift my hands up, shaking the cuffs. It's eating the cop alive that he has to let me go. It's all over him while he sticks the key in the lock, releasing my hands from the metal bracelets.

I don't give him another moment of my time, I have too much

going on as it is. Dealing with this asshole's bullshit isn't something I want to add to the list of things I need to do.

Walking towards the exit with Rook leading the way, I hear him open his mouth again.

"Caldwell," he says.

I turn my head just enough to let him know I'm listening.

"How's it feel to know your parents are the only ones who didn't pick up the phone? They busy? Aren't they visiting Dorian in Boston, he win another award?"

I hate the sound of his name.

*Dorian.*

The reason I turned out this way. The reason I was even born into my fucked-up family. I think I was the only person in the world who hated Dorian Caldwell.

However, I stopped caring about what they did a long fucking time ago and I didn't need to be updated on what it was they were doing with their beloved golden child.

Everyone in this town knows I'm the shadow of him. I see them whisper and murmur about it when I walk into crowded rooms. I'm nothing but the cheap replacement that never even stood a chance.

I know he's trying to get under my skin, trying to piss me off, but it doesn't warrant a reaction. It's not worth it and neither are they.

Instead of doing anything, I just keep walking out of the police station. Silas is sitting on the bench waiting for us, standing up once he sees us.

We were going to need to talk about this, but right now wasn't the time or place.

Thatcher walks out of one of the interrogation rooms, with Rook's father not far behind him. His coat draped over his shoulder and a smile on his face.

The rain had thankfully stopped by the time we walked

outside, Rook lighting a cigarette just for his father to snatch it out of his mouth and throw it on the ground.

"Arrested? On the first day of school, Rook? How much longer will this rebellion last? Another year? Two? Because I'm getting *very* tired of covering your ass! Don't you think you've put this family through enough?" He raises his voice only a little, he is after all, in public. With a shake of his head and a forced smile he finishes, "You know what, we can have this conversation tonight."

My fist tightens. This was not the first time I'd wanted to bash Mr. Van Doren's ratty face in. Wasn't the first time I'd offered either.

But for some reason, one that in our years of friendship we had never figured out, Rook wouldn't let us lay a hand on his father. Even after everything he'd put him through.

I had my opinions, though. I knew Rook enjoyed being hurt. When he'd call me at midnight and need me to rough him up. He said it was to let out tension. I knew better.

I knew he felt it was punishment for something he'd done in his life, something that had hurt his father at one point, but I was never sure what it was.

Theodore Van Doren bounces down the front steps of the station, walking with angry shoulders to his Cadillac.

"I have to catch up on all the work I missed out on because my son is an inconsiderate piece of shit, but I expect you to be at home when I get there. Is that clear, Rook?"

All he does is nod, not even looking his father in the eye.

"And you three," he turns, pointing a finger at us. "I'm this close to letting you all rot in prison; he should have never become friends with you. Everything chaotic he's ever done is because of you three," he accuses, like he's in court trying us for the corruption of his sweet, innocent Rook.

"Awful sanctimonious of you, Theodore," Thatcher replies, staring him down.

We don't need to say out loud that we know about the relationship Rook and his father share. He knows that we are well aware of what happens when he loses his temper.

There is nothing else exchanged between us until after his car pulls out of the parking lot.

I turn to Rook, tossing my arm around his shoulder, "Can we kill him yet?"

"I second that and, speaking for the mute, he thirds it," Thatcher adds.

He shakes his head, looking up to the gray sky like there is some message in those clouds for him.

"No. Death is a reward for him. I want him to suffer. Just like me."

# CHAPTER EIGHT
## *Applied Alistair-atics*

*Briar*

Since I was little, I'd always been good with numbers. While that may have something to do with my father teaching me how to count cards when I was young, I still preferred numbers over anything else.

Two plus two will always be four.

The square root of one hundred and sixty-nine will never not be thirteen.

In math, everything has a fixed resolution. Sure there are various ways to get to the answer, but most of the time you follow a set formula and it will yield the same solution every single time.

Math is easier than things like English or people. Both are too complex, they could have multiple responses, eighteen thousand different possibilities of how to break down a poem or read into what someone means when they say, "I'm okay."

In a world where everything has too many probabilities, I prefer numbers. Always.

I fiddle with the clean notebook in front of me, tapping the end of my pen onto the white sheets ready for class to start already. Everyone else around me is socializing, finding their way to the seats that circled the lecture hall. I'd picked a seat in the back, to the left of the front, because I hated feeling like someone was talking about me behind my back.

I also, admittedly, loved people watching.

Making myself busy, I start to pull my computer out of my book bag, sliding the brand-new MacBook onto the desk, in awe that I even have one of these. Thomas bought it for me as a gift. I'd almost refused to accept it, but I knew I'd need it for the courses I was taking.

"Briar, right?" I catch a voice to my right, unconsciously wincing before meeting a pair of delicate blue eyes.

My brows furrow because I'm not sure what he is doing talking to me or how he knows my name.

"I'm Easton. Lizzy mentioned you were new in town." He sticks his hand out to shake mine like it's some lawful business conference. The smile he had when he arrived hasn't dropped one inch.

I timidly return the gesture, grasping his warm hand in mine and following his movement of up and down. I'd showered this morning, but something about touching him made me feel dirty. He looks so clean, so poised and perfectly put together that I feel like sewer water next to him. Worried that I'll look down and see mud smeared on his unstained palm from my fingers.

"Uh, nice to meet you?" The way I say it, full of nerves, makes it sound more of a question than a statement.

He laughs effortlessly, his blond locks sway with the force, his large chest shaking a little.

"My father might kill me if I didn't give a formal welcome to a non-local. He's been trying to get out-of-state students here for years now. You a math major?"

Talking to people is a skill he'd mastered over the years. You can tell. In the way he holds himself. The confidence in his shoulders and the natural energy he's giving off make him seem easy to chat with. I'm just not sure why he's chosen to talk to me. Considering I'm pretty sure I'm at the bottom of the metaphoric food chain compared to him.

"Statistics actually."

"Intelligent *and* pretty. Quite a combination you have going on there." His smile becomes more flirtatious.

I could've sworn Lyra said he had a girlfriend.

Maybe she was wrong?

"Hardly," I mock, the tension in my joints easing up a bit. "What about you? Are you a math major?"

"Computer Science." He wiggles his fingers like he's typing, "I'm quite good with my fingers."

I know he's talking about his fingers on a keyboard, but I can't help the strawberry blush that begins to heat my cheeks. Even thinking about him with a pair of glasses on, white button-down with rolled-up sleeves, typing away on a computer, the glow of the screen illuminating the delicate points of his face.

It's enough to make any girl blush.

I notice the seat next to me is empty at this moment, chewing the inside of my cheek I decide what the heck? The worst he can say is no.

I motion to the chair next to me, "Do you want to take this se—"

"Easton! Babe, I got our seats up front!" A sugary, sweet voice echoes in the room, both of our heads peering in the direction it came from.

Molly? No, Mary!

That's his girlfriend, I warn myself. Knowing from what Lyra told me that I do not want to make an enemy out of her, even if she looks harmless with her Blair Waldorf-inspired wardrobe.

"You should probably grab your seat. I think it's about to start," I hurry out, not wanting any conflict between him and her. I do not need to be in the middle of an "it" couple. Not on my list of things to do.

"Yeah, it was good meeting you. Here," he grabs my pen out of my hands, tugging my open notebook towards him and scribbling something down quickly, "call me if you ever need anything or want to hit the library to study."

He's just being nice, Briar.

Guys are allowed to have friends who are girls. He's just being courteous, so don't read into it too much. His girlfriend is probably fine with it.

"Thanks, will do." I grab my stuff from him, pulling it back in front of me as he walks towards the front, sliding into his seat next to Mary. I'm assuming she's asking about our interaction, because her eyes swiftly dart to me before she begins whispering in his ear.

He plants a quick kiss on her cheek that acknowledges whatever question she was asking because she smiles and settles into her spot next to him.

I don't have much time to think about it because our professor walks in, his voice loud and controlling the room. Following close behind him is a younger guy who takes a seat in the corner of the room at his own desk.

"Welcome to Applied Mathematics. I'm Professor Sheridan and this is my TA, Mr. Crawford. Assuming everyone in here is studying some field involving math, it's safe to say this should be a very straightforward course for you. Any questions before we begin?" He clasps his hands behind his back, pacing in front of the long green chalkboard, allowing students time to raise their hands.

When silence follows, he nods, "Great, let's get started, shall we?"

My first day had started the way most firsts started. Natural. I had a tough professor who talked fast and wrote even quicker. Meaning my pen was working double time. Halfway through,

I'd decided to hit record on my computer to catch anything I missed.

I'd gotten through the hard part. The first day is always the most difficult and I'd made a friend, I think, so I take that as a win.

Well, I'd *thought* I'd made it through my first day without any obstacles. It was going so well, I was focused, I understood everything, I was satisfied, and then the air stirred.

We'd been in class for maybe thirty minutes when the door swayed open with a heavy creak. Booted steps stomp across the boarded floor as the same scorned face I'd seen the past several days every time I shut my eyes appeared inside the classroom. This wasn't confidence; he didn't carry himself in a charming light like Easton. His smile didn't make butterflies flutter in my stomach. He torched them. It was defiance and the power of *I don't give a fuck.*

He didn't mind he was late, that he was infringing, or that everyone was staring at him. He didn't care about anything.

The darkness I felt in the pit of my stomach that night comes back. It swells inside of me, eating its way up my throat.

I watch Professor Sheridan start to scold him for his tardiness, but when he realizes who he is, all he says is a mere, "Please, take a seat, Mr. Caldwell."

Alistair examines the room for a bit, stopping our teacher and his assistant for a second longer before shifting to the lecture hall, hunting for an empty chair.

The students in front of me have split reactions. Some of them, mostly girls, are moving their bags to clear a free spot next to them hoping he picks the seat beside them. Others are doing everything possible to evade his gaze.

Fear and admiration.

Two very diverse and very comparable emotions. Both of them are rooted in the same place—interest.

Watching everyone else means I've taken my eyes off him, so when they return to him, I see he's already making his way up the steps towards my section of seating.

There are various vacant chairs before me. He has to pick one of those. If he doesn't, it's going to be very clear he chose the seat beside me for a reason. The rest of the class will notice. I don't want to be known as the girl Alistair Caldwell picked out of the rest.

But good luck is too much to ask for because he slides into the chair next to mine. His large body fills up the space, smothering me, making me feel so tiny. Like I'm confined in a corner and a wild animal is keeping me in my place.

My grip on my pen is so tight that my knuckles are white. I can feel my heart beating erratically, crushing so hard on my ribs that I think I'll pass out.

I foolishly look around, watching people I hadn't even got a chance to talk to begin to gasp and whisper. Making assumptions about why he would sit here of all places. Their hushed voices and less than secretive stares make me uncomfortable in my seat.

"Is there a problem?" The deep pitch of those few words is enough to tell me that his voice resembles everything else about him.

Alarming.

The ogling and gossiping students flick around so fast I'm surprised they don't have whiplash.

Everything settles as our teacher proceeds to explain some formula that five seconds ago I fully understood and now I couldn't even recognize what class this was.

It's his smell. It's rattling me.

Not just a glimpse of it, like at the party, but his entire scent.

Spicy, like clove, and carnal. It's the smell of black magic at midnight. When witches stand around their brew at night with the moon and candles burning the room. Incense wisping in the air. Ancient spells and occult sorcery sting my nose. It's smoke and timber, and I hate how much I love this smell.

Stupid fucking hormones.

Forbidding myself to look over at him, I sink back in my seat, keeping my eyes ahead and pretending to focus on what Professor Sheridan is saying. But my peripheral vision sees plenty of him. Enough to keep me preoccupied. His meaty hands resting on the table casually. It's such an odd thing to notice. How his hands look normal right now and not like weapons. It just feels impossible to see him as anything but trouble.

The ring on his pointer finger has his initials on it, something I would call pretty on anyone else.

Good God, even in my side view he's gorgeous.

But not gorgeous like Easton. No. Easton is white picket fences, soccer dad, Sunday brunches, and sex with the lights off. And there is nothing wrong with that, that's something I want.

Something durable and safe. Reliable.

Alistair is gorgeous in a sinister kind of way. Reckless abandon, turmoil, broken hearts, but you'll never leave him because the way his mouth travels on your body while you're chained to his bed is enough to make any woman stay.

I didn't want trouble. I wanted safe.

This opportunity, this school, is my chance to have that one day. A life I don't have to run from. Yet, I was still allowing myself to be affected by him.

Even though I knew what would happen if I involved myself with a boy like him.

My hands are sweating, this itching feeling on my palms. The same feeling I get every time I'm about to steal something off someone. It puts the taste in your mouth like nectar. Sweet and addictive.

It's why walking away from the wrong side of the tracks is so hard.

You know how bad it is for you. You've seen what it can do to you. But it feels so fucking good that you just have to have it.

You crave it. You'd do anything for it. You'd die for it.

"You have a grudge against that pen?" he says, still facing the front of the classroom.

It would seem I'm not the only one using their peripheral vision at the moment.

His voice does nothing but agitate me more. I mean, why is he even here? Does he even take this class?

I'm annoyed that he is stirring me like this.

It's not unexpected, but you would think he would at least bring a sheet of paper and a pencil, a book even? Who shows up to class without supplies?

People like him have always bothered me. The ones who let their parents' money manage all their problems. Never grasping what struggle means because mommy and daddy bailed them out of everything.

Sure, the people in this town were afraid of him. Him and his frothing dogs.

But what were they except for four spoiled brats who relished in throwing tantrums? I mean, they weren't killers for Christ's sake; they'd be in jail if they were! They are just a pack of rich kids with bad attitudes.

"Are you even in this class?" As soon as I say it, I want to take it back. Not because I didn't mean it, but because I know he'll reply.

I shouldn't have even acknowledged him. But my mouth has never been good at keeping shut, especially when I'm annoyed.

We sit in silence and I hope, I fucking pray, he didn't hear me. That way I can forget I even spoke and get out of this class without a scratch.

He twists his head casually, looking directly at the side of my head as if he can't believe I said anything either.

"No," is all I get.

Just leave it alone, Briar. Leave him alone.

"So, what, you just sit in whatever class you want? Is that a perk of having your last name on a plaque outside of the library?" I glance over at him, his dark eyes observing my face.

Screw that. I'm going to make it clear to him that I'm not afraid of him or his friends. That messing with *me* is not a good idea.

A grin unfolds across his lips and I can't help but wonder what he would look like when he smiles. If the simple movement would soften his features at all.

"Careful," he suggests, "I wouldn't go around speaking about things you don't understand. You have no idea the *perks* I have because of my last name."

I roll my eyes, clutching my pen tighter in my hand like it's going to protect me somehow.

"Oh, I understand completely." The only way you get over what scares you is to face it, tear it down so it becomes nothing but a pest. "You're a posh boy who probably got his Amex taken away? Are you punishing mommy and daddy for grounding you from your Lambo? Bored of your extravagant lifestyle and wanna cause a little trouble? Get over yourself and welcome to every rich teen cliché. You're not special."

Yikes, Briar, that was harsh. Moreso than I would have liked to be, but I wanted to make it very clear I wasn't going to let him or his crazy-ass friends push me around. I refused to be Invisible Briar here.

It's not like they could do anything to me.

Nothing too damaging.

However, I'm not sure that's true as I count the ticks in his jaw.

One, does he work his jaw muscle out?

Two, he should shave his stubble.

Three, fuck.

He lets out a dark breath that flares his nose, tilting his neck just enough to crack it. Theoretically speaking, he isn't gonna hit me in front of all these people. Realistically, I don't know him well enough to know that he wouldn't.

Currently, I'm freaking out trying to figure out how to fix this before he explodes.

He shifts to face me once again, watching me with pits for eyes, reaching his hand out, seizing the leg of my chair and jerking me next to him. I can't tell if it's the chair squeaking or if it's me. Either way, my face flames a fierce red because I know people are watching.

I make an embarrassing *oof* sound when the corner of my seat clashes with his. That same hand I'd been staring at starts crawling up to clutch my thigh, his fingers squeezing roughly so that the denim of my jeans grates against me. And suddenly, I'm torn between the two halves of myself.

The side of me that wants to slap him for laying a hand on me, and the side of me that is throbbing from the heat of his fingers on my inner thigh. Dangerously close to my center.

His breath slaps me on the face, fanning across my lips and cheeks. I can smell the coffee on him, his morning cigarette, and the flavored gum he is chewing.

It's swirling around in my brain, jumbling my thoughts. Numbing the logical side of me just like the night I first saw him. I knew I should've left, but I stayed anyway. Just like I was doing right now.

My mouth is open, gaping at him as his dark eyes flick from my lips to my eyes, over and over again before he talks.

"There is a fine line between brave and stupid, girl. You are fucking toeing it." He breathes, my body recoiling from the insult, his face moves in even closer.

His lips desperately close to mine, an inch away maybe. I

can feel the warmth of his skin on my own and I know I should pull back, but I don't. My body won't let me. It refuses.

"They are not scared of me because of my money, they fear me because I could, and would, kill them if they crossed me. You should think about that before opening those cock-sucking lips again."

I inhale sharply, the lewd image of me on my knees in front of him while he said those exact words. My mouth wrapped snugly around the thick length in his jeans, his hand wound in my hair yanking me up and down it so he could pleasure himself.

"Don't be stupid. It'll get you killed," he ends, releasing my thigh and shoving my chair back to its place. Returning to face the board, crossing his arms across his chest like that didn't just happen.

A few students are turned around looking, our professor not noticing since we were all the way in the back and his back was turned to us.

I hold my breath, wanting to smack myself in the face, but also telling myself that I need to get laid as soon as possible because, obviously, I'm having a case of sexual deprivation if this psychopath is turning me on.

*I'm just projecting is all, that's it,* I tell myself as I try to calm my flushed cheeks and erratic breathing.

"You okay, Briar?" Easton's melodious voice comes as a safety blanket mixed with ice water, bringing me back to reality.

I blink, looking at the students who are charging out of the classroom and assembling their things. Apparently, I'd missed the dismissal. I didn't even hear if we had homework. I wordlessly thank myself for recording on my computer, saving the file instantly, and shove my things into my bag.

I stand up, "Yeah, I'm uh, fine. Totally fine."

Really believable, Briar. Honestly, where is your Oscar?

Easton looks down at Alistair, his once charming face

turning frigid. "Caldwell," he utters, giving him a less than stellar greeting.

"Sinclair." He sing-songs, looking up at him with a grin.

Next to each other, they look like the perfect representation of day and night. Ying and yang. Good and evil.

I'm grounded in my spot, not able to get past Alistair unless he moves his chair forward. So I just stand still, awkwardly watching them.

"How's your brother?" Easton asks smugly, like it's an inside joke or something.

Quick as a whip, Alistair responds with just as much irony, "How's your mom?"

For a few moments, they have a staring contest, neither of them speaking a word, only watching each other. It's clear they don't get along but know enough about one another to get under each other's skin.

"Come on, Briar, I'll help you find your next class," Easton snaps back to me, a friendly smile on his face.

I'm grateful for the help, wanting to get away from this situation as soon as possible, but Alistair has yet to move his chair.

"Let her out, asshole," he demands.

"If she asks me nicely, I'll think about it." This is directed at me.

Those dark eyes looking up at me and shining with a challenge. Daring me to do something about it.

I drink down the bile in my throat, not wanting to be late to my next class and needing some fresh air that doesn't smell like hot cloves. I hated being here, being in the middle of this.

I was not a girl who could be intimidated. My father raised me better than that.

You can do this, Briar.

I hitch my book bag up higher on my shoulder, pulling my hair to the side and taking a breath for courage.

With ease, I swing my leg over Alistair's lap trying to ignore the desire between my legs that's directly over his crotch. Our eyes meet for a split second, his jaw clenches and arms crossed at his chest, the veins bulging.

Easton grabs my hand for support, helping me pull my other leg over before I'm standing next to him on the outside row.

"I have Statistics with Gaines next," I tell him, already walking down the aisle towards the door, feeling the pair of ebony eyes follow my every move.

I try not to. I try to fight off the portion of me that looks for problems. The piece of me that misses the adrenaline of stealing and wandering in the shadows. I tell myself I can be different now, that I don't have to be that person.

But it wins. The fight is pointless.

Warily, I turn my head up to the top of the lecture hall, looking at the unmoving Alistair. His eyes never wavering from my own, like he knew I'd look back at him.

A smirk adorns his face just as he raises his hand, wiggling his fingers softly in a mock goodbye wave.

From down here, his eyes aren't as dark. They are a stunning brown color and I find it almost unfair that the boys stitched together with dark magic and cruel intentions always have the prettiest eyes.

# CHAPTER NINE
## Spade One

### Alistair

I went to therapy once.

Once as in, one single appointment that lasted maybe twenty-five minutes before the psychiatrist refused to work with me any longer.

I was twelve, five inches shorter than I was now, and I tried to stab my nineteen-year-old brother in our kitchen during a Christmas party, after I'd broken his nose and my right set of knuckles.

It's funny, I don't remember much of it besides what I've been told, and in perfect vision I recall sitting on the kitchen floor watching as connected people pulled strings, calling the best plastic surgeons and doctors money could buy.

My mother was bawling, holding Dorian's face in her hands while he held a blood-soaked handkerchief to his face, waving her away from him. They rushed out the door, everyone leaving shortly after and not a single person even looked for me. Not for punishment. Not for worry. Not even to ask why I did it. Nothing. The only reason I'd been put in therapy was because my grandmother insisted on it to save the Caldwell name. Claimed I had temporary explosive disorder, anything to make it look better.

They all waltzed right past the kitchen where I sat, clutching my shattered knuckles in my hand, watching them look right through me like I was nothing but glass. Something to only look through, never at. Not like Dorian, who was nothing but pure gold.

That had been my first punch. My first explosion of rage that I couldn't contain. I physically could not swallow it any longer, I had to do something. I wanted to hurt him. I wanted to kill him.

I'd walked to the fridge, grabbing a bag of frozen peas, knowing the cold would help the swelling go down. Rook had taught me that before I was even seven.

Dorian was in his second year at Hollow Heights and he'd decided he wanted an office, to study, fuck girls, whatever bullshit he'd told my parents. Instead of taking one of the fifteen thousand other free bedrooms, he took my conservatory. He picked it because he knew it was the only place in that fucking house I could stand. He didn't even want an office he just wanted to show me, once again, that everything in my life was nothing but his to take.

The conservatory was all the way on the west end of the house, it was a small circular extension of the original house. My grandfather had built it for my father when he was my age, and it had never been used until I was five.

When I was home, I stayed in there all the time.

I liked to listen to the rain pelt the glass case that surrounded it, watching the lightning strike trees and the thunder shake the small green couch inside. There wasn't much in there besides the couch. A few dead plants and useless bookshelves, but it was mine and it was the only place I had.

And he took it from me.

At the same age he was when I attempted to murder him, I still couldn't step into that room. When he left for graduate school, they left all of his shit in there and, truth be told, it stopped being mine the second he requested to have it.

The short list of places I could escape to had grown even shorter that day. It's still just as short.

The Graveyard was only for weekends, and I ruled the ring. Never beaten. Never touched. But it wasn't mine. Not really. Occasionally, I would go to Thatcher's house, but even there I felt out of place with all the one-of-a-kind sculptures and Victorian decorations.

The only place I had now was Spade One.

It was a tattoo shop just outside of Ponderosa Springs, shoved between an old barbershop and a general store. The neon sign that clung to the side of the window buzzed and cast a purple glow through the shop windows.

It had two stories, the bottom being the waiting room with black leather couches, the reception desk, and a small storage closet.

The upper floor was sectioned by tall glass plates, giving each artist their own space to decorate their station as they saw fit. Most of which was custom designs framed on the walls, stickers, and tattoo equipment. And in the back was a wooden desk where I stayed unless I was cleaning the shop or helping the tattoo artists.

The reason I'd been so furious at Dorian all those years ago, the reason he'd pushed me to throw my first punch, to truly awaken that rage inside me that won't leave, is because the conservatory was where I'd sketch.

I didn't keep it a secret because, well, it's not like my parents gave a fuck what I did. So, I would hang them on the glass panels of the conservatory walls. Each one covered with a cream sheet of paper and some sort of design I'd drawn. Dorian knew about it. He'd seen it.

By twelve, I had covered the space with them. So, when they remodeled it into his office, I never saw those pictures again. They had all been thrown away. Just another nail in my emotional coffin.

Not wanting him to win, never wanting my doodles to ever fall into their hands again, I started drawing on myself. My fingers, my hands, arms, and thighs. Wherever I could reach.

I often wondered if my father and mother even glanced at me, saw that I actually had talent. But I could have been an MIT graduate at ten with an IQ that rivaled Einstein and it still wouldn't have been enough to equal my brother. There was nothing I could ever do that would be good enough for them.

I think it was better I learned that at a young age instead of living my entire life vying for their attention when it would never happen. They had everything they needed in a child when they had Dorian. I was just a waste.

I'd started coming here, to Spade One, since I was seventeen. I found it one night while I was driving my car around late, contemplating running it over a popular jumping cliff with me inside of it. I had nothing I wanted to live for.

It's not nearly as sad as you think. I mean, it happens every day. People die, you get over it.

I'd been wanting to die since I found out the reason I was even given life. I mean, the boys would've had each other. I wasn't needed and I was tired of fighting for a life I hated. And that's when I saw the shop.

So, if you believed in Hollywood bullshit like fate, you could call it something like that.

When I walked in, met the owner, Shade, and started showing up with a fake ID just to get tattooed, I'd realized I finally found something that was truly mine.

Not my brother's. Not my parents'. Not even the boys'.

It was all mine, and no one could take that from me.

Shade let me work here when I had the time, free of charge on my part, and the only time I ever used a dime of my parents' money willingly was when I applied for my internship here after I found out I would be staying in Ponderosa Springs for the next year.

The original plan, before Rose, was leave for New York. Shade had taken a liking to my work and said he would set me up with a shop on the east coast for my internship. It was like someone had lifted a lifelong weight off my chest and I'd finally felt the wings they'd clipped as a child start to grow back.

Then someone had to go and murder my best friend's girl. A girl I'd seen as a little sister. And that entire plan was put on pause.

I was going to get the fuck out of this place, away from all the bullshit, and just start a life where nobody knew me. Where no one knew my last goddamn name.

The pencil in my hand snaps into two pieces, splintering onto the worktable and my unfinished tattoo design. It was a thigh piece I'd been working on since I got here today. Every tattoo that was on my body, I'd either done or drawn myself. My entire body was my portfolio. I'd let Shade do the ones I couldn't, but my legs were all me.

"Good time for a smoke break?" Shade says from his booth, looking up from the guy's leg he is blasting.

I nod, "I believe so." Pushing my chair back and standing up into a stretch.

"On your way back up, grab me some more gloves out of storage. Make sure—"

"The black ones. I do remember things, you know?" I call as my feet carry me down the steps and out the front door.

The foot traffic is slow, leaving me with some peace and

quiet as I light a Marlboro Red, letting the familiar smoke fill my lungs with the first draw.

I *thought* I was going to have peace and quiet.

My phone started buzzing in my front pocket on my second puff and I can't not answer. Not with everything going on.

I place the smoke on my lip, holding it between my teeth as I slide my finger across the screen, placing the speaker to my ear, "Yes, wife?"

I hear a scoff. "If I was your wife, you wouldn't dress like a retired motorcycle club president with a drinking problem," Thatcher informs me.

"You sure do bitch like a wife." I slide down the wall, squatting down and resting my back against the floor-to-ceiling windows outside the shop, "Why are you calling me?"

"Better question, where are you?"

"Why?" I answer his question with one of my own.

"Because you're supposed to be here helping us supervise Rook. You know, making sure he doesn't blow my house to tiny million-dollar pieces, while he makes chloroform in my basement."

Fuck.

I forgot about that.

Granted, it was pretty important, but I'm sure they could handle this one thing without having me there.

Chris Crawford, the teacher's assistant our snitching drug dealer told us about, was the only lead we had left. Saying it like that made us sound like vengeful detectives. Taking the law into our own hands, save the badge and give us knives.

All week we'd been following him around, just trying to catch him doing something out of the ordinary, and we'd almost stopped, given up on him, until Thatcher scored pictures of him going through product in his car after school. Whether he was our killer was to be determined. But he was supplying the drugs that killed Rose and that was better than nothing.

We had to have something to cling to. Anything. If we didn't, I was scared of what Silas would do.

"He's a chemistry major, Thatcher. It's just acetone and bleach. Your dead grandma could do it. As long as he doesn't get trigger happy, you'll be fine without me for a few hours."

As hungry as I was for retaliation, I couldn't help but hope this was the end. That Chris drugged Rosemary, trying to get in her pants, and it ended terribly. We could torture him until he died slowly. Then we could get on with our lives.

Except Silas, of course. It would take him years.

I'd watched them grow up together, Rose and him. She was the only one who really understood his schizophrenia. When they were together, it was like they were in their own little, twisted world.

I wasn't sure how long it would take for him to get over her. If ever.

"You never answered my original question, Alistair."

Oh, here it comes.

"I thought I made it very clear you'd make a shitty wife." Trying to distract him, but it's all in vain, I should know that by now.

"Where are you?" he deadpans, making it clear he doesn't want to ask again.

"I'm out," I exhale, looking around me.

Yeah, I *could* tell my best friend I was at a tattoo shop where I was doing an apprenticeship. It's not like I'm doing a drive-by, but it's the principle.

The fact I have this one thing to myself. Something I don't need to share or worry about being taken.

You never know how good ownership feels until you're the one who is never allowed to have anything, the one who's always being taken from.

"I needed a breather, went for a drive. You know what

Ponderosa Springs does to me. Why are you so keen on knowing?"

There is a silence, before he speaks again, "So, we are keeping secrets from each other now? That's what we are doing?"

"No." I breathe in the smoke, "If you needed to know, I'd tell you." Running a hand through my hair because I know he's about to catch an attitude with me.

I can practically hear his teeth grinding. I'm not even sure why he concerns himself with what I do, it's not like he's capable of actually caring about someone.

Everything inside of Thatcher is dead.

All emotion. Feeling. Remorse. Everything.

"Sure thing, friend," he mutters coldly.

"I'll meet you guys tomorrow," I say, but he doesn't hear it because I'm welcomed with the dial tone in my ear before I even finish my sentence.

"Fucking dickhead."

I stare down at my phone, seeing a missed text from Silas from earlier. I open it up, seeing a link and his text below it.

*The stuff you wanted.*

Tapping my thumb on the link, it takes me to a document folder that I'm assuming Silas put together. A smirk slowly forms on my face, like when you've been hunting something for months and you just start to sink your teeth into it.

On my screen is everything Silas was able to dig up about Briar Tatum Lowell.

Other than knowing she had a smart-ass mouth and Easton Sinclair had a hard-on for her, I knew jack shit and I hated that.

Unknowns weren't something I liked.

Her attitude towards me made it clear she wasn't a local, and while I liked a girl who could give it just as hard as she could take it, I wasn't joking when I said she was toeing a line.

In order to get under her skin the way I wanted to, I needed to know everything about my opponent. The one so brave and bold, so sure she wasn't afraid of me while her thighs quaked beneath my touch.

At first, I was going to let it go, but even after that class she was gnawing at me. Bugging me with her multicolored eyes. A mixture of gold, brown, and green swirled into one spiral. So, I checked Facebook before I messaged Silas. I hadn't been on Facebook in fucking years. I had to create a fake-ass account to even look her up. Turns out she isn't into social media either.

According to her high school transcript, she never missed a day of school, had a 4.0 GPA, and was on the swim team all four years. There was even an adorable picture from her freshman year when she had braces.

In all her school photos, there wasn't a single photo of her with a friend; it appeared my smart-ass was a loner. At her swim team senior night, she stood next to her parents, barely smiling, looking like she'd do anything to disappear into the crowd. Trying to make her body look smaller as to not take up much space. I would admit, the double braids she wore in the pool were making my cock twitch.

I continued thumbing through the files, curious how she was able to afford a school like Hollow Heights due to her parents' background. They barely had two coins to rub together. But I quickly caught up, finding out her uncle was a professor, Thomas Reid.

My eyebrows furrowed when a criminal record appeared, not just one, but three. My tongue running across my top lip. I knew there was something in her that craved me, now realizing it wasn't me, but the chaos that came with me.

She liked the shadows, too. Liked to lurk there. Stay there.

One count assault and battery, which is not only impressive on its own, but it was also on a guy who'd tried to attack her mother. Another charge of vandalism which just looked to be a prank of some kind. And one count of petty larceny.

So, she's a fighter and a thief. How interesting.

I wonder how many strings Thomas really had to pull in order to get a criminal into this school. In order for your application to even be glanced at here, you had to have thirteen fucking clubs and an insane GPA matched with stellar test scores.

And yet, she was here.

Here in Ponderosa Springs where she did not belong.

Running her pink mouth thinking I'd just sit and watch. Thinking Easton Sinclair will help her while she's being hunted by me. It's going to fill me with so much testosterone when she sees he's no help against me that I might combust. That little shit hasn't been able to do anything to me since kindergarten; there are some things daddy's money can't hide and that's pussy bitches.

I flick the butt of the cigarette onto the ground, embers dancing in the air as I do. I stand up to my full height and turn around to face the window of the shop.

The skull logo is transparent on my face, giving me a masked effect. The white skull covering my cheek bones and eyes. I tilt my head to the right and to the left, the skull seeming to move with me. A cruel representation of what I am on the inside.

Dead. Hollow. Empty. Merciless.

Except I don't need a mask to be any of those things. I just am.

Briar Lowell may think she isn't afraid of me because I haven't given her anything to be scared of.

Not yet anyway.

# CHAPTER TEN
## Hawthorne In The Woods With The Candlestick

### Briar

"How did you find this place?" I whisper naively, shaking my head at my ignorance.

I mean it's not like the dead can hear me, not that I'm aware of anyway.

When Lyra asked if I wanted to see something cool, I thought she meant a secret passageway in the university halls. Which wouldn't surprise me, I'm actually determined to find one. This place is too ancient not to have one.

I was not foreseeing hiking at least two miles into the woods behind the Rothchild buildings. We'd walked behind the buildings, sinking into the trees that swayed and keened.

The fog was right above our heads, settling lower and lower as the sun had begun to drop, melting into an obscure sunset of dusky purples and bitter oranges. We were walking near the coast; I could hear the crashing of waves against rocks nearby and smell the saltiness that coated the air. It was so powerful,

I could almost smell it above the rich scent of wet earth and sharp pine.

It wasn't until I saw the tombstones sprouting from the mossy ground that I really started to worry. There were ten, maybe twelve, graves marked with chipped and damaged markers, that were so covered in foliage and dirt you could barely make them out.

But that wasn't even the most unsettling part.

"My favorite part about Oregon is the bug population. When I was young, my mom would let me play in her garden and it never failed that I would return with a ladybug or some type of insect. So, when I was out looking for Scolopocryptops sexspinosus in the summer before school started . . ."

Even though it was somewhat unusual, I found it so fascinating how much she knew about bugs. Lyra was so intelligent that it sometimes made me jealous. The way her brain absorbed facts and spit them out from memory. It was remarkably impressive, yet she was so unaware of it that she didn't come off as a know-it-all. Just a girl who enjoyed talking about creepy crawly things.

I furrow my eyebrows, following her through the spongy marsh, "English, please."

She giggles, "Bark Centipedes. I needed one to finish my centipede specimen box and they are usually found in or around rotting wood. There had been a huge thunderstorm, so I went looking for fallen trees and I discovered this place." She holds the straps of her book bag, staring up at the towering building in front of us.

It was gray, gloomy, and looked like it might try to swallow me up if I wasn't careful. The thin alloy gate that acted as a door hung sideways off the hinges, and I saw a path of spiders slither along the top that sent a shiver down my spine.

"Is it a church or . . . ?" I asked, gazing up at it with her, a look of uncertainty on my face, the complete opposite on hers. She was beaming, exhilarated as she tugged on the metal gate, prying it open with impatient fingers.

"It's a mausoleum."

Oh, fuck that. Absolutely fucking not.

Lyra shifts to me, waving her flashlight teasingly, "Come on, don't be a wuss. It's cool inside."

Then she's off, disappearing inside the dark with a tiny glow to guide her way. My feet stay grounded outside. My brain trying to assure me that this was a disastrous idea, but my curiosity was greedy.

I looked up at the ominous clouds, the sky melting to black, and I started to feel a few chilly raindrops on my skin.

"I'm going to regret this," I mutter to myself, tossing my hood up onto my head and following after my strange friend in search of whatever it was we were coming here for.

I pull my own flashlight out, turning it on and brightening a set of narrow concrete steps that went down into the darkness. I took a breath, taking my first step cautiously to make sure I didn't fall.

Midway through, my Converse caught something, making me jerk forward. I hastily grabbed at the wall beside me, wincing as my hand encountered the damp surface. Steadying myself for a moment and wiping my hand on my jeans, I continued down the steps until I reached the bottom.

Lyra had already begun turning on oil lamps that I'm assuming she'd left here from her earlier visits, illuminating the room in a dim, warm glow. The smell was awful. It was moldy, dank, and the stench of rotting wood clung to the air like death.

The ceiling was much taller than I expected, the walls on either side of me layered with crypts, some of which were smashed open, and I was not about to check if the body was still in there. An unnecessarily large cross lay against the wall in front of me and in the center was a rectangular-fashioned granite table where Lyra laid all of her things down on.

"This is where I do my taxidermy. It's a lot more spacious and I don't have to worry about anyone barging in on me." She swirls in a small circle, arms outstretched as she looks up at the roof, like this place is some grand dining hall, and I suppose to Lyra, it is.

"So, why bugs?" I ask, grabbing a wooden crate and turning it on its top so I can sit down on it.

"Why not bugs?"

"Touché."

"My mom was a biologist, she worked with snakes in her medical research, so weird animals were common around my house. Probably why I take so well to your pet rat." She winks, using her flashlight to look around corners and underneath old boxes.

"Is your mom still . . . ?" I ask, dragging it out, hoping I haven't brought up a sensitive topic. Every time she talks about her, it's always in the past tense and I assumed that she had passed.

"Nope. Dead as a doornail." My eyes widen slightly at her crude words, but I know probably better than anyone that people cope with loss very differently. "She died when I was seven. I was put into foster care and when I turned eighteen I had full access to my inheritance and the insurance money. So, I enrolled, figured I'd already spent my entire youth here, might as well get my education here."

I nod, taking in all this new information, liking the fact that I was getting to know her. I'd never had a real friend before, and this was starting to feel a lot like a friendship that would last all through college.

She leaps towards a scuttering bug on the floor, her small hands skillfully picking it up and holding it in her palm as it crawls around on its six legs. Her flashlight shines on the exoskeleton, the insect's colors almost iridescent with its rich greens and shiny blues.

"Jewel Beetle. People used to use their carapace for jewelry in religious ceremonies. Now they're just a collector's item due to their color." She stares at the pretty bug, her eyes lit up with wonder and curiosity. She picks up a clear jar and slips it inside before shutting the lid tight.

"What about you? Is your mom dead? Your father? Siblings? You don't talk about yourself much, I've noticed. You're not a secret resident advisor, are you?" she jokes, her airy voice making me smile.

I'd never had anyone ask me that. My entire life no one had taken the liberty to ask me about who I was, about my life. I was struggling, trying to decide if I wanted to be honest about my parents, about what my father did, and who he made me into. Or if I wanted to lie because it's not like Lyra would ever know.

She would only know what I tell her.

I could make myself into anyone I wanted.

"My mom still lives in Texas and my dad is in state lockup, has been since I was thirteen." I breathe. "Grew up in the same broken-down trailer since I was born and I'm an only child. Not much to say about me, honestly."

"Is your dad in for something bad? Like killing someone?"

I shake my head, "Nope. He was a career thief. Pickpocketing, looting, that kinda stuff. One day he thought he could take on a bank. He was wrong."

"You miss him?"

"Yeah, every day. I know being a criminal is bad, stealing is wrong, but everything he ever did he did for me and my mom. He was just working with what he had. I did learn a few tricks from him, though," I say with a smirk.

Choosing to be honest with Lyra wasn't that troublesome. I didn't want the foundation of our friendship to be built on lies.

That's never healthy or good for anyone in the long run. Plus, I knew I could trust her not to judge me for anything I told her.

"Am I going to have to lock up my Cherry Coke and dark chocolate to prevent you from jacking it at night?" she says with a matching grin.

I laugh. "Your stash is safe. Scout's honor," raising three fingers and placing my hand on my heart.

The minutes pass, me watching her snoop around for interesting creatures that most would smash underneath a flip-flop. I even held a beetle that she swore would not bite me and it was kinda cool. The longer I'm down here the less creepy it becomes, once you get over the fact dead bodies are surrounding you it's not that bad.

It's kinda like a secluded hideaway, and because of that, we've decided to make it our gathering place for the Loner Society. A secret order of two people and two people only. Well, I guess until we make more friends, if that ever happens.

Everything was going fine until the sharp sound of someone screaming penetrated the air. It ricocheted off the walls, vibrating my feet, and the chambers of my heart constricted with panic. I jumped involuntarily, peering up at the steps from where the sound came. It was a cry for help, and the scariest part was it wasn't far away.

It was close.

Right outside the doors of the mausoleum.

They say you never know how your fight-or-flight instinct will work until it's triggered. It's easy enough to sit behind a movie screen and shout at the girl, "Don't go in the closet!"

But it's not that simple when *you're* the girl trapped in a creepy underground cemetery, and the only way out of the situation is to face whatever it is outside that's making a helpless human scream bloody murder.

"Did you—" I start.

"Yeah," Lyra finishes, nodding her head quickly. Her face is just as pale as mine.

We silently start to turn off the oil lamps, pulling our bags onto our shoulders without mumbling a word. Still not sure how we are going to get ourselves out of this situation when we don't even know what's outside waiting for us.

I look over at her, my hands sweating as I clutch my flashlight.

"We need to go see what's up there, then we can figure out a way to get away, okay?" I say, her face shining from the white glow of my flashlight.

She nods, clicking hers off, making the room much darker.

I take a shaky breath, recoiling as I hear another cry of agony. Like someone who's being shredded apart by an animal. Visions of the worst possible scenarios enter my head.

Someone being eaten alive by a blood-soaked bear or wolf. Even worse if they are being tortured by another human. Dragged out into the woods where no one could hear them scream because of the crashing waves and constant wind that howled.

I swallow the bile in my throat, clicking my flashlight off. I can't even see my hand in front of my face it's so dark. I feel Lyra reach out and grab the back of my book bag, clutching to me tightly as I start to feel my way to the steps.

My hands feel the filthy wall, my foot finding the first step. My teeth are clenched so tightly they are pulsating, trying so urgently to be quiet, terrified even the faintest of breaths will tell the thing outside we are down here.

I take each step gradually, seeing the metal gate still open and the cast of the moon gives us light to the outside. I can see the trees violently rocking, once again I can smell the ocean and I know we are about to see what is making that noise.

The farther up the steps we travel, the more I can hear. Like the low yelps and muffled groans. When we reach the top, both of us peering out to bear witness, the breath in my lungs ceases to exist.

The cords of dread inside me quiver.

Four tall men surround a body a few yards away. Their presence is an ominous one. That of evil and torment.

I lick my lips, their dryness coming on suddenly as cottonmouth sets up in my tongue.

"What are they—" I place a tender, yet firm hand over Lyra's mouth, silencing her beside me, my eyes wide as I shake my head, placing my free hand over my lips and making the *shh* face.

They are all dressed in black, head to toe. Their bodies blending into the night, one of them stands behind the man kneeling on the ground. From this distance, I can see how enlarged and beaten his face is. His eyes so bruised they are hardly open, dirt and blood coats his cheekbones.

The acid swishes around in my stomach and I want nothing more than to throw up right now. We are witnessing a crime. One that I'm not sure Lyra or I can stop.

I can only hear mumbling, nothing more. Just the hushed whispers and the sounds of one of their fists connecting to his bones. It's maddening, how powerful the impact is. I can actually hear his jaw break from over here.

It felt like a waiting game.

Do we run for it? Do we wait until they are done?

Lyra and I sit here, huddled down inside the mausoleum, straining our eyes to watch the horror in front of us. They beat him. Over and over again. No mercy, no sympathy. Just unadulterated rage and vigor.

This man, who would have to be identified by his teeth because his face was so unrecognizable, groaned. But he didn't beg for his life, he simply took it. Occasionally they would pause, possibly to ask a question, and when he didn't answer with what they wanted, it was another stroke to the face.

The pause this time was a little longer, their focus completely on him. A second later, I could hear the hiss of creatures most associated with the devil. One of them, the shorter of the group, drops a bag of colorful, slimy snakes on top of the guy. They wither and curl around his body, and I'd never heard terror like I did right then.

It wasn't just a scream of fear. He was horrified. This would traumatize this man for life. The memory of the snakes moving around his skin, hissing and striking at him. The sound ripped from his lungs and tore through the forest.

I grabbed Lyra's hand, guiding the way past the open gate noiselessly and to the left of the mausoleum. Keeping our distance from them, but still headed towards the direction of the school.

We needed to get help. We needed to get out of there before we were caught.

We crept leisurely, each leaf that cried beneath our shoes made us pause, hold our breath to make sure they hadn't heard before we kept moving. It was almost painful. How tightly I was straining my body. How careful I was being not to make a sound.

My jaw was sore from clenching and my head ached from all the blood pounding inside of it.

"Briar, is that a knife?" Lyra whispers nervously.

I turn to face the wicked group of people, even though I was trying to ignore them, hoping that if I did, the pressure in my chest would subside.

One of them had grabbed the man by his hair, dangling him out in front of everyone like a sacrificial lamb. His neck was exposed to the light, his Adam's apple that was coated in drops of blood protruded outward as they held his head back. Exposing him to the group.

I held my breath.

I watched in slow motion as the hooded figure lifted a blade that caught the glare of the moon, shimmering for a moment. My breath hung in the air, the seconds seemed to pass by in hours.

The knife ran across the man's windpipe, the thick crimson liquid beginning to leak out like a dam that had just released its floodgates. In an act of survival, he raised both hands to his neck, trying to hold pressure, attempting to prevent more blood loss, but it was no use.

He gurgled, frothing up even more blood from his mouth as he fought for his life. Withering and spurting. The last few moments of his existence leaving his body.

The blood had drenched the front of his clothing, pouring out of him at an unnatural speed and there was simply no stopping it.

My hand raised to my mouth, fingers trembling against my skin as scorching hot tears collected in my eyes. They fell of their own accord, and I had no intention of stopping them. Fear shrouded me. Unlike a shadow that just follows, fear infested my body. An infection that spread within milliseconds. It was consuming every fiber, every thought, every fleeting piece of hope, until there was nothing left between me and the shroud.

Only darkness.

Something else inside of me switched on. When asked about this moment years from now, hours from now maybe, I wouldn't know what to say. Because I was not in my own body.

My humanity had cut all ties to my soul. I felt no remorse. No sorrow. No pain. Like my brain had commanded my body to stop feeling entirely. Its sole purpose now was to get me out of this alive.

Seizing myself to move, I grabbed Lyra's arm hauling her towards the campus, only to be met with her resistance.

"H . . . e, he's de . . . dead," she mutters. "Really, dead. Like really, really—" Her eyes are glazed over. Possessed by something that is rooting her in place, something that's making her watch. If I wasn't there, I'd be afraid that she would stay here, watching them until they'd left.

"Dead, Lyra. I know. Now come on, we need to get out of here, please," I beg, jerking her arm.

The shaking in my voice must wake her up, finally turning her gaze from the scene and back to me. She nods once seeing my face and we both begin to pick up the pace in our exit.

I let Lyra go in front of me because she knows the way better than I do, but without flashlights, it's a guessing game.

You only see flashes of the moon's light between the trees, irregular and not enough to illuminate the ground in front of you. Which makes navigating through a forest a lot more difficult.

I think we are making headway. I think we might get out of this unharmed, but my shoelace gets caught on something, the abrupt tug at my leg makes me tumble to the ground with a heavy thud and light scream that I can't control.

My body hits the wet ground, my palms stinging with the impact, and I knew I'd cut myself from the blistering pain I felt. But the pain felt trivial. An afterthought honestly.

Because when my eyes looked up at Lyra, she wasn't looking down at me. She was staring beyond me towards the group of people who'd just murdered someone in cold blood.

Her mouth was slightly open and her eyes lustrous with tears. She was afraid.

And as my head shifted to look behind me, I understood why.

Like a pack of famished wolves who'd just inhaled fresh meat, all four of their heads were turned in our direction. Each one was locked onto us. Their hoods were still up, and I couldn't make out their faces in the dark, but I knew they were looking at us. At me.

A rush of adrenaline flew through my veins, my chest tightened and a strong wave of dizziness hit me. I was sure this time I was having an out-of-body experience.

Everything felt the necessity to work in overdrive, and I knew this was my body triggering my fight-or-flight. And when it came down to which one is selected, I thought it best not to argue.

I swung around to my friend, who still wasn't watching me.

"Lyra," I said calmly. "Run."

# CHAPTER ELEVEN
## *Come To Play?*

### *Alistair*

Everything was going according to plan. Everything was going fucking perfectly and I should have been prepared for it to go to shit.

Silas and Thatcher had grabbed Chris in the parking lot after he'd left late, the sun had set and the chloroform worked like a charm. He'd been unconscious in seconds.

They'd met me out here, miles beyond the school, Thatcher carrying his body over his shoulder. After Silas went through his phone, finding nothing useful besides Chris's anime porn search history, we tossed the phone into the car, so that it wouldn't be tracked back to us, and then Rook dumped his car off the side of Devil's Highway, a hundred-foot drop into the Pacific Ocean. They wouldn't find it for months, and by that time, they'd never be able to find his body.

When we all met out here in the woods and Chris had woken up, everything after that had also gone to plan.

Well, it took a minute or two for him to talk, after he finished screaming and I beat him to a literal pulp. He still just didn't get the fucking hint. We weren't taking no for an answer.

"Just tell us how your product ended up injected into the side of a dead girl's neck, Chris. You tell us that and this all goes away." I spat in his face, while he knelt on the ground in front of me.

He had one of those posh faces, where his nose was really thin and his eyes wide. I'd known Chris, prior to this moment and prior to starting at Hollow Heights. I knew him before I started going to classes I wasn't taking, just to watch him be a shit teaching assistant. Thumbing around on his phone playing Candy Crush.

He'd been friends with Dorian in high school. They ran in the same circles, were both on the swim team, and Chris had always been a douchebag. There are just some people that it sticks to like glue.

"Go fuck yourself, Caldwell. This won't be going away; my father will be hearing about this!" he complains, dyed blond hair coated with disgusting mud, his words coming out in a stutter because of his busted lip.

I grab the collar of his shirt with both of my hands, squeezing the material tightly as I lift him up towards my face.

"You think I'm scared of your fucking daddy? The only person who should be scared right now is you. Especially if you don't tell me what you know," I repeat.

There was a feeling in the air. A sorta buzz. It hummed and slithered through my body like a live-wire current, because I knew no matter what happened tonight, Chris Crawford would not be walking out of these woods alive.

A feeling of finding the truth about Rose. Of avenging a soul that never deserved what she got. My grip seems to tighten on his shirt, jaw twitching with impatience.

I wasn't surprised, I just didn't think he had the guts to do something like spit in my face. But sure enough, he reared back and spit right on the side of my cheek. The warm saliva mixed with blood was my breaking point.

He cackled as I turned my face from him, dropping him to the ground with a thud. The demons that live inside of my head raged. I was done playing my part. The truth was, I was the least dangerous of us. I'd always known that.

"I cannot tell you how much you're going to regret that," Thatcher says from behind me.

I lived for pain. For watching people crumple below my feet and succumb to the agony I warranted. If I never ate again, but could continue inflicting damage to others and feed off only the energy that came from their suffering, I promise I would.

But something that connected all four of us—something that we all enjoyed—was people's fear. We never wanted to be popular or homecoming kings. We wanted to scare everyone. So that when we walked into the room, they were terrified to look up. Afraid that eye contact would be the last straw before we did something horrific.

I made it a point to know the things that scared someone. What made their heart pound and their palms sweat.

While I knew Chris swam and enjoyed drugging girls at parties in high school just so he could get laid, I also knew something very important about him that was going to help me get what I wanted from him now.

Chris was deathly afraid of snakes.

He'd been over at the estate one summer, fucking around in the yard with my brother, when a simple, harmless garden snake made its way past them. Dorian had laughed about it for days, how Chris screamed like a girl running into the house without thinking twice about it.

I relished that memory. That gift I had been given at such a young age. To remember what it was that truly scared people. Not just superficially, but underneath it all. What made their skin crawl and caused them to have night terrors.

And then I'd exploit it. Because I ached for the power it gave me.

We all did.

The only real power in life is fear.

Money can be taken away. Titles can be stripped. But once you build a reputation the way we have, that fear that walks up everyone's spine when we walk into a room, can't be taken away.

I lifted the bottom of my shirt up, wiping roughly at my face. The spit coming off with ease.

"You bring them?" I ask Rook.

He lifts the brown sack up, shaking it a bit, the weight of it looked heavy. "Of course I did. This isn't my first rodeo. Are you forgetting about our senior prom?"

The prom we never attended. Well, not technically.

We did, however, release four fully-grown boa constrictors inside the building it was being held at. They didn't bite anyone, but it was fun to sit on top of the roof watching as students and teachers spilled out into the parking lot. Their screams echoing from the inside.

One of the many tricks we'd done.

Rook walks towards Chris, the bag in one hand. For a moment there is relief in Chris's eyes, thankful I'm done beating him. My toes curl thinking of how in just a few seconds, he'll be begging for me to kick the shit out of him if we'll stop what is happening. Rook makes his way behind Chris and says, "Death from snake bites isn't the way to go, Chris," before carefully turning the bag upside down and dumping the contents all over the kneeling man in front of him.

The black, red, and yellow snakes fell across his body. Covering his shoulders and lap. It took less than a millisecond before he realized what was happening. Registering that his worst fear had come true.

"How does that song go, Thatcher? Red and yellow can

kill a fellow?" Rook says as he squats behind him, saying it loud enough that he'd hear it over the hysteria.

The screams were so loud after that, he wouldn't have been able to hear us torment him. So acutely blaring I was positive he'd shattered the sound barrier. I wasn't even sure there was enough capacity in the human lungs to project screams like that.

He flung his arms wildly, throwing the silly creatures in multiple directions, their slinky bodies whirling in the wind. I doubt he knew that if he would have just sat calm, they would have minded their business and left him alone.

But coral snakes will bite when threatened, and being slung around seems pretty menacing when you're a snake. The first strike landed on his neck, the small mouth of the serpent opening to deliver the second most poisonous neurotoxin in the world. Another struck his hand. With two bites, he'd have less than three hours before his entire respiratory system shut down.

"Tell us what we want to know, Chris. You can walk out of this," I offer him. "The process of death from a neurotoxin is painful. Sweats, vomiting, excruciating pain. I can make it go away," I continue, walking towards his whitening body, so curious as to why he's so hell-bent on staying quiet about the drugs. What was it that he was hiding?

The screams had hushed, sobs had taken their place. His body shaking from the sheer force of his tears. He was looking up at me, pale face and milky eyes. Hopeless, broken, the will inside of him had snapped beneath my weight.

"I got a text! I got a te . . . text from my guy!" he wails, shaking. "Please just get them off! Get them off and I'll tell you!" He choked on his tears, the wetness allowed a stream down his face, cutting a path through the blood that had become a consistency like paint.

Rook comes to his rescue, well, as much as he can after snakebites. Using his foot, he moves them away from Crawford's shaking body. Picking a few of them up with his bare hands and laying them several feet away. Keeping one in his hand, playing with it,

"Will you put that shit down before you get bit," I scold.

He rolls his eyes, putting it down, "Yes, Captain Jackass."

My eyes return to Chris, watching him heave on his hands and knees. His entire stomach contents emptied out onto the ground. I wasn't sure if it was from the nerves or the bites. Either way, I found it hard to feel sorry for him.

I wondered if this is how Rose felt. If he'd been the one to end her life, if she felt scared like this. If she begged, if she cried for Silas. My nostrils flare, my boot pressing into Chris's side, kicking him over onto his back.

"Talk."

"I don't make the drugs." He coughs, "I don't . . . I just, I pick it up and drop it where it needs to go. When I started working there, I got a text from a random number. I thought it was bullshit, but there was always money in my account after the drops. This TA job doesn't pay shit and it's extra money." He breathes, wiping his mouth with the back of his hand.

"I got a text from my guy, I don't know who he is, I just know he tells me where to pick up the drugs and where they are headed. He told me he had something he needed me to take care of, I just thought . . . I thought it was another drug run or something. Told me he'd pay me twenty-five hundred for it."

Everything in this town comes down to money. Everything. This entire place had sold their soul to the devil for fucking nickels and dimes.

"Go on," I push.

He brings his hand to his neck, where the bite is swollen and red, wincing, "I showed up to the address, and there was a parked car. He had told me to check the trunk and that's when I found her. She was already dead!" he says, panicking.

"I told him I was out. I couldn't do it, but all he needed was for me to plant her body, make it look like an accidental OD. It was easy money, man! So I . . . I just, I . . . I left her at that trap house cause I knew that's where kids still partied."

His explanation just makes me angrier, it doesn't soothe or even help. It only makes it worse.

"So, we are just supposed to believe you didn't kill her? We are just supposed to take your word for it, Chris?" Thatcher accuses.

Chris raises his hand in defense, "I swear! I swear! That's all I know! I don't know who killed her." He weeps like a newborn baby, "The guy who texts me is a teacher. He's making the drugs, creating it in the school labs. I guess it's him, he did it! I don't know. Please, man, just don't let me die!" And he slowly turns into another blubbering mess, the pain beginning to set in. He rolls into a ball, cradling himself.

I run my hands down my face. I'm so fucking tired of running in circles. More dead ends. More people who don't fucking know anything. I ram my fist into the nearest tree, splintering the first layer of bark, and from the feel of it, slicing my knuckles wide the fuck open.

"God-fucking-dammit!" I yell into the sky.

And if I thought I was angry. If I thought my rage was unquenchable in this moment, I couldn't imagine what Silas was feeling as he appeared from the shadows.

He gives Chris no chance at pleading his case; he'd buried himself the moment he admitted to laying hands on Rose's dead body. There was no stopping him from walking behind Chris, grabbing his hair and yanking him up to his knees.

I couldn't argue when I watched the sharp blade slice straight across the flesh of Chris's neck. The thick liquid pouring from the wound, spilling onto the ground.

There was a moment of silence, our heavy breathing and

the sound of Chris's body spurting for help he was not going to receive from any of us before he was dead.

We took a second, to accept the fact Silas had just killed someone. For the first time, he'd ended a human's life, and it should have hit me harder than it did. Something inside of me should have changed if I was a normal person. But I wasn't. It just felt like an ordinary day.

And from that moment, that's when everything went to absolute shit.

I heard it.

The sound of a branch snapping, which could be an animal, but then I heard a girl's quick scream. It echoed around us, but I could tell it was close. Too close.

I jerked my head towards the sound, only seeing trees, until the moon gave me a perfect glimpse of where that scream had come from.

Not an animal, but a very scared Briar Lowell lying on the forest floor. A friend of hers, standing behind her, staring at us with her jaw on the ground.

I made eye contact with Briar. I saw the switch inside her brain shift to instinct over normal human reactions. She was about to dart.

There was a mixture of emotions that flooded my body. One was irritation. Why the fuck was she in the middle of these woods? Had she been following us? Irritation that I now had another problem I was going to need to handle. Irritation that she could be the reason we go down for murder.

She just went from an annoying pest that felt good beneath my fingers to public enemy number one.

However, the other emotion was raw.

It was the striking of flint inside the carnal part of me.

Like a wounded zebra, she held nothing but fear and survival in her eyes. They'd just witnessed everything we'd done to

Chris. They had just seen what we were capable of, and I highly doubt they planned to keep their mouths shut about it.

Like the night at the party, she knew what I would do next.

She knew I was the hunter and she was my prey, even more so now.

Natural selection at its finest.

A race to see who wants it more. They want to live and we are not going to get caught.

Predator versus prey.

And I never lose.

"The blonde is mine," I say arrogantly.

Rook howls into the night with laughter, the sinister cackle bouncing off the trees. The one who takes nothing seriously and is just excited to be a part of the chase. Thatcher has already started sprinting after them and Silas has made the executive decision to wait with Chris's body until we handle this problem.

My feet carry me through the winding trees, rain falling down in small drops, sliding down the back of my shirt. Boots thundering beneath my feet, pressing into the dirt to push me forward. I can see streaks of her wild honey-colored hair whipping behind her violently as she pumps her arms, willing her body to take her far away from me.

I'd entered into instinct mode. The burning in my chest from short spells of oxygen was ignored. I wasn't thinking of what would happen after this. The adrenaline that covers my insides is only allowing me to focus on one thing.

Catching her.

My reflexes help more in this moment than ever before as I dodge trees, fallen branches and rocks protruding from the ground. I watch as Briar's legs propel her forward, straining her tight jeans. Her red and black plaid button-down flapping in the wind.

My little red riding hood running from the big bad wolf.

Our story is inevitable.

I catch her.

I feast,

Her left foot ruins her. It catches an overgrown root, tripping her up just enough that I'm able to catch up.

I'm on her heels, she can feel me behind her now, all faith of getting away is slowly leaving her body and hopelessness will soon start to settle inside of her.

Taking a leap forward, I reach my arm forward, hooking it around her waist and yanking her to my body as we surge forward. My body twists instinctively so that my back will take the fall.

We tumble onto the ground, rolling to a stop. She pushes herself out of my arms, crawling on her hands and knees to get away from me. I snatch her ankle, yanking her back to me.

Quickly maneuvering my body to sit on top of her. Pinning her waist down with my own. Both of my knees planted firmly on either side of her body. Her arms and legs kick, she scratches, does everything she can possibly do to throw me off, but it's pointless.

A scream begins to rip from her chest, just as I slam my hand over her mouth, my palm pressing into her lips. My free hand gathering her hands and holding them over her head.

We are only twenty yards from campus, so that means we have to deal with this delicately. I can't have her screams waking the entire school up.

"Here I was thinking you were smart," I breathe, my chest heaving from the chase, a smile creeps up on my face, "You should know what happens when you run. It only makes me want to chase you more."

Her knee hits my ass, a sad attempt at pushing me off her body. I commended the effort, no matter how sad it was. I can admire someone who puts up a fight instead of begging for help. The kind of person who is their own savior.

She screams behind my palm, all of it muffled. It won't be long before she comes to terms with the fact that screaming isn't going to do anything.

I jerk her up from the ground, pushing her body in front of mine, her hands in my vise grip behind her back, my other still keeping her mouth shut.

Rook appears from the woods, her friend in a similar position in his arms. He's breathing heavily, his longish hair disheveled and flopping around. She also must have put up a hell of a fight.

"Well, it seems we have a small problem," Thatcher says sarcastically, adjusting his coat and clearing his throat. Placing his hands on his hips as he takes a deep breath.

"Small? They just watched us kill someone. So, what the fuck are we gonna do with them?" Rook breaths, the slight panic in his voice annoys me.

I'm going to take care of it. I always take care of it.

"I mean, we have options," Thatcher says, looking over at Briar. "It seems you caught the one you wanted, Ali," his eyes moving to Briar's friend.

I'd seen her around before, briefly, maybe twice in my entire life, but I knew she lived around here. I just wasn't sure who she was exactly.

Thatcher watches her and she returns that favor. Their eyes stuck on each other, in some weird satanic mating ritual.

"We can't fucking kill them, Thatch."

My blond friend, the one with more issues than hustler, smiled in the dark. The moon reflecting off it, blinding us.

"Says who?" He lifts his eyebrow, still looking at the small dark-haired girl. The flash of his pocketknife appears and Briar stiffens in my arms. Straight as a board. The hair on her arms pebbled.

Her friend was tiny compared to the lanky thing in my arms. Having her pressed into me showed me she was tall for a girl. I also noticed, through my deep breaths, that she smelt floral.

Soft, exotic, sweet.

Briar jerks in my arms, opposing Thatcher's statement. I wasn't sure if she was fighting for herself in this, or if she was fighting for her friend who had become a fascination to my psychopathic partner.

"Calm down, girl," I murmur into her hair. My voice holds a smirk, but I say it like you'd talk to a spooked horse.

"Says me, Thatcher. We kill them and we are no better than the scum we are after." Rook argues with him.

"Sweet, Rook. That's what you will never understand. I'm *not* any better than them," Thatcher croons.

"Will you two shut the fuck up so I can think," I grit out.

As easy as it would be to kill them right now, it wasn't the best idea. They, sadly, hadn't done anything, yet. So, killing them would be slaughtering innocent people, and that wasn't what I was into.

However, killing them would insure me and the boys were protected. I would do anything to make sure nothing would happen to them, even if it meant hurting someone innocent.

Goddammit.

"We aren't going to kill them. Because they are going to stay quiet, isn't that right, Briar?"

She shivers in my arms, like a cold chill just hit her.

*That's right, baby, I know everything about your sweet ass.*

I tighten my grip on her hands, leaning my head down to her shoulder, my breath zipping past her ear, "And if you don't, do you know what I'm going to do to you? Do you want to know what I'll do to your friend? What I'll let *him* do to your friend?" I nod towards Thatcher.

There is a small whimper that falls from her lips, one I doubt she meant to let out. I grind my teeth, my cock twitching in my jeans pressed against her ass.

"Show me how scared you are," I growl in her ear, the sound of my voice making her shake.

*Give it to me,* I want to whisper. *Let me feed off it.*

I want to see her on her knees, looking up at me with those kaleidoscope eyes, willing to do anything I want. I was so amped up in that moment.

I wanted to be beneath her skin. On top of her body. Between her legs. Feasting, conquering, showing her how hard she could come when she was shaking from pleasure and fear.

We weren't going to kill them. That's too easy. It's no fun.

We were going to do what we do best.

Scare people.

And secretly, I wasn't afraid of them snitching. What was a nobody from Texas and her friend going to say that anyone would actually believe?

"Fuck!" I hear Rook yell, his hands cupping his face as his captive takes off towards the school grounds. I'm too distracted by Rook to anticipate Briar sinking her teeth into the skin of my palm and shoving a forceful elbow into my gut, causing me to release her.

Both girls flee onto campus, dust left in their tracks.

Rook and Thatcher go to take off after them but I stop them.

"Don't."

"But what if they—"

"I have a plan" is all I say, and for them, it's enough.

They trust me. They know everything I ever do is for them.

# CHAPTER TWELVE
## *Snitches Get Stitches*

*Briar*

I felt sick.

Physically, mentally, spiritually, all of the "-allys" possible in the human body.

For the past two days, I'd been riddled with anxiety.

Constantly looking over my shoulder, expecting to see a police officer, or worse, one of them. Food barely had taste and I could hardly keep anything down.

Every time something hit the bottom of my stomach, I thought about the blood. I thought about the snakes and the screams, sending all I'd swallowed right back up my throat.

My insides were burning, acid reflux and the need to tell someone. Anyone. Keeping this secret that I had no business keeping was killing me on the inside. Eating me up.

My nights were haunted with dead bodies, death, and rotting corpses, tossing and turning until the dull sun cast into the dorm room.

Nightmares of how my heart nearly exploded out of my chest. How my feet ached from running so hard, and it still wasn't enough to keep me from his clutches. I saw his eyes in my sleep, I saw them when he was on top of me, peering into my soul.

So dark. Evil. Fueled by so much hatred.

It made me jolt from my bed, covered in sweat. His voice ringing in my ears, "*Show me how scared you are.*"

The way his hands held my wrists, his fingers digging into my skin. His palm over my mouth, the way his scent assaulted me in ways that made me ache. I could still feel his rough, hard body pushed into mine.

He felt dangerous. Like holding onto lightning. Everything about him made me feel unsafe and vulnerable. I had been at his mercy. He could have done anything he wanted to me, and I hated that.

I hated him for that power he had over me.

But what scared me more, more than his psycho friends, more than his murderous hands, was how, even though I was afraid for my life, it excited me.

In that moment I had felt alive. Every cell inside of me reverberated with vitality. I could have jumped off a cliff with no fear, robbed a bank. I felt superhuman with all the adrenaline that ran through me.

My body was still holding onto the attraction I felt for him the night of the party. My mind knew how crooked it was to be pulled to a guy like him, my brain understood the consequences. The destruction he would do.

But my body.

My body loved the flow of electricity. The endorphins.

Risking my life, my freedom, had been something I'd done since I was taught how to steal. It was a drug that I had quit before coming here, one I was determined not to run back to.

And Alistair Caldwell's hands felt like the worst kind of relapse.

I hated him most for that.

Thinking about him made me reach into my hoodie pocket, slipping my finger across the bulky ring that once adorned the king of my nightmares' hand. I could feel the hollow pieces from his carved initials, tracing them over and over again.

I stole it in case they did kill us. That way the police would know who to look for. If I was going down, I wouldn't go down alone.

For the past two days, I'd been waiting for the other shoe to drop. To see him walk inside my mathematics class, head straight towards me and suffocate me with his bare hands. Finishing the job he'd started in the woods.

I hadn't seen a single one of them and neither had Lyra.

The quiet creaks and groans of the nearly ancient library make me shiver. I quickly turn my head over my shoulder, making sure there is nothing, and no one, behind me.

Making my eyes strain to search between the rows and rows of dimly lit bookshelves, almost expecting him to be lurking in the shadows. However, there was nobody of importance, just other students searching for material.

I turn back in my seat, pulling my foot up in the chair and tucking it beneath me, my headphones in my ears as I return my gaze to the laminated newspaper articles.

The genealogy department inside the school library was way more extensive than I'd thought. I'd read through what felt like hundreds of articles about the history of this place and the town it sits upon.

Mostly, I'd looked for anything with the last names Caldwell, Van Doren, Hawthorne, and Pierson. This all felt like an elaborate chess game, and I was losing terribly because I didn't know my opponent properly.

From what I'd read, they were each a descendant from the town's original founders. Their families had been interwoven since the 1600s. Which meant old money and even older secrets. While there was basically nothing pertaining to them by themselves, there were a slew of reports surrounding their families.

Silas's father was one of the world's most successful technology owners. He'd created a system that protected big corporations from being cyber-hacked. It seemed any company that made money had invested in Hawthorne Tech. He also had two younger brothers, both in middle school and quite intelligent, winning awards left and right.

Rook's family was littered with lawyers and judges. The people in charge of balancing the scales of right and wrong. How could they have gotten it so wrong with this generation? There wasn't much about his mom, and I wasn't even sure she was around.

The Piersons, without a lack of a better word, were attention whores. There wasn't much on Thatcher, which didn't surprise me, but his multimillion-dollar grandparents were everywhere. They'd built a real estate empire after leaving the farming business in the fifties. But the biggest scandal surrounding that family was Thatcher's dad who was currently on death row after killing several women.

Here I was, thinking my family was screwed up. I was the poster child of happiness compared to some of these people. I mean, imagine growing up the son of a serial killer. You can't help but wonder what that does to a kid.

You can't help but understand how he turned out the way he is now.

It also made me question, is it nature? Or nurture? Is there something biologically coded into Thatcher's brain? Or did the sociopathic tendencies only surface after the world told him he was a monster?

Even though the other families had multiple features, the

Caldwells took the cake of most articles published in Ponderosa Springs.

Pages and pages of their story. How they came from nothing and built a legacy. The original migration to the area had been for religious freedom and from that they created one of the world's wealthiest towns. More than that, I'd found out that Alistair had an older brother named Dorian and he seemed to love the limelight.

All-star swimmer, valedictorian in high school and at Hollow Heights; he'd won just about every award you could think of. I almost gasped with how similar they looked. Almost like twins, even though Dorian was older. The main difference was Dorian was cheerful, a bright smile illuminating his features so his dark hair and eyes didn't look as dark as his brother's.

He was now living in Boston, a part of one of the best residency programs in the United States and would soon be a surgeon, according to this newest article.

I couldn't help but stare at the picture on the front page of a past write-up about family ties, Mr. and Mrs. Caldwell standing proud behind Dorian, each with a hand on his shoulder as he sat in a chair in front of them. All the while, Alistair was shoved to the side, no warmth, no attention, nothing was given to him.

He was an outsider everywhere. Including around his family.

"Hey, are you ready to go?"

I jump, placing my hand on my heart, the quick change of speed making me want to pass out. I'd been so on edge, restless, everything made me flinch.

"Sorry, I didn't mean to scare you." Lyra smiles softly, her hand still resting on my shoulder.

I quickly gather the research I'd been diving into, organizing it into a neat pile, before nodding.

"Yeah, let's get back before dark," I say.

Normally I wouldn't mind walking through campus at night. But *normally* I'm not worried about four killer assholes with a grudge against me either.

Together, we make our way out of the library. Instantly, I pull my clothing around me tighter to prevent the cool breeze from slicing through.

"I know you don't want to talk about it, but I think we need to. We need to figure out a plan, who we are gonna tell." My voice interrupts the silence of our walk.

To anyone passing by, we were just two girls chitchatting about life.

I had wanted to tell someone immediately after reaching safety. I still wanted to tell someone. I felt now would be the perfect time.

The only reason I hadn't was because Lyra was adamant about how horrible of an idea it was.

She was genuinely so terrified of them that even the thought of them finding out we said anything would send her into a breakdown.

"Not this again. I thought we agreed on not talking about it," she groans.

"No, no. *You* agreed. I never said that. It's our responsibility to tell someone. What about that man's family? Don't you think they deserve to know?"

It bothered me to think there was someone out there missing. Someone with a family missing them and we'd yet to inform anyone.

"You don't understand, Briar," Lyra tells me again as we walk through the grounds towards our dorm. My thin jacket is doing a shit job keeping the chilly wind from my skin. Summer is long gone, and fall has quickly arrived.

"I know they have money, but it doesn't protect them from everything," I argue for the hundredth time. "This isn't some

Tarantino flick. People don't just get away with this kind of stuff if you tell someone."

"They do if you have the right last name. Look," she breathes, looking around her quickly as if to make sure they aren't there, "they are the sons of founding families. Things are different in Ponderosa Springs than where you grew up. There is a hierarchy, unspoken rules, and one of those is those boys are untouchable."

It all sounded so unbelievable. Were they so protected that they could really get away with murder?

"I know all about it. Founding families. Rich bullshit. I know. We can go to authorities outside of Ponderosa Springs. We have options, Lyra. We can't just let them get away with this. Their legacy doesn't make them invisible to the law."

Her face is cold, serious, but I can still see the incline of fear in her eyes. "Yes, it does. They are above all of it. Sure, they each hate their wealth and family for the damage they've inflicted, but those last names shield them from *everything*. The fact they let us go in the first place is a gift. You don't know because you didn't grow up here, but they will do anything to protect each other. Lie, steal, cheat, kill. We are gum beneath their shoes. If it's them not going to jail or us living, they will not think twice about choosing each other."

My Converse pad against the cobblestones as we wind through the campus, other students walking past us. All of them worried about grades or parties, and we somehow drew the short straw. We were concerned about our lives and what we could have possibly done to curse God so wrongfully that he'd thrown us in the path of The Hollow Boys.

My clutch on Alistair's ring tightens.

"So, what, you really want to keep it to ourselves? Act like it never happened? You think you can do that?" I ask.

"Don't judge me! You don't see it but it's what is best for both of us," she responds, sliding through the door first.

"Lyra, we can't—"

"Briar! I already know what happens when you snitch on people like them. When you spill secrets about those families that are not your place to speak about." She slings her arm out, "My entire life was ruined because my mother thought the same way you did. And now she's six feet under rotting because of it." Her voice is shaky, her bottom lip wobbling as she turns to face me in the hallway.

My eyebrows furrow, "What are you talking about?"

I'd assumed her mother had died from a heart attack, maybe a car accident? What did they have to do with her mom dying?

She rakes her hand through her kinky hair, the rain making it frizz, her fingers getting caught in it as she frustratingly sighs.

"Henry Pierson is what I'm talking about. Thatcher's father. Butcher of the Spring. He murdered and raped women. Kept them in his basement for weeks at a time, just to prolong the torture as long as possible. He did unspeakable things to those women. And because my mother tried to be a hero, tried to be like you, she was one of those women."

My eyes widen, the bubbling of stomach acid making me ill.

A few weeks ago this place had been a dream. A land of opportunity.

It had quickly turned into my greatest nightmare.

"She saw him putting a body in his trunk while she was out for a run. Immediately, she went to the police thinking they would do something. Thinking they would protect," Lyra scoffs, biting her bottom lip hard and looking up at the ceiling.

"But she learned the hard way, there is no one who can protect you from someone like that. Here, there is nowhere to hide. Not from founding families." Angry tears well up in her eyes, gathering in the corners before a few of them fall, "I was there the night he showed up. Looking to tie up loose strings."

I gasp, my fingers covering my mouth, almost as if doing this will prevent the end of Lyra's story.

"He broke in and, my mom, she put me in her closet. I liked to sleep with her when I was little. She tried to call for help, but it was no use, he overpowered her. I watched what he did to her, Briar. I saw what men like them are capable of. I saw death that night. I laid next to her until the cleaning lady showed up the next day. I watched her decompose and swell up. I saw all of that. I saw what happened, and I'm trying to warn you, I'm trying to *save* you, by begging you not to say anything. It won't end the way you think."

Small tears drop from her eyes, dripping down her chin and onto the floor of our dorm hallway. I didn't even know what to say. How do you reply to something like that?

For the past two days I'd done nothing but bug her about telling someone, anyone, needing to release this off my chest, but I never realized what this might be doing to her.

How opening my mouth to the wrong people could affect her life and mine. I'd never been in this position before, at the mercy of someone else. There was nothing I could do to protect myself or Lyra. We couldn't call for help or reach out. We were all alone in this.

I hold my breath, reaching forward and grabbing Lyra's hand, showing my support. This unknown swelling in my stomach. Knots of nerves and anxiety because I didn't know what would happen next. I didn't know what my next move would be, but we would do it together.

Would they leave us alone? Would they finish what they started? What were they doing killing someone in the first place? What was it about their lives that were so bad it made them turn to murder?

These were lingering questions that I was afraid I'd never get the answers to.

"Okay, I understand. I won't say anything, I promise," I whisper softly, pulling her into a tight hug. Even though I didn't fully believe the words I said. I wouldn't say anything, not until I was positive nothing would happen to Lyra.

My eyes shut for a moment, thinking of how horrible it must have been for her. The nightmares she must have had, the hatred she must feel having to watch Thatcher waltz around the campus. Knowing that his father is the reason she became an orphan. There was rage in my stomach for her.

Her arms hugged me back, "How do you stand looking at him, Lyra? Why are you still staying here?" I question. If it was me, I feel like I would have darted away from this town as soon as possible.

She pulls back a bit, wiping her face clean of the tears, "It's hard to explain, but I feel close to her when I'm here. Leaving here is like leaving her, and I don't think I'm ready to do that yet."

I can tell there is more she wants to say, there is something she isn't telling me, but I don't push the subject. I believe she has shared quite enough family history for the day.

Silence returns as we walk to our room. Up the grand stairs to the third floor. I'd gotten sorta used to the extravagant decorations and over-the-top formalities. It was starting to become normal. Even though I'd only just started to settle in, I knew if these sleepless nights and haunted memories continued, I'd have to transfer next semester.

I couldn't stay here if I was constantly worried about who was watching me. Who was standing behind my back. But I also couldn't leave Lyra alone to fend off hungry wolves by herself.

There was noise in the hall when we reached the top step. At the end of the long corridor where our room sat on the left was a crowd of neighboring girls. Their voices bouncing off the walls and ricocheting towards us.

Utter panic begins to set in. I know it's not a coincidence

they are huddled around our dorm room, just like it wasn't a coincidence that I'd felt someone watching me in the library before Lyra showed up.

They were watching us. Toying with us.

Even though neither Lyra or I had seen them physically since the other night. They were still there. Prowling in the dark. Waiting patiently for the perfect time to strike. Ambush predators, animals that capture their prey with stealth and luring.

They'd become pursuit creatures that night out of necessity. But I knew, just as well as they did, men like them, they didn't chase. They *hunted.* Using the element of surprise to their advantage so that they strike when you least expect it, and the fear is freshly lit in the embers of your eyes.

That's what makes the hunt fun for them.

I don't let my fears deter me from finding out what exactly it was that had grabbed everyone's attention. What had been so interesting it caused everyone to leak out of their own spaces and into the hallway after a long day of classes.

"Excuse me," I mumble, parting through bodies. Navigating my way through them with Lyra on my heels. Her steps less anxious than mine, as if she already knew what was waiting.

"What is that?!"

"Fucking weirdos!"

"It reeks!"

There was one single nail piercing the skull of a skinned and sliced critter. Its medium-sized body dangles from silver nails, a stream of dark fluid flowing down the door and congealing in a blob on the floor. The smell had fermented due to the heat blasting through the halls.

Rotting meat and savage intent seeped into my body. My skin crawled with inevitability. My palms sweating, my mouth dry, and my heart striking my sternum like a drum. I pushed through, grabbing the doorknob and thrusting the door open.

I frantically made my way to the cage on my desk, flipping the lid open and clicking my tongue. Hope disintegrates in my chest. My sweet, all-white girl doesn't come skittering out of her hideaways for a treat as she normally does.

Desperately, I toss around the swings and houses, searching the entire space of her home. A sob rips from my throat as I pick up the metal cage, throwing it furiously to the ground. The pieces shatter on the floor.

I'd never felt such fury in my life. No one had ever done something like this to me before, came into my space and stolen from me. I'd always been the one doing the taking. *I'd* been in control of what someone could keep and what they couldn't.

"Briar . . ." Lyra whispers behind me, my shoulders rising and falling with massive breaths, tears running down my cheeks. My vision is blurry with anger and pain. Her eyes sad for me, but a piece of her wants to tell me, I told you so. I can see it.

I turn, seeing the entire floor watching me like I'm some circus act. I want to scream, to yell at them to get the hell out, and I'm about to.

But I see the paper. The white paper that's beneath my dead rat that's hanging from the door. I swipe my tears with the back of my hand, stalking to the door, the girls behind it jumping back at my aggressive nature.

I rip the note off the wall, peering down at the words scribbled in dark red, no doubt blood. There was no signature, nothing, because he knew I would identify who it was from. It wasn't from Rook, not Thatcher, or Silas.

No, it was from the one with the dark eyes.

*I'm coming for what's mine, Little Thief. Until then, keep quiet.*

# CHAPTER THIRTEEN
## Right On Target

### Alistair

*Pop-pop, pop-pop.*

The sharp sound propagates through the air and I don't have to message anyone to know where they are. A sound like heavy metal fireworks echoes as I walk around the side of Silas's house to the backyard where there is a section of the space dedicated to one of his many extracurricular activities.

The place we know he goes when the voices get too loud. When the things in his head start to seep out into the real world. The shooting range that his father designed for him is simple, targets at different yards, a booth that we are supposed to stand behind along with safety equipment that has never been touched. "Two hundred bucks says you won't stand in front of the fifteen-yard target," I hear Thatcher say as the gun stops going off.

"Make it five and you've got a deal," Rook bargains.

There is a quick shake of hands and I know I should say something. Tell them it's stupid and reckless, anyone else would. If I was a good friend, I would. We don't need someone shot on top of the shit we have on our plate, but if they are making the bet, I know who is shooting.

And he doesn't miss.

Ever.

Leaves have begun to fall on the ground, crunching beneath my feet as I make my way to the booth. I lean my arms on the bench, watching them. Silas is, surprisingly, out of his black hoodie, a gray T-shirt straining against his massive shoulders.

He always conceals himself. Never the kind of guy who struts around or shows off. Content being in the background. But when he's in his element, when he's doing what he enjoys, he loves to flaunt his talents.

Rook is holding a bag of chips, walking down the path of open trees standing in front of a black, white, and red target in the shape of a human's upper body. He turns to face us, smirking.

There is no fear. No anxiety. Just excitement for the adrenaline that's about to come. When you get over the obstacles your brain gives you when a fearful situation is present, when you face the panic head-on, fear can become the best aphrodisiac in the world.

It's called the flood.

A boost of endorphins through your system. Making your skin tingle and heart race. It's why there are adrenaline junkies in the world. Because they enjoy being scared. The rush of death.

Something we all have a taste for in one form or another.

Silas reloads his mag with a new clip, the clicking and clacking of the gun the only noise from him, even as he watches Rook grin like a cheeky bastard in front of him.

While Silas had gathered quite the collection of weapons over the years I've known him, he had a favorite. The one he used most often, the one he'd been given at fifteen.

The barrel of the Desert Eagle .50 catches the sunlight, the two sentences inscribed on each side reading,

*Non Timebo mala* on the left.

*Umbra et vallis tuae sunt* on the right.

It's Latin for, "*Fear no evil. The shadow and valley are yours.*"

It had been given as a birthday present from Rosemary. The custom red skull grip and polished chrome barrel had cost nothing less than three grand. It had been the perfect gift for someone like him, a testament to their relationship and the connection they had shared.

A connection meant to last a lifetime but was ripped viciously from both of them.

With ease he lifts the gun, the massive semi-automatic weapon was not something I was ever a fan of. I preferred to have full control over my destruction. Guns felt too impersonal. Not to mention, firing that thing felt like smacking a hammer against your hand.

Yet, he made it look easy. Simple. Like it was nothing.

Resting on my elbows, I waited, watching as he raised his right shoulder just below his cheek, holding the gun out in front of him expertly. Rook lifted his arms out wide, leaving Silas room to shoot around his body.

There is a pause for dramatic effect before the gun begins to go off. Barely jerking Silas's hands back as he fires over and over again, adjusting and positioning his aim to whiz past Rook's solid body.

Once the gun is empty, he points it down at the ground. Cracking his neck as he looks back up at his handiwork.

We all watch Rook step away from the target, a perfect line of bullet holes marking his silhouette behind him. I'd thought it was empty, until Silas fires two more bullets plunging two holes into the bag of chips.

"Tried to take a little off the top, didn't you, shithead?" Rook teases, pouting that his snack is now ruined.

A ghost of a smirk finds its way onto Silas's face and I smile a bit. The first real emotion besides rage or anguish evident that I'd seen since Rose died.

Rook was good at that. Making Silas smile, making him forget the pain for solitary moments at a time.

He needed this. Needed his friends. He needed to know that he would be okay and we would be there if he wasn't.

"Pay up, bitch." Rook puts a hand out to Thatcher who glides his hands into his slacks, thumbing through crisp hundred dollar bills, placing them in his palm.

"Shame he missed. I was hoping for a bit of blood."

"Course you were, Dracula," he says, folding the money into his back pocket.

I roll my tongue across the top of my teeth, "Not that I don't love spending time with you three, but any reason I received a 911 text?" I speak for the first time since arriving.

I'd planned on going to Spade One this evening, but I'd got an emergency meeting text from Silas, who rarely even messages in the group, so I knew it had to be important.

Thatcher is the first to acknowledge me, "It's about your little pet."

Briar Lowell.

Not a pet. Just a target.

I wasn't worried she'd opened her pretty mouth, I'd kept a close eye on both her and her friend. A testament to my abilities to stay out of sight because both of them couldn't stop looking over their shoulders.

Especially Briar.

She could feel me there and I think it was driving her insane she couldn't find me when she felt my eyes on her body. Hiding in the shadows of the library, through the windows of her classes. I'd made it a point to make sure she didn't mutter a single word.

I wasn't going to do anything severe, not until it was completely necessary. That was until I'd noticed a vital piece of me was missing. I'd thought maybe I'd lost it in the ruckus, but when the high settled, I realized I hadn't lost it.

It had been taken from me.

Her sticky fingers from years of thievery had stolen my ring. The girl who'd quickly shifted from a naive bystander with kaleidoscope eyes to the women who'd stolen from me.

I rubbed my finger where my missing ring used to sit, feeling naked without it. In my anger, I'd decided to kill two birds with one stone.

Sneaking into her room before I'd headed to the library to watch her. I'd planned on trashing the place to find what I had come for, but when it was nowhere to be found, I went with option B.

Prove a point and make sure they both knew what was to come if they spoke a word of what they'd witnessed.

I didn't even know she had a pet. That was luck on my end and a severe inconvenience for her.

Course, I let Thatcher handle the skinning of the animal, figured it'd be rude not to include him in something that bloody.

I hadn't seen her face when she found it. But I'd heard her, the wrathful scream, the crashing of throwing things around the room as I waited at the bottom of the steps of her hall.

That anger was all mine. I'd done that to her. Set a fire under her ass. And I owned every inch of that emotion. All of her emotions.

"What about it?" I ask, fist clenching at the need to get what belonged to me back.

"Silas finally got into the school badge access database," Rook says. "A joint and two bags of Doritos later and we found out that Briar's uncle, Thomas Reid, is a biology professor."

"And the study of organisms has to do with what exactly?" I say, not following.

"Look at you, Ali, paying attention in class. Mommy and Daddy would be so proud," Thatcher teases.

I grind my molars. Mommy and Daddy can go to Hell.

"Will you just fucking tell me what you found?"

"Thomas Reid has swiped in and out of the chemistry lab more than any science teacher at the university," Silas speaks, the click of metal ringing. Shocking me a bit that's he's actually talking.

"Over the past two years he's been in there after-hours. One, two in the morning. Hundreds of times."

I lick my bottom lip, "So we think he is the teacher who texted Chris? Not to state the obvious, but what if Chris was just lying so we didn't kill him? What if he's actually the one who did it."

I hated having to play this connect the dots shit. I felt like a corrupt detective and being a cop wasn't something I'd ever aspired to be.

"Why tell us about planting the body then? If he wanted to lie, wouldn't he have just denied all of it? Also, what teacher do you know who's headed into the chem lab at two in the morning? It would make sense for him to be, but we can't go chopping his head off," Rook smiles wickedly, "yet."

"But it's a lead. We can watch him, follow him, until we get the proof we need," he continues.

Rook's Zippo clicks, the flame lighting the end of his cigarette, "And we think his darling niece is involved or at least knows about it. I mean, think about it." He inhales, "She's broke as a fucking joke. You think a scholarship is what is paying for Hollow Heights? How'd she even get in to begin with, is an even better question. She's not exceptionally smart or wildly gifted. Thomas must have had quite a few strings he could pull to get her here. The kind of money that buys your homely-looking niece into a prestigious university. The kind of money that pays for people's silence."

I cross my arms across my chest, chewing the inside of my cheek.

This was it, a solid reason to go after her. Hard.

To show her what it's like when you get in over your head with people who don't give two fucks if you live or die.

Ideas crackled. Thoughts sparked.

Images of her wide eyes soaked with unshed tears and panic. Her rosy bottom lip trembling as she contemplates every life decision she ever made up to that point.

I was going to take everything from her.

Her joy. Her friends. Her secrets. Her fear.

It was all mine to take. All mine to steal.

"Yeah. I'm with you, but she wasn't even in Ponderosa Springs when Rose was killed. And I doubt her uncle is going around talking to her about murdering girls."

I did, however, need to proceed with caution. If we go after the wrong people, stepped on the wrong toes, harmed the wrong person, this entire operation would be over in twenty seconds flat.

"You defending her?"

I cut my eyes to Thatcher, his arms crossed over his chest, matching my stance. The wind pushing his slicked-back icy hair out of order. The gray turtleneck and black jacket made him look older. More sophisticated. It was just another layer of his intimidation process.

Look the part. Act the part. But inside, that's where you can rot in peace.

Inside you can be as evil and sinister as you desire. Thatcher believes in a mask. Hiding the world from what goes on beneath the surface.

I don't.

I wear who I am. I have no reason to hide.

He fits into the social food chain with appearance and communication. But we are the only three who have seen what is really beneath Thatch's frozen skin.

And because we know that, because we have him at a disadvantage, he despises the possibility of disloyalty. Of being betrayed.

"Does it sound like I'm defending her, asshole? I'm just stating facts." I furrow my eyebrows angrily, stepping from around the booth so we are on an equal playing field.

If there was one thing I hated, it was being questioned about my loyalty. Especially to them.

Rook places a hand on my chest, "Pipe down, boys. Nobody get their panties in a wad. I'm not saying she knows about the murder. Just saying, I have a good feeling that she knows something about the drugs. I mean," he scoffs out a laugh, "just look at her record. Not exactly a law-abiding citizen."

"Well, not all of us have daddies who clear our records." Now Thatcher is just being a dick. He is fully aware the price Rook pays at the end of the day for that favor from his father.

"How about we not get into daddy issues today, mm-kay American Psycho?"

I'd always admired that about Rook. His ability to laugh off pain, make a joke about something that would make anyone else angry.

Joining in on the fun, I sniff the air sarcastically, "Ignore him, it's shark week." I bump Rook's shoulder with a smirk and a chuckle.

Always the one to dish it and never the one to like taking it, an annoyed look settles in Thatcher's eye. Just as he raises both his fingers to each of us.

We had a direction, had another plan, another person of interest. As annoying as it was, we were getting closer. Each mark on our soul, all the blood we had spilled, it would be worth it in the end.

And now, I could have a little more fun with it.

"We have to be patient now," I say, making sure they are all listening to me. "We watch Thomas. See how he moves, what he does."

"And the girls?" Thatcher asks.

"We freak them out. Do what we need to insure their silence. Get whatever information from Briar we can in the process. But we do not lay a hand on them, not yet," I warn.

We had to build up to that. Have them so paranoid they could barely blink out of fear those seconds with their eyes closed would be the moment we would attack. Make them feel like every single moment we were watching, always there. Ready to pounce.

I wanted them haunted. I wanted them petrified and horror-ridden.

Only then, when we had the proof we needed, we could finish what we'd started.

The most exhilarated I have felt in a long time. My blood pumps, my mouth watering.

"Who doesn't love a little foreplay before the main event?" Rook wiggles his eyebrows, working of his own accord to take the gun from Silas, who is glaring at him for even touching it.

We have to get creative. We have to be sinister and stealthy.

We are going to make them wish we'd end them, just to get a break from the terror that wracked their bodies.

This was what I lived for.

# CHAPTER FOURTEEN

## By The Pricking Of The Thumbs

### Briar

I had officially hit extreme sleep deprivation. I'd started to heavily feel the effects of no sleep after forty-eight hours. Anxiety, irritability, and even hallucinating at the late hours of the night. Hearing the sounds of footsteps, creaking of doors, seeing shadows in my empty dorm room.

Even as I laid down in my bed, my eyes refused to close. My brain hell-bent on staying awake and alert. I didn't want to give them a chance to catch me vulnerable or at a disadvantage.

I felt like if I was always awake, I'd be ready at any given moment.

It'd been a few days since the commotion of my dead rat on the door. The whispers were still very loud, and people talked about me behind my back in class, but I'd learned to revert back to my old self. Blocking out everything that was being said, and really just started relying on Lyra for support who, thankfully, was fine with it, and leaned on me as well.

She took care of the mess on the door, quickly placing Ada

in a box and wiping up the blood she'd leaked. Together we buried her at the base of a tree behind one of the school buildings, throwing her a little funeral in the process before returning to our dorm and binge-watching the Harry Potter movies.

I tried to remain optimistic, but it didn't help. Every day felt like another waiting game, another day of catching a shadow move in the corner of my eye but turning to see no one was there.

Yesterday I'd had lunch with Uncle Thomas who was full of energy and talked the entire time. Which was fine, it meant all I had to do was smile and nod my head. He'd heard from my teachers I was a good student, and he was glad I was adjusting well.

And even though I wanted to tell him, I had promised Lyra I wouldn't. So, I kept it all to myself, swallowing it down with tasteless food as he continued talking about an upcoming annual school event that I didn't want to attend.

However, I told him I would go, hoping it was just an assembly of some sort. I wasn't in the mood to do anything but classes and hide in my dorm room.

I was living my life in a constant state of limbo now, always wondering when it would end.

After classes today I'd gone to the library to study, quickly realizing the warmth of the heater inside the large building, mixed with my tired eyes trying to read, was a terrible idea because I'd ended up falling asleep on one of my books and dreaming.

And, as had been the case lately, it was about him.

Not his wicked friends who walk with their heads high and grin like Cheshire cats as they strut around campus. Not even the one who thinks flipping his Zippo around is a personality trait.

I only dream of him.

I'm unsure of what it is about his demeanor that sets my spine straight or how he's able to make my senses heighten like a scared kitten. I'd never been fearful of a person the way I am with him.

There was just something about Alistair Caldwell that made me panic. Something inside of him was so dark, so damned, that it called to the deepest parts of my soul. The way he stared at me from across the courtyard, like he knew every single detail about my life.

What made me jump, what made me tick, my past, where I came from. He looked at me like he knew everything. What I would do before I even did it.

And he knew I'd stolen from him.

In retrospect, I wasn't sure I was making it out of his grasp alive and needed to have something on my body so they would know who killed me, I wasn't stealing because I wanted to. But because I had to.

I also couldn't walk up to him and throw the ring at him.

I liked having that edge on him.

I had something he wanted. Something he needed. If he wanted it back, he'd have to pry it from my dead hands. I felt like I had him at a disadvantage, maybe on a lesser scale than he had me, but a disadvantage nonetheless.

After I jolted awake from my quick slumber, I went for a swim, the cold water of the school pool had woken my muscles and given me a much-needed boost of energy. It felt nice to do something normal from my old life. I'd been a great swimmer in high school, not like it mattered to be a starter or anything because I didn't have the correct last name, but I was good.

My hair smelled like chemicals when I was finished, my fingers pruned, and even though I was nervous a shower would make me sleepy, I needed to wash off the pool water.

So, I'd slipped my clothes on over my damp bathing suit, planning to run all the way back to the dorms before I slipped beneath the hot water that would soothe my muscles. I shivered at the prospect as I pushed the door open from the pool, starting my walk across campus.

The wind bites at my skin harshly, goosebumps appearing automatically. My feet rushed across the campus, covering as much ground as I possibly could with my speed-walking. I could see the light escaping from the top window of my dorm hall door, almost to safety, when a different cold chill fell upon my shoulders.

I'd felt it too late, the presence of someone behind me. The sun was gone, I was all alone, and the urge to scream bubbled in my stomach. I quickly turned around, prepared to see what I always do, nothing.

He doesn't let me see him. He just stays long enough for me to know he's watching.

I am prepared though. I'm ready.

I ball my fist up, spinning around on my heels when I feel him close in on my body.

"Br—" I hear the beginning of my name from his mouth only a second before I slug my fist upward, hoping I make contact with something on his face.

My knuckles instantly throb, my face flashing hot when I see a swoosh of golden strung hair.

Oh God.

"What the fuck!" Easton hisses, holding his jaw where I'd thrown the best right hook of my life. Ronda Rousey would be proud.

My heart beats rapidly, nerves and the quick comedown from being frightened is a rush to my head. I place my hands over my mouth,

"Oh my shit. Oh my God, I'm so sorry," I mumble.

He turns his head to face me, still holding his face, rubbing the red area on his cheekbone.

"Damn girl. Wouldn't want to meet you in a dark alley," he jokes through the pain, and I laugh nervously.

"I'm so sorry, I didn't mean to, I just, I thought you were—" I freeze, thinking it's best not to finish that sentence the way I wanted to.

"Thought I was . . . ? A mugger?"

"Something like that. Are you okay?" I ask, worried. I feel like I'd just punched a guy who relies on his face more than most. Taking breaths, I tried to calm myself down.

"I'll survive. Better question, are you okay? You looked seriously spooked."

I run my hands down my face anxiously, sighing, "I'm tired is all. Haven't been sleeping well, my head is all over the place."

He nods in understanding, the redness growing, and I know it'll bruise by morning. "If it makes you feel any better, I think I broke my knuckle." I raise my hand so he can see the already swollen joint.

With ease, he grabs my hand, not giving me enough time to even flinch. Lowering his eyes to examine my knuckles, his thumb brushes over the sensitive skin and I wince slightly.

"I think you might have broken it. Do you want me to go grab you some ice?" He breathes his words onto my hand, his lips closer than they need to be. I can feel the warmth of his skin near my own, quickly retracting my hand.

I've stolen a lot of things.

A blender, a TV, a watch, I even stole batteries out of remotes.

Someone's boyfriend isn't one of the things I plan on adding to the list.

"I'll be okay, just a little scratch is all. You can just tell Mary the other guy looks worse than you do tomorrow," I slide in, smiling softly.

"Yeah," he nods, scratching the back of his neck in a boyish way, "I'll try that. It's all good, though. I shouldn't have run up on you like that. I think everyone is a little freaked out right now."

There it is again.

The panic.

"What for?" I ask the question I'm positive I know the answer to.

"The teaching assistant, Chris? The one from our Applied Mathematics class? He's missing. Has been for the past few days, and now Coraline Whittaker has gone missing. Her parents reported it yesterday, everyone's bugged out. This town loves to fuel rumors and scare non-locals with their ghost stories." He smirks, "They probably just ditched this place, wouldn't be the first time the pressure of Ponderosa Springs got to someone."

I'd already punched him in the face and now I was feeling the urge to upchuck on his shoes. This was the first time since we'd seen the murder that someone had mentioned it to me.

My mouth dried up completely. My head filling with images of the snakes crawling all over his body, their sharp teeth sinking into his skin. Watching the blood pour like a waterfall from his throat. The sounds of him gurgling for his life.

I quiver, stepping back from Easton, needing to get to my dorm room.

"Yeah, probably just needed a break from the school or something," I reply. "I've got to get back to my room, I'll see you in class tomorrow."

Clutching the strap of my bag, "And I'm sorry about your face! I'll make it up to you with homework answers sometime." I rush, wanting to leave this conversation.

He furrows his eyebrows in uncertainty. Probably thinking about how weird I am, considering I'd socked him in the face and was running away like a chicken with my head cut off.

I turn my back, moving my legs towards my hall.

"Briar!" he calls behind me.

Shifting my neck to look at him, "Yeah?"

"Be careful. Not everyone here is who they pretend to be." He lifts his hand in the air, rubbing his middle finger in reference to the ring that's adorning my own. I'd forgotten about it, forgotten that I'd slipped it on after my swim because I didn't have any pockets.

"Yeah, uh, thanks," I call back, disappearing into the safety of my dorm hall.

Great. Perfect.

He now thinks I'm with Alistair. Let's just add that to the list of things that don't need to be happening in my life right now.

I nearly sprint to my room, fumbling my way into the door. Everything begins to spin, I can't seem to catch up with the speed of things. The room is dark, besides Lyra's bedside lamp, the dim light casting a shadow onto her sleeping face. A book she'd been reading resting on her chest as she sleeps peacefully.

What I would give to do that.

To not dream of him.

To not think of him.

I lock myself in the bathroom, rushing to the toilet where I collapse hard on my knees. They dig into the tiles as I empty what little food I have in my body out into the white bowl.

My ribs tighten, my throat already sore from the stomach acid. My eyes shut as static flickers behind them. All the snakes. All the blood. The sound of them howling with laughter as they chased us through the woods.

It was a game to them.

They'd probably only killed Chris for fun. A joke. So bored with all their money and status they had to up the ante. Knowing their last names would save them from any backlash they'd receive.

They wouldn't even come close to getting caught, because in all the chaos is calculation. They have a reason for everything, a plan, always plotting their next move.

I don't stand until I'm sure I'm done, only then do I begin shedding my clothes and hopping into the white-tiled shower.

Pulling the stiff, plastic curtain closed, I close my eyes, lifting my head up to the showerhead as my fingers turn the cool metal to scorching hot water. I wanted to melt the memories off me.

"Uh," I gasp sharply. The water is a shock to my system, my freezing toes stinging underneath the heat. I almost moaned at how good it felt. Dropping my head, letting the stream cascade down my back and coat my hair.

I felt every drop bounce off my skin, silent beside from the pitter-patter of water smacking the tiles beneath my toes. I focused on my breathing, on the liquid, how warm I felt.

Since it had happened, I thought about why they'd committed murder. Were they truly that bored? Or had something else happened?

Were people really born monsters? Or were they conditioned to be that way?

And that girl, Coraline, they wouldn't have done something to her, would they? Which led me to wonder, if they had done something to her, were they the reason Silas's girlfriend wound up dead?

I couldn't imagine someone being so cruel they'd murder their own girlfriend, but I'd also never seen anyone like these four boys, so anything was possible.

Anything.

I was an outsider looking in on the secrets and treachery of this town. I was at a major disadvantage. Lyra knew the ins and outs. All I knew was what I was learning from day to day and it wasn't enough to prepare me for them.

My fingers raked the tangles out of my hair, the steam from the water clearing my chest. I opened my eyes, my intention was to grab the shampoo for my hair, but I was blinded by red, literally.

At first, I thought my knuckles were bleeding, but it was too much, there was so much blood surrounding me there was no way it was from me, I would have been dead.

It was like something out of a nightmare.

My hands were veiled with a thin layer of dark red fluid. It poured down my face, falling into my eyes making everything blurry. The color of blood enshrouds me.

I whip my hair to the left, watching it splatter on the white tiles, leaking down to race towards the drain. I smeared it down my arms, across my stomach, gaping at how much there was. How thick it felt against my smooth skin.

My heart raced, pounded, thumped, and tried running for its life.

Even though it was almost scentless, the smell of iron and old pennies burned my nose hairs. It felt too real. All of this felt so real.

I remembered Chris and all the blood that trickled from his neck. This was my karma for not telling, for letting him die like a slaughtered animal.

Tears mingled with the crimson water, my throat clogged from too many emotions. But soon animosity swells. It bubbles and froths in my stomach because I know this is not karma. This was done by someone with two arms and two legs, not destiny or some divine intervention.

I felt stupid for doubting them. For doubting the lengths they'd be willing to go to in order to ensure our cooperation. They had been inside our dorm again. Showing how easily they could sneak in and out of our home, proving how unprotected we really were.

My hands reach for the shower nozzle, unscrewing and yanking it into pieces. Five fake, plastic pods are shoved inside, dripping with false blood. I sling the nozzle onto the ground, not caring if I wake Lyra.

I find the tiles for support, resting both of my hands on them as I drop my head down, breathing deeply.

It cascades down me in rivers and puddles, crashing against my skin and seeping down the drain. The red color taunting me.

Their way of telling me I have blood on my hands. Showing me that I'm not innocent in this. I watched them do that to that man. I didn't scream for help or shout at them to stop, I just let it happen.

Chris's blood coats my hands just as much as theirs. I was guilty. I was no better than them and that's how they wanted it to be.

They wanted us to be dirty. Liars. Murderers. They wanted us to feel the guilt on our souls.

We are the puppets laced with their strings. Waiting for their next move. Our entire lives in their hands, who knows how long they'll continue to remind us of that with these small antics.

They have us right where they need us.

There was nowhere to hide, nowhere to run.

No way out.

# CHAPTER FIFTEEN

## *Something Wicked This Way Comes*

### *Briar*

The school function Thomas had made me promise I'd attend was, in fact, not an assembly.

The entire school, or I guess what looked like it, had gathered outside the back of the Bursley District, where I spent most of my time. It was where most of the mathematics classes were held.

Instead of an open common like the middle of the grounds, a recreational hall like behind the Irvine District, or the creepy mausoleum beyond the Rothchild District, there was instead a hedge maze.

Was it really a surprise that Hollow Heights would have a lavish maze, probably with some spooky story attached to its name? Not really.

I'd learned quickly it came with the territory.

Ponderosa Springs and the university that was built upon it was not for the faint of heart.

The seven concentric circles made of boxwood hedges

took up all the space behind the building before it faded into forest line. One single entrance into the encroaching formed grass, and what I assumed was one way out. In the center sat a tower with a double-helical external staircase, just to confuse people more.

Nighttime had come fast, students wearing glow in the dark bracelets and holding flashlights as they huddled in groups, laughing, enjoying another collegiate event they'd talk about on their wedding day.

I envied them.

Their oblivious nature and privilege.

I wondered how many people would show up if they knew students were being taken and teachers were being murdered in the woods.

Would they still enjoy themselves? Would the umbrella of wealth shield them from things even as cruel as death?

I wasn't so sure.

Slipping my thumbs neatly into the holes at the cuff of my long-sleeve shirt, the polyester felt smooth against my skin when the wind pressed it tighter into my body. Lyra had braided my hair tightly down my back, hiding the slight red that stained my dirty blonde strands.

We scrubbed the shower for hours on our hands and knees with little proof. The white tile had a faint pink layer now. Not to mention, my skin was still tinted the same color even after a clean shower.

"They call it the Labyrinth," Lyra speaks, walking in pace with me as we glide down the cobblestone steps to the damp grass in front of the soaring maze.

My stomach rumbled with lack of food and exhaustion, "Of course it is."

I cross my arms in front of my chest, leaning on my left foot to peer into the entrance, greeted with the sight of darkness and a scarce amount of moonlight. There was no way we could navigate our way through this without a flashlight.

"It was inspired by the Greek myth, you know Theseus and the Minotaur? The builders wanted it to be a replica of the one in Crete. They do this game for the freshmen every year, the challenge is always different and it's usually a puzzle of some sort. I had been looking forward to this when I was in high school." The use of the past tense does not escape me. Had been looking forward to, as in she could not care less now.

They hadn't only stolen our sense of safety, they'd stolen our sense of joy. We were so afraid to do anything fun, so scared they'd pop up around the corner and burn us to the ground.

Which sucked because I'd always considered myself pretty decent at puzzles.

"Welcome the freshman class of Hollow Heights!" one of the teachers announces with a microphone at the top of the cobblestone steps behind us.

"We are excited to include you in a century-old tradition here! Every single year is a different game, but the reward is always the same. If you find the golden key inside the Labyrinth, you win access to one of the school's many hidden rooms that have been remolded into private recreational halls."

There is a loud cheer and resounding enthusiasm from our peers, more excited for the competition than the reward, I'm sure. Although this is a renowned university with more plaques and awards than the fucking Pope, they don't offer organized sports, afraid athletics will become more of a priority than education, and that cannot happen at a school like this one.

If anyone for one single second thought Hollow Heights was doing anything to steer the greatest young minds of generations off-course, they'd be discredited immediately. People try for years to get their children in here, to even have their applications touched by a fucking paper clip.

This is where our future America would be coming from.

It messed with my mind to know four of those people already had a rap sheet bloody as a tampon, what did they plan to do after this? Would they be helping kids? Ruling the free world?

"Teams of two and three only! Each team will have fifteen minutes inside the maze to locate the key, if you are unsuccessful, after the air horn goes off, raise your flashlight up to the sky and wait for a teacher to come and guide you out of the maze. As always, we want to insure your safety during these fun times . . ." They go on to a list of safety precautions that more than half of us won't remember in twenty seconds, the rest didn't listen to the first time around.

My eyes scanned the sea of students, subconsciously searching for one of them. Another quick lesson I'd learned is if you saw one of The Hollow Boys, the other three were not far behind. There was never one without the others. Like sharks that hunted in a pack, it's never the shark you see you need to worry yourself about, it's the one lurking in the shadows that you can't spot that's more likely to take off a hunk of your leg.

I don't see Silas's black hoodie, Thatcher's frozen-tinted hair, or hear the click of Rook's Zippo over the noise. I didn't even feel the pressure that comes when Alistair's eyes are on me. That's usually how I know they are sniffing around.

The panic. The sweat. The adrenaline.

It's like every feeling I'd ever experienced combined into one, yet at the same time it was like nothing I'd ever experienced before.

God, I hated him for it.

But tonight, I didn't see them. I couldn't sense their presence. Organized school functions weren't exactly their thing anyway. Too many eyes, too many expectations to be upheld.

I nudge Lyra with my hip, smirking a bit, "We can still make this fun, yeah? It would be nice to have a secret place to hide."

She laughs breathily and it's the first sound of joy in the last few weeks.

"You really think we are going to find it before Try-hard Tracy and Golden Boy Garrett do?" Her eyes avert to Easton and Mary, a power couple in both vision and personality.

I don't miss the yellow-and-purple bruise adorning his otherwise perfect face, or the way Mary has intentionally matched her cardigan to the color of his shirt.

"This isn't about whose daddy can buy them the biggest yacht. This is about navigating a maze. No money. No status. Sure, from day-to-day they have the upper hand, but right now, we have the advantage."

"Our charming personalities?"

I push her shoulder lightly, the breeze catching her curls and pushing them behind her shoulder, "Besides that, smart-ass. Our advantage is street smarts. You think these kids have ever had to think on their feet before? Get themselves out of a tricky situation without their mom and dad? I doubt it." I wasn't being mean, just telling the truth.

It seemed to me Lyra and I were the only two people at this school who'd grown up below the millionaire line. Sure, Lyra had money now as an eighteen-year-old, but she grew up in the system and I knew how that was. I saw what foster care did to kids. What it turned them into and let them become.

From birth you're brought into this world without the ability to take care of yourself. You have to learn and adapt from watching others. Most have parents who guide and teach them. To show them the wrongs and rights of life.

Then there are others.

The outcasts, the castaways, the loners of the world who learn all these things themselves. We learn the hard way, we learn by failing, by mistakes. We grow claws and sharp teeth instead of warm hearts. We fight our way to the top. We take care of ourselves and our own. That's it.

"You're not worried about—" she pauses, looking over her shoulder to make sure no one is listening, "the maze catching fire or being hooked by a bear trap?"

I don't laugh, even though I should. I wouldn't put it past any of them to do something like that.

Was I worried? Yes.

Was I going to let that ruin this? I was going to try like hell not to.

"I doubt they'll be here tonight. Plus, they can't get into the maze when we are inside, there are teachers at both entrances. We should be safe to enjoy ourselves tonight, okay?" I reassure her.

She nods, not realizing that I plan on continuing, "But I really think we should consider telling someone, Lyra."

Nothing comes out of her mouth for a while, silence as we hear an air horn blare around us over and over again signaling the start and finish of people's time inside the Labyrinth.

"Let's take tonight. Just this moment. Just one night of normal and we can talk about what we need to do in the morning."

It was the closest I'd gotten to a yes from her. I knew she was more apt to say no right now, but I still felt like this was a small win. She was beginning to warm up to the idea of confiding in someone. The police. A teacher. Anyone who could help us.

I hook my arm through hers, "You gonna be able to keep up in that skirt?" The green-and-black plaid material brushed the top of her thighs, putting me in the mindset of Slytherin uniforms from *Harry Potter*.

It was cute the way Lyra was such a paradox. She wore plaid skirts and corduroy pants to collect creepy insects from the mud. Always coming into the dorm with dirt dusting her knees and palms. The way she crossed her legs when she sat with a book in her lap yet burped louder than any grown man I'd heard after downing a can of Coke. How she could be so soft, so feminine, yet do something that would be viewed as tomboyish. I admired the way she was able to balance out the pieces of herself so easily.

"Probably not, but we are gonna give it a shot." She laughs, pulling me towards the shortening line for the entrance to the maze.

We talked to pass the time, watched as students failed over and over again, the shrill air horn piercing the sky just before a teacher announced another team had yet to locate the key.

Our turn was next, and we stood between Lyra's psych teacher and my statistics professor, waiting for the go-ahead to enter the looming darkness between the plush green hedges.

A gust of wind hit me from the back, pushing me forward enough that I had to catch myself on the edge of the maze. It barreled through the trees, their achy limbs groaning and swaying beyond us.

I look down at my balled fists, the way my nails dig into the flesh of my palm, as the rhythm of my heart begins to pick up.

"Briar!" Lyra snaps her fingers in front of my face, attempting to bring me back to earth.

"We are up," she smiles, heading into the Labyrinth first.

The fog has settled low on the ground, sucking her up into the mist as she disappears inside. Fear licks the back of my neck, but I quickly shake it off, following after my friend.

My hand reaches out to run along the side of the hedge maze, my other clicking the on button on my flashlight. The glare hits Lyra in the face and she raises her hand to shield off the bright light.

I point the light towards the left, then back to the right seeing the two different paths. The fog making distant visibility nearly impossible.

"Wanna split up? We can cover more ground that way," she offers.

My first instinct is to say no. We are stronger in numbers always. But this is a school function, not a plan of escape from them. So, I nod.

"I'll take the left. Good luck." I give a smile in good spirits.

As we go our separate ways, I take a deep breath, tilting my head to crack my neck a bit. When I begin to navigate through the lefts and rights, everything becoming a bit blurred as I do so, I try to pick up the pace.

I know we only have so long inside here and I hate losing. The farther I get inside the more lost I feel, every turn, every change in direction feels like the wrong way. The height of the maze is too much for me to look up and over the hedges, so I can't even tell if I'm close to the middle or not.

I'm sure the air horn will be going off any second now, and that thought alone has me running faster.

"I am a lifetime rat owner, I should be able to get out of this stupid thing," I grumble, taking a deep breath and coughing a bit, my lungs wet from the fog. My heart ached a bit at the mention of Ada. If they let me graduate without killing me, I was coming back to stab him for killing my pet.

I place my hands on my knees, dropping my head to catch my breath.

When I lift it again, I lift it with my flashlight, scanning it in front of me. The light passes through the mist, catching the white paint of the tower that stands tall a few feet in front of me.

"I'll be fucking damned," I whisper, a grin on my face.

As I approach the structure I spot the golden skeleton key dangling from a single thread from the steps. Reaching on my tippy-toes, I wrap my fingers around the brisk metal, pride filling me to the brim.

I hear the pluck of the string letting the key go as it falls into my hands. There are a few seconds for me to admire the faux gold, but my action seems to trigger a horrible set of events. As if the string had been booby-trapped and I'd been the perfect victim.

Screams, high-pitched, ear-piercing shrieks erupt from around me. Voices shouting from outside the Labyrinth. I jump, spinning from left to right expecting someone to be near me. Instead, there is a consistent ring of shots fired into the night, a distinct sound of gunfire.

It's just fireworks, I rationalize, even though there is no sparkle or flicker of colorful light that ascends into the clouds. I can tell myself it's fireworks all I want, but it won't change the truth.

"Everyone remain calm and please head to the courtyard!" I hear one of the teachers announce over the microphone, the voice echoing towards me.

I wasn't sure what was worse.

Being trapped in this maze or not knowing what was happening outside of it.

My survival instincts had been triggered more in the past few weeks than ever before. This was nothing like getting busted by the cops or almost being caught by the guy you're stealing from.

This is much worse.

"Lyra!" I scream at the top of my lungs, my throat ringing painfully. "Lyra!!" I bail out, my flashlight guiding me as I start to retrace my steps that I'd already begun to forget.

My eyes are straining to see in the darkness, working to look for Lyra, while also trying to get me out of this maze safely. The fog and screaming had already discombobulated my senses enough, now there was blaring music that began to vibrate the walls of the Labyrinth. No lyrics, just discordant chords signaling a looming fate in my future. It sounded like music that was played on a carousel, meant to attract people to the bright colors and spinning horses.

It's just some joke the upperclassmen pull on the younger students, I think. That's all this is.

"Lyra!" I try again but hear nothing called back for me. The sound of a loud thud reaches my ear, just before my eyes dart to the right and onto a thin black cylinder that has just begun spewing bright red smoke from the top. It leaks and bubbles, spreading around me in thick waves.

Starting at my feet before escalating up my body, I didn't wait for it to continue taking up space. I started moving forward, my arms stuck out in front of me like a glorified mummy.

*Thud. Thud. Thud.*

More smoke bombs flying across the tops of the hedges, landing in random spots around me. The fumes have overtaken my vision, completely swarming me in an alarming bright red color.

Terror washes over me, raising the fine hairs on the back of my neck. My heart pounds in my ears as my eyes burn with irritation.

I was not frightened.

What I felt was beyond a useless adjective.

What I felt was a tangible, living force that crept over me like a hungry beast. It chewed at my raw flesh, tearing me limb from limb until it could feast on the immobilized heart inside my chest.

I could no longer control my hands as they trembled.

Coughs littered my lungs, waving my arms with little use, trying to move the smoke from my vision. Everything was a blur, all of it spinning too fast. I stood for a few moments, my stomach churning, closing my eyes and wishing I was little again. Wishing I was back home in Texas and seeking comfort in my father's arms. Allowing him to protect me.

I thought of my father and how he raised me to be stronger than this. Braver than the girl who lays down at the feet of those determined to knock her down. He showed me how to steal the wealth right under their upturned noses. I was taught to be unafraid of the bumps in the night. Because *I* was the bump in the night.

A shaky breath passes my lips, my flashlight doing nothing except illuminating the clouds of smoke directly in front of my face. I focused my ears to the sounds of screams, to where the voices echoed from. If I could head in the direction of them, it would lead me out of this maze.

"Lyra!" I choke out, hoping my strangled voice will alert someone.

I shove the key into my pocket, popping the flashlight into my mouth and holding it with my teeth as I tear my pullover off my head and toss it onto the ground.

A black wife-beater sticks to my skin with the help of some sweat that had trickled down between the valley of my breasts and onto my stomach. I steady my breath and try to calm the panic, moving towards the exit.

That's when I hear the snickering.

A dark, hooded chuckle that made my muscles tense. They cause me to move my legs faster. Knowing someone was close. They were close and I was trapped in here with them. The menacing aura from the sound had my bones shaking with panic. Echoes of laugher bouncing off the inside of my chest, buzzing in my head.

The carousel music spun faster, surging louder and louder with every step forward.

I felt a breeze of wind behind me, a ghost of a touch on my lower back, making me spin around, only to be met with more smoke. Another whisper of a hand against my left leg has me turning again. They were right there. Just beyond the wall of smoke, hiding, playing. I spun in circles while they grazed my body when I turned away from them.

I was stuck in a false reality. Shoved inside a haunted game I wanted no part of. My stomach swirled, my mind swimming as they cackled and brushed against me. Appearing and disappearing into the shadows.

They were everywhere and nowhere at the same time.

Impossible to keep up with.

"What the fuck do you want!" I scream, fed up with the games, tired of the cat-and-mouse torment. My flashlight pointed straight ahead as my chest heaved up and down with anger, "What do you want!" I yell again.

More laughter follows, my flashlight catching glimpses of their faces as they inch closer and closer. Walking side by side, their broad shoulders move in sync with one another. Bits of a clown mask cover the one on the far left, the one in the middle with the signature jigsaw face, and the last sported a simple plain white one that had blood leaking from where your eyes would be.

Vomit sits in my throat as they approach me. I back up, up, up, until I hit something solid. I was sure this is what Hell felt like. The one with the white mask, the tallest, reaches out and hooks a piece of my braid between his fingers, rubbing it between his thumb and pointer.

I stayed so still while he leaned into me, pressing my hair into the nose holes of his mask and inhaling desperately loud.

"What do you want?" I ask with a scratchy, broken voice.

What I thought was a piece of the maze, begins to move behind me. I step away from him, only to step closer into another body. I had nowhere to go, there was nothing I could do to prevent his arms encircling me, his palm clamping over my mouth as he pressed his hard body into mine.

The one who lurks in the shade and is a child of the night. Even with a mask, I knew which one he was. I could feel it.

I ready myself to scream at the horror in front of me.

"Your fear," his animalistic tone loud over the music and

commotion. I can taste the leather of his gloved palm as I wail into his large hand.

The front of his mask is touching my nose. My eyes crossing to make out the black-and-white skull on the upper portion of his face, the part where his lips should be is hidden by a thick, black gas mask that distorts his voice.

"Your silence," he continues.

The smell of plastic and smoke is almost overwhelming, but not as strong as the underlying scent of clove and black magic. Adrenaline pumps through my veins like liquid gold. Every nerve-ending firing, every atom shaking with energy. I was alive.

I was in the hands of death and I felt so fucking alive.

"The truth," he grunts.

What truth?

That he's a murderous son of a bitch? I could have already told him that.

Alistair's arm snakes around my waist, heaving me closer if possible, the labored sounds of his breathing through the mask, making me quake. I cringe as his dark eyes embed in my soul through the skull.

"I own you now, Little Thief. *We* own you. You belong to us. Be sure to remember that." The growl wobbles my bones, my bottom lip trembling.

I cower at his statement, knowing I couldn't do anything about it anyway. I couldn't save myself from this moment. I couldn't stop this from happening.

My heart thudded so hard, I knew he felt it against his own chest. Hot, wet fluid soaked between my thighs, my body sexually aroused from the charge of primal terror. I told myself it was just my body's natural reaction. That I couldn't help it. It was a biological response.

His grip on my body tightened, the hand over my mouth pressed harder, "You like being afraid, don't you, Briar? You like playing in the shadows with us monsters?" he questions, baiting me like a child.

I jerk against his grip, trying to show as much deviance as possible in my eyes. I was tired of being chased and him catching me. I was exhausted from running, from waiting for him to make a move. I didn't want to play the scared little girl anymore.

My body nearly refused, pieces of me wanting to seek out his warmth and the desire that wafted off him in waves, but I fought that back. With all the strength I had left in my body, I reared my head back before slamming it forward into his nose.

It's enough for his hold to loosen, before I am tearing away from his body and sprinting in the opposite direction, not stopping to see how he reacted to the headbutt that was making my skull throb in pain. I stumble into the maze, falling into the sides of the hedges, scratching and cutting my arms. I could hear him behind me, his heavy footsteps, the way his boots beat into the ground.

My chest ached for a clean breath of air, without the smoke, my legs burning as I rounded another corner.

I turned for a split second, just to see how close he was to me, and when I did my body collided with another. My immediate reaction was to fight them off, kicking, scratching, screaming bloody fucking murder.

"Briar! Briar!" my name is yelled by my attacker as they attempt to gather my hands in their grip, fighting my nails off their body.

"Help! Someone help!" I barrel out, continuing my fight. Delirious and broken.

"Briar! It's Dean Sinclair, I'm trying to help!" Who I thought was one of my attackers turns out to be the dean of our school. A dean who had wandered into the maze in search of the two students trapped inside after the commotion outside of it.

The walls surrounding me seem to cascade down as I slump

into the arms of someone that's not them. The devil could be reaching his hand out to help and I'd take it. Mr. Sinclair wraps his arms around me, holding me to his broad chest that smells of Old Spice, and cradles the back of my head, "It's okay, you're okay," he coos, probably feeling the erratic jumps of my heart and seeing my frazzled state.

I shut my eyes, tears escaping them, and it was at that moment I was so tired of crying.

I was so fed up with puking and feeling helpless. Playing a game they were experts at. Nothing but a pitiful little pawn in their chess match. They were ruling my life, my nightmares, taking over my life.

A life I fought to have, and I was just letting them take it.

They were spoiled assholes with vendettas I wasn't involved in. They wanted to kill me, fine. But I was done with their torments and their sick jokes.

I was done being the puppet. I was done being the mouse in this cat-dominated game.

If they want to play, then fine.

I'll play, too.

# CHAPTER SIXTEEN
## *Girl's Got Bite*

*Alistair*

I wasn't sketching her because she was attractive.

A lot of girls are attractive. There are a lot of girls who are pretty, and some who are hot, but that's not what matters right now. I don't care that she's pretty.

I repeated those words over and over again as I used my charcoal pencil to enhance the curve of her round face, extra detail in the way her cheeks tint when she's flustered. Her arched eyebrows, even the left one with a slit through it from a scar that refused to allow hair to grow over it. Easing on the pressure while I graphed the shape of her pink lips.

I was sketching her because she was another reminder of something beautiful that did nothing but make me bleed. My entire life was spent surrounded by shiny things, by stunning people with glittering smiles and beautiful homes. All they did was take from me, hurt me, until there was nothing left to take, nothing human to hurt.

It was fitting for her name to be Briar, a thorny fucking bush in my side. Poking, stabbing, annoying me.

The maze had been fun. Thrilling. My hands wrapped

around her scared body while she trembled beneath my touch. Even in the darkness, with the smoke pooling around us, I could see those colorful eyes dancing with terror.

They shook for me, they begged for mercy beneath the layer of dissent. She would not die easily, refusing to lay down and give up. Which was fine with me, more than fine.

I liked that she was willing to try and give it as much as she got it.

My pencil pressed harder into the paper, these drawings were just reminders. Warnings of what happens when you trust beauty over action.

Using my thumb, I began to blend the hard edges, shading them into skin texture, giving her more depth than she deserved.

My phone buzzed in my pocket, the only thing able to pull my head out of my sketchbook during class. I'd learned to drown out the sounds of those in power at a young age, school was a breeze for me now.

After pulling it from my pocket, I see a few messages from the guys, mostly talking about Silas and his slow ass. We'd been waiting for a few weeks to hear about the security footage he was trying to hack into.

Something about it was harder to do than other things; I think he mentioned something about a firewall? I don't fucking know. All I did know was that he was taking his precious little time.

We'd been following Thomas, taking turns keeping an eye on him, and we'd yet to catch him doing anything suspicious. No midnight runs from his condo apartment on Main Street, no smuggling of illegal drugs into his car after school, we hadn't even caught him going into the chemistry lab.

I figured he was keeping everything in his house now. Trying to lay low after Chris turned up missing and the Candy King nearly died from a fire that broke out in his house. Whoever was involved knew they might be a target. They knew someone was coming for them next and they were probably doing everything they could to keep their presence to a minimum.

Rook and I camped out for an entire night outside his place and there wasn't so much as a flicker of light in the wrong direction. I was starting to believe we were looking at the wrong guy, that the swipes in and out of the chem lab were just a coincidence.

I fire a text back, slipping my phone back into my pocket and picking up the pencil to finish what I was working on.

It was rare that I paid attention in class; even when I got lucky and had art as an elective in high school, I still drowned out the sounds of teachers and their directions. Not because I thought I was better, but because I didn't need their help. I didn't want their guidance.

Flipping to the next blank page in my book, I begin working on a few tattoo designs. Ones I'd like to have, ones I'd like to give to others. The more I worked, the more I was leaning towards black and gray illustrative designs, even a little surrealism where I could bend the creative spectrum onto skin.

Shade believed in mastering all techniques in tattooing, starting with the basics and building up. You could have a specialty, one category you're really good at, but you have to do the others just as well. So, even though I hated traditional Japanese-style work, I worked on sketching a dragon onto my paper.

"Mr. Caldwell." I hear my name seconds before my book is being shut by someone that is not me. The pages of my sketchbook tumble on top of my drawing hand and pencil.

The rest of the class seems to inhale simultaneously, all of them possibly in shock from watching someone else blatantly disrespect me. Sure, teachers are in charge at Hollow Heights. It's their job to dictate and guide us along our four-year journey.

Just not me.

Not me.

Not Silas.

Not Rook or Thatcher.

They leave us be. Letting the bad apples guide themselves, hoping our last names and money will cover any horrific damage we cause in the time we are here.

They don't bother bossing us because they know it would fall on deaf ears. Not only could we cause mayhem on our own, disciplining one of us would mean the possibility of upsetting our families. And with a name like Caldwell—one that is on half the town, the school library, and on the board of the university—mine was the last family you wanted to piss off.

"Would you mind telling me the definition of an Axon? Relative to the body, of course." Professor Thomas Reid stands tall in front of my desk. I hadn't even wanted to sit in the front, but by the time I got here, it was all that was left.

I drag my tongue across the front of my teeth, making a deep sucking noise as I do. Students around me hold their breath, watching me.

"Do you mind kissing my ass? Relative to the body, of course."

It's not the answer he wanted, but it's the answer he expected from me. He scoffs, the corners of his lips tipping into a satirical smile. I'd yet to see anything about Thomas and Briar that resembled one another except the dirty-blond color of their hair. If they didn't tell you, I don't think anyone would be able to tell.

"Clever, Alistair, very clever. You know what they say, sarcasm is the lowest form of wit."

I smirk, "And the highest form of intelligence. Maybe you should stick to teaching biology instead of lecturing students on Oscar Wilde. Doesn't seem to be your forte." Another failed dig at me has changed his attitude almost entirely.

The aggravation sitting on his shoulders as he imagines a

scenario where he can give me a piece of his mind without me smarting off back to him.

"You're right. This is biology. So, let's keep the doodles and sketches for art class. Pay attention or I'm kicking you out."

It's apparent Professor Reid, a teacher who has only been here a few years, doesn't care about the unruly reputation that surrounds me and my last name. I respect that. A man who makes his own assumptions, one who is not allowing others to scare him into not doing his job.

It's an honorable quality, and in any other situation, it might make me respect him more, but sadly, it's not and all it does is piss me the fuck off.

I scoot my chair back, the wood beneath it screeching noisily, grabbing my things, slipping my pencil behind my ear before looking him in the eye. If he's involved, I hope everything in my gaze is telling him:

*I'm coming for you.*

My jaw tightens as I stand to my full height, taller than him by more than a few inches, "Allow me," I murmur, not really giving a fuck if he kicked me out or not. I was leaving anyway.

I was going to leave without another word, walk to my car, drive all the way home and then take my frustration out on a punching bag or a wall. I knew his karma was coming, and knowing I could make him pay tenfold later on was what kept me from doing anything reckless in the moment.

That was until I felt his hand on my chest.

His fucking hand.

On my chest.

My blood is nearing a physical boiling point as I drop my head to look down at his slender fingers plastered to the front of my white shirt. My mind zones out for a few seconds, just spinning around the endless possibilities of how to break every bone in his body.

Each one crunching beneath my fist, underneath my shoe as I step down onto his windpipe, crushing it slowly. I wanted to rip him to pieces and use the leftover shreds as chew toys for Silas's dog, Samson.

My mouth watered with hunger for a food that didn't exist.

For pain. For broken bones. For cries of mercy.

"Your parents may be on the board, Alistair, but that does not make you untouchable. We all answer to someone," he says quietly, near my ear.

I raise my eyes leisurely, taking a deep breath, I feel my nostrils flare with the aggressive air passing through them.

"Get your hand off me," I grunt, suddenly losing every excuse in my head for why I don't collide my fist into every bone in his face. My control is slipping further and further away.

"Are you going to hit a teacher, Mr. Caldwell? That's grounds for expulsion no matter what your last name is."

What is it with this family and testing my fucking patience? First, his niece, who isn't going to know her ass from her head when I'm done with her, and then this fucking tool. Both of them, outsiders to this place, to how this works.

Thinking they are above the never-ending pedigree.

Dots of red begin to cloud my vision, the beast I don't bother locking away growls inside my chest, ready to gorge on my intended target.

Reaching my hand out to snake around his wrist, I grip him too tightly to be comfortable.

"There are not many limitations to what I can do, Professor Reid." My tongue spits his name out like rotten meat. For a split second, a firework of worry bursts in the center of his pupil before it dulls out.

I release his wrist, pushing past him with my shoulder a bit for good measure, and turn to look at him, the look on his face daring me to say anything that he could use to get me in trouble.

"You should be careful, Professor Reid. People going missing and all."

It was irresponsible to say in front of people, but I thought that was slightly better than killing him with my bare hands in this classroom. Throwing the door open, I stalk down the hallway, thankful it's empty and there is no one to shove out of the way as I make my way to the parking lot.

I doubted I would make it home before my fist slammed into something or someone. The urge to call Rook and tell him to meet me at the house for sparring was tempting. In the ways Thatcher and I butted heads, Rook and I seemed to mesh.

He needed to get hit sometimes and I needed to hit.

I guess there was something about being in control of who hit him that made it different. All I know is he needed it sometimes, he needed the pain, and I could give it to him.

And we would do anything for each other. No matter the favor. Even if it meant beating the shit out of one another.

Anger is pouring out of every single pore, my hands shaking as I click the unlock button on my key fob, my hand curling around the door and yanking it open.

I needed a second to catch my breath. I needed a moment to calm down.

What I didn't need was to open the door to my car just to find millions of bugs crawling around inside. Hundreds of the flat oval bodies scuttering along my dash and burrowing into my seats.

In my delusion, I thought there were snakes accompanying the gigantic alien-looking insects, but I quickly realized they were what was making the noise.

"What the fuck," I curse, inspecting the outside of my vehicle, making sure I hadn't run over something that might have attracted them to the inside of my car.

When I see nothing, I look back inside, eyes grazing a sheet of white paper with red ink splattered across it. I reach into the nest of maybe twenty of them, shaking the paper off until they fall down onto the floor-mats.

It would take me months to get the musty, wet smell out of my seats. I wasn't afraid of bugs, nor did they bother me, it was just highly irritating.

The world was intent on testing me today, apparently.

I scan the note a couple times, looking at the cockroaches, back to the note over and over again. An inkling of a smirk makes my lips twitch.

*I'm not scared of you, Caldwell. Fuck off and find a new hobby. I suggest starting with insect collection. Here, I'll give you a head start.*

I lick my bottom lip, shaking my head. What a fucking warrior she is.

A warrior that I was going to shatter beneath my combat boot. I'd watch that little smart-ass light that twinkles in her eyes when I'm not around disappear forever. I'd take everything she thought she knew and flip it.

And she was going to taste like honey on my tongue when it happened.

Human enough to be afraid, strong enough to not let it sway her. I wasn't stupid, I knew she was scared, but I had a strong inclination that she was finished letting us run all over her.

An itch on my hand causes me to look down and see that a chunky invertebrate had creeped onto my skin. I fling the bug onto the ground just before I smash it with my foot. It crunches under my weight.

She'd not only managed to get hundreds of cockroaches into my car, but also broke into my vehicle without triggering the alarm. It showed talent. Showed promise.

It was a fucking shame it was going to be wasted. That I

would have to take a girl who thought she knew everything and show her what life was really about.

Yank her into the darkness, into the shadows where I liked to hide, and show her exactly why she should be afraid of someone made of nightmares.

Someone like me.

# CHAPTER SEVENTEEN
## *Between The Waves*

*Briar*

Self-satisfaction had run through my blood strong today. I had a different pep in my step as of today. Walking around campus knowing Alistair was busy cleaning his car of roach shit.

Lyra was convinced this was just provoking them. Making it worse on ourselves. Maybe we were, maybe the prank was a mistake, but at the very least they knew now, we were not going to lie down for them to spit on us.

The maze had been the straw that broke the camel's back.

Fed up with being easy prey, tired of letting them win, even if I lost the war, I won a battle. I served Alistair a spoonful of his own medicine and I hoped it tasted like rotten milk.

I crept down the entryway to the school's recreational hall, the glass door with a simple lock the only thing keeping me from the pool. The glow of the lights beneath the water reflected off the walls as I approached.

With smooth fingers I pull two bobby pins out of my hair, taking the first one and pulling it apart with my teeth, making a ninety-degree angle with it. Squatting to the ground to work with the other, I stick it inside, turning to the left to create tension inside the standard padlock.

I slip the first pin over the top of the other, playing with the pins inside. It's simple math really, a standard lock has five pins, and each pin needs to be pressed up in order for the lock to open. However, there are seized pins, at least three, that are harder to release, so I start with those. Wiggling the bobby pin up and down, until I feel the right amount of resistance.

When I feel it, I press up hard, hearing the gratifying click.

"One down, two to go." I whisper, continuing the same process until all the pins are pulled and the lock gives, falling open on one side.

I smile smugly as I pull the padlock off the door setting it to the side before sliding inside the pool room. I take in the dark sky twinkling above me. English ivy climbs up the sides of the glass panels encroaching on the top of the roof where more see-through plates make up the top of the house.

During the day, light was shown inside every direction, it was inviting and warm. But at night, there was an edge. Looking out at the forest, wondering if anything is lingering between the trees, staring back at you. If you stared too long out there, you'd find exactly what you were searching for. Your mind entertains the darkness if you're not careful.

I clipped my phone into a small speaker, loud enough for me to hear but quiet enough not to alarm anyone of my presence. I'd decided against clicking on the indoor lights, the ones illuminating the pool seemed to be enough.

The bright, warm lights gave the pool a sea-foam green tint, making it more inviting.

Stripping my clothes excitedly, leaving me in my black two-piece. I'd been waiting all day to slip into the cool water. Swimming made me feel weightless. Nothing really mattered except the way my body moved. My brain could shut off for a little bit and I could just float.

I needed that.

No more Hollow Boys. No revenge plotting. No school or math problems.

Just to float for a bit.

My bare feet danced across the cold floors around the outside of the pool. Slightly damp and sticking to my feet, I inhale the chlorine that lingers in the wet air. The verbena and wild roses planted around the pool almost overwhelm it, but not entirely. I loved that smell. The chlorine that is. Huffing it like paint before meets as I readied myself on the diving board, prepared to launch into the water.

Music hung in the air, soft distorted melodies, with subversive lyrics and full of angst. The kind of songs that fueled broken hearts and brought castaways home.

Restless, I dive headfirst into the nine-foot-deep end of the Olympic-sized pool. The rush of water cocoons me, settling on the outside of my ears and making everything above the surface trivial.

The pressure of the water hugs me, showing me the comfort I lacked from being here. My family may have been poor, my father may have stolen for a job, but I grew up loved.

I grew up in a home where hugs were given freely and often. Where the grill was always on in the summer, the smell of charcoal wafting around the warm air. Where, in the winters, we'd find the largest hill in our trailer park and sled down it with plastic storage containers lids. Where my mom read me bedtime stories and tucked me in.

I was used to being invisible to everyone outside of my home. To feeling cold and unwanted at school, judged at the grocery store, but I knew I would walk into a two-bedroom trailer that felt like home and supported me. I had basically nothing to call my own except family, and now it felt like I didn't even have that.

I'd never felt more isolated.

Yeah, I had Lyra, I had Thomas, and I called my mom quite often, but it didn't feel like enough. Walking around here is a constant chill on my spine, always lugging the chip on my shoulder, ready to defend myself.

Minus being chased by psychotic men, I assumed most college freshmen felt this way.

Trying desperately to fit in, to find a place to belong in the world all alone. Going away from your family always sounds better in your head, until you're states away, alone, eating ramen in a hoodie that hasn't been washed in three days.

But it's a process. I know this too will pass, in one way or another. Either I start to get used to the torment or I let it scare me away.

I stay under until my lungs want to burst, until black spots began sprinkling behind my eyelids.

Piercing the water with a gasp for air, I push my hair out of my face, slicking it down my back. Chlorine stinging my eyes enough to make me wipe at them.

With a slow pace I make my way to the shallow end, stretching my legs out on the side of the pool, pulling my arms across my chest, working the muscles out.

I wanted to get my laps in for the night, I knew it would tire me out and I could possibly get some rest tonight. Which I needed, because I had a test tomorrow and I did not want to fail my first college test.

I picked the lane in the middle, number five, the song changing as I dived back underneath the water, starting with the breaststroke for my first hundred meters.

Five-hundred-meter medley was always my heat. I think it silently killed my swim coach that I was the only one on the team who could do all four swim styles. I won meets just to see the pissed-off look on her face because, just like everyone else, they expected me to fail.

And I guess that's what all of this comes down to.

It's why I haven't tucked tail and run far away from this homicidal school with kidnapping tendencies.

I didn't want to give them what they wanted from me.

Failure.

It's all anyone has ever seen when they look at me. When they get past the invisibility, all they see is trailer park trash destined for the gutters.

I wanted more for myself. I wanted to prove them all wrong. I lived for those moments, when I could see the shock on their faces. That's what I'm going to try to do here.

Build a better future for myself so that when people look at me, they see a woman riddled with success and confidence. They wouldn't be able to imagine me as anything else.

Those boys weren't going to take that from me. I wasn't going to let them see me fail either. Even if they look down at me from their respective thrones, thinking their terror pranks will run me off, ruin me. They would not be the end of me. They are not taking my future from me.

By the start of my backstroke, my arms were burning, I was taking sharper breaths, and staying beneath the surface for less and less time. Fatigue was settling deep into my muscles.

But I pushed through. I demanded more from my body because my mind wasn't finished yet. I swam because the water had always been a sort of freedom for me. A breakaway from the rules of gravity and the chance to feel absolutely weightless.

There is something about the motion of it, when you break past the burn, it starts to feel natural. The way the water swirls around me, the cool water as I move through a different medium than air.

I became a swimmer by accident.

I was eleven and my mom signed me up for a summer program, I spent the entire three months in the pool. And at the end of the program, there was a race, one that I had won by leaps and bounds.

It was the first positive label I'd ever been given.

The girl who could swim like a fish.

So, I never stopped.

I flip beneath the water one last time, pressing off the side of the pool with my toes and heels as hard as I could, propelling myself forward under the water like a swift dagger in the wind.

I reappear at the surface, rotating my arms in constant circles as I force my body to finish this last meter of freestyle. My arms glide in and out of the pool, my legs kicking with power as the last of my stamina begins to dwindle.

My fingers and hand slap the top of the concrete, marking the end of my medley. I stand straight up in the shallow water, my legs wobbly, as I take a deep breath. Holding myself up against the edge, regaining my sense of vision above the water.

With little effort I lay back, letting the water carry me. My breathing regulates as I stare up at the star-covered sky through the glass windows. Drifting off into a world all my own.

Envisioning myself as a woman with power. A business owner. A trailblazer. Someone important. Someone who can't be overlooked. I didn't know what I wanted to do for work after college, mostly because I didn't think I'd be able to afford college. Now the possibilities are endless.

I have never-ending choices with a fancy degree from Hollow Heights.

My eyes had shut on their own. Completely absorbed by

the water, the silence of the water soothing the chaos inside my head. I don't know how long I lay there, just floating, but I could feel my fingers beginning to prune.

When I reopen my eyes, the light from the pool beneath me is no longer bouncing off the windows. Everything is black.

In my swimmer's high, I think I still have my eyes closed. Only when I stand up in the pool, my feet sinking to the bottom, rubbing my lids, do I accept the fact I'm in the dark.

Not just dark, the pitch-black oblivion. I can't even see my hand in front of my face, not even the light from the stars is enough to stab through the black.

It's ridiculous. I know the pool lights probably went out or timed out, a simple explanation. But irrational fears drive up my spine, whispering in my ear.

What if this university has sharks they let out in here at night? Or crocodiles? They have about everything else dangerous and creepy, why should that be so far-fetched?

I look down at the water, the inky black liquid is only a sound in my ears. I can barely make out the top of it, let alone what's beneath me. My toes prickle, wanting me to take them out of this pool.

Blood pumps hard through me, pounding against my skin with every beat of my heart. My mouth starting to dry up, like balls of cotton had just been shoved inside my throat.

It's a normal human reaction. Anyone would feel this way. The feeling that something is going to reach out and grab my foot, yanking me beneath the water. Never seeing the surface ever again. Whether that be a ferocious great white or a human.

I can, thankfully, still touch, not sure how far away from the edge I am due to my reckless floating. I begin to toe my way forward, one arm outstretched, feeling for something solid that can help me out of the pool.

Looking behind me is out of the question, I know as soon as I see the never-ending bleakness over my shoulder it'll only make me panic more.

The light bulbs just burnt out, that's all—

*Splash*

I lick my parched lips, freezing almost immediately.

Whatever just entered the water with me did so ungracefully. Their weight vibrated the bottom of the pool, ringing up my already weak legs.

Giant anaconda?

Pissed off bull shark?

Vengeful human?

I'm facing the direction of the sound, slowly beginning to back up, measuring my distance by where the water sits on my waist. The farther I move back, the less water that pools around my stomach, meaning I'm headed towards the shallow end.

If it's an animal, I'm done for. They can see me in this darkness. They can feel my slight movements. My heart racing.

But if it's a human. One with a vendetta, then I have a chance because they can't see me any more than I can see them.

There was only one splash, meaning there was only one of them in here with me. But the other three could very well be standing around all my exits, waiting for me to make a move.

I hear the water ripple in front of me, a few feet away maybe, if my senses are good. Another ripple, then another, like it's moving towards me just as slowly as I'm moving back. Both of us careful for contrasting reasons.

Me, wanting to get out of this pool with minimal damage and as quietly as possible in the hopes they don't even notice I've left.

Them, not wanting to spook me so that I don't run, so that I don't escape.

The water is suddenly cold. Ice cold. How I imagine Alaskan waters run in the dead of winter. Little bumps riddle my thighs, my arms, my bottom lip trembles. I'd never wanted out of the water before. Not like I did right now.

My back lands against the side of the pool, relief flooding my soul. Lifting my arms, I press my palms into the slate ground, heaving myself up backwards ready to grab my stuff and sprint out of here.

Hands, human hands, wrench onto my hips, tugging me back into the water with no sympathy. I slide right back into the pool, as if I'd never left it. My lungs fill with a mighty scream, opening my mouth to yell for help only to have it covered by their palm.

"Quiet now, Briar. Wouldn't want anyone to know you're breaking into places you shouldn't be after campus curfew."

That voice. Those hands. This feeling.

Loathing, vile hatred simmers in my veins. The fact he's gotten me into this position again, that his hands have a hold on me and my body is eating it up. Frothing at the mouth, wondering what he will do next, like a naive little girl. He pins me to the wall easily, with one hand on my hip.

I feel his rough, soaked jeans rub against my naked thighs, his soft shirt sticking to my exposed arms. Who jumps in a pool with clothes on?

I tear my mouth away from his grip, "I think murder would take priority over breaking into a swimming pool, don't you, Alistair?"

I can't see him, only the obscure outline of his shape. The brawny shoulders, the way his head tilts in amusement at my response, and I know without needing to see, there is a fatal smirk sitting on his lips.

Rocks, massive rocks, weigh down my chest. Every breath hurts when I'm near him. He takes all the oxygen. Leaving me with nothing but his racy scent to inhale for fuel.

"Now why would you go running your mouth about something that doesn't involve you? I thought we were starting to become friends," he chides, with an underlying threat, making me nauseous. Making me dizzy.

I feel his thumb graze my revealed stomach, little shocks cascade through my belly. I ignore his questions completely. He doesn't deserve an answer.

"You come alone? Or did you bring your pets to help you take down little ol' me?"

Nerve struck because I feel his thumb dig into my skin, rugged and demanding. Making me gulp in pain. All his big red buttons, the ones I'm not supposed to mess with, surround his friends. You can attack him, but the second you turn your attention to his shit minions, he's ready to pounce.

I attempt to jerk out of his grip, only to be rewarded with a slam back in place. My back drilling into the side of the pool.

"Cockroaches. A bit juvenile, even for a bum like you."

"Clothes on in the pool. A bit insecure, even for a guy with a small dick."

He laughs, deep and rich like dark chocolate cake. Bitter at first, but it gradually melts on your tongue, turning sugary and sticky. My favorite type of chocolate.

My body shakes in his hands, once again my brain is at war with the rest of me. Endorphins fill me, tingling my thighs, sweeping across my core. I swallow my bile, holding my chin out, even though he can't see it.

The hand not on my waist begins to run along my shoulder, just his fingertips ghosting over my silhouette. Seeing me with his hands.

"You have something that belongs to me, Little Thief." All laughter is gone. All reminiscence of his humanity fading.

My eyes flick to the approximate location of my button-down on the chair, near the speaker where music still plays, knowing his ring is tucked in the front pocket of the shirt. Thankful for the first time that he can't see me.

"And I want it back," he snarls, his tone nips at my skin like feral wolves baring their teeth.

"I don't have shit." I buck at him, which is pointless, but I don't want him thinking I'm backing down. My heart thumps with the blatant lie.

His hand seizes the back of my head, gripping the hair back there with an intoxicatingly vicious hold. Pulling me down, so that my face is pointed up towards him. I can feel his mouth floating above mine, and I promise myself that if he kisses me, I'm going to bite his tongue clean off.

"You saw what we did to that teacher's assistant, didn't you?" The vivid images haunt me. "That's what happens to people who take things from me, Briar. They end up dead."

His breath is Novocain to my senses, numbing everything. The poison in his voice oozes into my pores, infecting me. All those images rush right back, the ones that plague me at night. Of the blood, of the snakes, of him.

The ones of him are the worst because I always wake up with sweat trickling down my lower back and damp panties.

"I'm not scared of you." I wince, another lie.

"Yeah? Prove it." I swear I feel his top lip hit mine when he pronounces the P in prove.

Winding his hand in my hair tighter, making it a leash for him to control me with. With speed and precision, he lodges his drenched right thigh between my legs. Wedging me open and lifting me at the same time.

I inhale a gasp, my breath hitching in my throat, my head falling back into his grip as the slight friction bolts from my center down to my toes. Lightning strikes my bones. Everything was completely void, every molecule was gone. This immense force of energy surges through me, it was only a second of touch but felt longer.

My entire body balances on his kneecap, all the pressure

directed to my core. His coarse jeans rub the delicate skin between my legs. It takes me a few moments to notice my hands resting on his covered shoulders.

"Are you scared yet, Little Thief?"

I grind my teeth, trying to breathe, but all I get is gulps of him. His smoky breath filling me up, up, up. I was going to explode. Tendrils of terror wrapped around my throat, choking me.

I was scared, yes. My mind, my heart.

But my body, my sick, fucked-up body, she liked it.

She liked it too much.

So much that I couldn't stop her from proving my point.

"Eat me," I bite out.

I feel his smug grin, right above my lips. Taunting me. Toying with me.

I feel it in waves. The way his knee begins to move in short circles, the tension never leaving my clit. I can feel everything like he's touching nothing but bare skin. The thin material of my bikini does nothing but aid his friction.

The intensity slowly begins to build. My tongue swelling in my mouth as I bite down on it, prohibiting any moans to escape. I felt hot all of a sudden; the water that had once turned to ice was now molten lava. Every movement of his knee stokes the flames higher and I can only watch. I can only feel as the inferno grows larger.

I am simply embers and ashes of pleasure in his hands.

God, and he fucking knows it.

He flicks his tongue across his bottom lip, catching mine in the process and I get the faintest taste of him. Do you know how scary it is to nearly taste the one drug on earth that could kill you?

I was hanging on the swing of life or death in Alistair's arms. Seeking pleasure from the one who seeks silence from me.

This is just to prove a point, I remind myself. I'm just

proving a point. I'm showing him that I'm not giving up and he can't scare me. Not anymore.

He jerks up, making a tortured moan rip from my throat. Alistair inhales sharply, absorbing my pleasure as we exchange heavy grunts and groans.

I couldn't deny the wetness that leaked from between my legs, maybe I could blame it on the pool, but he knew, he knew just as well as I did. My body craved this.

"Just tell me what I want to hear. Tell me you're afraid of me, bum," he mutters against my lips.

Heat surges inside my stomach at his crude insult, my cheeks burned red, or maybe they burn because I shamefully rotate my hips over his muscular thigh. It flexes and tenses beneath my weight, pushing me further and further towards the edge.

"Rot in Hell, trust-fund bitch." My curse is barely a threat with how breathy it comes out. Instead of the soft, supple sounds of a lover's name crossing my lips, it's a degrading term filled with so much loathing.

Hating him for making me love this.

My nails claw into his skin. Making sure when he leaves, he bears marks from me. So that when he looks in that golden mirror in the morning, he remembers that I have nails and sharp teeth.

How is it possible to be this turned on right now and my feelings so opposite? The tension inside of me only worsens when the desire escalates. My legs quivering, making the water splash around us.

My hips move of their own accord, chasing relief, chasing approval. I'd never felt like this.

I wasn't sure I ever wanted to feel like this again. This hot. This high. This reckless.

There was too much adrenaline. My heart couldn't take it.

A valiant cry builds in my chest. I tumble, no, I'm being

thrown into the deep end of a sticky, ambrosial pool of need. The coil inside my stomach compresses tighter, all because of the boy full of wicked games.

I didn't think he could get closer, but he does. His lips pressed into mine, but not in a kiss.

"You don't get to use me. Not to make your tight, pink cunt come. Not for silly games with your friend. Not for anything. I will get what is mine, Briar. Even if I have to kill you for it," he spews, my mouth moving with his every word.

Wait, what?

The water around me had become waves of pleasure, about to suck me under a tide of ecstasy, until it runs cold once more.

He lets me drop into the pool, the abrupt change has me falling fully into cool liquid, regaining my thoughts before shooting back up, coughing for air. For my sanity.

When I gather myself, I look around, the lights of the pool are on once again and there is no sign of Alistair Caldwell.

My chest heaves, my mind reels,

Was he really here? Did I fall asleep in the pool? Did I have another dream?

The ache between my thighs gives me my answer. The throb at the back of my skull from his grip tells me all of that was very real.

I was scared.

I was pissed.

I was empty.

How is he so angry over a ring? It's a piece of jewelry for fuck's sake. I despise feeling like there is more to his story than what I can see. I don't want to know his story. I don't care.

He is a sadistic brat who throws more tantrums than a two-year-old. There is no excuse for how he acts.

None.

Another song begins to play, as if the last thirty minutes

never happened. Life begins again and I'm pulled from the time warp he throws me in.

Frustration fills me so much that I sink to the bottom of the pool. I drop like a rock, swimming until I'm sitting at the bottom.

Then, I widen my eyes, letting the chlorine burn him from my memory, open my mouth and . . .

Scream.

# CHAPTER EIGHTEEN

## *Therapy Sessions*

### *Alistair*

"Harder."

"Harder!"

"Come on, man, I said harder! That's all you've got? No fucking wonder you're the spare." His spit lands on my bare chest, the redness in his face is the color of a fire hydrant. From yelling, from the fighting.

My wrapped hands jab into his exposed stomach, my eyes can't help but notice the deep lacerated scars that lay there and on his chest. I tuck my head into his shoulder, my left hooked around his neck to hold him still as I deliver punch after punch into his gut.

The spare.

I hate that godforsaken name.

I'd rather Thatcher call me Ali every day for the rest of my life than hear someone speak that word to me again.

It's all they see me as, it's all anyone has ever seen me as.

Sickly blows come from my fist, made to shatter bone. I don't know many people who could handle hits like these. I'd guess after years of abuse, he'd gotten used to it. It was a warped sense of bonding between friends.

Old wounds I love to bury with explosive rage, unearth in this basement. They are split wide open, leaving me to bleed out all the reasons why I wish I was never born.

Whether on purpose or by accident, my parents had named me after the chief executioner and torturer from Hell. Before I was even able to cognitively think, I'd been given a name that predestined who I'd become.

Someone who brought pain to souls. A name given to evil spirits and foul-tempered individuals.

It couldn't have been more perfect.

Rook propels my temper with his words, just like I knew he would. Just like I need him to.

"You're weak, Alistair." He groans; even though I'm causing enough damage to break him, he still wants more.

My head thumps with all the blood rushing to it, "Shut the fuck up, Rook."

This is where we transformed years of pain into moments of freedom; we were beating the torment from each other's bones.

Using the arm around his neck, I pull his face down towards my chest, connecting my hands at the base of his head, plunging my kneecap into the soft spot right below his ribcage. A receptive move that has my legs stinging from exhaustion. Welts begin to appear on his skin.

Our bodies stick together from the perspiration dripping from us. Using each other as the outlets we never had as children.

Sweat, smoke, and the lingering scent of rubber from the mat plug my nose. Just not enough to forget that exotic floral aroma that had stuck to my skin like leeches. It penetrated the chlorine. Even after my shower, I could still smell it. I could still smell *her*.

The vigor I felt after leaving her there, soaked to the core, knowing how badly she throbbed for an orgasm. I could feel the heat, the juices that poured from her cunt, even in the water. Knowing I'd twisted her little mind into knots.

I'd showed her that she was no better than us. A dirty, gritty girl who enjoyed the things that crept in the night. Watching her pant and whimper in the arms of the guy she hates.

Chasing an orgasm on the thigh of the man who was going to be her demise. It was intoxicating. I'd never felt power like that before.

My head isn't in the right space for this. It's slipping further away from this fight by the second.

In my distracted state, I give Rook the opportunity to place his hands on my chest, shoving me backwards and away from his body. He throws a sloppy left hook into my jaw, enough power behind it to clip my bottom lip. I feel the blood begin to dribble down my chin.

We freeze for a second, both of us in shock. Rook's eyes are opened slightly wider, and I raise my finger to my lip, pulling it away to inspect the bright red liquid left behind.

I'd never been struck before.

I'd never allowed anyone to hit me before.

I wasn't sure who was in more shock, me or Rook. For the first time since we were young teenagers, he'd landed a punch that brought blood.

She was ruining fucking everything. Her smell, the pathetic moans, over-eager hips, and panting were ruining my concentration. Her existence was fucking up my life.

So consumed with her, with getting rid of her, with keeping her quiet, that other women were a blur. All of them out of focus and hazy because my sights were so dialed in to what she was doing, where she was, who she was talking to.

The night in the pool, she'd done everything I'd wanted her to. A puppet on my wire. Showing her that she was nothing but a toy I could control. It wasn't my intention to have her ride my thigh, but it was my plan to watch her find out who exactly was in charge of this situation.

I knew she wouldn't back down. Not even if she was pissing her pants afraid. There is something in Briar Lowell that refuses to allow her to turn away from what frightens her.

And I want nothing more than to crush it with my bare fucking hands.

My thoughts are tangled, I am a frenzy of fury. I charge aggressively at Rook in my hysteria. Steamrolling him onto the mat and hearing him land with a hard smack to the ground.

I am sizzling beneath my skin, my core temperature skyrocketing. I am positive my skin would begin to melt soon.

I wanted to destroy her. I wanted to consume all of it.

I'd taken the power back after her little cockroach charade, but she would soon find something else to hit me back with. I wanted her so broken and lost, she had no choice but to submit and beg me to end her suffering.

On her knees all breathy and fragile.

Rook gargles for air under me, my technique sloppy as I rotate my body around his own, pulling him into a chokehold. My legs lace around his waist, my right arm circles his throat, while my left works as a pry bar to tighten my grip on his windpipe.

Demons, the hellions that I concealed inside me, crawled out, scratching my insides to shreds in the process. I could barely see, my vision blurry and brimming red.

There were barely shapes, only spots of light. The taste of my own blood on my tongue makes me wring his neck harder. The more I hurt him, the closer I got to catching her.

The closer I got to corrupting her completely. Until there was nothing left of who she was. When she looked in the mirror, she wouldn't even know herself. And maybe she would think twice about covering for her uncle and his shady business.

Maybe then she would regret being a part of Rose's death. Being a part of the destruction of one of my best friends.

"Ali . . . Alistair, I tap! Du-dude, I . . . I t . . . tap!" Rook gurgles through my grip, snapping me back to real life.

Reminding me that I'm ten seconds from killing him. I hadn't even felt his hand repeatedly smacking my forearm, until right now.

I let him go immediately, allowing him to sit up and crawl towards the benches on the other side of the room. His longish hair covered in sweat and swaying in front of his eyes.

I fall back into the wall behind me, staying seated on my ass. Dropping my face to look at the ground below me, holding my head between my hands. I've got to get a grip on my shit.

She is taking up too much space in my brain.

Taking up *all* the space in my brain.

"You alright?" I ask him as he gulps down a gallon of water in less than fifteen seconds.

"Never better," he says with a tired grin, the swelling and redness on his neck clear as day.

We sit in silence, catching our breath, gathering ourselves. Waiting for the euphoria of the moment to settle down and the adrenaline to wear out.

It reminds me of the first time he asked me to punch him when we were fourteen and in his backyard. His eye was already purple from the night before with his father, we were taking turns shooting his BB gun at birds that flew across the sky.

He'd turned to me with this, this look in his eyes. Like he needed me. Like he needed my help.

And I remember thinking how good that felt, to be needed. To be wanted as a friend and sought after for help, even if the help was something psychotic. In true Rook fashion, he made a joke of it at first, that he wanted to see how hard I could really hit.

But when I wasn't giving it my all, that's when I saw a side of him that rarely anyone saw. Including me and the rest of the boys. The part of him that's still a broken kid.

*"I need the pain, Alistair. I need it so I don't forget what I did."*

It was all I or anyone else had gotten from him.

We never talked about it again after that. I just showed up when he called and went to work like he was my personal moving punching bag.

"When are your parents coming home?" he asks, fingering his hair back out of his face.

I shrug, "Fuck if I know. Next week maybe. They have a board meeting for the school coming up and they wouldn't miss an opportunity to flash their accomplishments. And with the holidays coming up, my mother has to start planning her gaudy parties."

The holidays were always the worst.

Christmas, Thanksgiving, Halloween.

Any excuse to host a gathering where people could admire them. Any excuse to be in the spotlight, they took it.

The house was always full of people, swarming around like hornets disguised as butterflies. Always too loud, too bright, too fake. So, usually, I stayed with Thatcher and his grandparents for the holidays.

Because it wouldn't matter if I showed up for Christmas morning or not, they wouldn't care, nor bother to ask where I was. Plus, Thatch's grandma makes killer pancakes.

"Silas wouldn't blame you, you know."

My eyebrows come together, "What?"

"He wouldn't blame you if you decided to leave before we found out what happened to Rose. He knows what you go through here. None of us would blame you."

It had never been said out loud till this very moment, but I already knew that. We all knew that.

"Would you blame yourself? If you left him alone in his grief, before he got answers. Would you blame yourself?" I return the question.

"I'd fucking hate myself if I left him."

"Then what makes you think I feel any different?"

He nods, accepting my answer. It's not like he doubted it, but I think he felt like he needed to say it, to make sure I wasn't here because I had to be.

This town may have been cursed with lies and trash parents, but in it I found the people I'd tear down the gates of Hell for.

Family wasn't who you were born with. It was who you'd bleed for.

Thatcher. Silas. Rook.

They are the only people who mattered.

We make our way to the upper level of the house, both of us splitting up to shower, taking just enough time to clean up before my front door opened, and by the click of the Oxford shoes, I knew it was Thatcher.

"What the fuck are you wearing?" Rook comments from my kitchen where he is inhaling a sandwich with only a towel around his waist.

I tug my shirt over my head, looking at Thatcher who is wearing a brownish, cream-colored sweater thing that looks like it was shaved straight off a lamb's body.

"Italian luxury, honey. Costs more than your left testicle."

I blow out a laugh, seeing Silas walking in behind him, folders tucked beneath his arm. We'd all planned to meet here earlier today. Silas hadn't been at school and neither had Rook because the two of them had stayed up all night while Silas hacked into the security cameras.

He'd texted early that he had found something that would be of interest to us.

Rook stayed with him most of the time. Partly to keep an eye on him, the other part to make sure he was taking his meds. The last thing we needed was for him to be vengeful *and* unmedicated from his schizo drugs.

I follow both of them into the kitchen, slapping Silas on the back in greeting, before he lays out the folder on the marble island.

"Thomas and Briar aren't involved," is the first thing out of his mouth, before even opening what's inside.

The sound of her name makes my toes curl and the urge to bare my teeth hits me abruptly. I don't like the way other people say her name. Something about it rubs my gears the wrong direction.

"Sorry, what?" I say, shock evident in my tone.

Opening the white binder, he pulls out sheets of what looks like times, along with black-and-gray still photos.

"I finally got into the security cameras, and I found these," he spreads them out for all of us to look at.

My fingers grab one of the photos, seeing a teacher that isn't Thomas walking out of the labs. Which could mean anything at this point.

"It just looks like Mr. West, he's my organic chem teacher. What does he have to do with anything?" Rook asks.

"Greg West has been using Thomas's badge to swipe in and out of the labs. I'm not sure how he got it, but he's switched them. Look," he slides the sheet of times to the middle pointing to log-ins and log-outs.

"All the times Greg swipes in, it registers Thomas's ID number and vice versa. Greg is the one sneaking into the lab after midnight. This was his way of covering his ass in case someone found out about the drugs."

My stomach churns.

The excuse to beat Thomas Reid's face in until he hemorrhages to death has now flown out the window. Now he's just a teacher with a giant stick up his ass and a hard-on for pissing me off.

"Weeks of surveillance on the wrong goddamn people," I curse.

Thatch cuts his eyes to me, "Ah, ah," He clicks his tongue, "Let's not pretend you haven't enjoyed spying on Thomas's darling niece, Ali."

"You could always switch places with me. I'd tail a hot chick around rather than go through Thomas's office and apartment. He color-coordinates his underwear," Rook jokes, talking around a mouth full of food.

I grind my molars, ignoring Rook. "You want them to snitch? Someone has to keep an eye on them while you polish your fucking shoes, Thatch."

With a cunning smirk, he holds his hands up in the air, letting Silas continue to tell us what he'd been able to find.

"I went back a few months and you can see a few hours after Greg leaves, Chris shows up, swipes in and leaves with a duffle bag and goes to make whatever drop he needs to."

"So, Greg is the teacher who texted Chris about planting the body, which would mean he either did it or he knows who did. That's what we are saying?"

Silas nods, his fists clenching at the mention of her death, "He's the only person we've been able to connect to Chris. And why would he steal Thomas's badge, why not just use his own? Unless . . ."

"Unless he has something to hide," I finish.

We let the new information settle in. I run my fingers through my hair, pressing my palms into the sides of my head.

Frustrated, knowing we've wasted an entire month on looking at the wrong person, but we also knew this wouldn't be easy. We talked about this before it started. Knowing it could be years before we found out what happened to her, if at all.

But this, this felt like something closer to a lead. I could feel the end of this creeping up, knowing when we found the evidence we needed to, we would confront Greg and we'd find out exactly what happened that night.

We'd be able to let Rose rest in peace knowing whoever took her life met the same fate.

# CHAPTER NINETEEN
## *Tilly's Diner*

*Briar*

"Two double cheeseburgers, hold the onion, a basket of Tilly's Curly Frillys, and two strawberry milkshakes. That sound right, ladies?"

My stomach growls as our waitress repeats our order back to us. Greasy, delicious diner food was everything I needed in my life right now.

"Yup," Lyra and I say together, laughing a bit at our cohesiveness.

"I'll go plug it in!"

As she leaves, I turn my head to look out the window next to me, staring out at the dark road and parking lot full of cars. This little dive was the first thing in this town that reminded me of home.

The old school music that played from the jukebox in the corner, the checkered flooring, cherry-red booths, and bright blue neon lights took me back home to Texas and the Waffle Palace that was two miles from my house.

The smell of oil frying and laughter had a smile on my face since the first time we'd come here.

We'd both been studying for hours, so tired and hungry we piled into Lyra's car and took the twenty-minute drive to get here. It was only seven, so the dinner crowd was hot and heavy. The restaurant full of people you'd never expect to be in here.

Men in suits, ladies in heels.

It seemed to be a break from the luxury. Bringing everyone together in a humble establishment that was serving everything from funnel cakes to fish and chips.

We were a week and a half into October, and the leaves were fully turned. Except for the pines. They kept their dark, green coat year-round it seemed.

Since my last encounter with Satan's spawn in the pool, we'd yet to hear from them. We saw them on campus briefly, but the pranks, the letters, they had all stopped around the first of the month.

I could still feel Alistair's presence occasionally, watching, hovering, but it wasn't like it was before. Either they were planning something like our grandiose kidnapping and slaughtering, or they believed their torments had secured our silence.

Part of us wanted to forget everything we saw. I wanted off their radar and away from their gazes. Even if that meant staying quiet. I wanted to focus on school and act as if that night never happened, and it seemed Lyra was doing that much better than I was.

The other part of me felt like I would combust. To hold onto a secret like that for the rest of my life? I was sure it would eat me alive, but after the pool I promised myself I would graduate from here, have the means to protect myself, and *then* I would tell someone.

I would tell them everything I saw and hope justice would be served, but I couldn't do that now. I would just be the broke girl from nowhere Texas who was accusing the most important sons of Ponderosa Springs of murder.

No matter how many scenarios I ran through, that never ended well for me.

The promise I'd made had settled my anxiety some. Enough that my appetite had come back. Which was good for me because Thomas was beginning to worry about how frail I was becoming.

"Easton Sinclair asked about you in class today," Lyra announces, leaning her back against the glass window, her feet outstretched in front of her across the booth. "He hasn't spoken to me since we were in kindergarten when he asked to borrow my yellow crayon."

I pop an eyebrow, "Why was he asking about me?"

Since accidentally going Jackie Chan on his ass, I'd only seen him in class and once in the library where we went over answers on a study guide together. I didn't think I had done anything that would warrant him asking Lyra about me.

"He wanted your phone number," she giggles. "Someone's got a crush on youuuu," she sings in a soft voice, wiggling her pointer finger at me.

I swat it away, rolling my eyes with a soft chuckle, "He probably just needed answers to homework or something. Did you tell him to bug off and worry about his girlfriend?"

She shakes her head, "Nah, I told him if you wanted to give it to him, you would have."

I loved her even more for that.

"Plus, he doesn't seem like your type anyway."

"I have a type?" I ask, never really thinking about myself as the type of person with a *type*. I mean, minus the fact I required the guys I was interested in to be single and of legal age.

"You just don't look like the girl who ends up with a nine-to-five guy. You'd get too bored," she starts. "I think there are two types of women, those who seek comfort and those who seek love."

I'd never heard anyone say something like that before. I

mean, you could have both, right? You could have a stable relationship and be in love, it happened all the time.

"You don't think people can have both? Aren't you supposed to feel comfortable when you're in love? I don't think you can have one without the other."

About that time our waitress comes back with our tray of food, sliding everything in front of us and asking if she can get us anything else; when we decline, she leaves us to eat.

Lyra grabs the cherry off the top of her milkshake, popping it inside her mouth, "For me, love shouldn't be comfortable. Love should make you *uncomfortable,* it should challenge you, it should push your limits, make you grow as a person and all of those things you have to be out of your comfort zone to do. So, I don't think you can have both, no."

I love listening to her talk. I love hearing how she feels about life, love, philosophy, even when we have a full-on debate on a *Criminal Minds* episode. Everything she says is like it's been brewing in her brain for years. You wouldn't assume it when you first see her, because she is shy, but Lyra is funny. She is quick with sarcastic comebacks, and it makes me sad that I'm the only person at the school who knows that.

Everyone who passed up the opportunity to be her friend was severely missing out.

I grab a fry, dipping it in ketchup, "So you're the girl who wants love, right? An adventurous guy who helps you dig up worms and knows how to get dirty?" I roll my eyebrows teasingly, shoving the salty fried potato into my mouth and chewing.

A ghost of a smile passes her features, just as she snorts like she's thinking about a certain boy, or maybe a girl . . . I'd never asked her about her sexual orientation.

"Something like that. Who knows."

I pick up my burger, the melty cheese oozing from the side and the pieces of bacon peeking out from under the bun. My mouth was watering by the time I carried it towards my mouth, taking the largest bite of food in my life.

"Lyra Abbott! Is that you, sweet girl?"

I nearly choke, trying to chew this ungodly bite of food as a man in a pressed suit walks up to our table.

"Hey, Mayor Donahue," Lyra says softly, smiling up at the man with a neatly trimmed beard and soft red-colored hair who is looking at me now.

Of course I'd meet the mayor of one of the most prestigious towns in the country while I had my mouth stuffed with food. I place my hand over my mouth, chewing as quickly as possible.

"Hi," I mutter, swallowing painfully, "Sorry, I'm Briar." I wipe my hands on a napkin, then stick my hand out to shake his.

He returns it with a smile, moving my hand up and down gently, "Nice to meet you, Briar. I pride myself on knowing all the faces around here, but I can't say I know you! Are you new here?"

I nod, "Yes, sir. I'm attending Hollow Heights."

"Please, just call me Frank. It's exciting to know we have students from other places joining our corner of the world! Are you ladies enjoying your first semester so far? I heard there was an accidental misfiring of some fireworks the other night at the annual maze hunt."

Lyra and I look at each other with slightly hooded eyes, thinking back to that night. But she bounces back quickly.

"It's going well, just hitting the books and trying to meet the expectations set for us students," she covers.

"Well, I'll leave you girls to your dinner. Lyra, let me know if you need anything, okay?" he offers, and she nods in agreement, watching him walk away and towards the door to leave.

"You just casually know the mayor?" I say as we settle back into our booth, continuing to eat.

"He knew my mom back in the day. I was always in the same

classes as his daughters growing up." She pauses, taking a fry and dipping it into her milkshake. I crinkle my nose, confused by the combination, however I've learned not to question the oddities of my friend. "I feel so sorry for him."

"Why?"

Lyra looks around to make sure no one is around us, or listening to our conversation, before speaking, "Not only did his wife leave him for another man, but he lost both his daughters in the span of six months. He's lost everything and I'm not sure how he is able to keep smiling."

I begin to remember her talking about the mayor's daughter who died, reading it inside one of the news articles when I was looking up things on the boys. It said she was found at a local party house and the police ruled it as an accidental overdose, but apparently the rumor mill enjoyed adding salt to an already sore wound. If you asked anyone at the school, they'd tell you she killed herself or Silas killed her because she was sleeping with someone else.

If you asked me, it was just as sad either way.

A girl my age, one who hadn't even begun to live the best portion of her life, had people speculating and making up lies just to add drama to their own boring worlds. It was pathetic.

From the pictures in the articles, she was pretty, well-liked; from her obituary, just a regular girl whose time came too soon.

"Rosemary had a sister?" I couldn't imagine losing both of my children, but that close together?

"Twin sister," she cringes. "Her name is Sage. Mayor Donahue had to admit her into a psychiatric facility in Washington after Rose died. She just lost it, I guess. Just couldn't stop talking about her death and that someone had killed her. It was sad watching her in the hallways after. Like she'd lost half of herself, and I guess in a way she did." The sadness of the story makes my heart ache. "Even though I wasn't friends with her, it was our senior year. It was supposed to be fun and the moments we remembered when we were old. And all she'll remember it as is the year her sister died."

I had no siblings, but I couldn't imagine what losing a twin felt like. To be brought into the world together only to have them taken away at eighteen. She probably did lose half herself when she died. But a facility? That felt a little harsh.

"You don't think a psych ward is a little severe? I mean maybe she was just grieving. Losing someone like that could warrant some strange behavior."

I didn't want to come off as judgmental, I was just finding it hard to understand why a father who just lost one daughter would send another away. I mean wouldn't he want to hold onto her for as long as he could? Never letting her out of his sight? Helicopter-parent mode or something?

"I never really thought about it, honestly. I mean, maybe it is? I'm not sure on all the details, but someone said the mayor found her cutting herself in the bathtub. I think he was just doing the best he could, you know? Just doing what he could to protect her." She swirls another fry in her milkshake before taking a drink of it.

The words hang in the air as I push my leftover food to the side of my plate, fidgeting with something to make the silence not awkward. Just allowing my brain to absorb all this.

Everywhere I turn here, there is something dark, something morbid and sad.

Why the hell does anyone live here?

"Down to binge Netflix in the Loner Society Clubhouse?" she asks, changing the subject, a line of whipped cream giving her a mustache.

In the craziness of the maze, after Dean Sinclair escorted me out to safety and I saw that Lyra had already made it out, I remembered I had found the key. I'd presented it to the dean and he declared us the winners.

The key gave us access to what we dubbed the LS Clubhouse, a secret room inside the Rothchild District third floor. Inside had couches, a TV, tables and even a little popcorn machine.

We had the room until the end of our freshman year and it was where we'd started spending most of our time. Partly because it was ours, partly because we could lock the door with a key, and we felt safe.

"As long as I get first movie pick." I raise my milkshake glass towards her.

"Deal."

We click glasses and for a moment I feel like a regular college student.

I feel like a regular girl who was about to have a movie night with her roommate.

And I couldn't help but wonder if Lyra was right or wrong. Was I the girl who needed the challenge? Who needed to choose love? Did I need the extra drama my life had been given? A guy who is bad for me but good for my sense of adventure?

Because this, even as simple as this moment was, it felt like enough for me.

# CHAPTER TWENTY
## Territorial Predator

### Alistair

*Once, when I was eight, my grandfather took me hunting.*

*He was largely into big-game animals. Things he could gut, skin, and hang on his wall or plaster on the floor as a rug in front of one of his many fireplaces. Not because he enjoyed killing, because he enjoyed winning.*

*Without fail, when new people would show up to his home, he'd walk them into his study and brag about one of his many kills. Spewing an absurd story that always made him the hero. How he bravely fended off a bear from his buddies when he was only a teen or tracked a wounded elk for twenty miles.*

*My father got his boasting attitude honestly.*

*We stood in the middle of the woods from dawn till mid-afternoon when a flash of tawny fur rustled the trees in front of our tent.*

*"Nice-looking female." His smoker's voice always scratched along my ears like nails on a chalkboard.*

*The cougar's bright yellow eyes scanned the area in front of her, not thinking to look to her direct right. My grandfather shoved the outrageously large gun into my hands.*

*I looked over at him, confused about what he wanted me to do with this fucking thing because I'd never even shot a gun before.*

*"Go on. You have to become a man eventually." He nodded his head to the unsuspecting animal.*

*I never understood that. The need to kill something to prove your masculinity. It always seemed like a ploy to make people into serial killers. But because I felt honored he'd picked me to come with him that day, I lifted the heavy weapon.*

*Mimicking every western movie I'd ever watched, I pointed the barrel of the gun out, placing my small finger on the trigger and took a few deep breaths. Everything felt heavy, I felt awkward holding it.*

*I'd yet to grow into my body, all of me just limbs and bone. I didn't even feel strong enough to hold it up. I told myself it would be no different than the toy guns Silas played with, the ones that shot plastic bullets with rubber tips.*

*I hadn't meant to, but when I pressed the trigger and the explosion from the shotgun rocked my body, I shut my eyes. I closed them tight, wincing in immediate pain. My shoulder felt like it had been blown clean off and for ten seconds I thought I'd accidentally shot myself.*

*But even through the pain my eardrums rang aggressively.*

*I thought, like lions or tigers, the cougar would roar in defense. That it would have a deep, hollow voice that made the ground vibrate. Instead, it was a miserable shriek.*

*It sounded like a child wailing, shrieking over and over again.*

*Opening my eyes, I saw the animal fallen over in the clearing, tossing its head around and baring its teeth as it screamed in what I imagined was agonizing pain.*

*My grandfather taught me a very important lesson that day, the only one I ever remembered. He dragged me by my aching arm towards the crying animal, quickly removed a knife from his boot and showed me the long, thick blade.*

*"Sometimes putting something out of its misery is easy, Alistair. Like this cougar," he said. "It's obvious she's in pain, so we are going to help her." He swiftly plunged the dagger right beneath her ribcage, puncturing the heart, I think.*

*The sound dies in my ears, the eyes of the animal close, and just like that, its life is over.*

*"Other times, it's not as easy to tell when something needs to be put down. You may not see it right away, but it's always in the eyes. That's where you see if a person is already dead, even if they're completely healthy. Their heart is beating, but their eyes, they have already gone cold."*

*I've thought about what he said a lot over the years. Especially when I've looked into the mirror.*

*I'd thought about it even more as I walked behind Silas. I could only hear the crunching of dirt beneath our shoes and the echoes in my memory of Silas screaming. Just like that cougar when I was eight. Like he was being torn apart limb from limb. It wasn't a roar, it was a shriek that broke through glass. The pieces stabbing into my chest as I watched him sob over Rosemary's body.*

*His hands pumped into her chest, over and over again. I could barely watch knowing it was doing nothing. So painful that hope wasn't even an option. I cringed when the cracking of her ribs filled the air. It was at that moment Rook and I realized we had to do something, and Thatcher called for help. She was gone. She'd been gone for hours now. We all knew that when we saw her.*

*None of us had had the heart to tell him that, though, not until the point he was doing more harm than good.*

*My hands grabbed at his shoulders, "Silas." I think it was the softest my voice had been since I was a child, "You gotta stop. She's gone, she's gone."*

*"Fuck off! Fuck off, Alistair!" He wept, pushing down with*

*more force. Rose's body gave zero resistance to his strength. She shook with every chest compression, her normally flushed cheeks were a morbid gray and it made my eyes prick to see her like that.*

*I tugged harder, hooking underneath his armpit. Rook followed my lead, and I heard his voice, "Si, please, man." His voice was wet, the tears soaking his throat, "You're only gonna make it worse, just let her go."*

*Police sirens whined in the distance, the flashing red-and-blue lights bounceing off the trees outside, breaking through the destroyed house teenagers used to get wasted without their parents finding out.*

*"No! NO! Rosemary, wake up, Rosie, please! Let go of me! I have to help her, GODDAMMIT, ROSE!" My arms burned with the strain as we hauled him off her body, his feet kicking out as he fought us the entire way.*

*I'd done a lot for my friends. This was the hardest.*

*We held him down like a wild animal, nothing we could say would calm him down. He just kept howling her name into the night. Like the moon would hear his pleas and restore her life.*

*I wanted that for him.*

*If I could have traded places with Rose, if someone would have given me the option, I would have let them take me instead. Just so Silas would be okay.*

*The police, the EMTs, they came in like a swarm of bees. Buzzing around the scene, talking in hushed voices. When the shock faltered a bit, when he realized she wasn't coming back and there was nothing the medics could do but cover her with a sheet, he went silent.*

*My throat was sore for him, and even though we tried to get him to leave, to get in the car so we could help him, he refused to leave. And because I was drained mentally, I had no fight in me. I couldn't have wrestled him all the way to the car, so we waited with him.*

*We stood by until the police were finished, even after they questioned us. We didn't move. Not until they were about to lift her up onto the gurney, and that's when he moved again. Like a raging bull he pushed through them, shoving his way next to her again.*

*Officers reached for him, yelling at him that he wasn't allowed past the yellow tape like we hadn't already been there forty minutes prior to their investigation. He ignored them, like bullets ricocheting off metal, their voices did little to stop him.*

*Rook snatched his shoulder, "Silas, what are you doing, man?" Worry riddled him, afraid of his answer.*

*He turned, a few feet away from her cloth-covered body, facing the police and all his friends. It was like he was looking straight through us when he said, "I just wanna carry her one more time. Her feet get cold when she doesn't wear shoes outside."*

*Nobody, not a soul, tried to stop him as he scooped her up into his arms. Her sluggish arm falling out from underneath the white sheet, the tips of her fingers painted bright red.*

*We walked behind him, Thatcher, Rook, and me as he carried her to the ambulance. I watched her hand sway by his side, her hair spilling over his forearm, and I hated knowing she'd never laugh again. That she'd never tell a corny joke again or tease Rook about his hair. I hated that she'd never be around to make us feel . . . normal. Like regular guys instead of Ponderosa Springs's bastard sons.*

*How she'd crept into the spaces of my heart and become a friend, only to be removed so quickly. The way she didn't care about how people stared at her in the hallway when she held Silas's hand for the first time in middle school. The weird schizo holding hands with the mayor's daughter, they whispered.*

*But Rose didn't care.*

*She looked at Silas like none of that ever mattered.*

*He carried her body to one of her last stops before she would be buried six feet beneath the ground.*

*Her life ended, just like that. Without any warning.*

*Taken from us.*

*Stolen.*

"You take your meds?"

Rook's voice brings me back to the present. Reminding me that we have a very short window of opportunity which didn't include me daydreaming and him asking about medication.

Silas looks up to him from behind the desk, his hands full of papers as he searches through the drawers, dropping his head a bit as if to say, *Are you really asking me that right now?*

"Don't fucking look at me like that. It's twelve p.m., and if you don't take them now, you'll forget after you eat. You always forget after you eat," Rook argues as he pulls books off the built-in shelf.

"I don't have them on me, I'll take them later," Silas grunts.

I'd worried for months after that night if he'd ever look human again. If the bags beneath his eyes would retreat and he'd change back to his normal tan skin instead of the nasty pale he was sporting.

We all took turns sitting outside of his door, sliding food inside, water, medicine. Just waiting.

Three weeks.

We waited three weeks before he came outside of his room.

Feeble, noticeable weight loss, and a demand to figure out what happened to Rose.

When we agreed to help, it was like we were giving him something to work for. Maybe it was wrong of us to do this. Maybe we were making it worse by opening up a can of worms we didn't need to, but it was helping him.

He started eating again, he gained muscle back working out in the gym with me.

But even then, even now as I look over at his eyes, I can see it.

His eyes had gone cold the night Rose's heart stopped beating.

Rook abruptly stops what he is doing, as if we have all the time in the fucking world, walking over to his book bag and unzipping the side pocket, revealing a little baggie with two white pills inside of it.

"You're joking," Silas remarks as he watches him approach the desk.

"Do I look like I'm joking?" Rook challenges.

Rook Van Doren, the only one of us who could leave this town and actually become a decent person. Parts of me felt guilty that we fueled his chaotic side so much, his father's words having some truth among them.

Rook was already screwed up, but instead of telling him to cover it up like everyone else, we made him embrace it.

Depending on how you looked at it, that could be good, or it could just be doing more damage.

"Okay, Nurse Jackie," I butt in. "Take your goddamn pills so we can finish what we came here for."

Silas takes the medicine, mumbling a low thank you.

We had searched every nook, underneath rugs, beneath the couch cushions and were coming up empty-handed. Tensions were high as we were headed towards what looked like a severe dead end. If we couldn't connect Greg West to Rose, we didn't have much else to go on.

And we couldn't go around breaking into every single teacher's office. So, that would mean Rose's murder would go unsolved. With no police to investigate, no lead to follow, her death would sit on our consciences, on Silas's conscience forever.

Short of having Thatcher kill him just to kill him, we were screwed.

I watched Silas flip through pages, eyes scanning for anything, the smallest hint of something to give us an excuse to visit Greg late at night. Using whatever means necessary to get the information we needed.

He was desperate for answers, and I thought, was the knowing worse? Knowing now that she was murdered, but still not being able to catch her killer.

I couldn't help but wonder if we should have just left it alone in the first place. If we should have told him no and let him grieve. Then again, we would have been getting dressed for another funeral if we did that.

Silas, in his head, didn't have anything else to live for besides Rose. This hunt, it gave him another reason. I wasn't going to be the friend to take it away, just to have him kill himself moments later.

We searched for another ten minutes, the seconds ticking down quickly, too quickly. We were running out of time and patience.

"There is nothing in here! A few crinkled Hustlers with schoolgirls on them proves he's a fucking pervert, not a goddamn killer," Rook yells, frustration coming off all of us in waves.

"Well, what did you expect, numb nuts? There to be a message written on the wall in big letters, 'I killed Rosemary Donahue'?" I bite out. If anyone needs to be pissed, it's Silas. Our job as friends is to keep our shit together for him, not blow up when things don't go our way.

"You know, you don't have to be such a fucking cunt," Rook snaps.

"No big letters, but how about a metal safe hiding behind a curtain?" Thatcher's voice is the only reason I have not punched Rook's teeth in. That and that alone.

I turn to see Thatch holding back a curtain that I had assumed hid a window, which was what Mr. West had wanted me to assume. In the wall was a large safe equipped with a built-in combination lock.

The only way we were getting inside of it without being caught is to figure out the code and, from the looks of it, he didn't look like the kind of guy to just write down the password to his sketchy safe.

"Anyone know someone who can crack a safe?" Rook mutters from the corner.

Thc alarm on my phone begins to go off, alerting me that we need to leave because there are only ten minutes left before the security cameras cut back on.

"If we get caught, it won't matter if we know anyone. Let's go." I wave, making sure everything is put back in its original place before opening the door and looking both ways.

When I make sure no one is coming, we all slip out easily, locking the door behind us, making our way down the hallway of the Rothchild District and towards the exit of the building.

It wasn't a complete failure, and it wasn't the best news, but it was something. Another task, another name to hunt down. Whatever it took to keep Silas from turning his favorite weapon on himself.

I didn't want to bury another friend this year.

Rook was already texting half his contacts asking around about safe-crackers and people who specialized in it by the time we made it outside of the building, starting to walk past the commons when two bodies in front of the library, the library with my name on it, caught my attention.

I was quite close with the sin of wrath. If the devil was handing out awards for who represented which the most, I'd win the trophy with flying fucking colors. I knew about lust, my pride had gotten me into more fights than I could count, I think gluttony and greed went hand in hand, and I was a glutton for punishment.

Envy was one of the only sins I didn't practice often. Jealously and its green monster showed up around one person, and over the years it had slowly faded. I'd recognized there was nothing *he* had that I wanted as I got older, and soon my jealousy as the unwanted younger brother drifted into hatred. I couldn't care less if my dear older brother lived or died, I meant that in the worst way.

And right now, I'd never wanted to commit first degree murder so badly in my life. Dorian Caldwell.

The bane of my existence was having a conversation I couldn't hear with the thorn in *my* side.

I hadn't seen my brother since Christmas three years ago, I'd made it a point to be out of the house until he was gone. He stood a few feet away, a stupid fucking tweed jacket over his shoulders that looked like a burlap sack.

Success, wealth, it stuck to him the way flies lingered on shit. I despised him a little more for the way he styled his hair, the same charcoal color sitting on top of my own head, just less gel.

Two opposing forces, both I wanted to ruin in very different ways stood before me.

The weather was decent out, warm enough for Briar to be sporting a pair of shorts moms wore in the eighties. I traced her long legs all the way down to her busted-up Converse, the one on her left foot had a piece of silver duct tape along the side. Assuming it was there to cover up the big ass hole that was still evident.

Her hair caught a gust of wind, slipping it behind her as she smiled at my brother who was helping gather her books off the ground.

I wanted to rip his arms off for making her smile like that.

For having her attention.

My fingernails dug into my palm, squeezing so forcefully I thought I might have brought blood to the surface. The way she laughed at something he said, and how he purposely made sure their fingers touched as he handed over her books.

I wasn't sure if I wanted to kill him or punish her first.

Dorian wasn't supposed to be in for another week or two, at

least. He never showed up for holidays this goddamn early and the year he does, he's trying to take what is mine. Once again, he is ripping what belongs to me right out of my fucking hands.

Proving I was nothing but his spare. Everything I had was only his to take.

But not this time. Not her.

Briar was mine.

Mine to torment.

Mine to manipulate.

Mine to break.

It was about goddamn time she learned what happened when she didn't play by my rules.

I look over at the guys, feeling like I need to physically remove my eyes from the pair, "I think I know someone who can help us with that safe."

Whether she wants to or not.

# CHAPTER TWENTY-ONE
## Marked

Briar

The bag that covered my face is snatched off unexpectedly, rough enough to make my neck hiss in distress. Drips of water strike me on the cheek. I bare my teeth, blinking a few times, making my eyes adapt to the shady lighting.

Everything felt cloudy, my memory included, as I tried to put together how I ended up here. The last thing I remembered was leaving the library just as the sun had set. I'd made it just outside of my dorm hall before everything became murky.

I taste metal on my tongue, sharper than copper, more bitter than just blood.

Fear of the unknown rolls around in my mouth as I take in my surroundings. My Converse on the concrete floor, mold decorating it in obtuse patterns, and I can smell the dry rot of the building I'm in. Candles light the area sporadically, enough to show me the rest of what's inside.

The broken stained-glass windows, hollowed square spaces where caskets used to live, all these things tell me I've been here before.

The mausoleum where Lyra had dragged me to just

moments before witnessing someone die. Apparently, it was going to be my final resting place as well. How fitting. I glanced around, seeing no sign of my roommate, hoping that my absence would cause her enough alarm to tell someone I was missing. If, that is, she hasn't already been captured herself.

I only hoped that help got here before they completed what they'd started.

Alistair had officially grown bored with our back-and-forth games. I knew when they hadn't approached us or done anything for the past two weeks that they had been plotting something serious.

Bringing together the epic finale of this hell fest.

I gather all the fear in my mouth, refusing to die frightened. Especially not in front of these assholes. I'd given them enough of that fear since I'd arrived at Hollow Heights.

Heaving forward, I spit on someone's boot. And since Thatcher always wears Oxfords, Rook is partial to anything that makes him look like a playboy douche, and Silas keeps it simple with sneakers, I know my saliva has struck the intended victim.

My least favorite member of their satanic cult shakes his boot a bit.

"I've killed people for less than that," Thatcher's polished voice cracks through the silence.

I grunt, and if looks could kill, Thatcher Pierson would be six feet beneath the ground. "Good thing I didn't spit on yours then," I reply. My throat feels itchy, and I'd give my left toe for water.

Alistair strides closer to me, stooping down so that my static eyes meet the black pits in his face. Obsidian crystals that glow, sending crisis warnings to my soul. I twist my face defiantly, forcing myself to stare at Silas leaning against the wall, my eyes focused on the tattoo on his inner wrist. Rook flanking his left, playing with his lighter.

Those two were eerie in their own right. I knew if I made either of them mad, they might roast me over a fire only to feed me to their pets after. I knew Thatcher's reputation, and that solely was enough to warrant nightmares.

But as daunting as they were, as unnerving as they could be, they were still easier to look at.

All of them were so much easier to look at than him.

With heat in his touch, he sinks his fingers into my cheeks, puckering my lips together, forcing my head forward, demanding with his hands for me to meet his gaze once again.

"Eyes on me, Little Thief," he threatens with a tone so brisk it electrifies my skin. "Or have you forgotten that I own you?"

I hold his glare, not backing down for even a second. I let his ebony eyes pierce my own. The possessive nature of his grasp elevates my defiance.

*He* owns my fear. Not them. That's what he's saying with his eyes.

"Your fear ends and begins with me, only me," he goes on, relishing in the power that comes from that statement. Alistair knows no matter what happens, his friends will never scare me the way he does.

They will never make my heart race or heat boil under my skin the way he can. They won't ever control me the way he has secured.

We both know he's right, and it makes me fidgety admitting it, even internally. For such a tight-knit group of sociopaths, this one doesn't share so well.

"Don't," I lean my face close to his, our breaths mixing like it did in the pool, "flatter yourself," I conclude, resting in the chair. "You don't own shit, Alistair. That's your parents' money. You have nothing without that last name," I sneer, keeping my heart rate under control.

They were going to kill me anyway, right? I might as well go down telling them exactly what I think about every one of them.

"I don't believe you're in a place to be making cynical remarks, hick," Thatcher defends his friend, arms crossed over his chest, his white button-down rolled up to his elbows. The veins in his forearms are an alarming cobalt blue.

"Oh, yeah?" I cut my eyes to him. "And what are you going to do about it, Norman Bates? Cut me up because your mommy and daddy didn't love you?" I pout sarcastically.

When Lyra speaks about Thatcher, it's always in a muffled manner. Like he's a boogeyman who's always listening beneath your bed. I'd yet to see that in action, so I never took him seriously. The way he waltzed around in his coats and turtlenecks.

To me, he was just a guy with raging mommy issues that needed to be treated urgently.

Until right now, when his mask of sophistication drops like an anchor to the sea floor, lugging me down with it. Vomit slides up my throat as he threatens me with eyes so void of any emotion, I'm not sure he even has a soul.

"Don't."

They know each other so well that Alistair doesn't even need to turn around to say it. He already knew Thatcher was going to do something hasty.

Alastair's hands drop to my thighs, crushing them, securing them. My stomach flips, body melting. I jerk in my chair, bucking at him, wanting to get away from his touch. Only causing the zip ties to gouge into the tender skin of my wrist.

"If you're gonna kill me then do it, just fucking do it! I'm tired of this!" I exclaim, or try to, but with the lack of water in my throat, it just comes out cracked.

Rook laughs from the corner, like an explosion, loud and intrusive.

"Anyone gonna tell her what she's won?" He rotates the Zippo across his knuckles like a domino.

I stopped moving, peering intently at each of them. Puzzled by what it was I had supposedly won. This felt like the very opposite of a prize.

"What is he talking about?" I direct my question at Alistair, looking down at him in front of me. The grip on my thighs becomes tighter as he holds me there for another moment before releasing me.

He takes a step back, "We aren't going to kill you." Waltzing around my back while Thatcher rolls his eyes at me.

"The jury is still out on that," Thatcher adds.

"Fuck you," I hiss.

Alistair is now standing behind me, making me anxious. I'm humming with anticipation as he bends at the waist, his mouth lowering near my ear. Simmering air heats the sensitive skin of my neck, a chain reaction of goosebumps riddling my body.

Every time he is close it feels like the warning signs before a tornado or thunderstorm. Sirens blasting in my head, keeping me on my toes.

"So, what then? You're gonna continue toying with me? What fucking pussies," I growl, leaning my upper body away from him.

The tip of a knife rubs against my wrists, "We need your help."

He must be fucking delusional. They had to have been dropped directly on their damn heads as children and cracked their fucking skulls wide the hell open. They could ask me till they were blue in the face and I'd still spit in their faces.

It's so humorous, that they are asking, I start actually laughing.

"You're joking. You have to be joking," I cackle. "You crazy-ass psychos expect me to believe you've been doing all this just to get me to help you? Whoa, you sure know how to treat a lady!"

I feel the tension in my wrists release as the knife cuts through the plastic. If he thought I was going to just sit here and listen to this dumb shit, he was severely mistaken.

But Alistair is already prepared for me to retaliate, he clutches onto my shoulder, prodding into my muscle, keeping me glued to the chair.

Leaning down, his cheek pressed into the side of my head, "How about you keep your sweet ass right there. Be a good girl, you're gonna wanna hear what I have to say."

I can't exactly make a run for it. If my memory serves me well, the last time I ran from him, I was tackled to the ground and I ripped a hole in my favorite jeans. I pull my arms in front of me as a shield, rubbing my wrists soothingly.

My hands were sore, my shoulders throbbed painfully from the uncomfortable position they were in. I wiggle my fingers, stretching them out and catching a glimpse of something black on my right middle finger.

I squint my eyes bringing my hand closer to my face. On the top of my finger below my knuckle are the initials, A.C., about the size of a penny. I'm horrified, rapidly trying to rub off what I hope is a sharpie.

I'm not even paying attention to anything else, just trying to clean off my finger. My finger that has Alistair's initials on it.

"It's going to heal like shit if you keep rubbing it," Alistair's face is sporting a smug grin that I want to knock right the fuck off.

"You tattooed me?" I shriek, standing up and pressing my chest into his. I lift my chin up into his face, fuming. His dark eyes burn against mine, pieces of his dark hair falling in front of his face a bit, as he dips his head towards my lips,

"Can't have you forgetting who you belong to. I told you Briar," he breathes, "you're mine."

"I'm gonna rip that silver fucking spoon right out of your mouth just to feed you back all your territorial bullshit."

"Little Thief, there is no spoon. I learned to lick wealth from knives."

We stand there, staring each other down, trying to see who would blink first. My breathing was erratic, my heart couldn't possibly beat any faster. He tattooed me, something so permanent, something so visible. The entire world would be able to see it.

I felt branded. Stamped as his property. I'd never be able to get rid of him, even if he left me alone. I'd always look down at the black ink on my hand and be reminded of how dark his eyes are or the way he smells pressed against me.

That's why he did this. So a piece of me would always belong to him.

"I'm about to go grab some lotion, this is like premium porn," Rook announces, making it clear that we are not alone in the bottom of this mausoleum.

"I'm leaving." I shove my shoulder into Alistair's chest, pushing past him and towards the stairs. I'm stopped from proceeding by Silas, who doesn't say a word to me. Only standing in front of the exit, crossing his arms and looking down at me with a blank look.

"You walk out of here, you and your uncle can start packing your shit."

My spine stiffens as I grind my teeth, curving my head to look over my shoulder, "Excuse me?"

"We need someone to help us get into a safe. If you don't want to help, that's fine. But you can kiss that scholarship goodbye and Thomas can go ahead and start searching for another teaching job," he says with little emotion in his tone.

Alistair was not bluffing; he could easily pull the strings needed to kick me out. His father and mother are on the school board—with a snap of his fingers, not only my life, but Thomas's life could be ruined.

He'd worked so hard to get himself out of the gutter. To go to school and better himself, only for me to come here and ruin it for him? To take away all the things he worked for within a blink of an eye?

"A safe? What makes you think I can help? I don't even know how to do that!" I lie straight through my teeth. The only thing he knew I stole was his ring, I didn't think he knew anything else.

"You can run from your past, but not your criminal record," Rook says, lighting a cigarette and releasing the smoke from his mouth.

I felt exposed. Vulnerable as they all looked at me. Every one of them knew everything about me and I only knew what the papers said about them. I was at a severe disadvantage.

"Well, there is your answer. If I have a record, obviously I'm not good at stealing." Another lie.

All of the times I'd been arrested or caught was when I was young, before I'd perfected the art of thievery. Depending on the safe, I knew I could easily crack inside it. I just needed time and a stethoscope. But I didn't want to help these guys. I didn't want to help them with anything. I did not want anything to do with whatever it was they had gotten themselves involved in. Some type of gang, drugs, murder, I didn't want any of it.

"I'm going to have to sadly agree. How exactly do we know she can do what we need? She's an illiterate, poorly dressed hick. Would bad be out of the realm of possibilities here?" Thatcher's voice is starting to sound more and more annoying, the itch to punch him was building by the second.

"Steal his wallet."

I turn to Alistair, lifting an eyebrow, "I can't."

"Okay then, leave. Kiss your future out of the slums good-bye. You'll be on a plane tomorrow."

I had to make a choice. I had to make it right now.

Help them, then be done with it. They would leave me alone

because they knew I wouldn't say anything, because if I did, they would throw me under the bus with them. This was their way of dirtying my hands right along with theirs.

I would be just as guilty now.

Or I go home. I leave this place and all my hopes and dreams go down the drain.

"I can't steal his wallet right now. That's not how it works," I lick my bottom lip, trying to give myself some moisture. I could barely breathe without feeling like cotton balls were stuck in my throat.

"I wouldn't just go up to a guy and say, 'Hey, I'm gonna steal your wallet.' I have to catch him off guard."

"See, I told you, she's a liar."

Fed up with Thatcher's mouth, I lunge at him, shoving him hard with two hands. My emotions were so high, the slightest movement would have set me off. My explosion of rage moves his tall body only a little. Pissing me off even more, but I got my message across.

"Will you just do it," Alistair orders, ignoring my outburst.

Annoyed, tired, and wanting to get this over with. I take a breath, walking closer to him while he watches my every move like a hawk. Yeah, this is definitely the ideal situation to jack someone's wallet.

"I just walk up to the guy, avoid eye contact, step to the side," I act out everything I'm explaining, looking at the ground as I step across Thatcher's body, "look them in the eye once, then boom I'm gone."

I stride past him, spinning on my heels to face everyone once again. Holding my hands out as if to ta-da at the end of a magic trick. Thatcher reaches into his pants, pulling out his wallet, wiggling it around in the air.

"It's still there, swine. See, I told you, let's just get rid—"

"Check the inside," I say with a smug look on my face. I

swing my arms behind myself as he does it, opening the billfold only to find it empty. Reaching carefully into my back pocket, I pull out a couple hundred-dollar bills.

"It's all about the distraction," I hum as the crisp bills slide along my fingers as I count them out loud.

When I shoved Thatcher, I'd easily jacked the wallet. Slipping my hand into his pocket and getting the billfold before he even realized what was happening. To everyone else it just looked like I was fed up with his shit, which I was, but it also gave me a way in.

Then I'd snuck it right back inside where I found it, only empty. The money looked pretty in my hands. I toss the Benjamins into the air towards him, watching them flutter around the space, falling onto the dirty floor.

I didn't want to do this. This was not something I imagined for myself after leaving Texas. I wanted to leave the stealing behind me and maybe I could after this. When this was all over, I could have the fresh start I needed.

I just had to make a deal with a group of devils first.

"So, what safe am I breaking into?"

# CHAPTER TWENTY-TWO
## *Family Tree*

*Alistair*

"Make sure you pack a suit."

I hear as I shove another T-shirt into the duffle bag, scanning my room for things I might have missed so that I don't have to come back here for anything else for the next several months.

Snorting, "Yeah, right."

Collecting a new sketchpad and a set of pens off my desk, tossing them in there as well. Most of my things were already in my dorm, but when the Christmas and Thanksgiving breaks rolled around everyone left the school grounds and I was going to need something to keep me busy while we were visiting Thatcher's family.

All of his distant relatives on his mother's side flew in to visit and I normally locked myself in my room by day two of the festivities. Even though it was loud and there were more people than I was comfortable with, I still preferred it over my own home.

While I didn't celebrate with them, the holidays always felt more authentic at Thatch's. There was no insanely decorated ballroom or catered meal for a hundred people. It was a normal family dinner, with Christmas trees and Jingle Bells playing in the background.

Had his father not been a raging psycho, Thatch might have grown up to be an ordinary wealthy dickhead. If things had gone differently, I know I would have hated him. We probably would have ended up being lifelong enemies.

Just so I didn't have to hear him, I walk to my closet, clicking the light on and searching through the rows of clothing I've never worn.

Mostly suits, tuxes, gifted to me or purchased when I was young and could be forced to wear them.

"You're not showing up to a masquerade ball in jeans, Alistair. It's tasteless and you'll stick out even more than you already do. We need to blend in." He makes a good point, but it doesn't mean my skin stops itching when I think about wearing a collared shirt.

"I don't even see why we need to go. Besides giving you an excuse to wear something ridiculous," I grunt, pulling a black set off a hanger, needing to see if it will even fit before I worry about packing it.

Hopefully, it would be too small, that way I had a reason not to wear one.

"Because it's our safest bet. We know where all the teachers and students will be. It will give us more time just in case your pet tries to do something ignorant."

My pet.

She's the worst behaved pet ever. A beaten dog that won't stop pissing on the couch just to make me angry.

The All Hallows' Eve ball was one of many outrageous traditions held by Hollow Heights. It was like college prom, but much worse. My mother still has pictures of herself and my father when they attended. It happens every year and it only grows more extravagant as the years go on.

Clearly it was not on my list of things to do, but like I said, Thatcher had a point. Everyone agreed it would be the best time to sneak back into Greg's office, guaranteeing us more time for Briar to do what we'd asked of her.

Shedding my clothes and stepping into the slacks with my phone tucked between my ear and shoulder, I thought about how naive she had been.

Making demands I had no intention of keeping. We knew she would be telling Lyra, which was fine with us. She wouldn't talk and she'd already seen too much to not be involved.

It was when she spoke like we were expected to leave her alone after she did this for us. Sure, the other guys would comply. But the stick and poke tattoo I'd decorated her finger with while she was passed out from chlorophyll was there for a reason.

She was mine. For however long I saw fit.

Knowing she wasn't a part of Rosemary's death made her less of an enemy and more of a girl in need of breaking. Swinging her finger around ordering us to leave her be, never to bother her again.

Did she really think I would stop? After coming so close to having her break into pieces in front of me in the pool, did she really think my reign of terror would end that easily? That I meant what I said when I shook her hand?

The tattoo had been for the possessive man inside of me. So that when Easton Sinclair asked her to study in the library again, he'd know who she belonged to. And if my brother crossed paths with her again, which wouldn't be happening if I could help it, he would know that Briar Lowell was one of the few things he'd never have.

I watched her, seeing her try desperately to hide the parts of herself she felt didn't belong in a place like this. Like her dark desires were something filthy to hide away. But I knew, I could see it, she was not the kind of woman who ended up with a douche like Easton.

He wouldn't be able to feed the curiosity that lurked beneath her skin. Not the way I could.

I had no plans on stopping. When I was finished, she'd see just how twisted she really was, and she'd love every second of it after it was all said and done.

I'd slipped the black button down over my shoulders, listening to Thatcher from my room.

"Are you listening to me?"

Not at all.

"Yeah, something about your shirts are missing. Are you asking me if I've taken them? Because that would be a seriously misguided question. I would never, and I mean this in the worst way, never wear anything you own."

"Pardon me for thinking my roommate was going through my closet. Maybe it was Rook. Anyway, I'll see you later. What time are you gonna be here?" he asks, and I can't help but roll my eyes. Yeah, the pyromaniac is burning shit down in your ten-thousand-dollar cashmere shirts.

But now that I think about it, Rook's probably using it for flint.

"The next few hours. I'll text when I'm on the way." We say our goodbyes before I toss the phone onto the bed, buttoning the rest of my shirt up, tucking it into the pants. Snagging the jacket off the chair, I stand in front of the full-length mirror as I shrug it on.

When I glance up at myself, I catch the reflection of my mother behind me. Her shoulder resting against my door frame, wearing a dark purple nightgown that shows just how much starving herself over the years has done to her body.

I should have heard her by now, or at least noticed her presence that's normally given away by the clinking of the whiskey tumbler or the smell of her Virginia Slims cigarettes that waft off her in waves, even when she tries to cover it up with Chanel perfume.

Choosing to stay silent as she watches me, her eyes looking me up and down before her feet pad into my room completely. I look down at the buttons on my shirt, pretending to be doing something with them.

A cloud of smoke hits the front of my face and I lift my gaze with contempt. There isn't a word spoken, nothing is said while she looks over the edges of my face like this is the first time she's really seeing me. As if I was a stranger in her own home, and to her, I probably was.

For the first time in years, she lifts her hand, skimming her knuckles across my cheekbone and the coldness from her skin makes my jaw tense.

"Beautiful boy . . ." she whispers, her voice murky and filled with fog.

I used to ask myself a lot why my mother never looked at or touched me like other kids' moms did. I watched as children would run into their mother's arms seeking comfort and praise. The love that should be shared between the two, and I used to wonder what I had done that made my mother hate me so much.

Why her touch always felt like wet slime and her gaze never felt warm, always chilled and judgmental. Why instead of chasing the bad dreams away, she brought them upon me.

I pull my face back, glaring down at her, one thing they hadn't planned on was me being so tall.

"Yet so rotten to the core," she adds. The thing is, she wasn't even trying to be mean. She wasn't trying to hurt me; she just genuinely didn't care enough to think about what she said to me. Hurting me would require her to give a shit, and she didn't.

"A shame a face like yours was wasted. At the very least, your father and I can say we made handsome children."

I sneer, my nostrils flaring, "That's what happens when you raise a child in another's shadow, mother. They become nightmares."

She lifts the white stick to her mouth, inhaling deeply, her eyes crinkling in the corners as she smiles a bit. Smoke swirling in the air between us. I didn't bother changing out of the suit. I walked over to the bed, grabbed the duffle bag and slung it over my shoulder.

"You should stay where you are headed until after Christmas. It's for the best, darling."

Leave it to my faulty parent to require my absences instead of asking where it was I was going. For all they know, I could be going to a drug deal. I think I have finally accepted that they would probably encourage me to go somewhere dangerous, me being killed would be a clean way to get rid of me. So they could stop keeping me around to save face.

"Mom, have you seen my medical bag—"

Apparently, I was overdue for a family reunion because Dorian walked by the bedroom door, only to stop when he caught a glimpse of us inside.

I was silently begging my father didn't pop his graying hair around the corner. Even if he did, he'd look over me for a moment and then continue acting like I didn't exist. I preferred him out of anyone. He didn't even try to pretend he liked me.

It's a kid's dream to have an older brother he can look up to. Someone who will defend him against bigger bullies and teach him how to throw a punch. Someone they can annoy until they give in and play video games with you.

That's what an older brother should be. A protector. A guide. Someone you can count on.

I think mine's just the antichrist.

After graduating from Hollow Heights, he left for Boston to attend medical school, I think he's an intern or some shit like that now. I find it almost comical that he's being trusted with people's lives.

How anyone can look at him and not see what a selfish, vile prick he is.

And knowing that my parents made me to be just like him. Creating me in his image. I wanted to skin myself thinking about it.

He pauses, looking at me with revulsion, "You're still here? Figured they would have already found you dead in a ditch by now."

"That would give you too much joy, Dorian. Can't have that, can we?"

"How anyone thinks we look similar is beyond me. It's an insult to my genes."

"Believe me, I don't want anyone telling me I look like a monkey's ass either, but you work with what you're dealt," I say, giving a disparaging smile.

"They should have just broken the mold with me. Instead I'm stuck having to stare at my spare parts every time I come home."

I wanted to hit him for reminding me, but I didn't want to deal with the backlash. "As fun as this was, I'd rather go kill myself than stand here with you two any longer."

I stride out of my room, perfectly fine if those are the last words I ever speak to either of them. Harsh, I know, but it doesn't make it any less true.

"Make sure you cut vertical. That way the likelihood of you surviving is slim," Dorian adds, his voice bouncing off the back of my head as I descend the steps, trying to put as much distance between myself and them as possible.

Slinging my stuff into my passenger seat as I jump into the driver's side, starting my vehicle and flinging gravel behind me as I tear out of the driveway. Hoping I smash a window or two in the process.

I don't breathe until I'm off the estate and speeding down the road adjacent to my house. When I'm sure they can no longer hear or see me.

I stopped feeling sorry for myself after I met the boys. When I was shown that family isn't who you're born with. It's who you'd kill for. That even though my parents and brother are like living with actual demons, I still had the guys.

We were six and at a country club summer bash with our families. That's the first time I met them. When I found Rook and Silas trying to set off a small firework, while Thatcher distracted anyone who walked by.

Three boys who all came from wealth but were still searching for the chaos in life. Needing the anarchy to cope with the horrors at home, in their minds. Even at that age. These people who wouldn't view me differently or try to change who I was, three people who took me how I was and made me embrace who I am.

We never made each other hide. We saw the good, the bad, and the worst.

Underneath all the trouble, the torment, the evil, we were just boys who'd been broken. Innocent children who were thrown into this world with no protection. They gave us no choice, not really.

So now, the monsters protect each other.

And only each other.

# CHAPTER TWENTY-THREE

## Will You Go To The Ball With Me?

### Briar

The month of October had begun to fade away as quickly as it arrived. The halls were decorated for the occasion, everything sporting something spooky or orange. Carved pumpkins in the commons, punny lines written on the chalkboards.

Fall had fully wrapped its arms around seaside Oregon, making it impossible to walk outside without a jacket, and as Halloween approached, the less excited I became.

Finals were already posted for all of my classes, all of them somewhere in the first week of December, which meant I was already studying for them. November would be nothing but flash cards and highlighters.

I used to love Halloween.

Not the dressing up, but because of Syfy's *Thirty-One Days of Halloween*. Curling up on the couch after school with my parents with a bag of candy corn and popcorn to watch old horror films. All of us laughing at the shitty graphics or the cheesy plots. There wasn't much that could beat that.

This year I'd barely watched any of them.

My life felt enough like a thriller movie as it was.

Then there was this ball that was coming up next week. I'd always wanted to try dressing up in a fancy dress, because it wasn't something I'd been able to do before. But knowing I was only going just to disappear seconds after it started, all in order to help four people I couldn't care less about, well, it took away the fun.

Even when Thomas gave me money to go shopping for a dress. Even after Lyra and I had picked them out, I still couldn't make myself excited for this. Vindictively, I hoped I couldn't get into the safe or there was an alarm so they would get caught.

On the other hand, if they got busted, so would I. They would get a slap on the wrist and I'd be expelled. Lyra had been right from the start—they were untouchable here. Years and years of reputation built off their last names made punishing them impossible.

"True or false, a recursive function must have some way to control the number of times it repeats," Lyra asks from across the library table, a Twizzlers hanging from the side of her mouth as she leans back in her chair, the legs lifting off the ground a bit.

I rest my head on my hands as I look down at the table, "True."

"Correct! Another one right for the math whiz," she announces, tossing the flash card onto the pile in front of us. We sat across from each other, both of us with open laptops and at least three books apiece open, also notes, pens, highlighters. We'd thought mingling finals studies into our time made sense, until we were trying to focus on three things at once while trying to write four-page papers.

*How is it that I'm a math major and I'm still writing fucking papers?*

I pick up one of the blue index cards, "Tell me the lipids structure."

Lyra was majoring in entomology, of course, with a minor in biology. When she graduates, she wants to do clinical research on how certain insects may have potential medical significance.

When she told me, I thought she was a little crazy, but then I thought about how snake venom is used in some heart medications, so why couldn't we use insects?

"Monomer, glycerol and three fatty acids. Elements include carbon, hydrogen, and oxygen." She chews a piece of the red twisty candy, swallowing, before I nod.

"Do you even need to study?" I arch my eyebrow, smiling.

"Probably not," she shrugs, throwing her candy at me. It hits me in the chest, causing us both to laugh.

It was moments like these where I felt the most comfort. When my life had become everything I'd wanted. Study sessions with someone I could call my friend.

Absent-mindedly, I rub my thumb over my middle finger like I'm playing with a ring. The slightly raised skin under my knuckle makes me look down. Still in shock that it's even there to begin with.

"Does it hurt?" Lyra asks curiously.

The makeup I'd put over it was starting to fade and I'd need to reapply it soon.

"No. I think it would be better if it did hurt."

"Why?"

"Then I'd be more inclined to hate it."

I'd promised myself that I'd be open and honest with Lyra about everything. Including the fact that the tattoo itself was beautiful. I loved the way the letters fit in the space of my finger, the A and C designed to swirl around like vines around rose bushes.

I thought about getting it covered up with an actual rose when this was all said and done. Just to shove it back into Alistair's face that anything he threw at me I could handle.

Even if it was a permanent memory of him.

"Should I be offended that I wasn't invited to this study session?" Easton Sinclair's voice reminds me of coffee in the morning. Smooth, warm, everything you need to start your day.

I lift my head, looking over at him with a smile, "Extremely offended." I joke, "I lost your number or I would have invited you."

Small white lie. I did lose it. After purposely throwing it away. Easton was nice, I'm sure he was a great guy, and given the opportunity I might accept a date offer from him, but not while he had a girlfriend.

One who, from what I've seen, is pretty nice. I mean, she looks at me like I should be shining her shoes, but she still seems nice. And no one deserves to be cheated on, ever.

My mama taught me that if he cheats with ya, he'll cheat *on* ya. Cue the Texas accent.

"No worries," he replies smoothly. "Hey Lyra," waving softly to acknowledge my roommate's presence.

"Hello," she flutters her fingertips in a wave back, picking up another piece of candy and chewing it.

"I asked my dad about the fruit trees for next year and I think I've won him over with the idea of a cherry tree. No more waiting on shipments to the grocery store."

Lyra's eyes burst with light, fireworks exploding inside of them. I crinkle my eyes at him suspiciously; winning over my friend was a smooth move, I'll admit.

"That's so cool. Thanks, Easton," she replies, excitement in her voice. The ability to just walk outside her dorm and pick cherries off the tree was all Lyra needed to be happy. And bugs, obviously.

"I'm actually glad I ran into you, I wanted to ask you something," He returns his attention to me, placing his hands behind his back, rocking on his heels a bit.

"Sure, what's up?" I close my Applied Mathematics book, giving him my attention.

"The All Hallows' Eve ball next Friday, if you haven't already sworn off going, I wanted to know if you'd go with me. I'll even make sure to let you poke me with the corsage my mother will inevitably buy for us." His floppy blond hair falls in front of his face a bit, blue eyes confident.

He knows I'll say yes.

I mean who would say no to Easton Sinclair?

I wasn't sure if I found the confidence attractive or annoying.

"I'm shocked, I mean, flattered," I laugh out, tucking a piece of hair behind my ear, "but aren't you going with Mary? I'm pretty sure I voted for you two for Hallow Queen and King."

"Mary and I broke up last week." He sighs, running a hand through his hair. "It just wasn't working out, we felt it would be best if we were just friends."

"So, you're single?" I stall.

"As single as one could be. Is that a yes?"

Did I want to go with him to this? Possibly. Easton was cute, he was likable, and everyone loved him. I'm sure he'd be a perfect gentleman, hold the door open for me, call me pretty when he saw me in my dress.

There wasn't a reason to say no, not anymore.

Yet, I still wanted to say no, and not just because I'd have to ditch him once we arrived. I was attracted to Easton, I just didn't *like* him. Not enough to date him. When you think about guys you like, you are supposed to think about what it feels like for them to kiss you, how your body will fit with theirs, the way they make your heart race.

All I think about with him is platonic friendship.

"I'd love to, but I—"

"She already has a date."

The squealing of chairs rings in my ears, the one directly beside me gets pulled out roughly before someone's weight is dropped into the wooden seat. Rook slides into the chair next to Lyra, a smirk on his lips as he rolls the match around with his tongue.

My shadow returns behind me, casting over everything else around me. He absorbs it all, stealing all the light and pulling me deeper into the dark with him. That's where he wants me. Right there in the shadows with him. They always said in movies the light defeats the dark. That good wins over evil, so why is it that he is able to destroy anything that even tries to challenge him?

Good, light, it was no match for him.

"Ladies," Rook offers with a sly wink. I watch Lyra look at him out of the corner of her eye, picking her chair up and moving it farther away from him.

"I'm sorry, what?" Easton asks, trying to play catch up with this situation. I'm sure when he thought about asking me, Alistair Caldwell and his friends were not a part of the equation.

"I said," Alistair grabs the edge of my seat, tugging it closer to him, pulling me further into his web, "she already has a date."

I feel his head right next to my head. The way he leans into my body, smelling my hair, and I only make it worse by falling into his chest. Completely by accident of course, the jolt of sudden movement rattles my balance.

His toned arm slinks over the top of my shoulder and around my neck, dangling over my body, his fingers swinging confidently right above my belly button.

I bite hard on the inside of my cheek, "Easton this isn't . . . he . . . ," I wave my hands softly, trying not to make this look any worse than it already is.

"He isn't what? Your boyfriend?" he spits out, disgusted that I'm even allowing Alistair to touch me. Even though he probably has more money than Easton could imagine, he still looked down on the man behind me. Like he was somehow better than him.

"No, he's not," I grind my teeth, turning my head a bit to throw a sideways glance over my shoulder. "We are just . . ." I drag out the word tasting funky on my tongue, "friends."

I feel his lips move against my hair, tilting up into a smirk.

Cocky fucking bastard. When Easton walks away, I'm punching him right in the dick for this. I knew we had to look friendly so it wasn't strange to anyone why we were together at the ball, but this was crossing a line.

"Come on, Little Thief. We're more than friends," he whispers for only my ears, "You haven't told the golden retriever about how your little pussy was dripping on my knee the other night? Practically begging me for it."

I shiver and not because it's cold.

"She's mine, Sinclair. I'm sure you can find another hopeless girl you can con with your whack-ass knight in shining armor act," Alistair says loudly, never moving his head from next to mine.

Easton's eyes have become a hurricane of anger. The once light blue color that looked like happy skies, have become dark, veracious warning signs before a storm tears through the land.

"This is the kind of guy you want to spend your time with, Briar? A fucking asshole with no morals? His own family can't even stand him, he's a nobody." Easton slings the harsh words out like a whip, hoping to clip someone in the process.

I didn't know much about Alistair in the family department, but I also didn't think it was Easton's place to be judging other people. He has no idea what goes on behind the closed door of the Caldwell home.

Was Alistair a hellion with anger issues who made me want to run far away from him? Yes.

But I doubt he became that way after being raised by a loving family.

Everyone has secrets. Everyone has a story.

Even the heroes.

Even the villains.

"A nobody who's fucking the girl you're drooling over."

I gasp at his response, ready to deny that immediately, but Easton is already firing back. Shaking with disbelief, a switch flipping in his demeanor, "Drooling? Please. She's a new girl with a nice ass, but not even that is worth dealing with you or your deranged friends."

I shouldn't be surprised.

But it still stings.

Boys like Easton are a dime a dozen. The pretty ones who seem to have it all, who smooth talk their way right into your heart only to step on it when you don't give them what they want.

I could at least respect Alistair and the fact he was upfront about what an asshole he was. He never tried to be something he wasn't. What you saw is what you got, even if you didn't like it.

"You probably weren't even a good lay anyways," he grumbles, looking down at me like I was dirt beneath his shoe.

"I thought we were friends," I say a little loudly, causing the librarian to shush me, her eyes slitted and filled with aggravation. I glance around at the other students watching us, my cheeks warming up.

"Friends? You looked gullible and like an easy lay. You're just a girl from the gutter." He states, "There's no Prince Charming for you. Welcome to your life, Briar. One-night stands and quick fucks, it's what you were made for."

"Rook." Alistair grunts, nodding his head towards his friend.

Quickly, so fast I barely see it, Rook Van Doren has Easton slammed onto the table. Pens and highlighters rolling onto the floor. Those in the library watching quiet as mice, afraid one noise will have one of these rabid dogs tearing into them next.

Alistair stands to his full height, a looming shadow as he bends to speak to Easton who is fighting against Rook's hold, his cheek smooshed into the wood.

"Say her name again," Alistair bites, "and I'll make you swallow your fucking teeth."

Rook lets him up, Easton jerks upwards. Straightening his shirt and dusting off the imaginary lint, embarrassment tinging his cheeks.

"Fucking freaks." He mutters.

I don't get a second to even think of retaliating because Lyra has already jumped to my defense, "Eat a dick. Take your bruised ego somewhere people give a shit."

He leaves without another word, letting all of us settle into what just happened.

I look up, leaving my seat, staring up at Alistair.

"And you," I point my finger at him, "I'm doing this one thing for you. That's it. We are not friends, we sure as hell are not fucking. You cannot come around pissing on me like you're marking your territory."

It seems I'm failing miserably at being serious from the looks of it. I swallow nervously as he slants his head, arching an eyebrow up at me as if to ask without words, what did you just say to me?

My pointer finger retracts, just as he curls his hand around my wrist. The lights in the library illuminate his eyes, showing me the chocolate swirls inside of them. I'd become so used to the midnight black shade, that the newfound color was a shock.

He inclines forward, his breath skating across my skin as he keeps our eyes locked together. Surprising me, he slides my middle finger into his mouth.

A gasp flies from my lips as I watch him. The way his warm mouth encases my finger and how his soft tongue swirls around the base makes my toes tingle. I bite down hard on the inside of my lip.

Leisurely, he removes his mouth from me. Dropping my wrist and swiping his thumb across his bottom lip, "Don't cover that up," he looks down at the tattoo on my finger, "and I won't have to go pissing anywhere."

I try to ignore how attractive he is in the daylight. How the sun almost makes him seem normal. The way it reflects off his tanned skin and highlights the edges of his lean body.

I ball my hands into fists before briefly looking down at where he'd licked. The makeup that was once there is gone, thanks to his saliva that had dissolved the product. Which was what he wanted to happen of course.

Fucking prick.

The sound of his boots falls away on my ears, signaling his departure, but not before he turns around to face me, walking backwards as he speaks,

"And Briar," he starts, "make sure you wear something pretty for me Friday."

# CHAPTER TWENTY-FOUR
## Master At Work

### Alistair

Violins echo in the distance as I lean my back against the outside of the Rothchild District, where the Salvatore Dining Hall has been transformed from its normal rectangular tables and dull atmosphere into something Gatsby might actually want to attend.

I hadn't been inside yet, but I just knew dangling chandeliers and overpriced decorations awaited me. We only needed to make an entrance, just long enough for people to see that we had attended.

The sooner we could do that, the quicker we could get to the task at hand.

"She could have decided not to show up."

"She'll be here," I tell Thatcher as I throw the butt of my cigarette out onto the ground, stomping on it, crushing the embers beneath my weight.

And if she didn't show up, then whatever happened to her after she had done to herself.

Rook and Silas were busy shutting down security cameras, which left Thatcher and I to escort Briar and Lyra into the pretentious Halloween ball. It was basically a way for students and teachers to openly judge each other. On their outfits, their dates, anything their self-righteous eyes could see, they would tear apart.

It's always the people in glasshouses who throw the most stones.

My phone hummed in my pocket; I pulled it out, checking the illuminated screen. There's a message from Shade making me furrow my eyebrows as I click on the green messenger app.

*I sent in my recommendation, you should think about applying.*

Attached was a link to a shop in New York that was hiring new tattoo artists. They were looking for someone who specialized in black and gray. I thought about what my life would be like if I could accept this offer.

I was a few months away from getting my licenses and then I could work anywhere I wanted. Had Rose not been killed, I would have already been on the east coast. Probably in New York, already working at a shop, living in a one-bedroom apartment, walking to work where there wasn't a single person who knew my name.

I'd be all alone.

Would I even like my life without the boys? I mean, I had no doubt Thatcher was already going to move east, and so was Rook, but Silas had planned on staying here with Rose. Could we all head out together? Start new lives where the trail of blood would stop following us and we could just . . . live?

I wanted to say yes, but that was being optimistic.

"What's that about?" Thatcher asks, sticking his nose towards my phone.

"Have you always been this fucking nosey?" I jerk the screen away, shoving it back into my pocket away from his eyes.

"I've never had to be. You've never been this secretive before." He looks down at me like I stole something from him. This deranged need for him to know everything about us gets old fast.

"Listen . . . I don't ask you what you've been up to when you come home with blood on your hands, okay? We all have things we keep to ourselves, even you."

I don't think he's killing people. I mean, he might be, but I doubt it. I just think he has his own ways of releasing steam like the rest of us. Thatcher's is just a little more . . . gruesome.

This makes him drop it, because even he's not ready to own up to his own secrets.

"Here, I picked the most basic one I could find." He tosses me a mask, solid black with swirls of silver across the front.

"I'm not wearing this."

I look over to see him attaching the dark red and black one to his face, tying it behind his head. The mask covers the upper half of his face, matching his corresponding-colored suit.

"Don't be such a wimp, just put the mask on."

Grunting in irritation as I fumble with the string, pressing the plastic onto my face and tying it tightly behind my head. Mine shields most of my left side, leaving some of my nose uncovered, along with my right cheekbone and lips.

I just knew I looked fucking laughable in this thing.

The click of heels in step makes me turn my head, hoping it's not another girl wearing a variation of the same dress clinging to her date because she can't walk in her shoes.

Lyra's dress is tulle on tulle, the crimson lace stretches around her waist exposing a full figure she hides beneath her normal wardrobe. She reminded me of a girl who'd grown up listening to fairy tales. Just not the ones of kissing frogs and happily ever afters.

The Brothers Grimm variety.

Ones that told stories of brutality and death. Not of gold and stolen kisses, but blood and the power of dark magic.

The fabric fades into a rich black color at the bottom as the ball gown style dress grazes the ground as she walks towards us. Even I can admit that the way her blunt bangs drape above her black glittered mask, exposing the pale skin of her face, matched with red lipstick is hot.

"Looks like someone is stealing your signature color, Thatch." I mutter, leaning back into him covertly.

"Evidently," he breathes, like it took all his oxygen just to say that simple word.

Surprisingly the bug queen carries herself well in her heels as she approaches us, looking sour, or at least looking sour towards me.

I open my mouth, but she interrupts me, "Briar had to stop and see her uncle. He wanted to take pictures to send to her mother. She'll be here soon."

The awkward silence that fills the air is enough to kill someone. Lyra and Thatcher have engaged in some weird eye contact. Neither of them speaking, just staring, waiting for the other to blink.

I almost laugh thinking about Lyra, the girl who enjoys picking up bugs and having mud on her hands, hooking up with Thatcher, one of the cleanest people I know. Obsessively clean. Clothes organized by brand, then color. Bed always made, everything has a place. Yet, they were standing here fucking each other with their eyes.

"Thatcher," I cough, "this is Lyra. Lyra this is Thatcher." I introduce the two of them sarcastically, but from the looks of it she is very aware of who he is.

"Yeah, I know who he is. I mean," she clears her throat, looking at me, "I know who you all are."

The way she watches him, like she's staring straight

into his soul through the holes in her mask. It's not fear, it's . . . inquisitiveness that settles in her gaze. Even though she wants her distance from him, she still finds him interesting.

Which was more than most girls would have the balls to do. Our freshman year of high school, a girl ran out of the boys' locker room naked after Thatcher pulled a knife on her while she was about to go down on him.

"Pleasure to meet you," he chides with a smirk on his lips, reaching his hand out for hers.

"Now you're introducing yourself? I didn't realize introductions came after spray painting someone's car and chasing them through the woods."

I face the familiar voice, peering at Briar whose heels are ticking against the walkway as she makes her way towards us. Her eyes burning, teeth bared like she's ready to rip Thatcher apart for looking in Lyra's direction.

Even though she's braced with aggression, looking like she's ready to go to war against my friend, I'm taken aback by how graceful she looks.

My mouth waters while I follow the neckline down the front of her dress that halts right above her navel.

I shoved my hands into my pockets to prevent them from racing across her skin. Skin that looked so soft, like flower petals in the summer. I was foaming at the mouth for a taste of her.

Just one.

One agonizingly slow lick up the valley of her breasts where her skin lay exposed. Purple fabric wraps delicately around her throat exactly where my hands would rest when I was making her sweat beneath me. Her tits were barely covered with strips of material, the cool wind, or maybe my gaze, had tweaked her nipples, making them hard for me.

Instead of the ball gown direction, she's opted for something simple. Silk material that clung to her, chasing the curves of her figure all the way down her body. The purple that was more of a lilac shade, made the green in her kaleidoscopic eyes shimmer.

Blood rushes to my dick, my boxers suddenly becoming extremely tight around my groin, and not because of her erect nipples or pretty eyes.

No, it's the way her small hand raises to her ear, re-tucking a few pieces of hair behind it. My tattoo caught in the light and, even though it was small, the decorative font I picked matched her dress too well.

How dainty my initials looked on her body. How fucking good they looked on her finger. It only made me stiffer thinking about covering her body with my name, stamping my initials on the entirety of her skin.

I wanted to smell her. To see if she'd put on that perfume she didn't know I liked. The one with exotic flowers and something sweet. Striding closer until I was standing directly in front of her.

The heels made her a bit taller, her head right beneath my nose. I laid my hand flat against the corner of her neck, my finger splayed across her collarbone and lower throat. My fingertips fluttered against her pulse, squeezing just enough to let her feel me.

The mask around her eyes does little to hide the way her cheeks flush at the feeling of my touch. The makeup on her face just enhancing what was already there in the first place.

A lot of girls were hot. Being hot was easy.

Not a lot of girls could wear my name the way she does.

"I like your hair like this," I say, staring down at her, feeling her heart race beneath my touch.

The honey-colored strands are all pushed to the right side of her head, falling in deep waves across her shoulder, a shiny hair piece holding it back near her left ear. I liked the way it exposed her neck to me. Slender and creamy.

She smiles, "I'll make sure to never wear it like this again then. I think if you keep that mask on, I might just be able to get through this night without gagging."

I grin, rolling my tongue across the bottom of my teeth, "Feeling feisty today?"

Using little force, she removes my hand from her chest, swatting me away, "Just tired of your bullshit and ready to get this over with."

A shame that even when she was done with this favor, I still wouldn't be finished with her.

I hold my elbow out, motioning for her to take it. "Then let's get it over with," I say coldly.

Together we walk into the entrance of the ball. As I suspected, the lights from the crystal chandeliers glint with a soft glow. Candles illuminate the windows in threes, and everything looks like it was purchased at a 16th-century Renaissance fair. The students and teachers are all wearing similar masks, dancing, chatting, the normal social cues that happen at these kinds of events.

That is until we happen to be noticed by bystanders. Both Thatcher and I arm in arm with girls, dressed for an event no one expected us to show up for. I can't help the smirk that sits on my face, most of them are probably afraid we've done something. Pulled some prank that we wanted a front row seat to.

Briar's hand clutches onto the material of my suit as I guide her towards an empty table, away from dancing bodies in the center of the room. Tchaikovsky's "Swan Lake" track swarms the room, and I only know that because it's constantly played in my house when my father is home.

It was the only thing he knew how to play and, somehow, he felt it made him more polished when he showed guests.

"Why are they staring at you? It's like you're the Pope for Christ's sake," she breathes, trying to keep her head down and away from prying eyes. Shying away from the attention she would never be getting if she hadn't walked into this room with me.

Eyes from every direction stay glued to us and I just know Thatcher is adoring every second of this. The way everyone has paused their evening to give us their undivided attention.

I lean towards her ear, brushing the top with my lips, "Because we are everything they wish they were, Little Thief."

Taking me by surprise, she snorts, laughing softly, "Just when I think you can't get any more stuck up."

"I'm not saying it's because of my parents' money," I reassure. "We refuse to abide by the rules Ponderosa Springs laid out for us as children. When they look at us, they see the freedom, the rebellion they will never have. Girls look at you and wonder—" my breath is heavy on her skin, I can tell by the way her breathing shallows.

"—'What does she have that could possibly have grabbed his attention? How can I be more like her?' We are crack to rich girls. Because at night, when they lay down with their polo-wearing boyfriends, the ones who will buy them mansions and cheat on them with their secretaries, it's guys like me they think about."

My arm snakes around her waist, letting the soft fabric of her dress itch my palm, "Gritty, terrifying, shady men like me who make their panties wet. They come harder thinking about me breaking their hearts, than they do while their boyfriends are fucking them. So, yes, they are looking at me, but they are also staring at you." I knead her hip, pulling her into my body more just so I don't lose the smell of her, "Make sure you are giving them a show they'll remember."

All of that is true.

The girls around us, who would be more than willing, but all of them are too scared to admit it to themselves. Too afraid their daddies and priests will find out they like to be fucked by the bastards of this town.

That's what we spend the first hour of our time doing, watching our peers spin around us like puppets, casting their stones in our direction as we sit at the table keeping to ourselves.

Well, that's what Briar and I do.

Thatcher asked Lyra to dance fifteen minutes ago and he's spinning her in circles on the marble floor, her brown hair swaying behind her as she tries to keep up with him. Briar was watching them like a hawk, her eyes moving with Thatcher's hands like she's ready to cut them off if they make the wrong move.

They looked like mismatched socks out there.

I pulled my phone out of my pocket just in time to see a message show up from Silas giving me the all clear for the next few hours. They were headed down to the party to help Thatch and Lyra keep an eye out in case Mr. West left the party for any reason. That way they could text us to head out before he came back to his office.

This plan was foolproof.

Hopefully.

"Show time, Little T," I mumbled to her as we snuck ourselves out of the main hall and towards the exit. We stopped by Thatcher's car, grabbing the stethoscope she requested before embarking on the short walk to the adjacent building where his office was, the wind blowing her hair as we walked. I wasn't sure if her shivering was from the cold or if she was just nervous.

The dark surrounded us, the little light from the moon beyond the windows was what helped guide our feet up the center staircase. Shadows of trees reach out for our walking bodies as we crept down the halls. Our feet in step with one another the entire way.

We finally make it to the door, so I reach inside of my pocket to pull out the tool Rook had given me to help me unlock it, but

Briar had already pulled out bobby pins. Gliding the metal past her plump lips, using her teeth to bend them the way she needs them to go.

With finesse, she makes quick work of the lock, lifting and pushing all the correct pins inside to make the door click, letting us know it's open.

Once we are inside, I choose to leave the light off in case anyone is to look up to the windows. I didn't need them seeing a glow coming from Mr. West's office when he was supposed to be at the party.

"Grab me a pen and some paper," she says after I show her the safe behind the curtain.

"Is 'please' not a part of your vocabulary?" I walk to the mahogany desk, opening the drawers until I find a pad of paper and a pen.

"Do you want the safe open or not?" Her eyes turn back to me, arching a thick eyebrow, everything about her presence tells me she's in work mode and she needs to focus.

"Touché."

I hand her the things she asked for, leaning on the wall next to the safe, looking down at her as she begins to play with the dial. Spinning it left a few times, then right. Feeling the gears inside shift and click into place.

Placing the stethoscope in both ears, placing the chest piece right above the dial. From here, I witness what could only be called pure genius. The way she sticks her tongue out, biting down on it absent-mindedly as she listens for what she needs from the machine.

Then she begins writing down numbers, creating graphs on the paper, plugging them into formulas, and my mind is twisted with misunderstanding. In movies, they just twist the dial with the stethoscope, listening to the right ticks. Apparently, that's not all you have to do in order to get the correct combination.

Taking the earpieces out and laying them on the ground as she scribbles numbers down on the page, doing math most would need calculators for in her head.

"Where'd you learn how to do this?" I ask, curious how one gets into the hobby of stealing.

"Shouldn't you already know? You read my criminal record, I'd assume you read other things about me."

I roll my eyes, "Sorry, there wasn't a section in your file about hobbies. Well, minus your sophomore team swimming picture." I crack a small smile in the darkness, catching a glimpse of her tinted cheeks.

"My dad," she breathes, scratching out a set of numbers and rewriting them, "He was in and out of jail my entire life, but when he was home he taught me the skills of the trade. Pick-pocketing, safe-cracking, card counting, if it involved quick cash he showed me."

"Odd bonding technique," I note, her fingers starting to try different combinations in the lock. I imagined a smaller version of Briar sitting in the floor of her house playing with locks and stealing wallets.

We were proof that survival had little to do with money and everything to do with the environment where you grow up.

"Well, not all of us can bond with our parents over winters in the Swiss Alps and summers in Prague."

I click my tongue. "Yup, that's me," I say as I flex my fists, stretching out my fingers. "Spoiled, arrogant, rich boy with the entire world at his feet. What more could I want in life?"

She looks up at me, pausing her work, "You expect me to believe that your life hasn't been golden platters and butlers? Don't stand there and pretend you had it rough. You have no idea what it was like growing up without enough money to keep the lights on, worried about when you'd be able to eat again, or when the next time the police would bang on your door wanting to know where your dad was. You're no better than any of those people out there, you and your friends just happen to be more unhinged than the rest."

"You wanna sit here and argue about whose life is sadder? Whose childhood was worse? You think you're the only one who has been through shit? If it makes you feel better to think all those things about me, go ahead. I won't stop you," I retort.

By all accounts she's right.

I don't know what it's like to be poor.

I have always had money, I've always had food in the house when I was hungry. I had the basic necessities of life and then some.

But what she doesn't know, what she doesn't deserve to know with her snotty, woe-is-me attitude, is that when I was a kid, I begged to trade all the money I had for parents who loved me. For a family who cared. I would have rather been starved and loved, than starving *for* love.

Then you grow up and you realize you work with the cards you are dealt. You shut the fuck up and you move forward because all the pleading, all the praying, won't get you anywhere. Sometimes you are just the bad apple that didn't fall far from the tree.

I wasn't going to argue with her.

It wasn't worth it. There are just some things people will never understand.

We don't talk again, just letting the noise of the safe dial twisting fill the void. Not until she finally puts in the right order of numbers, pulling the door open with a loud groan.

"Piece of cake," she whispers, patting herself on the back. Which I'm glad she did because I wouldn't be doing it for her.

I squat down, looking inside, hoping something in here will give me the information we need.

Grabbing the phone and manila envelope out of the safe,

walking it to his desk so I can lay them down. My first action is turning the phone on, waiting for the white apple to go away before a basic lock screen appears.

I'm not surprised to find there is a password protecting the information inside. I grind my teeth, "What was the combination to the safe?" I ask Briar.

"5749."

Tapping the numbers out on the phone only to have it vibrate and tell me it's the wrong one. Knowing I'm not going to get anything out of it but more frustration, I set it down opening the envelope instead.

Inside is a couple hundred dollars, along with a flash drive that seems promising. Carefully plunging it into the desktop computer, waiting for the file to pop up while Briar comes around to stand behind me, watching the screen over my shoulder.

"What the fuck do you think you are doing?" I turn my head to look back at her, eyebrows furrowed.

"I'm the one who got in the safe. I should be able to see what I helped steal." Crossing her arms in front of her as if this power stance will intimidate me.

"Go watch the door," I toss my head towards the entry. I didn't need her seeing what was on this, even if it was nothing. If it happened to be something that gave away information about Rose and her death, Briar would be way more involved than she needed to be.

Bad luck threw her in my path the first time when she was at the mausoleum. The wrong lead kept her there, and her helping me into this safe was the last role she'd play in our journey of revenge.

I'd kept her on a string, a puppet I could play with from time to time, but she would have nothing to do with Rose and what we would be doing to the people who had a hand in her death.

"No." She stands her ground, "Either you let me watch or I scream."

"You willing to take the fall for this?" I quirk an eyebrow, knowing good and well we could throw her under the bus for what we were doing.

"If it means you don't get the information on this flash drive, then sure."

I think she's bluffing, the way her spine stiffens and she stares me dead in the eyes is convincing, though. Weighing my options back and forth, knowing I don't have the time for this.

"Fine, but whatever we find on this stays inside that thick skull of yours, got it?"

Nodding in agreement, we both turn to face the computer again.

I can feel her breasts rub against my shoulder as she leans over me to see the screen, her smell so close to my nose that my cock can't help but stiffen. I wonder if she'd stop me from tossing her on this desk and showing her how hard she could come when she was afraid of being caught.

How fast her heart would race as I watched adrenaline flow through her body.

I sink my teeth into my bottom lip, like I would her skin, just to keep the images at bay.

When the file pops up with a ding, I double-click, pulling up a surveillance video. I'm not sure where it's from, but it looks like a warehouse or construction site. The concrete floors and tall ceilings leave me nothing to go on.

There is a man tied to a chair in the center of the room while Greg West stands above him, walking in circles. I turn the volume up, hearing his voice filter through the speakers.

"I think we have been more than flexible with you. Now you owe us quite a lot of money," he says, just before mystery man lifts his head and exposes his face to the camera.

Briar's breath runs cold against my neck as she gasps, "Is that?"

I nod, biting the inside of my cheek, "Yeah, it is."

Together we watch Mayor Donahue struggle against the ropes that bind him, wriggling around as he speaks, "I just need a little more time, Greg! Just a little more time and I'll have it all to you, in full."

Acid burns the inside of my throat, my brain not being able to comprehend what my eyes are seeing. Because I know the man I watched sob over his daughter's casket isn't involved in her death. The man I took pity on. One I felt fucking sorry for.

My hand finds the edge of the desk, pressing my fingertips into it as I squeeze tightly to keep myself from throwing this computer at the wall.

"You said that six months ago. We have no more time to give you, Frank. The boss is tired of waiting. You either hand over the money now, you give us something else we could use, or," Greg pauses, standing in front of the mayor shrugging, "well, if it comes to that option, I'm not sure you're gonna want to know what we will do to you."

Frank Donahue, a man who'd raised his daughters alone for as long as I can remember, one of the only people in this fucking town I respected, becomes everything I despise in less than twenty seconds.

"Fuck!" He groans, "What do you want? Just name it and it's yours!"

My stomach boils, demons scratching the inside of my chest, ready to rip me apart so they can get out.

"Well, you borrowed a lot of money from us for your last campaign, Mayor." Greg toys with him.

"I had to! I was going to go bankrupt if I didn't," he argues, his voice cracking a bit.

"Plenty of people go bankrupt, Frank, and they still don't borrow money from people they don't intend on repaying. Considering the money we lent you would have gone to buying another girl, we need product."

I can feel a whoosh of air as Briar's hand rushes to cover her mouth, muffling the sound of a gasp as a revelation we both were not expecting comes out.

"That's where Coraline went. She was taken," she mumbles, fear shaking her voice. I can even hear the tears that are threatening to fall down her cheeks.

I'd only heard about Coraline Whittaker being missing in passing a few weeks ago. Thinking exactly what everyone else did—she hit the road and left this cursed town. My mind was going a million miles a minute . . . were there more missing girls?

"The boss doesn't want to be too greedy, so he's being nice here, Frank, and is only requesting one of your daughters. You give one of them up and you can consider your debt paid." Greg places his hands on the arms of the chair, leaning his face towards the mayor, "In full."

The battle of Heaven and Hell attempts to tear my soul in half. A war I was never expecting to go on rages in my head.

I was going to crush Frank Donahue.

Every bone would be dust beneath my hands and when I was done making sure he'd never walk again, I'd let Thatcher slice him up real nice and serve him to this fucking town on a golden platter.

"You want one of my girls?" his voice shakes.

"Or the money. Your choice."

"What will . . . will you kill her?"

I'm sick that he even needs to ask that question. I'm sick that he's even debating it. I'm even more sick that I know what he's going to do, because this answer leads directly to Rose's death.

Sweet, innocent Rose who never deserved any of this shit.

My friend, my best goddamn friend who stayed up at night worried something he did, someone he crossed was the reason his girl wound up dead.

"Don't be naive, Frank. You'd be selling one of them to a sex operation. We sell and trade girls. What their owners do after we collect them, well, that's out of our hands."

"Oh my God," Briar whimpers.

Greg pulls out a gun, holding it to Frank's skull, making it clear he isn't waiting for an answer.

"Wait, wa . . . wait! I need a second, just a second!"

"We've given you plenty of time. Your time is up." I hear the tick of the gun being cocked back, the brief silence before Frank says the statement that changes the course of everyone's life.

Forever.

"Rose. Take Rosemary."

# CHAPTER TWENTY-FIVE

## *What Happens In The Dark*

### *Briar*

The next several minutes of my life go by in a blur of hasty decisions. Moments ago, I'd witnessed Alistair almost combust from the video we'd both watched. My stomach was queasy just thinking about it.

It made me nauseous to think he'd hugged Lyra, how sorry she'd felt for him when in reality he'd done all of this to himself. The reason he'd lost a daughter to death and driven his other one to the brink of insanity.

Yet even in my state of utter shock, I couldn't quite follow Alistair. The way he paced a hole in the floor, sleeves rolled to his elbows. His blood was pumping so strong that the veins in his forearms were thick vines asphyxiating a tree.

There were links chaining together. I pieced the narrative in my head, weaving all the parts I'd witnessed and what I'd heard. It all finally coming together to make one shocking image.

They weren't just killing people for the hell of it. They weren't murdering teachers and abducting girls because they could, they were doing it so they could figure out what happened to Rosemary.

I saw the way his black eyes fragmented, cracking like the earth above lava. The glow from the magma below blazed through the obscurity when he listened to Frank give up his daughter like she was some pig for sale.

It had evoked this real, raw, vulnerability I'd never seen on his face before. Even if he tried to mask it with anger and wrath. I could still feel his hurt as he stared at that screen.

Rose had been important to him.

And she'd been taken away.

I of all people should know what happens when you take something from Alistair Caldwell, it almost always doesn't end well.

I thought he would have time to cool down before we headed back downstairs. I was going to give him space, let him punch something, but we didn't even get out of the office.

We had been so absorbed with the video that neither of us heard our phones buzzing in our pockets until it was too late.

Lyra had blown my phone up with texts and calls, all of them reading the same thing, "Get the hell out of that office."

Greg was on his way from the party, and by the time we had read the messages, he was already messing with the doorknob.

My heart dropped to my feet as we rushed to shove everything back into the safe, shutting it as quietly and quickly as possible. My wild eyes searched for places to hide, the sound of the lock wiggling making a trail of sweat race down my back.

We were screwed.

Until Alistair palmed my elbow, jerking me into the closet across the room. He shut the door, the plantation shutter door allowing us to see bits and pieces of what was happening outside.

I couldn't breathe, I felt weak and light-headed as I rested my hands against the tight walls, my back cemented to Alistair's chest as we waited with charged panting breaths. I was frozen as I watched Mr. West waltz into his office.

His expensive shoes floated across the carpet as he made his way around to his desk. I could feel the fury sweeping off Alistair's chest, his heart beating vigorously against my spine.

He wanted to do something stupid. His anger was getting the best of him at that moment. The man who'd made a deal that ended his friend's life was only a few feet away and I was nothing but a toothpick holding the dam back.

I felt him shift his weight and I panicked.

My hand darted down to his, wrapping around his long fingers like a child seeking solace. I folded my hand around him, clutching harshly. I wasn't doing it to protect him, I was doing it to protect myself.

If he busted out of here, we were both fucked, and I wasn't going down with him. As much as I hated it, we were in this position together.

Greg fiddled with his computer, sitting in his chair and making himself comfortable. I had no idea how long he'd be there and I didn't know if I could stand here forever.

I shut my eyes, pinching them as I tried to imagine anywhere else instead of this claustrophobic room with the one man on earth I couldn't stand. My breaths came out erratic and it felt like there was nothing I could do to calm my galloping heart.

My brain was flooded with distress signals. The ability to process this anxiety was shutting down my system. Everything felt scattered and normal function felt unlikely.

Just beyond my shut eyes, Alistair let go of my hand and both of his hands come down to my hips stopping there with authority, grounding me to my spot. I felt my breath in my stomach, the collapsing of my ribcage over and over again.

With gentle strokes, he followed the curves of my body like a reserved path. Fingertips ghosting over the material of my dress, all the way to my chest where he paused.

I was cast in a daydream, nothing here felt real.

Not even when his hands slip below the fabric, callused palms brushing my tender nipples, and it sending tiny bolts of lightning to my center. Somewhere in the back of my mind, I knew I should have been furious. I should have stopped him, but it was as if another person had taken over my body.

An alter-ego had come out to guard me against the terror.

I tilted my head back onto his shoulder, my nose brushing his razor-sharp jawline and I swore it almost cut me.

"Can you feel that, Little Thief?" he murmurs, so inaudibly that I think I might be hallucinating.

I nod, agreeing so that he'll continue to knead my breasts, maneuvering in small circles, lifting the weight of them up as the pads of his fingers dive more firmly into my skin. My daze of warmth begins to fizzle out as I hear Mr. West move in his chair, leaning up to type something into the keyboard.

"It's called the flood." My legs twitch at his voice. "That rush of endorphins that's filling you up. Your brain does that before you're about to die, so it'll be less painful. Making you all tipsy and aroused. It's why you like being scared. It's why under it all," his chest expands with a breath, "We are the same."

I could feel it.

This sensation of ecstasy that baptized me from head to toe. Drowning me in need. How alive the stir between my thighs felt. The way it was all elevated because Mr. West was but a few feet away. At any instant, he could catch us, Alistair's hands assaulting my breast, my back arched into him as I panted like a dog in heat.

I felt so near to death, yet so fucking alive.

Swallowing hard as he moved his study south, hands tugging the skirt of my dress up and around my waist, exposing the lacy top of my black thong. I was grateful for the dark color, hoping the arousal already pooled there wasn't visible to him in the dark.

"I can smell how wet you are, Briar. Your cunt was needy for me in the pool and she's needy for me now and I've barely even fucking touched you." He talks to me like I'm in trouble. Speaking down to me, as his palm traced the curve of my ass.

My body trembled from the feeling, making me shift so that I could feel his clothed cock pushing into me from behind. I could feel my mouth hanging open in silent pleasure, my body betraying all forms of control I'd previously had over myself.

Yet my lips just wouldn't give in to him. Not yet.

"Fuck you, Alistair." I hiss through bared teeth.

The way his mouth came down over mine was a rush of flame. A clash of tongues and teeth as we stirred each other. Our lips blending in pursuit of passion and resentment. I wanted to moan how good he tasted, just like dark chocolate.

Biting my tongue when he latches onto my bottom lip with his white teeth, sucking on it before releasing me. I could taste the blood in my mouth, the metallic edge burning me alive. My fingers grab onto his clothing, unsure if it's from anger or desire.

"Stop lying to yourself, it's getting old." His tone leaving no room for argument, "You need this. You've been craving this."

Heartless fingers reached between my legs, shoving my thong aside before slipping across the crease of my pussy, making me tremble in his hold. I'd never felt so small, so tiny in his brawny arms. Everything he was sucked me in and refused to let me go.

I wiggled, chasing the little bits of friction he was delivering. My mouth, my pride would never let me admit it out loud. That he was right.

That at night when I woke up sweltering, the only way I could get rest was if I placed my fingers between my thighs and let them dance to thoughts of him. That after the night in the pool, I couldn't come without picturing his face.

The twinge in my stomach was heavy, but so, so good.

And I wanted it all.

I looked up at him in this tight space, our lips floating over each other,

"Fight me or fuck me, Caldwell. I'm done playing games."

I'd deliberately unleashed a furious beast with those words. I'd never felt power like that, it engulfed me whole. Taking all my willpower against him and setting it ablaze.

Reaching between my legs from the back, two fingers drew patterns at my core, parting my lips and spreading my juices. Lazy, intentional strokes as he explored my sopping cunt. I can hear the faint sounds I made between my thighs as he drags my natural lubricant from clit all the way to the puckered hole closest to him.

He played with me, teasing me, and I could hear his throaty breaths as he watched me. Looking down watching the way my hips grinded on his fingers, chasing that high.

My hands mounted to the edges of the closet frame, clutching for stability as my body leaned forward. My head barely scraped the door, pieces of flyway hairs seemed to poke through the slits in the entry. My eyes kept surveillance on the teacher who would only have to click the light on in this room to see us beyond the shutters.

He would see my flushed cheeks and the shine from the liquid that poured between my legs, dripping, racing down to my ankles.

I quivered in Alistair's grip, the fire of my heat only grew with each passing moment. There was a second of clarity when he stopped touching me to unzip his pants, pulling them down just enough to remove his dick, when I asked myself what the fuck I was doing.

God, Briar, what the fuck *were* you doing?

Then, like it had never appeared in the first place, it dissolves the second I felt his length press between my folds, slipping between my thighs, slicking his shaft with my sweet-smelling fluid.

The veins in his ridged cock stroked against the tender parts of me, tickling my clit with every rock of his hips. Ragged breaths tumble from both of us.

I glimpsed down to the view, as he penetrated through the gap he created in my thighs, the tip of his cock gliding beyond my mound, revealing just how hard it would be to keep quiet when he buried himself inside my compact walls. It was the most erotic experience of my life.

"Are you scared?" His voice felt like thunder in my eardrum.

I shook my head no because I wasn't. I was hot. Driven mad with desire. Delusional. And fucking desperate but I wasn't scared, for the first time being around him, I wasn't afraid.

With calculation, he stretches forward knocking his fist against the closet wall.

Once.

Twice.

Three times.

The sound ricocheting around in the room making Mr. West elevate his gaze in our direction. He couldn't see us from his desk but his eyebrows were furrowed in confusion, contemplating the need to investigate whatever it was that he just heard.

Oh my God.

What was he doing?!

"Alist—"

I felt his palm cover my mouth just as he sheathed himself entirely inside of me. Leaving me no time to adjust, no time to settle.

Alistair wasn't having sex with me. He was fucking me. He was taking every emotion I had and feasting on it.

My wetness helped aid his violent thrust, but I could still feel the discomfort from the abrupt action. My fingers dug into the wood of the frame, eyes wide with horror as Greg stood from his desk.

Icy fear trickles into my veins at the promise of getting caught. Alistair knows what he is doing, what I could lose if we are found. I think those thoughts are what fuel his vicious onslaught.

Cruel deep blows from behind me leave me reeling. I could feel him everywhere. His scent strangling me, his cock so deep that I didn't know how I'd ever feel empty again.

"Are you scared?" he grunted to me.

I was submerged in too many feelings. It was all too much. My heart hammered at the dread of being caught, we were going to be discovered not only breaking into his office, but fucking in his closet.

I knew the consequences for myself if that happened.

But even as Mr. West began to walk towards us, I couldn't tell Alistair to slow down. I wouldn't even tell him to stop if I had the chance.

There was a burning in my stomach that only flew higher the harder he pressed into me. Short, ruthless drives that I was shocked no one could hear. My cries were swallowed by his palm over my mouth, and as much as I wanted to, I couldn't shut my eyes. I had to keep watching.

It was like watching a head-on collision. My eyes just couldn't be peeled away from the horror. I had to see how it ended.

Every step Mr. West took, the closer I got to my climax. The more intensely I felt Alistair's shaft brush against the sensitive spot inside of me. The harder I pressed back into him, giving him something solid to slam into.

Chills racked down my body as I heard his low grunts of pleasure, the way his free hand held my hips steady. His lips blazed the trail of my throat with urgency. I can feel the way he inhales my scent deep into his lungs. Trapping me there.

I wanted to come.

I wanted it so badly that I didn't care if I got busted.

My mind went empty, my body utterly boneless in his grasp. Everything was spinning, flickers of white spots filled my vision as euphoria licked at my heels. My walls clenching around him tighter and tighter.

"Tell me, Little Thief. I wanna hear it. Tell me right fucking now."

Tears brimmed my eyes from the powerful emotions. His hand pulling from my mouth, leaving me free to scream for help or tell him exactly what he wanted to hear. I was so wound up, that I was already close to falling over the edge. The rubber band inside my stomach began to snap. So, when his thumb found my clit, rubbing it mercilessly I couldn't restrain myself.

"Yes, I'm afraid," I whispered in a frail voice that frightened me because it didn't sound like myself.

The ultimate high had been reached when Mr. West grasped his hand around the closet doorknob. Ready to open it and watch me shatter into a million pieces while Alistair continued fucking me from behind. My orgasm hit me hard, an onslaught of pleasure that vibrated every inch of my body.

Sticky, nectar ambrosia leaked down my legs, drowning Alistair's cock. My pussy convulsed, sucking him inside of me and refusing to let him go. I could feel every dip and curve of his length within my walls as I drew my orgasm from him.

"Fuck, I need to pull out," his voice is strained, raspy and strangled. He seems to be saying that more to himself than to me.

Teeth sunk into the flesh of my shoulder, not just a tiny love bite, but a ferocious bite that left my skin stinging. Alistair pumped his hips into me a few more times, before sliding out of me easily, another shock wave of fulfillment fills my chest as I hear my name on his lips as he comes.

I can't help but wonder if that happens often. When he's in the shower if his hand is wrapped around his cock, jerking until he comes.

Beyond the point of ecstasy, I didn't even register the sound of a fire alarm blasting that had concealed my whimpers of pleasure and our last whispered confessions. I was coming back to earth, the consequences of my actions becoming more and more real as I heard the alarm echo. It sounded all around campus.

Mr. West curses, so close that he's basically breathing the same air as me. He quickly forgets about the thumps from his closet, rushing to go help with the apparent fire that has saved my pride and reputation.

I burst out of the closet, the clean air outside of our sweat and hormones is a brutal reminder of what I just did. What if he had a fucking STD? We didn't even use a condom. My God I can't end up pregnant.

Placing my hand on my chest, forcing myself to calm down as I turn to look at him, my dress sticking to my thighs from the perspiration.

"Please tell me you're clean." I breathe, wincing as I try not to check him out while he pulls his pants up, zipping them and shaking a hand through his hair. Waltzing out of the tight space as if none of this bothered him.

There is something that flashes over his eyes. Annoyance? Frustration?

He breathes, "I'm clean."

Relief floods me, taking care of one of the major glaring issues I'm dealing with right now. The siren continues to blare as I jog slightly to the window, seeing that one of the trees in the commons is encased in a rage of orange flames. The fire crackled and hissed loudly, rising higher and higher as it consumed the old tree.

"Oh my God, Lyra." I breathe, worry filling me for my friend that I left with three out of the four psychos.

I spin ready to bolt out of this office and back to where I left her in the grand hall. Alistair's arms catch me before I can, stopping me with his tall frame, hands holding my forearms tightly.

"Lyra's fine." The human in his eyes is gone, returned are the black orbs that leave no room for anything but darkness.

"Yeah? And you know that how?" I argue.

A knowing smirk builds onto his face, twisting his face into the stunning villain he is. My stomach rolls. God, I had sex with him. I had the best sex of my life with him and now what?

"Because she helped Rook set the fire."

# CHAPTER TWENTY-SIX
## Stays In The Dark

### Alistair

"Don't you have your own dorm?" I recline in my desk chair, "And your own bed?"

Rook lifts his head from my pillow, raising his eyebrows, "Can't I hang out with my two best friends?"

"Thatcher is in the shower and I'm practically ignoring you. You just don't want to sit alone in your room."

"Silas is at The Graveyard, he wanted to go alone. I've got to learn to trust him to do things by himself, but if I sit in our room without a distraction, I'll end up following him to make sure he doesn't do anything stupid." He admits, tossing his Zippo into the air above his head, catching it smoothly as it falls back down.

I nod, turning back to the sketch on the table, my pencil pressing into the paper shading the outside of the rose to give it more dimension.

"Speaking of Silas," Rook continues, sitting up and hanging his feet off the edge of my bed. "We are already taking care of Greg, I know. But what are we gonna do about the mayor? We're just gonna let him live, knowing what he did?"

The lead of my pencil snaps from the pressure I'm applying.

"It's not our call," I say, still looking at the drawing. "It's Si's. We handle Greg, get what we can out of him, then we leave it up to Silas if we go after Frank. This is his war. We're just soldiers."

I knew when I told them what I'd seen that it would take a minute for it to soak in. Let the truth burn the already bleeding wounds we were sporting. Once we confronted Greg about his involvement, once we figured out if he was the one who injected the drugs and wound up killing Rose, I knew Silas would begin shifting directions.

The plan was to kill Greg, grab the USB before anyone else could, and keep it for when we were ready to anonymously send it to the police. We wanted the ones who had been entangled in Rosemary's death, not a sex ring. That wasn't on our agenda, but we couldn't keep the information to ourselves when we knew there were other girls missing. We would let the police take care of that once we were done getting the revenge we deserved.

Mayor Donahue would get what was coming to him either way. Whether that be at the hands of me or by the hands of the prison system, he wouldn't make it out alive.

I thought about that video for hours upon hours over the past few days. Replaying how easy of a decision it was for Frank. How quickly he'd chosen one of his daughters to bargain.

Deep down I felt guilty.

I felt partly to blame because Rosemary's relationship with us was probably the reason he picked her over her sister. Sage Donahue did not run in, or even around, our circle. While Rose didn't mind getting dirty, hanging with those of us who had a bad reputation and letting our antics slide, her sister couldn't have been more opposite.

Sage had been a cheerleader, Ponderosa Springs's Sweetheart, and wouldn't have been caught dead around people like me. She hadn't been a bitch to us, rather pretended we didn't exist. Which was fine, we weren't going out of our way to be welcoming to her either.

Silas had said she always made herself scarce when he came over to see Rose. While they were twins who shared DNA, they couldn't have been more opposite.

"Would you have done it?" Rook asks, looking over at me, his jaw tight. A storm brewing in his mind.

"Done what?"

"Would you have chosen if you were Frank? Would you have picked between your kids?"

I jam my pencil behind my ear, pushing my sketchpad away. Crossing my arms in front of my chest and staring at the ceiling. Biting at the skin on the inside of my cheek.

"I would have let Greg kill me before I was the reason one of my daughters wound up dead."

The product of a family who'd chosen early on which son they loved. Not just a small line of favoritism, but I wasn't even in the running for most loved child. I questioned my existence from my youth. If they hated me so much from the second I came into the world, why would they even have me?

If Dorian was so perfect, why would they even have another kid? They got it right the first time, right?

Secrets have a way of creeping up on you in this town and the answer to that was no different.

Even as the person who is depicted as evil in everyone's story. I'd still sacrifice myself before harming someone I cared about.

A knock at the door stopped this conversation before it could even get started.

"It's probably Silas," Rook announces, hopping out of the bed to open the door.

Why would he knock, though? Wouldn't he just walk in?

The door opens slowly, Rook's stature blocking the hallway from my vision so all I hear is his voice.

"Well, well, well, I knew you'd come knocking on the devil's door eventually." I can practically see the smirk on his face from here.

Briar's snarky voice drifts into the room, making me that much more aware of my surroundings.

Rook turns to face me, jerking his thumb behind him, "That's all you, dude."

I take a breath, pushing myself out of the chair and walking to the cracked door. I wrap my fingers around the top, pulling it open and leaning on the frame as I stare down at Briar.

Her eyes are glued to my naked chest, taking me in, the tattoos she hadn't seen before, all of it, and I let her.

This allows me to watch her openly, the straight-legged jeans she wears all the time, her long-sleeved striped shirt that's cut at the navel, exposing the flesh of her stomach. I wonder how many guys in this dorm hall looked at that exact piece of skin as she made her way to my room.

My fingers tighten on the door, "Finished staring?" It comes out harsher than I intended, but oh well.

"Yeah, um, yeah, I just . . . cool tattoos." She tries to cover her blatant eye-fucking, failing miserably.

I peer down at my chest piece, really the only thing on my front half, besides the coin on my lower abdomen. The ram skull and thorns were something I designed myself, Shade got the honors of holding me down for the seven hours it took.

"Thanks," I grunt. "Is there a reason you're here? Or do you just enjoy ending up in places you shouldn't be?" I raise my eyebrow, watching her rock back and forth on her heels.

She looks up and down the hallway making sure there is no one around, "I just wanted to say thank you." The shit lighting in the dorm makes her eyes look dull.

I knew what she was saying thank you for, but I decided to be an asshole anyway.

"For making you come? No thanks needed," I don't bother fighting the smile when she starts turning pink. Her round cheeks tinted and flushed.

"That's not what I meant and you know it," she hisses. "I'm thanking you for Ada."

I sigh, stepping out into the hall, shutting the door behind me and resting my back on it. My arms crossed in front of me. After we bolted from Greg's office I had the privilege of explaining to her that before we fucked in the closet, I texted Rook to do something so we could get out of there.

I didn't know he would burn down a courtyard tree, but it did the trick. Poor Lyra had become an accomplice to arson all because she was trying to wrestle the match out of Rook's hand, only to knock the flame onto the gas that ignited it. This was also the reason I felt so confident giving away our position while I was buried inside of her. I couldn't have planned for any better timing, but even if we had gotten caught, I wasn't worried.

Greg West was dead in my book, what was he going to do to either me or Briar if he was six feet under?

"Don't make a big deal out of it."

"But it is. You know what . . ." she holds her hands up, like she's stopping herself from talking by doing that, reaching into her pocket, "it doesn't matter. I just wanted to return this, a truce of sorts." The light catches my ring in her palm as she holds it out for me to take.

I fucking knew she had it.

After the office, after the sex, after the aftermath, the torment of her dead rat wasn't necessary. I had enough on her that if she wanted to talk, I'd ruin her. So, it wasn't a big deal that I returned the dumb rodent.

I should've killed it to begin with, it would have been easier than buying supplies and food for the damn thing. A fucking thing that bit me within the first three days I had it in my dorm room.

I'd had a full-on argument with the white rat, while Thatcher was in class, about how it better get its shit together or I was gonna let my roommate really skin it. I hadn't lied when I said I let Thatcher skin an animal, a squirrel I think. That's what we used for the note on their dorm door.

"Now we have our hands clean of each other," she finishes, waiting for me to take the jewelry from her. "You go your way and I'll go mine."

I almost wanted to laugh. Our hands clean of each other?

We'd done quite the opposite in that closet. I'd dirtied my hands and cock with her. My fingers, my lips, they were covered in her smell. The shower after had only made my dick hard. Standing under the burning hot stream of water, her scent rolling off me into the mist making it that much easier to fuck my hand.

I was stained with her.

There was no getting clean.

Not now.

"You know what people here see when they look at you, Briar?"

The question catches both of us off guard.

She recoils, rolling her eyes at me, "I can't wait to hear this,"

I lean my neck towards her, sweeping a piece of her hair behind her ear as I let my eyes glide down her slender throat, towards her shoulder where my teeth marks probably lay.

"Nothing. They see nothing," I mutter.

Her reaction is warranted, the way she swats my hand away, sucking her teeth and standing in a defensive position, already regretting coming here to try and offer an olive branch.

"That's so sweet of you, Alistair. Really, thank you for reminding me of what a piece of shit you are."

I let her walk away from me, just enough for her to feel

better about herself, before following after her. My pace steady, knowing I'll catch her eventually.

"They see trash," I continue, "A cast-off."

These words seem to push her faster until she's swinging around the banister, about to head down the steps. I follow close behind, so that she'll hear every single word I say.

"A girl from a nowhere town who doesn't belong here. An invisible girl with no purpose, no future."

My words are harsh.

But they are honest.

The teachers don't look at her with potential like they do other students. They look at her as if she's already made it as far as she'll ever go in life. Just her being here is enough. They don't see her as intelligent or talented.

They barely even see her.

She spins abruptly, frustration and pain twinkling in her eyes. Even though she's stopped, I don't. I continue to pursue her, step-by-step, until she's pressed into the front of my body.

Until her back is on the wall and I can smell her.

"I just wanted this to be over, Alistair. Why are you telling me this? Why are you still doing this?" There is a crack in her voice as she searches my eyes for answers.

I keep my jaw set, my face impassive. There is nothing for her to see inside of me.

"Can I tell you something?" I ignore her questions completely.

"No."

I don't listen, I grab her belt loops hooking my fingers into them and slowly pulling her into me. My mouth breathing the same air as she is, our noses brushing each other.

"They look at me like that, too," I whisper, my tone grainy.

I'd come from generations of wealth and was still treated the same as the girl with practically nothing. It had nothing to do with money and everything to do with what was inside of us.

"They look at me like I'll be nothing. I've learned over the years, I like it. I love being the person they shove in the shadows."

Her eyes ignite with passion, as our hips press into one another. My right hand resting at the base of her throat, fingers curling around her neck just a little. I could feel her heartbeat beneath my hand, the fast paced pitter-patter.

My tongue swipes across my bottom lip, catching hers in the process, "I thrive there. We can do whatever we want inside of the shadows. It's where I belong. Our invisibility doesn't make us weak, Little Thief."

The pressure of my hand increases, a small whimper falling from her lips.

"It gives us power."

The look in her eyes tests my self-control, it's the look of need. She wants me to kiss her. Kiss her lips, her neck, the sweet place between her shoulder and throat, her ample tits, the curve of her spine. She wants me all over her, inside of her.

We can never be clean of each other again.

I want my words to soak into her skin. Seep into her system so that she understands what damage she can do when she recognizes the dark and twisty pieces of her are not something that need to be hidden away. They need to be what propels her forward.

It's the only way she'll make it out of this place alive.

I release my grip, pushing off the wall behind her to put distance between us, my cock hating me for taking it away from her warmth.

Standing there for a moment longer, staring at her, the way her chest rises and falls. How her flushed cheeks make her look even more innocent than she already is. It would be so easy to take her, right here in this hallway.

Instead, I turn around, forcing my legs to move me back towards my dorm room where Rook and Thatcher are probably trying to listen through the door with a glass cup.

"Wait—Alistair—wait." I pause giving her the floor to speak, only for a second though, and she knows that.

"I wanna know," she breathes, "I wanna know what it is that makes the shadows so great. I want you to show me."

My fists clench as fire rushes through my veins, excitement pumping through my blood. I bite my tongue, holding in a smile.

I knew who Briar was. I knew the girl she was and who she could be the moment I saw her at that party. I knew the damage she could wreak on this place.

Now it was time for her to see that for herself.

# CHAPTER TWENTY-SEVEN
## *God Of Wrath*

*Briar*

The roar of engines vibrated the concrete stadium I walked into. The smell of burnt rubber and weed. I'd been amazed when we walked up from the parking lot at the bottom of a small hill to see the towering lights still worked at this place. Assuming it had been someone's parents' money that got them powered up again. Underground rap to death metal, the music that clamored into the night.

People who looked no older than fourteen smoked cigarettes by the center of the track, even people who looked close to thirty huddled together placing bets on the lunatics that raced around the cracked and broken track.

The Graveyard was everything I expected it to be.

Chaos. Mayhem. Rebellion.

"How have the police not shut this place down?" I yell to Lyra over the craziness as she leads me to a row of concrete seats that are open. They aren't too far up, so we can see everything pretty clearly.

Including the makeshift boxing ring that sits in the center of the stadium. A large patch of dirt in the middle of the grass from where the green refused to grow after it had been stepped on too many times.

I cringed as I watched a kid my age crumple to the ground after a knee to the face.

If something like this was in my small town in Texas, the sheriff and half the county cops would be on it like white on rice.

"They know they won't be able to do anything about it. You can't arrest all of us that are here, and even if you do, most of the people here have enough money to be out of the handcuffs before they are even booked. It's pointless."

The night air is chilly and I'm thanking myself for wearing layers. The soft material of the hoodie paired with the large button up coat I'd thrown over it was doing the perfect job of keeping me warm.

My uninsulated Converse were a different story, I was pretty sure my feet might freeze off before the night was over.

Shoving my hands into my pockets to heat my fingers, I watched as two cars line up at the starting line.

"Ladies, gentlemen, whores and bastards, welcome to The Graveyard!!"

*Well, that's pleasant,* I think as the surrounding crowd begins to rumble and scream. Clapping hands, hoots and chants make my stomach bubble with excitement. Lyra bumps my shoulder as she joins in on the clapping, encouraging me.

"As always, if you're racing you should already be waiting in one of the pits. Please, no one walk on the track during the action, I don't feel like scraping brains off the asphalt tonight," he announces with a joking tone that makes the crowd cheer louder.

That should have scared them, but it only ignited their exhilaration.

The first heat of cars rev their engines, the motors purring. We spend the first thirty minutes applauding as vehicles from

Mustangs to Ferraris tear down the track. We weren't even sure who we were rooting for, but we knew it was fun.

I'd be lying if I said I wasn't looking over between races for Alistair. The signature leather jacket was nowhere to be found and neither were his friends, not yet at least.

My curiosity wouldn't let me leave it be. Leave him be.

I showed up to his dorm with a plan. Thank him for not killing my rat and returning her unharmed, she actually looked a little chunkier which meant he was feeding her a little too much, but I thought that was kinda cute.

I'd return the ring and we'd go our separate ways.

He knew I wasn't involved in Rose's death, he'd ensured I wouldn't talk about Chris, and we'd cured whatever sexual tension had sizzled between us. There was no reason for us to keep in contact.

I was supposed to be done with him.

Then he did what Alistair does best. He pushed me. He tempted me.

My brain wanted nothing to do with him. It knew that everything Alistair was would be nothing but trouble and pain for me. But my curiosity, my body, they wanted just a little bit more.

Secretly, I also wanted to know about what they were up to. I wanted to understand why they were looking so hard into Rose's death and how it landed them in Mr. West's office. And if they didn't plan on saying anything, I would, because there were more missing girls out there apparently, and we couldn't just let them be sold.

With timing I couldn't have planned any better myself, I saw Thatcher's blond hair reflect in the moonlight, appearing from the entrance of the stadium. Silas was in step behind him, wearing his hood down for the first time that I've seen.

Girls took immediate notice of this just as I had.

The gray skullcap beanie, a cigarette tucked into his lips and a skintight white workout shirt that did little to hide what he has beneath it.

I thought about that video, I thought about how terrible the pain he keeps inside must be. And even though they'd given me no reason to feel sorry for them, even though they'd been a living hell, I felt sorry for Silas.

They take a minute to scan the crowd, looking for where they are going to sit, I think, when Thatcher's eyes land on me.

It would take a lot for me to feel sorry for *him*. Even if I was civil with Alistair, I couldn't stand Thatcher Pierson. Maybe it was because of his father, maybe it was because he allowed the reputation of his father to rub off on him. Like the fact his dad took lives didn't even phase him.

And even though he didn't know who Lyra was to him, I still hated the way he looked at her.

He begins the incline up the stairs, heading straight in our direction. My spine stiffens, preparing for an inevitable insult war that is coming for me.

"Ladies," he coos, sliding into the row behind us and rubbing his hands together with excitement, "Who is ready for a little bloodbath?"

"I think you're out of luck, Dahmer. I haven't seen much blood since I got here," I sneer, looking over my shoulder and giving him a sarcastic smile.

He returns the same smile, matching my energy, "That's just because Alistair hasn't fought yet. There is always blood when he gets into the ring."

Silas sits beside him quietly, puffing the brown end of his cigarette, my eyes locking with his for longer than I would have liked. We sit there staring at each other, until he reaches into his pocket, pulling out the pack of cancer sticks and leaning them towards me.

I think he thought I wanted one since I was looking at him so hard.

Shaking my head, "I don't smoke. Thanks, though."

"The only thing we seem to have in common," Thatcher adds.

"You don't smoke?" Lyra asks Thatcher, making conversation with the wolf in sheep's clothing as if he wasn't the scary kind of handsome that all successful serial killers possessed.

He looked over at her, tilting his head as if admiring a child, so I automatically leaned closer to her. Feeling the need to protect her from him.

"I don't believe in killing yourself slowly, Lyra darling. If you're going to do it, I say," he runs his thumb across his throat, licking his canine teeth because the thought of blood probably made him hungry, "do it quickly."

"Like father like son, I guess," I say with a razor-sharp tone.

He moves his eyes off her, cutting them in my direction. Like it kills him to pull his attention from her. All of them had a different soft spot, something that sent them over the edge and Thatcher's was his dad.

An icy glare slices through my hardened exterior and for a split second I think he might kill me. My blood runs cold as his lips turn up into a vicious smile that rivals Heath Ledger's in *The Dark Knight*.

He struck fear in me because of what I knew he was capable of outside the gates of Hollow Heights. He'd graduate from here, inherit a company, marry a dull, pretty woman, and have three kids. He would live an essentially normal life, wealthy friends, golf on Saturday, and brunch on Sunday. Except at night, in his basement where his wife thinks he's working on small projects, he'll be torturing innocent people. He will never be suspected, the man everyone adores, but he has a vile personality trait.

They won't ever catch him either. Because he's stunning but twice as bright.

"No, sweets. My father didn't have a type, he just wanted to end as many female lives as possible. Ya know, mommy issues and all," he jokes.

He leans towards me, his face close to mine. My heart pounds into my chest, over and over again, he elevates his index finger to wrap around a strand of my golden hair. The urge to vomit hits me hard.

"I prefer dark hair, and I like to take my time with them. Bleed them slowly, cut them up. The dismemberment just," he inhales deeply, shivering as he does, "gets me going."

I can smell his oaky scent at this distance, like the forest after it rains.

His eyes darken and he has wound my hair around his finger so tight it's starting to pull at the roots of my scalp.

"I'll look over your tasteless, moronic comments because Alistair likes handling you himself and he's made it very clear no one else can touch you, but if you get in my way, I'll kill you and dye your hair after."

The revving of bike engines drowns out the sound of anything else as he leans back into his seat, my throat dries with anxiety. It took all the strength in my muscles to swallow. It would seem Thatcher was over our banter; I'd crossed one too many lines with him.

I turn back around to face the track, uncomfortable with having him behind me. I had no idea what he could be doing back there. Planning to cut my hair with scissors, slice my back up.

"Van Doren better not lose. I have hella money on that fucker," some guy in front of us complains to his girlfriend, and I look harder towards the racers lining up.

Both of them are sitting on top of sport bikes, their feet planted firmly on the ground on either side as they wait for their green light. I recognize Rook's black-on-black bike almost immediately. I hear it pulling into the school parking lot most mornings when I'm sitting in class, turning my head and looking out the window to see him arriving late.

"How does he even see out of that thing?" Lyra asks me, taking in his appearance of black jeans, black hoodie with orange flames drawn on the sleeves. His helmet is matte, the face shield reflects in the night, and I'm not sure any light is even allowed through that visor.

"Luck?" I answer, unsure myself.

The Christmas-tree-shaped light that dangles between them begins blinking from red to yellow, and I hold my breath a little as I watch Rook rotate his wrists to rev his engine, the sound making my eardrums buzz.

When the light drops to green, he releases his clutch, propelling him forward at an insanely quick speed, both feet coming up to rest on the pedals as his tires eat the pavement beneath.

The whining of the motor blends perfectly with everyone's cheers, and as my eyes begin to follow him around the track, I catch sight of a large skull tattoo on someone's back in the middle of the stadium.

Standing in the grassy center, where fights had taken place all night, is Alistair. A small circle of people gathered around him and his opponent. I take in his shirtless stature, the way his muscles tensed with every breath and sweat made him glisten in the night.

My attention has shifted completely from Rook to him.

Even as I heard the bikes whizzing around and around in circles, creating this tornado effect in my mind, I couldn't pull my eyes away from him. There was something electrifying about watching him.

Alistair's opponent towered over him in both height and weight. A man with tree trunks as arms and buildings as legs, the difference in bodies seemed unfair to me. One punch to the face and Alistair would have his jaw shattered.

But the way Alistair moved didn't allow for anything to even skim his body. Agile and quick as he ducked underneath monster punches, countering with lower body strikes that had to have broken ribs.

They rotated around one another, like animals ready to strike, always keeping their eyes on each other, never allowing the other to circle behind them. Alistair's face came into view just before he launched a right hook that made the entire crowd around him cringe.

I didn't even watch as the other guy fell. I could barely see anything as he took the opportunity to slam fist after fist into his opponent's face, burying his skull into the dirt beneath both of them.

Blood speckled his naked chest. The people watching couldn't look away but their faces all stared with horror in their eyes. If he continued this pace he would kill this man.

Yet, all I could focus on was the curves of his face, the bend in his brow, and the curl of his upper lip.

I'd never seen anyone so wrathful, but he made it look beautiful.

This sort of molten anger rolled through his body, leaking from all his pores so it was all you could see. A cruel volcano of human rage that incinerated anyone he touched, yet you still stood there admiring how nature could be so incredible, even when it was wreaking havoc.

A god of wrath.

This was the reason I'd shown up.

So that Alistair could remind me of the bits of me I'd left back in Texas, pieces I thought had to die there in order to make it in a place like Ponderosa Springs.

The parts of myself that loved the way my stomach tightened

and my core ached while I watched him hurt someone. Someone who thrived in the trouble most wouldn't even attempt.

I didn't need to be a thief anymore, but that didn't mean I had to leave the lifestyle behind. It didn't mean I had to settle for a boring life without adventure.

Hands tear him away from the man on the ground, pulling him up; it took seven people just to get him to stop. Even then it still looked like he allowed them to stop him. If he wanted, he could've kept going until that entire crowd was yanking at his skin.

Rook steals the attention from mostly everyone, though, his winning lap consisting of him lifting the front tire of his bike up off the ground, riding a wheelie up and down the track. Lyra hides her face as he places both his feet at the back of his seat, standing straight up on the motorcycle, continuing to ride it around.

When I look back for Alistair, he's nowhere to be found.

The night becomes frigid as we sit out here for another thirty minutes, watching the races, the fights. Almost everyone is wasted off their asses at this point. Just as Lyra and I stand up to leave, Thatcher and Silas do the same.

"Following us?" I arch an eyebrow, suspicious.

"Coincidence," Thatcher replies.

The four of us make our way out of the stadium, them heading in a separate direction to us as we stop to use the bathroom before we start the walk to Lyra's car. The walk is short, filled with us talking to keep our bodies warm.

I see her car a few feet away in one of the grass parking spots and a few spots over I see Alistair leaning against the hood of his vehicle, talking to his friends. I notice the extreme redness on his knuckles, a few of them bleeding. He's still shirtless from the fight, making it hard not to stare.

Knowing I should ignore him and just get in the car with

Lyra, I know I should just leave, but I can't. Something inside of me just will not let me leave until I say something to him.

"I'll be right back," I say to Lyra as I walk around her car and head in his direction.

Rook is the first to notice me, the smirk on his face making me want to slap him. A blush tints my cheeks as I begin to think, *has he told them what we did?*

Oh my God, do they *all* know what we did?

I suddenly feel exposed even more in this night air and the urge to tuck tail and cut my losses is strong, but I can't do that now that one of them has noticed me.

They all begin to shift, turning to face me, and it's the most awkward fifteen seconds of my life as we all stand there staring at one another. My eyes refusing to even look in Alistair's direction because I know he's probably smirking.

"Well, that's our cue boys." Rook slaps them on the back, looking at Alistair, "Happy birthday, dude."

Birthday?

They begin to walk away as I tuck my arm behind my back, holding onto my shirt nervously.

"Today's your birthday?" It seems to be the best way to segue into conversation with him. I can't exactly start out by saying, *Hey, watching you bash someone's face in got me hot and bothered because I think I'm attracted to dangerous things.*

He nods, clicking a button on his phone to display the time, "As of three minutes ago, anyway."

"You're not having a party with your friends and half the town tonight?" It's a joke, one that was supposed to lighten his mood, but apparently it failed.

Grabbing his shirt off the hood, pulling it over his head before looking me in the eyes, "I don't celebrate it."

Seriousness weighs down his shoulders, his tone flat.

"Come on, you're what, nineteen? It's a law that you're not supposed to start hating your birthday until at least forty."

He scoffs, a short laugh falling from his lips, "Birthdays are about celebrating the day you were brought into the world, right?"

I nod.

"Why would I celebrate that when I didn't want to be brought into the world?"

The riddle of who Alistair Caldwell really is beneath all of his bravado continues. I only had sections of him, ones I'd got from watching him and being on his bad side.

I knew he was angry. That he was loyal until death to those three boys. And anytime his family was spoken about, he avoided it.

Growing up, my life was shit. It was tough, but I never wanted to end my life. I never wanted to not be here. For someone to want that, they'd need a reason and a damn good one.

He was a mystery, and to a girl who is curious, he's kryptonite.

"The tattoo on your hip. I've seen it before, Silas has one, too, doesn't he?" I change the topic, hoping to gather another piece of his puzzle.

Slowly, he lifts just the bottom of his t-shirt up, exposing the coin with a skeleton on the front. I squint, reading the words written across the top and bottom,

"Admit one, Styx Ferryman." I read out loud.

Without thinking, my fingers extend on their own, grazing the ink on his skin.

"It's Charon's obol. There are myths in many cultures about how you must have a coin to pay the ferryman who takes souls from the land of the living to the land of the dead. It's why some people put coins over people's eyes when they die."

"Like the river Styx in Greek mythology," I say, pulling my

hand away. "So why do you two have one? I doubt either of you are short on coins for when the time comes."

His shirt drops, covering the tattoo again, "We all have one. That way we can bribe our way back to each other. Even in death."

I'd never seen loyalty like theirs before. I'd heard of it, when people talked about being loyal this is how they would explain it, but none of them would actually do it. Not the way Alistair and his friends did.

They would die for each other in a heartbeat, and it was evident in everything they did. Like all the broken pieces of themselves lined up perfectly with each other. They could cultivate together in the dark, protecting each other there where no one would attempt to hurt them.

I thought about how sad it was he wasn't doing anything for his birthday. Someone young and with opportunities. My parents threw me a party every year in the trailer park, everyone would come together for potlucks. There would be music and a Slip'n Slide. It wasn't Disney World, but it was special to me.

No one deserved to hate the day they were born.

Not even Alistair.

"Let's go do something," I propose, looking up at him as he gives me a *you're kidding* look.

"Do what?" he runs his tongue across his teeth, smirking like he's up to no good and I allow the excitement to course through me as he does, instead of trying to stop it.

"Whatever you want. It's your birthday, you should enjoy at least one of them before you need to use that coin."

"I told you I don't celebrate," his breath fanning across my face as I step in front of him.

"Yeah, and I don't care. Plus, you owe me," a grin finds its way to my face, taking over. I wasn't sure what we would get into, but I knew I would enjoy it.

"What could I possibly owe you, Briar?" The way he says my name is smooth and I like the sound of it on his tongue, especially as he raises both his eyebrows, baiting me.

Slowly, I lift my middle finger up showing off the initials that mark my skin, flipping him off.

"You owe me for stealing my first tattoo experience from me. So really, this isn't even about your birthday, it's about you making it up to me."

A laugh that felt like thunder escaped from his mouth. My breath hitched at the abrupt sound and my stomach fluttered because of how much I liked it.

And it was a sound that I wanted more of.

# CHAPTER TWENTY-EIGHT
## *Find Me*

*Alistair*

I'd never brought anyone to this house before besides the guys, and even then they didn't stay for long. I wasn't sure why I'd brought her here in the first place, there was no reason to come here. No reason to show her the house because it's not like it was a home to me.

Maybe some part of me wanted to show her what all the wealth had bought me.

A gigantic house with no one inside. With no love and no warmth in sight.

It was just expensive furniture and overpriced light fixtures.

"This could house the entire town I grew up in," she says, looking into the kitchen while I run warm water over my bloody knuckles.

Her eyes fan across it, walking around, running her fingers across everything on the counter while I lean against the sink, wondering what she's thinking.

"It's nice, but . . ."

"Not what you expected?"

She nods, "Your home is supposed to be where you can be

self-expressive. No photos of your family, nothing comforting, this," spinning, her arms extended, "looks like a house for showings. It doesn't feel like anyone lives inside here."

I could laugh at how ironic that is.

"It's a house. Not a home," I say honestly.

"Is that why you hate them? That's why you hate your family?" She doesn't look at me when she asks, probably shocking herself with the boldness to ask me a question like that.

"I don't hate them for treating me like an outsider. I loathe them for having me to begin with, for having a son they knew they would detest the rest of his life." I could feel her slowly trying to unwind the snakes that coiled around my body. Timidly trying to figure out ways to get inside of my head, beneath my skin even more than she already had.

"You can't say that. There had to be something good before, parents don't just despise their children from birth, Alistair. There has to be a reason."

My fists begin to ache for violence. I look down at the dried blood, running down the drain into the sink.

Naive.

That's what she is.

Even her, a girl who grew up with nothing thinking she'd possibly seen every bad thing the world could offer, was still naive to the cruelty of human beings.

That's what I want to tell her. Not everyone has a reason for doing shitty things. They are just fucked up people in the world because they can be.

"We aren't talking about this," I end the conversation. Not needing her to poke around any more than she already has.

"Alright then," she mutters quietly. "Where's the bathroom?"

After pointing her in the correct direction, I pick up my phone to check the messages from the guys.

Silas has sent a photo of us when we were kids, maybe eight

or nine years old, that his dad had taken after we'd spent the day shooting each other with nerf guns. Rook's hair is still long, our faces have aged, but it's still us. There wasn't a happy memory in my brain that they weren't a part of. There was no good without them, even through all the bad.

He'd added a quick, "*HB.*"

Thatcher made a comment about how I still dress like an eight-year-old, to that I replied with a middle finger emoji.

The sound of the shower running before a loud crash echoes down the hall immediately puts me on high alert. Dorian and my parents were in Seattle for the weekend for some conference. Had they not been, Briar wouldn't have stepped foot on the property, even if I wanted to show her the reality of growing up here.

So, my question was . . . what the hell was she doing?

I walk towards the bathroom, the door is cracked slightly, just enough to let the light escape.

"It's not polite to take showers at people's homes without inviting them first," I say loudly.

When I don't hear a reply, I move a little faster, pressing the door completely open and finding it empty, even the glass shower is void of the person who had been here just moments ago.

What the fuck?

Only when I see the mirror above the sink am I rewarded with a clue to the location of my missing houseguest.

*Come Find Me.*

Soft, delicate handwriting in the fog of the glass that makes excitement flood my system.

This is the game she wanted to play? In my territory?

What a stupid move for a smart girl.

I turn the shower off, walking back to the kitchen to toss my jacket onto the kitchen island with my phone and begin my search. I know she didn't go up the stairs because she would've had to walk past me to make it into the foyer. Which leaves the back portion of the house fair play.

A low whistle finds itself falling from my lips as I take my time. I'm in no rush to find my little thief. I search each room checking behind doors, beneath beds in the spare rooms.

There is no spot left unturned when I leave them.

When I find her, I want her breath to be held, hands over her mouth as she attempts to stop even the slightest of sounds from falling past her lips. I want her heart to be racing with adrenaline and her skin to be flushed from the mixture of fear and excitement.

The sound of my boots echoes off the walls as I work my way towards what used to be my favorite place in the home.

I push the door open with my fingertips, the untouched office consisting of a desk, some thrown-around books, and an older-than-dirt coffee table. The glass dome covering this portion of the house allowed the stars and moon to shine in the room.

I looked out at the forest around my house, so dark that it would be impossible to see what was creeping behind the trees. Anything could see us inside of here.

Even in the scant lighting, I spot what looks like a shoelace peeking out from underneath the side of the desk, like someone is kneeling beneath it, trying to hide from all the monsters outside.

As quietly as I can, I creep up to the side of the desk, stopping my whistle, right before I slam my palm on the top of it, dipping down to look beneath, a smirk on my lips until I see there is nothing there.

I furrow my eyebrows, confused for a second. Her Converse sat face down at the edge of the desk, a trick I should have thought of. I just don't put two and two together. Well, that is, until I feel hands squeeze my sides.

"Boo." She whispers quietly, "How do you like being scared, Alistair?"

Turning in her hands, looking down at the grin on her face, my eyebrow lifts slightly.

"That was you trying to scare me?" My fingers rest beneath her chin, tilting her head up towards me as I lean down, "You're gonna have to do better than that, Little Thief."

And I do the one thing I'd been dying to do since I saw her in the stands at The Graveyard. The only thing I wanted for my birthday.

I press my mouth to hers, molding us together and tasting her on my tongue immediately.

I take her head between my hands, pulling her into me more so I can taste her deeper. My tongue moving inside of her mouth; I planned on pushing her onto the desk, spreading her legs and tasting her second set of lips, but she had other plans apparently.

With much more force than I anticipated, she presses her hands into my chest, pushing me backwards. Instinctively, I reach behind me, feeling for something solid to fall onto and finding the armrest of the swivel chair.

I'm seated, looking up at her, as she stands between my legs looking a lot like the kind of trouble I want to get lost in. The moon highlights the right side of her body, showing me all the parts of her I want to touch.

The way her low-rise jeans sit below her hip bones, her tight shirt wrapped around her breasts in a way that made them look heavy and supple. I notice her nipples are hard, visible through the material of her shirt.

My jaw and cock strained at the same time. Thinking about all the other men that might have seen her like that. Nipples erect from the cold, flushed from the air. I wanted to rip out the eyes of men I didn't even know, just for glancing at her like this.

She is the female form perfected. There is nothing more erotic. Nothing more beautiful.

With deliberate movements she flips her hair to the side,

hands moving down on my chest, nails scratching the surface of my skin with the force. Confidence pours from her as she sways her hips to the sound of silence, falling until she's resting on her knees in front of me.

She looks like a ticket straight to heaven and I would have walked through hellfire to get it.

I feel her fingers rake up and down my jean-clad thighs, peering up at me with those kaleidoscope eyes. The moon shows me every filthy, dirty thought she's having inside them.

"You plan to do something while you're down there?" I ask, arching an eyebrow and looking at her like she *needs* to do something. Like she needs to impress me. Looking at her like she won't be able to handle pleasuring me, even though I know she's capable.

But my little thief enjoys a challenge.

"No one ever taught you how to be patient did they, Alistair?"

She leans her body forward, dipping her head towards the thick outline in my jeans. I can feel her hot breath through the material, making me twitch with anticipation. I lick my bottom lip, catching it with my teeth.

"Careful. I'll only let you tease me for so long before I take what I want."

Just as I say that, her tongue flicks from her pink mouth, grazing over my length. I dig my fingers into the armrest to prevent myself from grabbing the back of her hair and sliding myself all the way down her throat.

I wanted inside of her. Any hole. All of them.

Dropping my head to my chest, watching as she plays with the button of my jeans, all the while her mouth is toying with my wallet chain. Steadily she rolls her tongue up and down the cold metal, lacing it through the links of the chain.

*Fuck, that's hot,* I think to myself, not wanting to give my pleasure away before she's even really touched me.

"This how you steal men's wallets?" My tongue rests against my upper lip hiding a smile. "Good technique," I add.

I can see her smile from this angle, only some of it, mostly her blonde hair flowing over my lap, the tip of her nose and her tongue when it extends out of her warm mouth. But even still, I spot the smile.

"Very funny," she laughs. The vibration between my legs makes my hips jerk just a bit.

Her mouth doesn't make any more coherent words, because after unbuttoning my jeans she has me help jerk them down just enough to pull my cock out. My throbbing length stands straight up, the tip angry and swollen with anticipation.

Briar's eyes widen a bit, fixing her gaze on my dick. I smirk thinking about how she'd already had it inside of her, reaching the deepest parts of her. I'm continually impressed by her eagerness.

The way she wraps her hand around my base, a shock racing straight to my balls. I fight to sit still when she takes her time to lick the little white bead of come off the tip before wrapping her lips fully around me.

I groan through gritted teeth, my jaw clenching as she accommodates my size perfectly. I can feel her mouth stretching around me as she sinks lower and lower onto my shaft. My hand reacts of its own accord, grabbing her hair and twisting it back around my fist.

Her tongue quickly lathering my shaft in her slick saliva, I can feel her hand pumping my base in time with the entry and exit of my cock between her hot, pink lips.

I let my head fall back as she continues to work between my legs.

Letting her control the pace for a bit, allowing her to play as she runs her wet tongue along the underside, her mouth tight and warm around me. When she falls all the way down, my cock hitting the back of her throat, I can't help but hold her there for a second longer.

When she doesn't fight to come back up, allowing me to stay rooted in her throat, I take it a bit further. My hand in her hair controls the movement of her mouth on my length, working her lips up and down me.

"Fuck," I groan, her slick mouth taking me so well. My grip tightens, my speed increasing a bit before my cock can't take the teasing anymore.

I stand up, placing both of my hands at the back of her head, her bright eyes looking up at me with need as she moans while I slide further down her throat. I feel her nails dig into my thighs as she helps tug me closer to her.

"You helping me fuck your tight little mouth, Briar? Is that what you want, doll? You want it rough?" I ask, holding her at the root of my shaft, waiting for her answer before I release her for a breath.

I want to come just looking at her eyes watering, how needy she is down on the ground for me. Eagerly she nods, giving me the permission I need.

My hips rock forward, sending my entire length down her throat, feeling it constrict around me. I keep myself buried inside of her, jerking my hips with short thrusts, using my hands to hold her face in one spot.

Allowing my gaze to wander down to where she is working diligently between my legs, my soaked cock slipping in and out quickly between her lips, her cheeks hollow with suction.

Continuing to use her mouth however I can, I shove myself into the back of her throat so I hear that satisfying soft gag from her. Every thrust she keeps her lips sealed around my cock, flicking her tongue when she can.

Everything I was giving, she took. She ate it up willingly,

giving it just as good as she was getting it. There was nothing hotter than seeing her on her knees for me.

Almost as if she knew I was watching, her eyes open, green orbs finding my gaze and holding it. Throughout it all she doesn't stop sucking, she stays there just for me. Head bobbing up and down, never missing the rhythm of my hips.

I'd never felt so exhilarated. Sex never felt like this. Nothing had ever felt like this.

The sloppy sounds echo in the air, making my hands curl into her hair, wanting more of her every second she's down there. I'm too big for her to breathe through her nose forever, so I pull back, letting her gasp for air once I'm out of her mouth.

"Holy shit," she chokes, voice croaky, coughing a bit as she wipes her chin, looking up at me with tears streaming down her face from the aggressive nature. If I had my phone, I would've taken a picture so I could jerk off to it every day for the rest of my life.

Her red-rimmed eyes, crimson cheeks, swollen lips, and saliva dripping from the corners of her mouth. She was ruined, gasping for air beneath me and all I wanted was more.

I wanted her shattered, to collect her tears in a jar and use them as lube to jerk my cock later. Everything she was, I wanted to inhale, break, use up until I was finished.

I bend down, pressing my fingers into her cheeks, guiding her up from her knees and towards my lips. My kiss is painful, punishing her mouth with my own as our tongues wind around each other like snakes.

Sitting myself back into the chair, pulling her back between my thighs so that I can undo the button of her jeans. My fingers hooking the loops and tugging them down her slender legs.

Stepping out of them gracefully, holding my shoulders for guidance as she removes her panties, taking control once again and crawling into my lap. I feel the heat from her cunt pulsating against my stiff rod.

I reach my hand up, wrapping it around her throat, pulling her towards my mouth once again, "You're gonna take my cock aren't you, Briar? Let me fuck you until I come?"

Reaching into my back pocket, finding the condom I slipped inside there, I raise the package up between my lips, tearing it open with my teeth and sliding it down my shaft. Never once taking my eyes off her.

She nods softly, reaching between us to grasp my cock in her right hand, dragging the head of my dick from the top of her slit all the way down to the bottom, coating me in her juices.

My tip pushes between her lips, a single moment of just that inside of her, before I press my hands into the sides of her narrow hips, slamming her down the entire length of my shaft.

I drop my head to her shoulder, groaning in pleasure as she gasps in surprise in both pleasure and obvious discomfort as she adjusts to my size. I can hear her breathing heavily into my ear, gentle moans flooding my senses as she begins to rock her hips above me.

I can feel her nipples poking through her shirt into my body, her warm torso and those full, round thighs pressed into my own. A wordless moan escapes her mouth with every dip of her hips that sends my cock thrusting into her, once more filling her tight walls.

Fingernails dig into my shoulder blades, her momentum picking up, leaning forward as she concentrates every muscle in her body into fucking herself on my shaft. I run my tongue along the column of her throat, gathering the drops of sweat, relishing in the salty-sweet taste of her on my tongue.

"Alistair, I—" She whimpers, losing her rhythm and I know it's because she is craving more. She needs more.

"What baby? Tell me what you need and I'll give it to you," I coo into her ear, a smirk adorning my lips. I just want to hear her say it. I want to hear her break down and ask me.

"I . . . I, fuck this feels so good. How does this feel so good?" she cries, moving in a figure eight, trying to find that perfect spot for my cock to hit.

I curl my left arm around her waist, pushing her down on my dick, forcing her to take every single inch, stretching her little pussy around my length.

"Tell me what you want, Briar." I demand.

"Fuck me, please? I want you to fuck me," she says all needy and soft.

It's the only thing I need to piston my hips up to meet hers. Keeping her held down, so my cock is the only thing moving in and out of her slick tunnel. Gliding through her pussy like it was fucking made for me.

My thighs slap against her ass, echoing around the conservatory, my orgasm building with speed. I just need her to come first, I need to feel her clenched all around me screaming my name before I busted.

I use my free hand to wind around her throat, squeezing the sides of her neck near the base, putting pressure on her ability to breath. I increase the pressure, holding tightly, watching her eyes roll into the back of her head as she tries to fight the urge to need oxygen.

I'm triggering that fight-or-flight instinct in her brain. Giving her that safe kind of high she can overdose on. The kind that makes her toes curl and her blood feel like it's on fire.

She looked like a fucking goddess.

Taking my cock like such a good girl, body arched towards me, head tilted back, mouth gaped open and her eyes shut tightly as I'm sure stars flashed behind her eyelids.

The way her hourglass figure sits on my lap, my dick disappearing inside of her over and over again . . . I was going to die if I didn't come.

"Oh my God . . ." Her voice is strangled and quiet as she goes almost completely limp in my arms, coming all over my dick, soaking my lap with her orgasmic liquid. Her walls clamp around me, making it nearly impossible to even thrust back into her.

I release her throat, hearing her struggle to moan, and choke for air.

My climax takes me, overwhelming my senses as I bury myself as deeply as I can inside of her body. My cock spasms and pulsates, my abs lock down as pleasure drowns out everything else in the world for a few solid moments.

Her hands ease up on my body, her body sagging down onto mine as she drops her head onto my shoulder, catching her breath.

It's quiet as we gather ourselves, neither of us moving. I don't even think I blinked, too afraid this moment would be over if I did.

There was a wave of emotion that overcame me, different than a post-orgasm high. It felt like my mind had ceased war with itself for the time being. Nothing felt heavy and everything just . . . was.

I felt her head move, turning towards my ear.

"Happy birthday, Alistair," she whispered, a huff of a laugh trickling into the air.

For the first time . . .

It actually was.

# CHAPTER TWENTY-NINE

## *Carnie Rides*

*Briar*

"Cotton candy is the closest thing to divine food humans can have, did you know that?" I shovel another handful of the sticky, pink-colored fluff into my mouth, moaning at the way it dissolves on my tongue.

"I would argue with you, but this tastes so good that I don't think I can," Lyra replies, munching on her blue cloud of sweetness.

"Girls! Are you even working or just laying around on the job?" my uncle says as he walks up with a box of old green wine bottles, setting them down on the bench in front of us.

Lyra and I look at each other before laughing loudly. Taking a minute to sober up, "Sorry, Thomas. We were taking our lunch, it's illegal to work people without a thirty-minute break," I joke.

He rolls his eyes playfully, grinning at the both of us, "You've not even been here thirty minutes!"

Both of us set our cotton candy down, continuing to laugh as we start helping put the booth together. I could hear the music start to wind up as the sun began to set, lights illuminating the sky, the air filled with the smell of greasy food and sweet treats.

Ponderosa Springs's Carnival was being hosted by Hollow Heights this year as a way for students to pitch in. Mostly upperclassmen who made booths or ran the games like bottle stands.

We were helping my uncle set up the Ring Toss before we headed into the carnival to hit a few rides before we had to go back to the dorms.

I was organizing the bottles on the table when I heard Thomas say my name. I turn slightly, "What's up?" I ask, smiling softly.

He scratches the back of his neck, standing next to me and fiddling with the bottles I am messing with.

"I know that I wasn't around much when you were growing up and I'm not your parent," he starts, looking even more nervous, "but I'm sorta your guardian here, or at least I feel like it, ya know?"

I quirk my eyebrow, "Are you trying to have the birds and bees talk with me? Because my mom already explained all that."

"No, no, no," violently shaking his head, holding his hands out in front of him, "I'm not saying that. I just," he takes a breath, "I know you've been hanging around Alistair Caldwell and his friends lately."

I'm more shocked than I should be.

I mean, I wasn't frolicking around campus holding his hand, but we had been seen together, even from my first day of class. I knew people were going to talk. It'd been a few weeks since his birthday, and we'd spent most of it trying to find places to get our hands on each other.

His car, my dorm when Lyra was in class, the shower, I couldn't remember the last time I'd had this amount of sex in such a short period of time.

Yet, every time I tried talking to him about himself, asking about Rosemary, or just about who he was, I was shut down immediately. And I hated that I was settling for just sex.

Every time I told myself I would walk away, I would leave him alone if he didn't give me something to go on.

I just couldn't do it.

Shamefully, I was willing to settle, as long as I had certain parts of him. Deep down I knew there was something there, he just wasn't letting me see it. I had known it the moment I saw him, Alistair was addictive. I just didn't know how much, until I finally had a taste.

Quitting him wasn't easy, especially with the way he touched me. The way he held me when we were together and the way I caught him soften his gaze when we laid next to each other after our orgasms.

He was winding his web tighter and tighter around me and I was letting him.

"We are just friends," I say, brushing it off as nothing. I wasn't lying, we didn't have a label, so friends was closer to the truth.

"And that's fine. I just want you to be careful, okay? Alistair has a particular notoriety here. His family, too. I just don't want you getting hurt, Briar."

I knew if it were my dad, he would have said the same thing. My dad would have already tried beating Alistair up, but he would have said this to me beforehand and even though he was telling me to steer clear of him, I was still thankful.

Wrapping my arms around his waist, I hug him quickly, "I'll be careful. Thank you, Thomas."

This seems to bring relief to his shoulders, the breath he releases rolls across the top of my head as he hugs me back.

"I missed out on group hugs?" Lyra says, walking over with other boxes, pouting jokingly.

We spend the next hour helping Thomas put the game together, even helping get his first few customers started before we begin taking on the carnival rides that we know are probably not the safest.

My hair is wind-blown, my cheeks feel chapped from the last ride, and I haven't stopped laughing since we got here.

I'm talking to Lyra, walking around, when my shoulder grazes someone else.

"Oh, I'm sorry," I mutter, turning around and reaching my hands out to catch whoever I'd hit.

"It seems we are just destined to keep meeting like this," he says. "I'm starting to think you're running into me on purpose."

I'm nearly blinded by his smile, but even that's not enough to distract me from the fact I know his face.

I ran into him outside of the library such a long while ago, I didn't think he'd remember me. We'd had a quick conversation about my chosen major while I gathered my books and he told me if I ever needed help with my classes to reach out to him.

Having only seen him in pictures up till that point made it even more shocking at the resemblance between him and Alistair. Dorian could've been his twin, minus the way his nose tilts to the left a little too much, and his cheeks are soft compared to Alistair's sharp ones.

"How are your classes going? Any teachers giving you trouble? I know Mr. Gabble can be quite the stickler."

"They are going fine. No problems, yet." I force a smile onto my face, hoping if I keep the conversation light I can shuffle away from him quicker.

"Oh, I'm being rude. I'm Dorian." He sticks his hand out for Lyra to shake, which she returns, "Dorian Caldwell."

"Lyra," she replies, moving her hand up and down with his.

"Are you ladies enjoying the carnival? I swear every year it gets more and more attractions. Hollow Heights is going to need a bigger fairground if it's here next year," he laughs, placing his hands in his pockets.

"It seems that way," I say awkwardly.

Dorian had never given me a reason to find him odd, but I couldn't shake the feeling that he was a part of the reason Alistair hated his family so much.

"You both are freshmen, right? So you know my brother, Alistair?"

The way he asks the question makes me think he knows the answer already. This glint in his eye that's daring me to lie to him. Watching to see how I would react.

"Of course we know him. Well, know *of* him. Your last name is pretty popular around this area." I cover my lie with a joke, hoping my fake laughter will be enough to convince him.

"Consider yourself lucky you met the more charming brother first then." He adds a wink for good measure.

I know he's being nice, but the comment makes my skin crawl in all the wrong ways.

"I guess so," I lie easily.

"I meant to ask you at the library the other day, but . . ." he reaches into his pocket, pulling his phone out, "I'd love to get your number, maybe take you to dinner? I know this great restaurant—"

"I'm sorry, but I have a boyfriend. Thank you for the offer, though," I interrupt before he can finish, slowly starting to back away from him, pulling Lyra with me.

A flare of something wicked turns his smile from polite to twisted in less than ten seconds. The annoyance of my rejection sits on his face, but soon it's gone, his regular charming face back in place.

"Maybe another time then," he chuckles. "You ladies be safe tonight. I'm sure I'll be seeing you around."

Just as quickly as he appeared, he's gone. Disappearing into the crowd of carnival guests.

Together we make our way through the rest of the rides, I'm almost dizzy from the amount of times I watch Lyra on Tilt-A-Whirl. Either way we were having fun, enjoying ourselves as the night started to get a little colder.

I stood outside the bathroom waiting on Lyra, thumbing through my phone, when the feeling of being watched made the hairs on the back of my neck stand straight up. I raise my eyes, looking through the crowd in front of me but seeing no one that would have been staring at me.

The feeling of someone curling their hand around my arm sends me into high alert.

"Don't scream," I hear whispered in my ear.

I'm jerked backwards, being pulled to the backside of the bathroom building, away from the noise of the carnival. I feel his body press into mine, backing me into the side of the brick. Instantly comforted by the smell of clove and spice.

"I can't leave Lyra," I whisper-yell, pressing my hands into the leather of his jacket, trying to put space between us.

"The guys will be with her until we are finished," Alistair replies, his frame shielding me from anyone who might walk past us back here.

Our eyes meet, matching smirks adorning our faces. "Thought you didn't come to school functions," I insist.

"Rook wanted a funnel cake."

That's the last thing he says to me before he presses his lips to mine in a scorching kiss that sears all my thoughts. I melt like ice on the hot pavement as his body bends me back, allowing me to feel every muscle against my soft skin.

My fingers grip onto the collar of his leather jacket, heaving him closer to me. Needing to feel him everywhere.

One more hit. One more high.

I repeated that in my mind.

"Just for Rook, huh?" I whisper when our lips part.

He snaps at my bottom lip with his teeth, before dipping his head into the crook of my neck, making me gasp loudly as his wet tongue runs along the column of my neck.

"Just for Rook," he grunts.

"Liar," I moan tenderly, dropping my hands to his toned stomach, fingers sneaking up the hem of his shirt to touch his bare skin that burns beneath it. He's always so warm. On fire all the time.

The smile on his lips grows as he marks my throat with his mouth "Truth?" he rumbles in a deep voice that makes lightning strike my core.

"Please."

My voice comes out more needy than I expected, but I think that was all I really wanted from Alistair. The truth, answers, something that proved this was more than some sex fest. That I was something more to him than the invisible poor girl who was an easy lay.

"I've got some things to take care of tonight, but I need to taste you first. Wanted to get my head right. And I need to ask you something," he starts.

"What body wash do you use?" he asks, inhaling me like I'm the finest strain of cocaine he could acquire.

I can't help the laugh that escapes my mouth, "What?"

"What is that smell on you all the time. It's like fucking flowers."

The way he traces the veins in my neck with the tip of his nose makes me shiver in his arms.

"It's—ugh," I stumble, distracted as his hands fall on my hip bones, rubbing circles into them, "Olay. Blackcurrant and orchid. I think."

A mental note is made to keep using that scent as we stand there, hands reaching for exposed skin, tugging each other closer, short breaths, gentle moans as we work each other up.

I loved this. I wanted this to be enough, but as my head falls back against the wall, my brain makes it impossible for me to concentrate. *What does he mean by something to take care of? What is he going to do?*

This couldn't be enough for me. I needed more. I needed answers.

I wanted to be selfish because I wanted all of Alistair. Not just pieces.

Pressing my hands into his chest and pushing lightly, putting a gap between the two of us, "Alistair, wait—" I start, swallowing the nerves in my throat, "What are you going to take care of tonight?"

I make the mistake of connecting my eyes to his. Dark, rich, bitter brown eyes that remind me of fresh earth after a heavy rain. So dark they are inky, almost black, full of depths I can't even understand.

The lust that tinted them begins to lose its luster and I know he understands what I'm asking.

"Don't," he says, shaking his head. "Don't do this right now."

"Is it about Rose? Are you going to the police about what we found on that flash drive, you're gonna turn Mr. West in? Is that what you are going to do?"

His hands retract from my body, "It's taken care of."

"How? Did you tell someone?" I push, "I need to know that something is being done, there are probably hundreds of missing girls out there. This is the evidence people need to resolve unsolved kidnappings! You have to say something." It had been buzzing in the back of my mind since I saw the video.

"You aren't a part of this. You did your job and now it's being handled. That's all you need to know."

I furrow my eyebrows, "That's all I need to know? Are you fucking kidding me? I broke into a safe for you! I could've been expelled, hell, arrested! I deserve to know!"

The way he steps away from me, like I've made him sick, has this sharp pain moving across my chest, the way jellyfish wrap their tentacles around your body before shocking you. I can already feel the burn.

"No, you broke into a safe because I blackmailed you. Don't act like you've done me any favors, Briar."

"Are you serious?" I spit out, a harsh laugh following. "That's how you're going to be about this?"

"What did you expect? We start fucking and I owe you an explanation to everything I do?"

I flinch at how harsh his tone is, how harsh his words are.

"I don't owe you anything. If you're looking for a boyfriend who is gonna call you pretty and tell you you're the reason he believes in love, you are in for a rude awakening cause that's not me. This," he waves his finger between the two of us, "is sex. That's it, just sex. Don't try to convince yourself it's anything more."

I thought the moment my heart broke it would be this loud crashing sound in my chest. That it would make a commotion like smashing glass onto the floor.

It didn't. Instead, it was this silent moment of mourning as the pieces fell apart. There shouldn't have been a reason I was so affected by this.

Why should I?

Alistair Caldwell is bad news. He is trouble. He tormented me. He is involved in murders and sex rings. There is nothing redeemable about him.

But there was a brief time between the wrath, between the hate, that he was *my* bad news. *My* trouble.

I thought, stupidly, I was special. I mean he tattooed me, didn't he? Marked me for the entire fucking world to see?

This dull ache begins to radiate all throughout my body. Hearing him say that aloud stings, even if I knew that was how he felt about it on the inside.

But this is Alistair. He probably tattoos every girl he fucks just to mark the conquest. To show he owns everything he touches.

It was my mistake for thinking a zebra would ever change his stripes.

"It's easier for you, isn't it?" I say. "For me to hate you?" My eyes are stinging, but I am refusing to let a single tear fall for him. He doesn't get those.

He scoffs, shaking his head, "I don't want you to feel anything towards me. That would make it easier."

"You'd rather me hate you than open up. Than to explain why you're such an asshole all the time! It's why you won't tell me about your family, isn't it? They made you like this, didn't they?"

"I don't tell you because it's not your damn business. Stop trying to get more from me! I'm not going to sit here and tell you about how my mommy and daddy don't love me while you pet my head. Leave it the fuck alone."

"You're just scared," I counter "You know that if you tell me, if you let me in," I poke his chest with my finger, "I'll understand why you did the things you've done. I won't have a reason to hate you anymore, and for some reason you don't want that."

Pure, unbridled anger contorts his face, "Because you *should* hate me, Briar! I'm not a person you should like. I'm not someone you should be friends with." He stalks towards me, eyes blazing into me as my body stumbles back at his sudden movement.

"I am not a good person. I hurt people. I enjoy hurting them, and guess what? I'm enjoying hurting you. I fucking love taking pleasure in hurting you, Little Thief."

The words fire off into my chest like bullets. Cracking the shield I'd built over my heart.

I don't move, still standing stiff as a board, staring up at him with a blank look. Trying to search for the light inside of his eyes. Searching for something I think died a long time ago.

Something that may not even exist.

"What did they do to you?" I croak, shaking my head in disbelief.

That was it then. I was just a puppet he could play with, just someone to toy with and manipulate. I didn't mean anything. It was all just a part of his fucking game.

"Hey, lover boy! You done? We need to head out." Rook's voice is a saving grace, giving me an excuse to get out of this conversation. Away from Alistair's eyes.

Wrapping my arms around myself, ready to curl up in my dorm room with a pint of Ben & Jerry's, I start walking back towards the noise of the carnival.

*I shouldn't hurt this much. I shouldn't feel like this,* I think as I pull my phone out of my pocket to shoot a text to Lyra.

Midway through typing the word, "Where," a sweet smell filled my senses and I could feel the softness of cloth pressed into my nose.

Then, the world went black.

# CHAPTER THIRTY
## Judgment Day

### Alistair

Usually after I hurt people, I have this rush of elation that floods my entire system. It takes away the hunger, it feeds the anger, just long enough that I can regain control over my life.

I get my fix for the day and I'm set until the next time I feel the need to destroy someone.

Right now, all I was feeling was self-loathing. So much of it that every breath felt like I was inhaling gasoline. More fuel to the fire inside of my chest that was not going out any time soon.

My left hand wound tighter around the steering wheel, my foot punching the gas as my car tore across the asphalt. The gauge on my dash was trying to let me know this vehicle couldn't go any faster, but even so I kept my foot to the floor.

Music busted through my speakers, and I could see out of the corner of my eye, Rook, air-drumming against the dash, slinging his head back and forth to the beat. I watched my headlights peer down the nearly empty two-way road, trees on either side as we approached our destination.

When you're going that fast, one slip of your wrist would send you rolling, the car would fly into the trees killing both of us almost instantly. But neither of us could be bothered. We focused on the dense sound of music, the drums that thundered and shook the glass of my windows.

I told myself the feeling would dissipate after tonight. I would wreak havoc, end a life, and the annoying tugging inside of my chest would leave. Pressing on the brake for the first time since leaving the carnival, I began to slow down just enough to not flip the car as I make a right.

Briar was a pawn in a large game of chess. A piece that had surprised me and had been fun to play with. I'd gotten what I wanted. I'd had her down on her knees with those pretty little eyes staring up at me, I had her twisted around my fist, I had my fingers deep in her cunt and watched as she found a high like never before with my name cursing her lips.

I had broken her.

Showed her that she is no better than I am.

Just another person addicted to how it feels when you do something bad. I ripped away her idea of what she thought she wanted, shedding light on how all the dark parts of her were her power.

I tore her down, just to build her up, only to yank the flooring right out from underneath her. Watching her crumble before my eyes.

But that was what had to be done.

I could not afford to have her poking around, getting involved where she shouldn't be, asking me shit she doesn't understand.

It was better to break her heart now. Get it out of the way before something worse happened. Before she built this imaginary world with me in it, shoving me into a dream I had no business being a part of. Expecting me to be something I am not. Something I will never be.

I wanted this, I thought.

So, why the fuck did I feel this way.

With ease I pull into the driveway of the condemned house, right outside the weak metal gate that does a shit job of keeping people out. The no trespassing signs are so old that rust holes have started to eat away the words.

Rook is out of the vehicle before I'm even in park. Electricity courses down my arms as I look up at the small two-story brick house. The night had come fast, it always does during this time of the year, and the liberating task at hand we'd all been anticipating was only a few minutes away.

A gust of strong wind picks up a pile of leaves, carrying them across the brown yard. The draft howls through the house, slipping inside the damaged roof and between the cracks of the boarded windows.

The last time I saw this place it housed a dead body. Tonight, it would do the same.

I step around to the back of my car, while Rook opens the trunk. Headlights blind me as Thatcher's vehicle comes into view. Both him and Silas pull in next to me, cutting the engine and stepping out.

We don't talk, no words need to be said. We know why we are here, and that pressure hangs heavy on each of our shoulders.

"Catch," Rook mutters, tossing a long-handled axe in my direction.

I calmly snatch it from the air, squeezing the wood in my palm, feeling the weight of the weapon in my hand. The chisel-shaped blade flashed in the night. And ideas for all the ways I could kill someone with this appeared in my mind's eye.

Hearing the sound of distorted wails as Thatcher and Silas walk from the back of their car, each of them carrying half of a restless Greg West. He fights, trying to kick his duct-taped feet free.

We follow their lead through the dead yard, up the unstable front steps and through the entrance of the trap house where we had found Rose.

Stepping inside was similar to walking into a time machine. We toss Greg onto the same floor where a motionless Rose had been laid the last time we were here. The boards on the floor creak with his weight, head banging onto the ground as he tries rolling around.

Thatcher and Silas had waited outside of his house after we left the carnival, waiting for the perfect moment to snatch him up as he walked to his front door. Just when he thought he was going to be able to kick his feet up on the couch, click through the sports channel, Thatch had ruined it. Grabbing him up and throwing him in his trunk.

The consequences of all of his actions up to this point made the air thick.

Spilling blood for our revenge. Tempting the degree-scale of our moral compasses just to feel the relief of vengeance on our souls. If I ever got caught, I wouldn't regret it.

Even if I rotted in a prison cell for the rest of my days, this would have been worth it.

They would always be worth it.

I was ready to hear Greg say the words. We had followed the breadcrumbs and they'd led us to the person we'd been looking for. I just needed to hear the words.

Rook rips the tape off his mouth, the sound of skin and hair tearing echoes, and shit immediately begins to pour out of his mouth.

"What the fuck is wrong with you?!"

"As a unit?" Thatcher asks. "Too many things to count."

Greg shoves his feet into the ground, trying his hardest to push himself away from the four of us. It's kind of pathetic actually, the last feeble attempts of a trash human being.

"Did you mean to kill her, Greg?" Thatcher asks. "Or was it just dumb luck that she was allergic to the Ecstasy?"

It's interesting watching someone who had up to this point been completely confident that no one would ever know what they did. It's interesting seeing the shock register in their ratty eyes and they begin to think, *Oh shit, I'm in trouble.*

"I . . . I don't know—"

"We saw the flash drive," I stop him from even trying to deny it. I wasn't here to question him or get more information on the dealings of what he was into. I had enough evidence with the drive to know the police would look into anything we didn't take care of ourselves. I came here to listen to him confess.

I was prepared to become judge, jury, and executioner.

Like most evil disguised as humans, his mask melts right off his face. He knows he can't deny it, he is aware of what we have seen. It's either own up to it, hope that we respect him for admitting it, or go out like a bitch.

"I'm assuming one of you was fucking her? That's why I'm here?" he mocks, rolling his body so he is sitting up on his knees, his greasy hair falling in his face a bit as he spits on the floor,

"The X was just to make her more pliable for the buyer. She'd been sold the day I picked her up from the library. I didn't know the dumb bitch would die from it. Cost us money we didn't have to lose."

Blind rage takes hold of Rook at the sound of someone insulting Rose, so he takes the opportunity to acquaint himself with Greg. He twirls his bat, swinging the aluminum stick like a knife through butter, and crushing it across Greg's side, sending him flapping in the air with a harsh thump.

I silently hoped it punctured a lung.

"You don't get to speak about her. Not like that, fucking crook."

It was the first of many painful lessons we would be teaching our professor tonight.

He mewls at the group of us, pressing his forehead into the dirt, eyes crossed in searing pain. Thatcher takes the sole of his Oxford shoe, pressing it into the same set of ribs that had just taken a major league swing, and punts him onto his back. I felt the tightening in my chest, the pressure increasing across my entire body. Feeling it in my hands, my neck and jaw muscles, as my fury built higher the longer he spoke.

"You think killing me makes it any better? You'll be just as bad as me, nothing but a killer. This won't bring her back!" he yells, spit flying from his mouth like white bugs. "She's dead. Nothing you do will change that."

I'd been waiting months for this. Spent sleepless nights thinking about what I would do if given the opportunity to get my hands on the person who took Rosemary from us. Bursts of memories play in my mind. Of Silas, of Rose, all the good, all the bad.

That was what no one was getting.

We knew she was gone. We knew that no matter how much blood we spilled, she wouldn't come back. She was truly gone.

We just didn't fucking care.

I stride forward, "No, it won't," twisting the axe in my hands so the blunt end points outward. "But it'll make me feel a fuck-ton better." I slam the end of the weapon into his throat.

The sound of kindling breaking over a tree crackles through the bottom floor of the house. Greg's windpipe splinters in his throat from the strike from the back of the axe. The brutal choking sound that falls from his mouth would make me cringe if I wasn't so amped up on how good this felt.

High-pitched breaths and wheezes is all he can manage. Not another word will come from his mouth.

It's then that Silas steps forward.

Hands calm, eyes like coal. He stands over Greg, peering

down at him so that he can take a peek into what a living human looks like when they lose their soul.

The Grim Reaper gave up his duties for tonight, handing them over to Silas so that he could sentence a dirty soul to whatever hell awaited him.

This had always been the plan. This had always been his kill. The retaliation he felt would make it up to Rose, because in his mind, he should have been there that night.

Rose was walking home from the library because of a fight they had. I still didn't know what it was over, but instead of waiting for Silas to pick her up, she left on her own.

Whatever his last words were to her, they were said in anger.

I'd give anything to know the thoughts that swirled in his mind right now as he stood face-to-face with the man who ended his girlfriend's life.

With subtle grace, he drops one knee down beside him, straddling his chest and pinning him to the floor with his weight. The floorboards creaked with the disturbance and all we could do was watch, waiting for the moment Silas needed us.

"I hope it's hard to breathe." His voice is gravelly as he wipes the dust off his vocal cords, "I hope every single breath feels like razor blades carving your throat wide open."

His hands, wide, large and powerful, sink down onto Greg's face. Slipping his fingers behind his skull to hold him steady, and allowing his thumbs to brush over his eyelids.

Greg coughed and fought for air, fear of death becoming more apparent, and he couldn't even scream for the help that might've saved him.

He wiggles, bucking off the ground, the last attempts of a man about to meet whatever maker he believed in. Never to take another breath again.

"I want you to remember this fear in Hell. Remember this pain for eons as you roast alive in the pits of the underworld."

With unimaginable strength, he sinks his thumbs into the sockets of Greg's eyes. Pressing into the hollows, digging through the delicate skin of the eyelid, seeping farther into the spongy muscles.

Guttural screams, like a static TV, come from Greg's chest. A pain that would have anyone begging for mercy. Yet, Silas barely flinches. Even as blood vessels begin to pop open, allowing blood to squirt onto his chest, coating his thumbs as he gouges his eyes out.

"Fuck," Rook whispers under his breath as he stands beside me, Thatcher looking at it as if it's some sort of demonstration and he should be taking notes.

"I hope you think about her, how you could have avoided this had you never laid a hand on her." He continues, looking unshaken, as if he's digging into a peach to pry the pit out of the center, the soft flesh giving way to his pressure.

Crimson liquid replaces the hollows of his eyes, streams of the sticky blood race down the sides of his cheeks. The way he curls his thumbs beneath the side of the eye, pulling upwards abruptly. When Silas removes his fingers from inside the sockets, it looks like a digital horror effect.

The way Greg's eyes dangled from the sockets by tiny nerve endings, jiggling with the momentum of his body's violent shakes.

Without another word spoken, Silas wraps his hands around Greg's throat and begins to compress. It takes four minutes to end his life. Four quiet minutes before his legs stop moving, his throat stops making gargled noises, and his heart rate completely stops.

In those four minutes, it felt like it was finally over.

For now.

Together we helped follow Thatcher's instructions on cleaning up the body, picking up any traces of us being here, while he drowned the body in bleach. Making sure any form of DNA evidence we had left on his body was melted away by the chemicals.

As our last measure of covering up our tracks, we let Rook douse him in lighter fluid, before setting Greg on fire. The smell of burnt flesh and fried blood took over any other smell. It came off as a perfume of death and my nose would still be smelling it years from now.

I stood outside of the house, waiting for the body to disintegrate, smoking a cigarette against the brick when Silas came walking outside, hood up and head facing the sky, like he was looking for her in the stars.

"You good?" I ask him as I exhale the smoke from my lungs.

"I asked you to stay a year, stay till we figured out who did it, and we did that tonight. So, I'm not gonna ask you to stay any longer," he says, still not looking down from the night, "but I'm going after Frank."

I wasn't offended by what he said. He knew what being here was like for me. Having to stay longer in a town that raised me to be an outcast with a family that put me there to begin with. I knew he was just trying to look out for me.

But I told him I'd stay till he was done. I promised him.

And I wouldn't break it. Not even if it meant dealing with the trauma that comes with this place.

I walk up behind him, placing my hand on his shoulder, "I'm with you, until the very end of this. I'm with you, Si." And I meant that. I would be here until the end, whatever that meant for us.

He nods, accepting my answer. "She used to say you were the most like the older brother."

I furrow my eyebrows, my throat suddenly clogged, "What?"

"Rose. She used to say that you took on the older brother role so that you could be what you never had. Always looking out, making sure nothing ever happened. It was one of her favorite things about you, because she knew I'd be alright as long as you were in charge." There is a faint smile as he stares up into the night, telling me something I'd never heard before.

I'd never told Rosemary about my family, but when you grow up around someone, it's hard not to notice the inner workings of someone's life. She knew enough to put certain things together.

I let silence take over. Allowing him some space, some time to think about what just happened. To come down from the adrenaline high we all were experiencing.

Somewhere deep down, I knew Rose was in the clouds angry with us. Angry with Silas for risking our lives just to avenge someone who was already dead. I could see her slitted eyes and furrowed brow.

But even so, we could die knowing her killer met the same fate.

That was enough.

"Alistair!" Rook shouts from inside of the house, barreling through the entryway to the front porch.

"What?" I ask, suddenly snapping back to high alert. Ready to fix whatever problem had just arisen.

"Lyra, she called me on messenger," he announces.

"Lyra Abbott? What does she want?"

"Just take it. Here." He shoves his phone at me, letting me grab it and place it to my ear.

"Hello?" I say, confused being a massive understatement.

If she is calling me to bitch me out over Briar, I'm going to let her know very quickly this is not the right time for it.

"Alistair! Oh, thank God. I've been trying to reach you for an hour. I didn't have your number, and you don't have Facebook, so I just started calling the other guys on here hoping you'd—"

"Lyra, what the fuck is going on?"

I end her rambling, hoping she can get to the point.

"It's Briar," she says on a breath. "Is she with you?"

I'd delivered enough punishments to earn me a title in Hell. I'd sent fear through more people than I could count. Pain in random men's bodies just for fun during fights.

I had gone my entire life almost without feeling this for myself.

Absolute panic.

I feel it in my chest. Like someone stabbing it with knives, each burning and digging into my flesh. My heart pounds so hard it vibrates my entire ribcage, the rapid thumping echoing in my ears.

There is a ringing there as well, like a siren. So loud and high it nearly bursts my eardrums. Pins and needles prick my fingers, my toes, everything turning to numbness in less than twenty seconds.

It was as if I'd submerged myself into water for a little too long. Held my head beneath the surface so long that when I came up, gasping for air, my throat burned and my brain was screaming at me to never stay under that long ever again.

I'd never been scared before.

And I imagine this is what terror feels like for others.

"No. She didn't leave the carnival with you?" I manage.

"Oh God, Briar." She starts to weep into the speaker, sounding out of breath. "After you guys left, I waited by the bathrooms and she never came back. I got a message from her phone saying she was going to your house, but it's almost two in the morning and she hasn't checked in. She's not answering her phone either, Alistair what if—"

"Stop." I don't need her to say the words. I don't want to hear them out loud.

I knew what she was going to say and the reality that it could be true made me want to hurl. I'd just watched a man have his eyes gouged out of his skull and I barely flinched.

Yet the prospect of Briar being kidnapped and possibly sold as a sex slave was enough to send my stomach into a fit of kick-flips. I pictured her fighting, doing everything she could think of to defend herself.

Cause she was a fighter and I knew she wouldn't go easy.

But even so, all I could see was them using her. Touching her. Violating her.

"Wait," I say out loud, my brain spinning. "You said she texted you? Said she was going to my house?"

Lightbulbs explode inside of my mind.

The urge to throw up is quickly replaced with a bomb of fury that is seconds from exploding.

"Yeah, why?"

"I know who has her," I tell her. "And I'm going to fucking kill him for taking her."

# CHAPTER THIRTY-ONE
## *The Reckoning*

*Briar*

Good and Evil.

An early concept that many try to say has a certain likeness.

They like to tell you that good encompasses all the light. It's the halo of life that does no wrong. It's the sound of newborn babies crying, soft strands of woven golden hair, and church pews on Sunday.

While evil is the root of sin. It's the creatures that lurk in the night, screams from the misty woods, and crows squawking over fresh meat. Evil has an image. It is the shade, black, oblivion.

Your whole life they depict these for you, so that when you develop a mind of your own you will be able to see the difference. You will see someone and know whether their intentions are sinister or pure.

They are fucking wrong.

Evil has no fixed image and neither does good.

If that were the case, Alistair wouldn't be breaking through the door of his family home ready to tear through Hell. Dorian wouldn't have me tethered to a chair with a gag in my mouth, looming over me with wicked intent.

By the world's standard, the man almost holding a PhD, the homecoming king, the man with light brown eyes, a million-dollar smile, and well-dressed stature, should be my knight in shining armor.

And the morally gray brother, the one with cold eyes and a damning reputation who believes killing people will avenge his friend's girl, is the crooked villain ready to rob me of my innocence.

The moment I'd stepped foot into Hollow Heights, the second I heard about Alistair, he had been painted as the evil one. I was guilty of it myself as he stood beside Easton in that classroom.

I took what they said about him and made assumptions. Granted, anyone in their right mind would think of him as the bad guy after watching him participate in a murder. And maybe that did make him evil. The ability to wipe someone off the face of the earth. At the same time, had someone killed my mom, like Lyra's, I wasn't so sure I wouldn't do the exact same thing.

This entire town had made him into something he wasn't. They started a war within his soul and expected him to find peace. Shocked when he chose violence over harmony.

Raised by a family that he had no chance of surviving unless he became cruel.

My eyes said words my mouth couldn't as Alistair came into view, stalking into the living room with animosity in his harsh glare.

I thought his white t-shirt would melt off his body, the way it spread across his defined shoulders, and tapered into his lean waist. His hair wasn't pushed out of his face, instead single pieces crossed his forehead as if he'd been running his fingers through it.

His boots thudded across the floor.

Dorian barely moved from his seat, swirling the melting ice

in the whiskey tumbler, looking up at his younger brother with contempt. The barrel of the gun resting against the leather chair.

"I was starting to think you wouldn't show up." Dorian speaks first, watching the way Alistair abruptly stops as he sees the gun in his hand. He stood in front of us, his eyes flicking to me and back to his brother.

I know the swelling on my eye has started to show, the blood had stopped running down my face an hour ago and I could feel how stiff my eyebrow was from the caked blood that sat there.

Refusing to let him touch me warranted a pistol whip to the face that left me unconscious for what felt like days but had really only been a few hours. When I woke up, I was tied to this chair, listening to Dorian rant on and on about how mistaken I was.

How stupid I was for choosing Alistair over him, for denying him when he was better in every way. How appalled he was by my inability to see that for myself. He paced back and forth in front of me, until he'd finally decided to sit down, leading me to believe he'd had some sort of psychotic break.

He had to have.

"What are you doing?" Alistair questions, fists balled by his side as he keeps his cool, knowing he's at a disadvantage because of the explosive weapon.

"Doing what I do best, little brother." I don't have to look over to see the grin on his face, "Taking what's yours. Taking what has always been mine."

My mouth ached from straining around this cloth wrapped around my head, preventing me from speaking anything other than disgruntled mumbles. Tears stung my eyes and even though I had tried to remain as calm as possible, I felt their hot slickness run down my cheeks.

"You're fucking delusional, Dorian. We aren't kids anymore and this isn't a game. Let her go," Alistair argues.

I feel Dorian's eyes on me, "She's pretty, isn't she?" he murmurs and I want to vomit at the thoughts he's having about me in his head. "It was one of the first things I noticed about her. How her Cupid's bow is perfectly symmetrical and her eyes, they shine like jewels. Then she had to go and ruin it."

The creak of leather bowing beneath his weight echoes in the room as he stands up, leaving the whiskey on the side table and keeping the gun in his dominant hand. My heart beats in tune with his steps as he waltzes behind my chair.

I can feel the cold metal of the gun pressed into my hair, the way he draws patterns in my scalp with the barrel, making me wince with fear. I tried to suck in the tears, to silence the cries but I could only handle so much.

I couldn't believe that this was where I might die. Pinned between a man I care about and the man who hates him.

"What the fuck are you talking about?"

"I saw you two in the conservatory the other night. When you thought no one was watching." Delusional rage spews from his mouth, I can feel the gun shaking in my hair from the force of his voice. "When she let you touch her! Let you defile her. How her body molded against yours and I couldn't believe she'd do something like that. I couldn't believe she'd choose you. I mean," he scoffs, "if she looks that good with the copy, imagine how stunning she'd look beside the original."

He had taken a night that I wanted to be special and turned it into something sinister. I'd never be able to think of Alistair's birthday without thinking about where Dorian had stood when he watched us. How long he'd stayed there.

"She's not mine," Alistair says, refusing to make eye contact with me. "She's just a girl. You'd be ruining your life, your legacy, for a girl who means nothing to me."

I grimace from his words, pulling my eyes from him to look at the ground. My chest aching so fiercely because I might die meaning nothing to someone who means more to me than he was supposed to.

"She was mine first!" Dorian bellows, my spine shaking from fear. "I saw her first! She was supposed to be mine and you took her from me!"

I wasn't sure if the confusion was coming from the concussion I was sure I had or the words coming from his mouth.

I could feel his hand press into the side of my head, crying out slightly as he dropped his head to my hair and inhaled deeply. "I saw her on her very first day in Hollow Heights," he mutters, like he's talking to me. "I knew at that moment, I had to have her. I had to have you, Briar."

All I heard was him raising the gun, the sound of it smacking against something solid over and over again as he continued, "But you chose him! You opened up your legs for my extra! He is nothing compared to me!"

This fantasy he had built in his head of us had quickly come falling down without my realization. Only having talked to him twice, I never knew he was watching me. Fueling hallucinations I wanted no part of.

My first day when I felt someone staring, it had been him. Pins and needles poked my skin thinking about all the times I felt someone looking at me and how I had assumed it was Alistair.

The gun is returned to the side of my head, the force of the barrel digging into my skin, and I can feel my body trembling. My heart thumping. Sweat trickling my forehead.

"Dorian—" Alistair starts.

"I see the way you look at her! Like she belongs to you! The tattoo on her finger! You marked her!" he practically screams. "You don't deserve her, you deserve nothing. You're just a gutter rat, the backup in case I failed. You don't get to have anything!"

The temperature rises as his movements become more

frantic. The countdown on the bomb that is Dorian Caldwell ticking down closer to a massive explosion.

"Dorian! Listen to me," he steps forward, hand out in a truce. "We can get you help. You don't need to do this."

"I don't need fucking help! I want her!" I flinch. "And if I can't have her, neither can you."

It had all been moving so fast, heated words, rushed movements. Everything was spinning on fast forward, and it was then that it all decided to slow down. It felt like I'd dropped beneath the surface of the pool, falling to the bottom and just sitting in the depths. Everything in the water was slower.

I watched Alistair charge forward, the word "No" screaming from his lips.

A gust of breath escaped my mouth in slow motion, shutting my eyes before the end came tumbling towards me.

I thought I would have flashes of my future, of my past, all the things I'd never experience, but instead I just saw him. I saw him and conceived a world where I could love him without repercussions.

The way he lunged for me, how fear and pain blossomed across his face like a freshly grown rose. A rose bloomed just before the cold winter, where it would soon die. I wondered if after my death he'd become like Silas, or if I really was just nothing to him.

I saw how he'd been a boy before he was a monster, before he'd been painted as the face of evil. I saw what they all had forgotten—that he was loyal, made of flesh and blood, of crooked grins and onyx eyes.

Beneath it all, a boy with dreams, with friends, who laughed.

A boy who had once loved his brother.

And I thought how lucky I was in that moment, to see him as nothing but a boy.

The gun's blast pierced my ears, bursting the drum inside.

Warm, wet splatters of liquid coated the side of my face, and I expected there to be more pain.

My eyes opened, still able to see.

I must be a ghost, right? I didn't expect it to happen that quickly, I thought there would be a light, a gate I needed to walk through.

Instead, there was Alistair falling to his knees in front of the chair, hands inching towards my face.

"Briar, Briar, Briar."

*Briar*

*Briar*

*Briar*

It felt so real, my name on his lips, echoing in my head as the gag on my mouth was pulled away and the ties wrapping me to the chair fell off. I felt his hands, hotter than coals, press into my cheeks, directing my attention towards his gaze.

The world started moving normally once again. I had breached the surface, just in time to hear guttural groans of pain and the shuffling of feet.

"You're okay," he whispered. "You're gonna be okay, Little Thief."

As if I was a feather, he scooped me up into his arms, cradling me to his chest. My nose seeking out the comforting smell of his cologne and burying my head into his neck as he carried me. Chasing that scent.

My vision was spotty, but I could see on the ground, behind the chair I'd just been sitting in, lay Dorian. On his side, eyes wide open, clutching his shoulder where blood was staining his white button down. So much blood it didn't look real. Seeping between his fingers as he rocked on the floor in pain.

Just before my eyes closed, I saw them.

Three shadows moved across the living room, dressed in

black and, as always, the children of the dark came to protect their own.

## Alistair

The shower had shut off twenty minutes ago.

I wanted to give her time. Allow her to absorb everything, let the dust settle, and I knew once she came out, the adrenaline would have wiped her to the point of exhaustion.

Staying in the guest house at Thatcher's meant she would have a bedroom to herself without any of the awkward, *where am I sleeping?* conversations occurring. Even though I knew she needed space, I refused to let her sleep at the dorms tonight.

Just for tonight, I wanted her under the same roof as me. I needed to make sure for tonight at least, she was safe.

The creaking of the bathroom door made my knee quit bouncing, long enough to follow the trail of her long legs, steam pouring out from behind her. The shirt and boxers I'd given her to wear were a few sizes too big and they swallowed her body.

A goddess. An angel. All the good left in a wicked world.

Gently grabbing her wet hair and pulling it to the side, giving me a clearer view of the bruise on her eye.

I hated myself more then.

That I had been the reason a girl who represented all the things I'd ever wanted was hurting. A girl who had everything I needed and I was too afraid to accept. Because, just as Dorian said, I didn't deserve anything.

That's all I've been taught. So how would I have believed for even a second that Briar and I could have been something?

Looking at the bright purple wound and scratch on her face threw me below rock bottom. I didn't question that I'd been more worried about that bruise than about my brother bleeding on the floor.

Even though there had been a solitary moment tonight when I was looking at Dorian that I saw myself. A son who'd been raised to be something he never wanted to be.

He was the other extreme.

Raised with the pressure of being the successor, having to be perfect, never allowed to fail because if he did, they would replace him. I knew what pressure like that felt like for a young kid, and it had done just as much damage to him as it had done to me.

And for that moment, I hated him a little less, because for the very first time, I related to him.

My head aches with repercussions I knew I'd be dealing with come tomorrow. Answering questions from our parents, listening to what story they would spin to cover all this up.

But for right now, I would let the guys handle Dorian's hospital journey, and I would deal with everything else in the morning. Right now, I wanted to make sure she was okay.

That she would make it out of this with some sort of normalcy.

"The bed is clean and the door locks." I stood from the chair, not being able to look at her for longer than a few moments. "I'll be right down the hall if you need anything throughout the night."

"Alistair?" she whispers, halting my stroll to the door with just the sound of her voice.

"Yeah?"

"I'm sorry."

*I'm sorry.*

As if this had been her fault. As if she could have possibly done anything to stop my brother. Even if she hadn't fallen in my path, he still would have done this. Maybe even succeeded in his goal of making her his.

I shake my head, "Stop, this isn't your fault. Don't do that."

I let out a breath. "Dorian needs help. He's fucked in the head. Don't be sorry, you did nothing wrong."

Tears stream down her freshly cleaned face, "I'm not sorry about him. I'm sorry about whatever it was that happened to you as children that made you two this way. That made you have to shoot your brother for me."

I wanted to leave.

I should have left.

But I physically couldn't stop myself from moving towards her. It was like gravity pulled me in her direction, refusing to let go until my hand cupped the side of her face, rubbing the tears away from her cheeks.

"Technically, I didn't shoot him," I smile gently. "Silas did."

A laugh that she probably didn't expect escapes her throat, "You know what I meant."

We stood there while I held her face, staring at one another and I thought about everything I'd done to her up to that point. How beneath it all, I was just attempting to destroy her because she represented what I could never have.

And similar to Dorian, if I couldn't have her, no one could.

How right now, all I wanted was to really have her. Not just to toy with, more than a game. But I wanted to have her laughs.

I wanted to swallow them whole and see if they would heal all the rage in my soul. I wanted to bathe in the peace that came with being next to her after sex, when we'd draw lazy circles on each other's bodies and nothing else mattered except the steady sound of her breath on my skin.

I knew her fear, but I wanted to know what drove her.

What made her smile, why she always wore the same pair of shoes, and what she wanted to be when she grew up. I wanted to be more than the man who scared her.

I wanted to be a man she could love even if I had no idea what that meant for me.

"Will you stay with me tonight? I . . . I just, I don't—"

"Yes." I don't let her finish, she doesn't need to.

She gets in the bed first, moving smoothly and quietly. Her long limbs trailing random patterns in the cotton waves, navigating the sea of navy-blue fabric with grace that reminded me a bit of a shark gliding effortlessly through the deep blue ocean.

I kicked my shoes off, reaching behind my head and removing my shirt, tossing it onto the floor and making my way onto my side of the bed. I shove the pillow under my head, laying on my side so we are staring at each other.

"I always wanted siblings," she says. "Being an only child is lonely and I think that's why it was so hard for me to make friends. I've always just felt alone, and as weird as this sounds, I didn't feel that way here. Even when you and your friends were being raging assholes."

I chuckle, my chest vibrating with warmth.

"Siblings are overrated," I joke. "I never really had a sibling either, not in the way most people do. I had a blood-bound older brother, but that didn't make us siblings."

"But you have Rook, you have Thatcher, Silas," she points out.

"Yeah. I do have them."

Those were my brothers. Family that was chosen. Who woke up and chose to be a part of my life every day.

"Is Dorian—" she stumbles. "Is he going to be alright?"

I sigh, "Yeah, Silas just hit some muscle in his shoulder. He'll need a blood transfusion and some fluids, but he'll be alright."

She nods, accepting my answer and I see that the knowledge of him being alive makes her feel relief. Even though he almost killed her, she still didn't want anyone dying because of her.

If I wanted her—if I *really* wanted her—I'd have to make sure she knew me. More than just what I wanted the world to see.

"He's got hemophilia."

"What?"

"Dorian. He was born with a rare condition called hemophilia. It's just where his blood doesn't clot as fast as regular people's does. When he was seven, he was at a lacrosse practice and took a hit to the ribs, no big deal for most kids, but he ended up in the hospital with severe internal bleeding."

I remember hearing my parents talk about it. I remember hearing it for the first time and thinking, I hate that my brother is sick. That I wish I could fix him.

"That's when they found out and my grandfather, Alaric, refused to allow the Caldwell name to rest on the shoulders of a sick boy. What if he died? What if he couldn't handle all the assets he was set to inherit? At the very least, he told my parents they needed to have a backup in case something happened."

I fucking hated talking about this. I hated thinking about how devastated I had been as a kid when I found out why I was born. I hated how no one cared after I was told. How it was just something I was supposed to live with.

"Alistair—" she mutters, sadness in her voice.

"So, my parents basically made me in a petri dish. Genetically modifying my genes so that I was the exact blood type, so that I was initially a replica of my older brother. So that if something did happen, I could give him blood, donate an organ. I was only born to be spare parts. The heir and the spare, that's what my grandfather called us." My voice felt like it gave out towards the end, like all the gas in my tank was finally gone. I was now running on empty.

I make myself look at her, look her in the eyes, "I've been wanting to kill myself since I found out. I didn't want to live a life where I was only meant to be a backup. Extra. Only important if an organ was needed. No one deserves to live like that. And then I met the guys and—"

"They gave you a reason to live," she finishes, taking the

words I didn't want to say out of my mouth. Knowing that admitting out loud that I need someone isn't easy.

"Yeah. They did."

Her hand reaches forward, pushing my hair out of my face, running her fingers through my dark locks.

"I'm glad you met them. I'm glad you're alive, Alistair."

Something happened inside of me in that moment.

All these dark clouds herded over me and it began to pour with rain. Rain that fell hard and fast over the inside of my chest, wetting an organ that I thought had shriveled up and died.

My heart was a desert. Deserted, dry, without nurture or care. Nothing but sand and blistering heat. And it had just started raining for the first time in my life. The beating no longer felt painful, but smooth, the way it was always meant to beat.

"When I first saw you at that party," I pause, not sure how to explain what I'm feeling, "you made me feel alive. You excited me. You electrified me in a way no one had before."

The way she stood in the middle of that dance floor, surrounded by people, smoke falling in front of her, and the flashing lights only giving me pieces of her face. Even through all that, I could still see her clearly.

Her hands rub circles into my chest coaxing the words from my throat, "And tonight, when I saw you in that chair, all I could think about was the last things I'd said to you. How I let my past dictate how I felt about you. I've never been so fucking—" I tightened my hold, "scared, and I hated it. I don't ever want to feel like that again. I refuse to feel that way again."

And I meant that. I was never going to feel that again. I wouldn't let her be put in that position.

"We can't predict the future, Alistair. And it's okay to be afraid of that. Being scared doesn't make you weak, letting it stop you does."

I thought about that.

How she was the definition of that statement. Even though I'd put her through hell mentally—I'd scared her—she never stopped fighting me. Never let it stop her from moving forward.

"I will tear through the sky, rip Heaven's gates apart if that's what it takes to prevent you from being at risk again. They will have to raise Hell to stop me from protecting you. You understand?"

She nods, looking up at me, eyes coated with exhaustion. I pull her closer to my body, curling my arms around her so that her head is resting on my chest.

"Get some sleep, Little Thief."

"What does this mean, you know, for us? I don't want to be that girl who wants the label, but I just need to know what I mean to you." Her lips move across my bare skin as she talks, distracting me for a moment.

I won't lie to her, and I hope at the end of this, she'll be able to accept that.

"I don't know what any of this means if I'm being honest, Briar. I'm not sure how to describe how when I'm around you my heart feels like it's beating for the first time, or how you make me feel alive." My eyebrows furrow as I continue, "I'm not sure how to take any of that, what that means for you, for me, for us."

And that was the hardest part.

How was I supposed to know what love felt like when I'd never been shown it? When I'd never been taught how to receive or give it? My version of caring for others was beating up Rook when he needed to hurt, helping Thatcher skin a deer, and letting Silas shoot pop cans out of my hands.

That wasn't enough for Briar, she deserved more.

"But I do know, I'm obsessed with the way you feel pressed against me. The way your lip curls when you're angry makes me want to piss you off just so I can see it. I'm constantly angry when I hear other people make you laugh, it makes me want to hurt them, because for a moment they were making you happy and I want that job."

She smiles against my skin as I continue.

"And right now, I could stay here for a lifetime just feeling your heartbeat. I'm not sure what I can give you, but whatever is left of me, whatever I have, it's yours, for as long as you want it."

And I meant it. Every word. Even though I wasn't sure if I'd just made a huge mistake by laying out my cards so openly.

There is a beat of silence before I feel her lips against my skin in a gentle kiss.

"And if I want it forever?"

"Then it's forever, Little Thief."

"That sounds an awful lot like love, Alistair Caldwell."

Pins poke my skin, like a full body numbness that overcomes me. The waves of peace settle into my shoulders and the euphoria that comes with being next to her sucks me in.

No killing. No history. No psycho brothers. Just me, a guy who would do anything to keep this girl next to him.

"It's something," I mumble, pressing my lips into the top of her head and inhaling deeply, filling my lungs with her scent.

"Then that's all that matters. That's all I need," she whispers. "The rest is just fluff anyway." I glance down at my initials adorning her finger, pissed I put it on the middle one and not the one directly to the left.

"Whatever you have to give, I want all of it. All the dark, all the scary. I want it. Forever."

Just like that, the shadow child learned that you don't have to step into the light to find happiness. You just need to find the person willing to step into the gray area.

"It's yours. Every warped part of me. It's yours, Little Thief. I hope you like playing in the shadows, we will be staying here for a while."

# CHAPTER THIRTY-TWO
## *Happy Holidays*

*Briar*

It took till the week before Christmas for officers to finally identify the body that had been torched at the local party house. In that week, students and faculty had assembled together in the snow-filled courtyard to create a memorial for Greg West.

As I walked past the balloons, pictures, "we miss you" cards and all the other memorabilia, I couldn't make myself feel sorry for him. The man who lived alone and helped sell girls into sex slavery.

My fingers were wrapped tightly around two cups of coffee as I pushed the heavy door to the dining hall open with my shoulder, moving my way through the rows until I saw Lyra with her nose in a book, the seat in front of her empty for me.

"Wild first semester, huh?" I say, as I drop down into the chair, sliding the extra cup towards her.

"Passed my exams, witnessed murder, committed arson. I'd say it's one for the books." She looks up, thanking me for the coffee.

I wasn't sure what the term was for bonding over chaos, but Lyra and I had made our loner society a forever kind of thing.

After all the messes we muddled through this last semester, I couldn't imagine going through the rest of my college days without her by my side.

"Did you see the cops on campus? I heard they were interviewing girls who were friends with Coraline. There have just been too many missing and dead bodies for them to not look into it," she says, flipping the page in her book.

"Yeah." Dread filled my stomach. "It was bound to happen eventually."

Everything about how Alistair and I did things was completely backwards. But that didn't mean I cared for him any less, it didn't mean my worry for him going to jail lessened because we'd just gone on our first date a few weeks ago.

I knew I had this deep, profound connection to him. Our souls linked through the different types of invisibility we experienced as children. But it was at Thanksgiving that I knew I loved him.

When he walked into Thomas's apartment wearing slacks and a button-down, carrying a pie that Thatcher's grandmother forced him to bring. I saw him step out of his comfort zone for something that made me happy.

All I wanted was for him to stop by, I didn't expect everything else.

We spent the day together and it felt like something a real, normal couple would do. Helping around the kitchen as Thomas told stories of his youth and we tried to relate. There had been thirty minutes of awkward tension, but it quickly melted once Alistair began warming up to the situation.

I loved him because of what I knew he'd give up in order to protect me. In order to make me happy. And even though I may never hear those three little words from him, I know he feels them.

Alistair Caldwell will never be the man who will shower

me with pretty words and love poems. The man who says every emotion he feels or the one who says I love you. But he is the man who will walk through a blizzard just to get me pie from Tilly's Diner during finals. The man who will break the noses of men like Easton Sinclair for not leaving me alone.

He is the man who is savagery and security. The perfect balance to make me feel alive, yet safe. The only drug on the planet that's good for you. Lyra had been right, to an extent, in that diner.

I wasn't the girl who just wanted comfort. I needed the challenge. And that's what he was. A challenge every single day.

I didn't know when it happened, when the hate and lust shifted to love, when my heart started drawing his name on the inside walls, not with distaste but with admiration.

It would just severely blow if the guy I just started dating went to jail for murder, but being with him was knowing I was taking that risk.

"So . . ." I start, reaching into my side bag and pulling out a neatly wrapped present. The rectangular box is decorated with black and purple wrapping paper.

"Briar! I thought we said no gifts!" she scolds.

"I had to get you something. I saw it and it was too perfect. It practically jumped off the shelf."

Small white lie. I'd had this custom made, but she didn't need to know that.

"I thought I was going to get to surprise you," she pouts as she pulls out a much larger box, sliding it across the table towards me.

We share a laugh, realizing we are the type of people who couldn't *not* give gifts to the ones we care about.

Together we begin opening our respective gifts, inside mine is a soft red pullover. The vintage looking material makes my toes curl with happiness and I run my fingers across the embroidering on the front that spells, *Loner Society.*

If I wasn't already wearing what felt like ten layers of clothing, I would've put it on, that's how much I loved it.

Lyra's present was a silver charm bracelet, four charms already adorning the chain. A cute beetle, a cherry, a little knife for her obsession with Criminal Minds, and a raven for Edgar Allan Poe, her lover.

I walk to the opposite side of the table, wrapping my arms around her and hugging her tightly to my body. I was beyond thankful that my first friend was someone like Lyra.

We sat catching up over coffee, planning an entire Christmas movie marathon, and enjoying the company of each other.

It's only when I get a notification on my phone that I have to leave. The text was a simple, *Labyrinth in five.*

I told Lyra bye, it's not like I wouldn't see her tonight before we all left for Christmas break.

Not being able to help the excitement bubbling in my stomach or the butterflies that fluttered in there, I speed-walk out of the dining hall, rushing across the school grounds towards the Bursley District.

The snow came down hard, huge snowflakes stacking onto the already white ground. My shoe prints leaving a trail behind me as I started a light jog. My breath coming out in visible smoke clouds.

I flew around the side of the building heading towards the entrance of the Labyrinth; the last time I'd been inside I'd been clawing to get out, now I was rushing through the semi-circles, ready to see who awaited me in the center.

Pine trees carried the weight of the snow, their dark needles still poking through, giving me the first real winter of my life and making it beautiful in the process. I came skidding to a stop when I made my way around the last portion of the maze.

Alistair stood with his hands shoved deep into his dark jeans, his hood pulled up over his head to shield his face from the harsh weather, a leather jacket over the black hoodie.

He was a stark contrast from the white falling around him, sticking out like a sore thumb.

Snow crunched beneath my feet, making him raise his gaze in my direction. I was almost taken aback by how unfairly stunning he was standing there. Everything faded when he looked at me, when the little bit of sunlight hits his eyes they become this brilliant, almost clear black. Like perfectly worn sea glass or water in a stream running over stones.

I take my time walking towards him and he stands perfectly still, eyes zoned in on every single step, and as soon as I'm within distance, he attacks. Wrapping a toned arm around my waist and pulling me snug against his body.

As if it's a greeting, he drops his head to my hair, inhaling my scent before saying, "Hello, Little Thief."

I love the way my skin warms when he talks, heating me up from the inside out.

"Caldwell," I throw back, pulling back so I can look up at him. I tuck my arms around his waist beneath his leather jacket, keeping my hands warm. This is what a safe place felt like.

"See all the cops on campus?" I ask casually, even though it makes my stomach roll.

"I did," he says easily, looking down at me. "It was a risk we knew about before we did this. I won't apologize for it if they find out what happened, but I doubt they will."

I didn't expect anything less from him. It was the one thing about Alistair that didn't change from the moment I met him, he never apologized for who he was. You either took him as is or you hated him for it.

"Still working on Frank?"

He nods casually in answer. I didn't need him to change, I

didn't need him to tell me he loved me or shower me with flowers. But I did ask for the truth, no matter how bloody it got, he promised he wouldn't lie to me.

And he'd kept that promise.

He told me everything. All the things they did before Greg, everything that happened to Rose and what they had planned to do with the mayor. Which wasn't much at the moment because they were waiting on Silas to call the shots for the next move.

All they did know was that he wasn't getting away with it and his time was coming, soon.

"I'm scared. I don't like not knowing things," I whisper, resting my chin on his chest.

His fingers push my hair behind my ears, thumbs swiping across my cheek bones.

"I'm not sure where we go from here, Briar, or what will happen, but I know no matter what, I'll protect you. I'll protect this," he says, soothing the anguish that sits in my heart when I think about him being taken away, or worse, winding up dead.

Hollow Heights had been nothing like I thought it would be. Everything I guessed would happen wasn't even close to what I got. Never in a million years did I think I'd be standing here. Never thought I would be the girl who protected murderers.

I guess some people are just born to run with criminals. I guess that person is me.

"It's funny, I thought when I came here it would all make sense. What I wanted to do with my life, where I wanted to end up later in life," I drift off. "I'd never had anything good like this happen to me before, so I never really thought anything good would be possible for me in the future. But I'm starting to like figuring it out as I go."

"Yeah? You don't have any idea what the future looks like for you?" he asks, raising an eyebrow, a mischievous twinkling in his eyes like stars in the night sky.

"I mean," I sigh sarcastically, "the idea of you and I apartment hunting next year doesn't sound too bad. Snagging an internship with the data science program might be nice, throwing surprise birthday parties for you . . ."

"Briar," he growls, interrupting me.

"No birthday parties?" I ask with a smile.

"No parties. I enjoyed the way I spent this one," leaning towards my face, moving his warm lips across my own. "Fucking you."

Heat surges between my legs, that dull ache that never leaves increases and I'm suddenly thinking about all the things we could do inside this maze. I bite at his bottom lip playfully.

"What about you, Mr. Caldwell? Any ideas for your future?"

"Continuing to tell my parents to shove their business ventures up their ass," he grunts and I can't help but laugh. "Making sure the boys don't end up in jail and spend every moment I can trying to find new ways to scare you."

I thought about the last time we had sex, in the parking lot of the school at midday with students walking around campus. The tinted windows shielded us from eyes, but it set me on fire thinking they could maybe see me with my thighs wrapped around his waist as he thrust inside me over and over again in the back seat of his car.

He knew I liked to test limits and I trusted him enough to let him do that.

My safe high.

My adrenaline rush.

"Still haven't come around to your parents?" I ask, trying not to let the images of us distract me.

"Dorian's been in rehab for three weeks and they are already trying to replace him. I don't want anything to do with their money or business. They made their bed. They can lie in it for all I fucking care."

According to the Caldwells, their oldest suffered a traumatic injury that had left him addicted to painkillers and he was working hard in rehab to rid himself of the filthy habit. That's what they told everyone anyway.

The truth was the pressure of being Dorian Caldwell drove him to start taking drugs. Mixing and matching uppers and downers. Whatever he could get his hands on. He hadn't been sober in years and his parents didn't even care to notice as long as he fit the image.

Now, they were scrambling to find an heir.

It was a shame they saw their flesh and blood as assets, versus human beings, their children.

Anytime I asked him, Alistair said he didn't think there was much hope in rekindling a relationship with Dorian. Not because he didn't understand and not because he kidnapped me with plans of killing me, but because even before the drugs he'd done exactly what his parents did. Made him the outcast. It was a long road that he didn't want to travel down. Not any time soon anyway.

"I have your Christmas present," I say, pulling us away from the depressing topic, grinning from ear to ear.

"Are you wearing a bow underneath your clothes?"

I snort, rolling my eyes, "No, you perv. It's in my back pocket. But you'll have to grab it yourself."

He arches his eyebrows with the challenge, slipping his hands lower on my body. I shiver as his hands rub up and down my back side, falling down to my butt and grabbing it roughly.

I moan softly, his head dipping to the side of my neck, the little kisses left on my collarbone make my head buzz. Carefully he sticks his fingers into my back pocket, retrieving the gift with two fingers.

He pulls it between us, the golden chain dangling in front of me, and I have flashes of it brushing my nose as he crawls on top of me, pressing his body into mine, rocking inside of me over and over again.

"This your way of branding me, Little Thief?"

The tiny B in the center of the necklace catches the light, making me grin.

"Figured I'd return the favor, considering I have to walk around with your initials on my finger forever."

He chuckles, unclipping the hook and wrapping it around his neck. The chain hugs his neck in all the right ways, dangling a few inches below his Adam's apple and I want to lick it.

I loved the way my initial seemed to fit perfectly on his chest. My fingers reaching up and running along the golden chain. In my mind he was already mine, but now, I was marking him publicly.

Alistair Caldwell was mine, mine, mine.

"Speaking of that, my present requires a little bit of a drive, you up for it?"

"You gonna let me drive?" I raise my eyebrow, knowing he hates my driving. It makes him nervous the way I take curves.

"Tell ya what . . . make it through the maze without me catching you and the keys are all yours."

The challenge sparks my excitement. I take an eager step back from him, a Cheshire cat grin eating at my face. I could feel my heart start to pump a little faster, I slowly start backing away from him,

"Deal," I say quickly, before turning and taking off back through the maze.

Knowing that even though I really wanted to drive, I'd always let him catch me.

# CHAPTER THIRTY-THREE

## Wrap Me Up

### Alistair

"What is this place?" she asks as I shut the door of the shop behind us.

Her Converse squeak against the hardwood floor as she spins in a short circle, snow-chapped face making me smile.

"It's called Spade One," I tell her. "It's a tattoo shop I apprentice at."

She gasps, "You jerk! You let me shove tattoo shop applications down your throat for a week and you didn't tell me?"

I admired that about her.

How even though it seemed impossible to anyone else, she believed that I deserved the best out of everything. Stealing my sketches and hanging them up in her dorm room, showing them off to Lyra.

It felt nice to have someone believe in you.

"I've been working here for a while now." I lead her up the steps, where my table is already set up. I'd come by earlier, cleaned it up, got everything ready for this today.

"I can't believe you didn't tell me!"

"No one knew."

"Not even the boys?"

"Not even them," I say honestly, sitting down in the swivel chair near the tattoo bench. "This was the only place I had to myself."

When she's done looking around, she makes her way towards me, sitting on my lap, the chair rolling backwards with her weight.

"So why tell me? I know all about how protective you are over the things that are yours." She pushes my hair out of my eyes.

My hands sitting right above her backside, resting on her hips, fingers hooked in her belt loops.

"I promised that everything I have is yours, remember? No secrets."

I squeeze her hips, rolling her body on my lap, quickly pressing my lips to hers in a rush of a kiss, "I want you to have all of me. So I can have all of you."

Slinging her arms around my neck, looking up and around the shop, "And this is all of you? You wanna own one of these one day?"

I nod, "Something like that. I really just want to give people art that's there forever. Tattoos are the ultimate commitment to art and I like the weight of that."

When Shade gave me a spare key to this place, I doubt it was for the use of me tattooing my girlfriend on Christmas, but I think it would make him worry less about my mental stability if he found out.

At least he knew I was capable of holding down a relationship.

I thought about having my own shop when my apprenticeship is done, hiring the artists I wanted, putting out a certain product. I liked the idea of being in charge. In charge of something positive, of a dream.

"Want your present?" I ask, running my tongue along her bottom lip.

Briar chews the inside of her cheek, trying to contain her excitement but I know her, and how much she loves surprises. Even when she says she doesn't. I also enjoy the slight O her mouth makes when she's in shock, it reminds me of what she looks like when she comes.

"What is it?" she asks, and I toss my head towards the black leather tattoo table.

"There are two technically, but one of them is beneath the table."

With enthusiasm, she rushes off my lap, leaving me cold without her presence near me. Her nimble fingers pull the black box up and onto the table. Not bothering to take her time as she begins to rip it open.

I can see the white laces as soon as she pulls the top off, her squeal of excitement has this buzzing feeling going off in my chest. A form of gratification I'm still trying to get used to.

She pulls up the red shoes, hugging them to her chest, barely looking at them before she says, "I love them!"

I roll my eyes, "You haven't even seen the best part."

Standing up and meeting her halfway as she flips the shoes over, looking at the soles that have my name on the left and her name on the right. I felt it was too much of a narcissistic asshole move to put my first and last on both shoes.

"Tired of seeing you walk around in busted-up shoes."

It was just another thing that made Briar so different. How a pair of shoes that would mean nothing to kids around here meant so much to her. She gushed and ogled the custom Converse, slipping them on her feet and dancing in front of the mirror.

I'd never seen a pair of shoes make someone so happy.

"One more gift," I tell her, walking behind the mirror. "I'm gonna tattoo you," My hands reach for her, rubbing my initials on her finger, "Whatever you want."

Leaning into me, she hums, "You mean I get to be conscious for this one?"

A deep laugh reverberates my chest, echoing as I dip my head to the bend in her neck, "If you want to be . . ."

I let her decide what she wanted, where she wanted it. Figuring I should make up for the first tattoo she was given considering she was passed out. I don't regret marking her, though. Showing the entire world she was mine. I'd spend the rest of my life doing that.

She lays on the table, her shirt rolled up just below her bra, revealing her ribs to the cold air of the shop. I start the process of sanitizing everything, prepping my needles, getting all the ink. It's not a large tattoo, four little words on her upper ribcage would take maybe twenty minutes.

When I'm ready, I look down at her on the table, "You ready?"

"I think I can handle a little pain."

I smirk as I press my foot into the pedal, the hum of the machine filling the shop. I pulled her skin tight, starting to work over the stencil I'd already placed on her. I fell into this sorta trance when I was drawing or tattooing.

But it was different with her.

Like I was placing a piece of me onto her skin. By showing her this place, by letting her into my world, into my head. It was more than just my initials with a stick and poke.

This was a tattoo that meant something to her, and I was helping her memorialize it forever. Every time she looked at either of them, she'd think of me. And that's what I wanted, for her to never stop thinking of me.

To never stop being mine.

Because I would never stop being hers.

Her body vibrates beneath me, a short little whimper escaping that makes my cock twitch, listening to her mouth release shaky breaths.

When I was done, I quickly cleaned her up telling her she could hop up and check it out in the mirror if she wanted.

There is always this uncontrollable urge I get when I'm around her. I had it the first time I ever saw her. Wanting to touch her, break her will, test just how far she'd be willing to go to find pleasure.

I admire her, shirt still tucked beneath her bra exposing her taut stomach. Jeans sitting low on her hips, the lettering riding her ribcage like it was made to be there.

*We are all thieves.*

Art on Art.

"Like it?" I ask, even though I watch her eyes light up like diamonds when she sees the script in the mirror.

"Love it," she whispers.

I stand in front of her, pulling the plastic wrap open, and looping it around her back. My body inches away from hers, the smell of her igniting the hunger in my stomach.

I yank her closer as I begin to wind the clear plastic around her body, taking my time, watching the way her eyes drop to my lips, ready to steal a kiss from me.

My fingers running along her skin makes her shiver, my eyes fixated on her movements as she starts to lift her shirt higher, exposing her white bra to me.

Like two supple fruits ready for feasting, her tits lay exposed to me, the tops nearly spilling over the edge.

"You said no one comes in during Christmas, right?"

Lust, passion, wickedness flashes in her eyes, the golden specks making my cock stiffen. I lean my head towards her face, keeping my distance between our chests so I can keep winding the plastic around her.

"You wanna play, Little Thief?" I question, her head nodding up and down slowly, her nose brushing mine.

I loved how willing she was. How unafraid of testing her

limits she was. Letting me push her until she was ready to shatter in my arms.

My grip tightened around the cylinder of plastic, looking down at her, "You trust me, yeah?"

"I trust you." She repeats, waiting for me to make a move.

"I'm gonna scare you, okay? But I promise I'll make it feel good after. Be brave for me okay, baby?"

Her eager nod has the head of my dick pressing into my jeans, aching to be released, dying to be inside of her.

My hands worked in circles around her body, wrapping the clear plastic over her breasts, high on her chest, before moving around her shoulder, coming around and pausing as I stare at her.

She watches me with anticipation as I wind it around her throat, then her soft pink lips that press against it like she's kissing a glass window. I continue, until it's wrapped right above her nose, making sure it's tight on her body.

The urge to panic should be building as I limit her oxygen for a moment, the plastic covering both her nose and mouth as I dip my head towards her lips.

I grab her throat in my hand, pulling her covered mouth to my own, kissing her over the elastic that acts as a barrier between us.

Her lips try to move with my own, making me smirk. *What a good girl*, I think.

She chokes against the plastic, trying not to panic for air, my lips still pressed on hers,

"Shh, baby, it's gonna be okay," I tell her as I take my finger, slipping it into her mouth, poking a hole and allowing air to flow freely.

Gasping as I begin to carefully undo the button on her jeans, her free limbs helping her step out of them. With her panties exposed to me, I walk her back to the floor-length mirror, pressing her ass into the cool glass.

Taking the cellophane and wrapping it a few more times around her throat before I toss it onto the floor. I use the tail end of the plastic as a leash of sorts, pulling her towards me and tightening its hold on her neck.

"Alistair," she whimpers, her free arms grabbing for my t-shirt desperately trying to tug me closer to her body.

My left hand skates down her delicate body, falling between her legs, under her panties and feeling just how needy she is for me. Using the pad of my fingers to smear her wetness all around the soft mound of her pussy.

I spin her around, hold her face to the glass, her breath fogging up the mirror as I groan in her ear, "You feel how soaked this pussy is for me?"

With ease I stick two fingers inside of her tight walls from the back, feeling her push back into my hand, wanting me deeper already. So greedy, so fucking mine. I pull back on the leash, cutting off more of her airflow and I hear her gasp.

One of her hands shoots back, gripping onto my forearm, nails digging in as I see those eyes start to roll back. Cutting off just enough circulation to make her feel like she's fucking flying all while I finger-fuck her from behind.

I release my hold, allowing her to get a rush of oxygen, her back falling as she holds onto the mirror for support. This is what I wanted every day of my life, watching her fall deeper and deeper into pleasure.

My eyes trailed the deep curve of her back, her tight little panties shoved to the side on her round ass, and God, her face was a dream. Flushed and tinted red with adrenaline, my ink sunk into her skin.

This was the closest to heaven a man like me would ever get.

Retracting my fingers from her cunt which makes her whine at the loss, I very quickly slip them into her mouth, through the hole in the plastic, allowing her to taste how very sweet she is.

"Like nectar of the gods, Briar. You're their sweetest gift," I murmur as she suckles on my digits, licking them clean before I start to pull my pants down, releasing my cock from their jean-clad prison.

It springs out, landing right between the slick, full cheeks of her ass, the thick red tip dripping pre-come. I keep one hand on the leash, while the other pulls to the root of my shaft smudging her spit and juices all around me.

"I'm going to fuck you just like this," I snarl darkly into her ear, lining my eager cock up with her snug entrance, my body energized by the promise of ravaging her. "Tell me you want it, Briar."

She doesn't miss a beat, "I want it, fuck, I want it, please." Practically shaking when I thrust hard inside of her, filling her to the hilt. She spreads her thighs more, letting me reach deeper at this angle and we both fall into an ocean of pleasure.

I revel in the sounds of her whimpering in both pleasure and discomfort. Breathing heavily through her teeth as her body is forced to adjust to me. I don't give her much time to think about it, because I'm already starting to find a brutal pace as I piston my hips in and out of her.

That's what we did. In the middle of my tattoo shop, we fucked. I stole her breath, while I shoved my cock so deep inside of her she'd feel me for years. We didn't need the Christmas carols and the tree. We just need each other and this. This furious, soul-destroying bond that I would rather die than lose.

"Fuck—" she gasps breathlessly, her body unable to do anything other than moan and urge me forward with her willing pussy. "So close."

I yank back on the leash, pull the air from her lungs abruptly, her entire back plastered to my front as I thrust upward, my free arm wrapped tightly around her waist. The lewd sounds of our bodies coming together over and over again fuels me to give her more.

I fuck her into the mirror, my body and cock pinning her the way she liked. Briar loved it when I shoved her into unforgiving surfaces.

Her legs start shaking, her body going limp as she struggles to scream when she comes on my shaft, milking me for all I'm worth. I let go of the plastic completely, my hand immediately finding her hip to grip her so I can pound into her ruthlessly, chasing my own orgasm.

The pulsating tightness of her cunt pushes me over the edge, the hand on her hip travels up to her scalp, grabbing a fistful of honey blonde hair and pulling upward. Her head tilting from the mirror, worn down, flushed. "Mine," I groan, as I look into the mirror, making eye contact with her.

"Yours," she mumbles.

My orgasm takes me. Just as I pull out, thick, warm strings of come paint her back. I spasm and pulsate, quivering from the force. I keep a hold of her hair, tilting her face so that she's looking over her shoulder.

My lips pressing into her hot mouth, my tongue dipping inside, pouring all of my emotion down her throat. Hoping it will be enough to keep her close, keep her by my side.

"Forever, Little Thief," I say, as I bite at her bottom lip. "This is forever."

I heard her heartbeat, just like I did the night she ran from me in the woods. It was beating for the darkness. Beating for me.

I tried to catch my breath, listening to my own heart.

Listening to it match her rhythm.

Two hearts destined to be alone found one another, joined hands and kept beating.

Together.

# CHAPTER THIRTY-FOUR
## *From Thief To Arson*

### *Briar*

If I saw one more welcome back poster I was going to hurl my coffee at it.

The Christmas break was over, which meant waking up at the crack of dawn instead of going to sleep. It would take me months to get my sleep schedule back in order after the three weeks I'd had off.

Between Lyra and Alistair, I rarely went to sleep before five in the morning. My boyfriend and best friend were night owls that had pulled me over to the dark side. Now I trudged up the steps of my first lecture hall, Lyra skipping in front of me like she isn't sleep-deprived. We both were taking a foreign language class this year and we'd thankfully ended up with the same professor.

I slumped down into the chair, slamming my head down onto the desk in front of me and shielding my eyes from the bright lights inside the room. All I wanted was to be curled up in bed sleeping and Alistair's hoodie was doing nothing at all to wake me up.

The scent that stuck to it only made me warm, sleepier.

When he told me he didn't have class till ten, I debated on throwing a textbook at him. Whoever thought Latin at 8:30 in the morning was a good idea could fall in a hole.

"I'm going to die of sleep deprivation," I groan.

"How about you don't do that. Alistair will be up our asses with depression if you die." I lift my head just an inch to see Rook sliding into the row with us, sporting a black eye and busted lip.

"I hope the other guy looks worse than you do," Lyra notes.

He just shrugs, giving us a lopsided grin before sitting down, and leaning back in his chair. I can smell weed sticking to his clothing like cologne, the red rim of his eyes making the color stand out.

Lyra, the rest of the boys, and I had slowly started to become friends. I say slowly only because of Thatcher, who I still had a love–hate relationship with. There were times I could envision myself strangling him to death and other times I didn't know what the group would look like without him.

I'd spent an entire day at Thatcher's house, meeting his very normal grandparents for Christmas. When I tell you it was the oddest day of my life, I mean it. Four of the most chaotic, damaged men I'd ever met acting like the perfect gentlemen for a little ol' lady named May.

It just proved even more that they all had souls, no matter how hard they tried to conceal them.

Our professor chose this time to walk in, gathering all of our eyes to the front and pointing to the chalkboard where she began writing. The Latin words were nothing but gibberish in my head, from lack of sleep and understanding.

Second semester had finally begun. What that meant for me was a new set of courses, another step closer to my future, but it always meant stepping into the unknown.

As normal as the past few weeks had been, I knew what

Alistair was doing when he stayed out with the guys. Plotting, devising a plan that would end with the mayor of Ponderosa Springs six feet under.

Except now, there were investigators looking into it. The stakes were higher and even though it made me nervous, it barely phased them. They knew what they had done and they would be willing to pay for those actions if the time came for it.

I squint my eyes, reading the words in the chalk.

*Temet nosce*

"Does anyone know what this means?" the middle-aged, successful-looking woman asks from the front, scanning the crowd for a brave hand.

When nothing but silence answers her, she sighs, ready to give us the translation, only to be interrupted by the lecture hall door opening with a heavy creak.

It's human nature to be curious, to uncover the unknown. It's why everyone turns their heads to the entrance, looking at the person who is walking in late.

Strawberry blonde hair hangs in a blunt shoulder-length cut, brushing the tops of her shoulders as she walks in holding books close to her chest. Walking with practiced grace and femininity that I would kill for. It's not her beauty that has piqued my interest, it's the way everyone in the class gasps and stares.

Everyone seems to be frozen, staring at this poor girl who doesn't know what to do but stare back. It's like they've seen a ghost.

"Who is that?" I ask Lyra in a whisper.

I hear the clock on the wall tick.

One.

Two.

Three.

"Sage Donahue."

# Rook

Remember when you were a child and they would yell at you for poking the fire? Told you that you'd piss the bed if you kept doing it, or worse, it would hurt you. Then you grew up in fear of the crackling heat, knowing if you touched it, there would be repercussions.

I am that fire. The flame. The blaze.

Unpredictable in ways you could never imagine. There is no taming me, it's impossible. I burn way too high, way too hot, to ever be put out.

You play with me and you are left burned. Roasted alive, left only with seared skin and blisters to remember me by.

The match in my mouth snaps clean in two between my teeth. Split right down the middle, the only sound to be heard in this class.

I thought it was the weed that was making me trip, my brain playing a sick trick. But everyone else seemed to be trapped in my hallucination as well, meaning my worst nightmare had just walked right back into my fucking life.

She was back.

Lyra and Briar sat adjacent to me, whispering about the new student who had stolen everyone's attention.

Yeah, she used to be really good at that. Being the apple of everyone's eye with that natural strawberry-tinted hair that always looked like flames wrapped around my hand.

Everyone's golden girl, queen bee, rally girl, homecoming sweetheart. All sweet and sugar that had gotten stuck in my teeth, before I ripped it out. I'm sure I was the only one who hated her. Probably because I was the only one who really knew her.

Miss Americana had demons. Skeletons. Things she'd die if she knew anyone had found out about.

Empty, ruthless, blue eyes drift to mine and I feel the twitch in my hand start. Blue eyes like the hottest flame, and I of all people knew what playing with that flame felt like.

Ticking in my muscles began building as I refused to move my gaze from her. I was seconds from grabbing my lighter and torching this place. Ready to burn all the memories she brought inside this room.

Memories that danced around me like shadows.

The urge built higher and higher.

It was a part of me.

I was born to make things burn.

Dainty limbs, peppered pale skin with flame-colored freckles, heart-shaped lips.

My greatest-kept secret.

My worst mistake.

The girl who once burned my sad memories, only to become the gasoline that fueled them.

Tomorrow the birds will sing, Sage.

I repeated the words her voice said the last time we spoke.

And I will set every last one of them on fucking fire.

# ACKNOWLEDGMENTS

Creativity-wise this book was the easiest for me to write. I've had this idea in my head for a few years now and being able to put it down on paper was unlike anything I've experienced before. This world is something I'm proud to say I've created, these characters and all their flaws mean so much to me. I hope you enjoyed them.

Fletcher, for lending me a hand in the weaponry department. I still don't want to know how you are so well-informed on the different types of knives.

B, Noah, Clay, for guiding me in the art of torture, murder and the shady side of life. Thank you for always answering my questions Google didn't have answers for.

Saffron, I'm not sure who should thank you more, me or my readers. You gave me the courage I needed to write this story, to believe in my art. I'm forever thankful we became friends.

Steph, for getting excited when I get excited. Always knowing what to say and being with me on this journey.

Amber, Mary, Jen, Autumn, Jess, five of the best Betas a girl could ask for.

To everyone who helped make this book come together, amazing cover designers, editors, formatters, all of the above. Thank you.

And of course, to you, the readers unafraid to travel in the dark with me. From hockey, to a rockstar, now this. Every word you read, every page you love, is me falling a little more in love with you. I mean it when I say, you're the reason my dreams came true. Thank you, and as always,

With all my love,
**MJ**

# evermore

Love, spice and sleepless nights.

The hottest new romance publisher at Penguin Random House UK.

Prepare for excessive swooning, devouring love stories and dangerously high standards for your own happily-ever-afters.

Proceed with caution... and an open heart.

FOLLOW US ON SOCIALS:

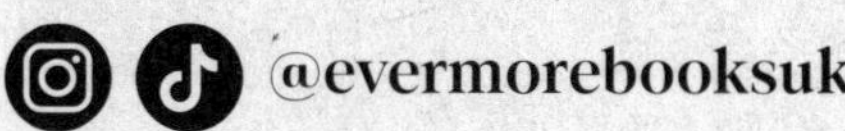

On a station platform, with nothing to read, and a four-hour train journey stretching ahead of him...

That's where the story began for Penguin founder Allen Lane. With only 'shabby reprints of shoddy novels' on offer, he resolved to make better books for readers everywhere.

By the time his train pulled into London, the idea was formed. He would bring the best writing, in stylish and affordable formats, to everyone. His books would be sold in bookstores, stationers and tobacconists, for no more than the price of a ten-pack of cigarettes.

And on every book would be a Penguin, a bird with a certain 'dignified flippancy', and a friendly invitation to anyone who wished to spend their time reading.

In 1935, the first ten Penguin paperbacks were published. Just a year later, three million Penguins had made their way onto our shelves.

Reading was changed forever.

—

A lot has changed since 1935, including Penguin, but in the most important ways we're still the same. We still believe that books and reading are for everyone. And we still believe that whether you're seeking an afternoon's escape, a vigorous debate or a soothing bedtime story, all possibilities open with a book.

Whoever you are, whatever you're looking for, you can find it with Penguin.